THE AMAZON MURDERS

A RAINFOREST MYSTERY

To my good friend, Diana!
Hope you enjoy. Take care!
Best wishes & happy reading!

S.W. LEE

Love,
Sue

A PERMUTED PRESS book

ISBN (trade paperback): 978-1-61868-456-1
ISBN (eBook): 978-1-61868-457-8

Cover art by Hunter Walker

This book is a work of fiction. People, places, events, and situations are the product of the author's imagination. Any resemblance to actual persons, living or dead, or historical events, is purely coincidental.

PERMUTED PRESS

For Gary W. Cole
my soul mate

You lifted my spirits when they were down, encouraged me when I felt lost, and cheered me on for the ten years it took from penning the first words to publishing this final manuscript. Thank you for lovingly pushing me to write by countless times admonishing, "Go to your room!" You kept me focused and moving forward, and not one time did you give up on me. This book is as much yours as it is mine.

PHOTO CREDITS

Page 2 – Map of Brazil. NASA image courtesy Jeff Schmaltz, MODIS Rapid Response Team at NASA GSFC.

Counter. http://treefoundation.org/canopy_education.htm

Quote. *Dr. Margaret Lowman, Canopy Biologist*, January 17, 2000

Page 15 – Map of Amazon Rainforest. Mongabay.com

Page 376 – Figure 1 The Cutting edge of the rainforest. Damon Winter / The New York Times / Redux

Figure 2 The wonder of the Amazon. Sue Lee, photographer.

ACKNOWLEDGMENTS

The first time I met Corinda Carfora, my literary agent, she told me that the best book she had read in a while was an unpublished manuscript. It was *The Amazon Murders*, the book you are about to read. I want to thank Corinda for not only believing in the theory presented in the book but for putting her own blood, sweat, and tears into the editing of it. Thanks also for your patience with a first time author, and "here's to many more books to come!"

When I met Richard Gallen, the doors of publishing opened. Richard loved the science in The Amazon Murders (He came up with the title.) but asked me to strip out the story and drop in a new one (What an exercise in editing!). I did, and he was right. Richard also introduced me to Corinda. He graciously allowed me to camp out in his 5th Avenue loft office twice for five days for free while he, Corinda, and I met, discussed, and edited the manuscript. The world lost Richard Gallen on December 3, 2013, from complications of Parkinson's Disease.

I want to thank my editor, Bobbie Metevier for the hours of hard work and editing and marketing advice. An author herself, Bobbie graciously offered her own experiences as I crept through the publishing maze.

Debbie Wiygul Ring has always believed in this work, encouraged me at every step, always been an amazing sister, and…knew someone…who knew someone…who knew Richard Gallen. Jennifer Lee gave me the idea for the first chapter and has been a great critique. She, my daughter, Catie Lee, and my granddaughter, Alexis Couch, have never stopped loving me for just being a parent and grandparent, encouraging me, and believing in me. Son, Tommy, Katie, and Cooper Lee and sister, Cindy Wiygul Richie. Other family members who have been completely supportive are Marcie, Cary, and Baylee Calenberg, Renee and Philip Cole, Tommie R. Lee, my nephews, Willis Ring, Jr. and Morgan Adams, and my beloved mother, Catherine Breedlove Wiygul, who entered eternal life on February 25, 2010, always believing but never knowing for sure the novel would be published. My father, Eph Wiygul, ever the skeptic, wasn't sure about this rainforest book, but knew when we lost him the book would be published. Thanks to Tom Lord, an in-law, or maybe an out-law, long-time Athens funeral director, for never questioning why I called him one summer afternoon while he and his family were vacationing and asked, "What would happen to a body hanging from a tree in 100% humidity in 90° heat?" After a thoughtful pause, he muttered, "Well…after a few days, I suppose the muscles would start sliding from the bones...." I definitely used that one!

Many thanks for the hours of science discussions go to Dr. James Grogan, Frank and Jerusa Pantoja, and Dr. William Delaune. Their endorsements with their titles are on a separate page. I'd also like to thank Dr. Jim Maruniak, professor in the Entomology and Nematology Department, University of Florida. Thanks to Scott Paul, of Greenpeace, who got me in touch with Dr. Grogan.

I can't forget Marian Rees, who validated the theory and characters when I had written a mere 75 pages.

I am indebted to John Maruniak, cousin and friend, who diligently worked through the first mammoth edit, raising the bar on quality with a commitment to excellence and a willing heart, poet, Dr. Eleanor Hoomes, who read the book faster than I thought possible, found five major areas to strengthen, and gave great encouragement, and fellow author, Jay Jones, who tediously and quite effectively worked through the manuscript one last time before it was sent to the publisher. Thank you all.

I am so happy to be in a relationship with Permuted Press. Thank you for what you have done so far with the design and publishing of this manuscript, and I look forward to working with you for many years to come.

I appreciate my other readers, proofers, and commentators:

Mike Elmore, Charlie Felts, Dr. Leslie Latham, Dr. Janet Cotter Atha, Anne Peppers, Tera Duval, Kathy Codding, Connie Cannon, Carolyn Meadows, Chris Maruniak, Stephen Merrifield, Jackie Scarborough, Sandra Norred, Rachel Wells, Cindy Watts, and Mae Whitlock.

I'd also like to thank the Carroll County Writing Club in Carrollton, Georgia, for listening and critiquing over the years.

Last, but not least, I beg forgiveness from anyone who has helped me over the years who I may have forgotten to mention. Thank you all.

Now…READ…and enjoy!

SCIENTISTS' ENDORSEMENTS

The natural world is full of strange and beautiful relationships whose purpose is always more life, even in death. Who's to say what is possible when what we know represents the smallest fraction of what is? I am intrigued and entertained by the ideas S. W. Lee sets forth in this new novel. The salvation of biological diversity on this planet, nowhere richer than in the forests of Amazonia, may indeed require push-back against the greatest threat to it, which is us.

Dr. James Grogan
Mount Holyoke College, Massachusetts & Instituto Floresta Tropical.
Formerly, Yale University School of Forestry & Environmental Studies

(Translated from Portuguese)

This book presents a provocative, fantastic theory, a strange journey into the waves and tides that nature surely hides from the eyes of humankind. I've never thought in this way before! Imagine: even as humanity exploits and degrades the Amazonian forest environment for whatever price available, we fail to anticipate that this betrayal could generate a forceful reaction, a blind, out-of-control response that mankind is incapable of countering....

Frank S. Pantoja
biologist,
Instructor in Natural Resources from Amazon,
Federal University of Western Para & Susthentar – Environmental Services and Tourist Amazon

It seems that most non-scientists believe that scientists either know everything about the natural world or are diligently trudging down a linear path while filling in the few remaining gaps in that knowledge. Far from it. Every day we are being bombarded with new discoveries and are confronted with the underlying logical inconsistency of achieving absolute knowledge of a system that contains the observer. This is not a bad thing. Ignorance, the ever present and seductive unknown, provides the fuel for scientific progress. While the author's theory of the killers in this story may not be scientifically probable, it is seductively possible. Immerse yourself in this novel and perhaps pursue some of the provided resources. You'll learn something while enjoying a wonderfully entertaining ride.

Dr. William Delaune
Private Research Methodologist and Design Consultant,
retired, Senior Research Scientist for the Department of Veterans Affairs.

On the 23rd of August, 2010, smoke obscured a 1500 mile corridor in southern Argentina up through Brazil, Bolivia, and Peru. In an image shot from its Aqua satellite, which measures fire to a greater sensitivity than other satellites, NASA detected 148,946 fires.

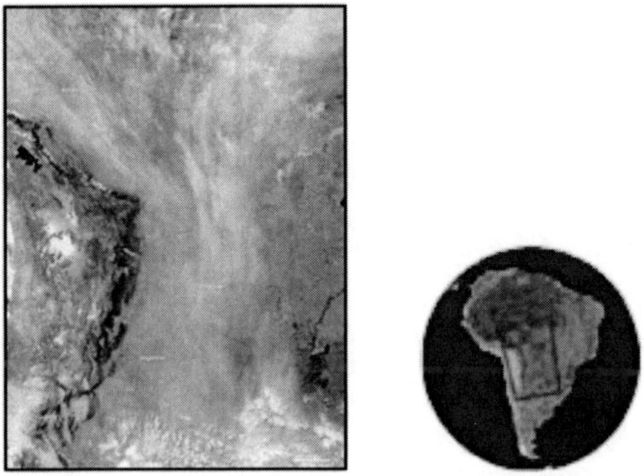

NASA image courtesy Jeff Schmaltz, MODIS Rapid Response Team at NASA GSFC.

"If nothing is done, the rain forests of the world will no longer exist in 25 years." - *Dr. Margaret Lowman*, *Canopy Biologist*, January 17, 2000

Days	Hours	Min.	Sec.
4537	20	48	13

Counter (http://treefoundation.org/canopy_education.htm) counting down the seconds.

In the Amazon Rainforest lives a spirit of protection. Humankind, the sole abuser of the forest, has yet to earn this protection, so it is not the protected. That gift is reserved for the extraordinary flora and fauna. From where did the protector arise? From the spirits of those who took their last breaths in the forest. The apparition appears and begins to whistle—always the exact same melody. If by chance one mimics the tune, the spirit will react. If one is well-behaved, causing no harm to the forest, the spirit will merely frighten and move on. However, if one destroys the forest with abandon, pollutes the air, or displaces creatures from their environment, beware! Death will be forthcoming.

The Curse of El Tunchi

1

Fear twisted in the man's chest as he struggled for air and ran through the darkness. *How long has it been*? Thump. Thump. Thump. Thump. His head twisted from side to side trying to catch a glimpse of the creature. *Where…is…it*? *Breathe. Breathe.* Thump. Thump. *No…keep running*! He heard his own heart pounding like a drum, twice as fast as the rhythmic plodding of his feet on the dirt path. This was a run for his life.

Move! *Move*! *Hide*! Thump. Thump. *No, move*! *Move*! *Keep moving*! Thump. Thump. In a moment of clarity, he marveled at a realization: *I'm screaming, but I can't hear my voice. Please let this be a wicked nightmare.* As quickly as the thought flashed through his mind, he knew this wasn't a dream. Wondering if a situation was a nightmare never happened in dreams. His battle for life was unquestionable.

He heard the hissing sound, then rapid movement behind him, like nylon swishing between thighs.

Oh, God! *Please help me*! *It's coming*! *Hide*! *Where*? *Oh, God*! *Where*? His eyes darted for a place to hide. *No, keep moving*! He raced on.

The man tried to sprint, but he was almost spent. Yet, he could not slow down or the monster would overtake him in an instant.

Help me! *Someone please help me*!

The creature chasing him was unlike any he had ever encountered, one so large he could envision it easily killing a 500 pound croc, and he was much smaller than a crocodile. He could almost feel the fangs digging into his shoulder, on his neck, into his back.

Waiting. Waiting. Waiting for it to happen. Thump. Thump. *Where is it*? His head swiveled around giving him the appearance of an owl—a floundering owl dodging the talons of an eagle, sure of its death but still fighting for its life. But this was no eagle.

The green anaconda! *A giant*! *Move*! *Run*! *Keep running*!

Infant vines reached out grabbing at him as he raced over the barren path, trying to wrap sticky tendrils about his legs, his ankles, his feet, anywhere to pull him down—tendrils as agile and strong as the tentacles of a giant squid. Like the squid, they might suck the very marrow from his bones if their hold became firm enough. Or could they be the tails of the other jungle snakes, laying a gauntlet that would eventually be his end? One vine stopped him dead as it wrapped tightly around one ankle. He fell, face first onto the dirt path.

His head jerked upward as a new sound assaulted him. *Oh*, *God*, *help me*! *What now*? *Shrieking*? *Shrieking*? Thump. Thump. He was on his knees, then flipping over and tugging at the vine that was snaking up his leg. His head swung back and forth, back and forth…looking for the new sound. *What is that shrieking*? Loud piercing cries—as if thousands of velociraptors had escaped from Isla Nublar and the infamous *Jurassic Park*—announced that something even more horrifying was coming. The vine loosened as if trying to gather strength for another death grip.

The man jumped to his feet. The shrieking was even louder. *There's something more*! *Now*, *THEY are coming*! *THEY*! *THEEEY*! *Run*! *Run*! He jerked free, tumbling forward, flailing his arms as he continued his onward momentum…but to where? He focused, trying to see anything as he peered into the night.

Engulfed in terror, he stopped and turned in all directions. *Now what*? *Eyes*? *Yes*, *eyes are everywhere*! *Everywhere*! *Piercing eyes*! *They're all staring at me*! *Why*? Every color of the rainbow. Only eyes shone out at him from the thick blackness.

Go! *Move*! *Don't think*! *Just keep going*! Thump. Thump. Thump. Thump. He was running again. He gained momentum. His lungs were on fire as goliath cyclones of whirling, choking smoke reeled around him. He continued down the path until it seemed a fog was lifting, revealing there was no more forest. He slowed his pace and examined his surroundings. Where lush greenness once curtained about him, there was only choking smoke from glowing, smoldering stumps, as if a fireball had charred the Earth. His chest burned with every wheezing breath.

No forest. Where am I? He sucked air. Smoky, dusty air. *Breathe*! *Breathe*! *Why is the forest gone*? He was gasping. Gasping for hope. Gasping for one more chance at life. He ran on.

A massive mouth snapped just inches to the left of his face and his voiceless scream recoiled. He ducked as an immense rope of slimy green and black muscle flipped over and began to curl around him. He sidestepped the second loop and twisted free, spiraling as if he were a ninja, a remarkable feat for him.

Unexpectedly, his heavy panting and thumping heartbeat were interrupted by a whistling noise. He froze in place when he heard an eerie tune. *Is someone whistling*? He tried to quiet his breathing and still his racing heartbeat. He looked down at his feet and watched in horror as his legs were covered in bark and his toes began to root into the ground. *Oh*, *God*! *I'm so screwed.* He couldn't move; it was still coming. Adrenaline surged through him when he heard a branch snap. He gathered his strength into a tight spring, and when he released, he felt his toes snap off. He sprinted forward in agony on his bleeding feet, and he realized that the warm liquid trailing after his missing toes was not runny like normal blood. The fluid was viscous, like resin. He couldn't dwell on his feet. He had to get away. He kept running.

What is that whistling? That sound. That sound. Where is it coming from? He could barely make out the tune before the shrieks erupted again. Renewed terror threatened to force the thickened blood through his heart, up his neck to burst the vessels in his brain.

What's happening? What…is…happening? The darkness! The eyes! No forest! The shrieking! And now? What is that? The whistling… He screamed out the words, but there was still no sound.

He stopped abruptly, sniffed and wrinkled his face in disgust. *What…is…that…smell?* There was an awful odor that tasted metallic. He salivated, running his tongue in and out of his mouth trying to suck more of his saliva, swallowing several times hoping to rinse the taste away.

He reached his hands out flat, like a blind man trying to find a wall or a tree, anything except the blackness, or the snake, or the screaming. *Could this be Hell? Am I already dead? Where am I? Need to see…*

The man stumbled from the path and slipped in a gelatinous puddle. A long, thin shape lay nearby. The moon pierced the smoky haze casting a light on the object. Only the shabby clothing and outline of a skeleton announced that what lay before him had once been a living, breathing human. Actually, it looked more like a mummy.

He pondered for a split second. *What is a mummy doing here?* Scrambling to his feet, he tripped again, this time landing in one of the reeking piles, this time his hand landing on leathery skin over a protruding bone. *Another body!*

Lifting his arm from the human sludge, he vomited. As the sky began to lighten, his eyes darted around in trepidation of what lay ahead. He pushed himself from the ground and shuffled forward encountering another bony corpse, skin tight against its skeletal frame.

The sun was climbing higher. The smoke was lifting to reveal…no more rainforest. Turning in a slow circle, he saw no more luscious plants or palms; no more choruses of insects or frogs or other forest creatures. But what of the eyes of the night? They were gone. Only dry, desolate ground with curling threads of smoke rose from where centuries-old undergrowth and canopy trees once thrived.

The shrieking started again and renewed its foreboding with vigor.

The man ran on. *So loud! Too loud!* He covered his ears as he stumbled again but kept moving forward. From the corner of his eye, he glimpsed the end of a tail trying to reach him. Something tightened around his ankle, and he was on the ground again.

Two large demonic eyes of sparkling gold swayed above him as spirals of a muscular vice encased his body. Immediately the enormous snake began to tighten its grip. It raised its head above his face with a menacing grin.

The snake's eyes! *The eyes. Those eyes.* The man finally embraced his imminent death. The eerie tune rolled off the snake's undulating, forked tongue.

Mimic the tune. Mimic the tune, his subconscious prodded him. *If I do…maybe…I will live.* With his dying breath, he traced the notes emanating from the snake. As his soul began to leave his body, the sky flared with fireworks of bright colors, all flashing in his vision.

The snake opened its mouth, about to devour him. If he thought he was afraid before, what happened next was beyond horrifying. A legion of huge, shrieking ants poured from the snake's mouth. The noise was so extreme the man would have covered his ears again had his hands not been pinned to his sides by the constricting monster.

Ants continued to surge from the serpent onto the man, and as they began to sting, each barb felt like a bullet shot deep into his body.

The pain! *Oh, God, the pain*! *On fire*! *Burning everywhere*! *The pressure. I…can't…breathe…*

His eyes flew open. The last thing his mind registered was a powdery film covering his eyes as the ants continued to swarm over him.

Just before the man slipped into unconsciousness, he heard the snake's hissing voice proclaim, "Feel the curse of *El Tunchi.*"

* * *

Will lay on his back with his arms stiff at his sides.

Carlos was unsure whether it was safe to touch him or not. He had seen men come out of a vision ceremony and attack those nearby, and he'd also seen men die. Will looked dead, with no rise and fall of his chest. Carlos leaned cautiously over his friend's body hoping there was still a pulse. He pushed against Will's shoulder with the tip of his boot.

Will gave no response.

"Will?" Carlos continued prodding his friend in broken English, "Must wake up, Will! No good sleep soon after drink the *ayahuasca*." Poking and shouting he yelled, "Wake up! Will, wake up!" He leaned forward and slapped Will's face before jumping back. He yelled as loudly as he could, "Must no die!"

Will's eyes shot open and he drew in a deep, lungful of air. Then he began swinging his arms wildly screaming, "Get it off me! Get it off me!"

Carlos jumped back. "It okay, Will. What you say? Nothing on you!" he shouted.

Will struggled to get to his feet before collapsing and rolling hard onto the ground. He closed his eyes and opened his mouth, inhaling another huge gulp of fresh, pungent rainforest air like a fish floundering on a riverbank. He could still feel the snake's grip around him, the ants pouring over him. The agonizing stings. He brushed wildly at his face and arms.

In Will's mind, his own voice sounded like he was under water. "Get them off!" He furiously wiped his sleeves and shivered as he listened to the dwindling shrieks echoing through his head.

"Nothing on you, Will!" Carlos shouted as he squatted nearby. He tried to reassure him, "You okay, Will. Open eyes. Stay open."

Will rolled to the side and grabbed onto Carlos, wrenching his face close. "The eyes! Do you see the eyes?" His own wide-eyed gaze searched all around for the spectacle that surrounded him earlier until slowly it dawned on him…it was no longer there. Even so, Will had a nagging fear that he was in danger, still seeing the bodies and feeling the panic, ants treading over his skin, the jungle eyes watching him as he ran for his life, the agony as his toes snapped from his feet.

He pulled at Carlos again. "I don't…want to see it…again." His raspy voice was scarcely above a whisper.

"What you see?" a shaman asked, finally stepping forward.

Will released Carlos, "Where…" Will panted as he combed the forest around him, his heart pounding hard, "is…the snake?"

The shaman leaned down. "You vision was snake?"

Will nodded. He swiped at the sweat running down his forehead and burning his eyes. He blinked and tried to focus on the man but couldn't. The man appeared like the gaping mouth, and Will shrank away.

"Noooo!" Will covered his face with his trembling hands.

"It okay," Carlos assured him, trying to comfort again, this time touching Will's shoulder with his hand, wishing he could leave this place, mindful of the Indian's interpretation of evil when a snake appeared in a vision.

The shaman clutched the front of Will's shirt. "Tell me. You see snake in vision? Tell me!"

Will blinked several times, focusing on the shaman for the first time. The fear was fading. His thoughts were settling down. He was alive. There was no giant snake. No hideous ants.

"Yes," he coughed as the shaman released his grip.

Carlos handed Will a bottle of water, which he drank heartily. He wiped his mouth with the palm of a shaky hand as water rolled down his chin, dripping onto his chest.

"Cobra? Snake?" The shaman asked, panic appearing in his own eyes.

"Hell, yes, I saw a snake." Will was coming back to himself. "The damn thing chased me. Hell, it almost killed me." He shuddered at the thought. "It wasn't no cobra though. It was a giant, green anaconda and," he gestured wildly as another quick shiver ran from his neck down his back, "screaming ants poured out of its mouth!" He glared at the man. "They were all over me! They stung like hell!"

Will turned his anger on Carlos. "Why didn't you tell me I could see something like that? Damn snake! I thought this was just going to be a good high!" His voice drifted off, and he fell backward onto one elbow.

Carlos recoiled, stunned by Will's admonition. "No high," he corrected, "healing ceremony."

Will coughed again loudly. "Healing, my ass. I don't give a...," he wheezed, still gasping for breath.

The shaman stood and nodded. "Bullet ant." He began to shake his fan of *chiripanga* leaves over Will, chanting as he moved in slow circles, the rattle rhythmically complementing his mantra.

Will became aware of an unpleasant scent, which somehow registered as his own. "Damn," Will muttered as he looked down and saw the wetness between his legs. He tried to stand again but rolled over onto his right side instead. It was too soon to get up.

The shaman stopped his motion, "*Cobra conversa*?"

Carlos knelt back down. He knew Will was angry, but he could also see he was having trouble concentrating. "He ask if snake talk."

Will had been so frightened and in such pain he had almost forgotten. Finally righting himself to a sitting position he growled, "*El Tunchi*." He could still hear the words. "He said, 'Feel the curse of *El Tunchi*.'"

The shaman straightened. Under his breath he said, "Bullet ant. *El Tunchi*?" He dropped his fan and backed away, narrowing his eyes and staring at Will for a moment longer before holding up his arms in the air and speaking in a language even Carlos could not understand.

Will studied Carlos, expecting him to translate.

Carlos simply shrugged his lack of understanding.

When they looked toward the shaman, they saw only the fan on the ground and the surrounding forest. The shaman was gone.

2

At the cutting edge of the Amazon Rainforest…

… a platoon of ants came and went to an underground nest. Their steady frenzy created a furrow in the ground as wide as the palm of someone's hand. The ants moved forward, a fluttering parade of green leaves heading for the entrance hole into an underworld. As though on a busy two-lane highway, ants without leaves raced away from the entrance on one side of the furrow, while ants carrying leaf pieces instinctively scurried toward the nest on the other side, climbing over exiting ants that might wander into the incoming lane.

The ants practiced a type of sustainable leaf harvest, slicing off only part of a leaf from various plants and trees to avoid exhausting vegetation. They were hauling pieces of leaves ten times their own size, the equivalent of a man carrying two full-grown horses above his head.

The ants descended deep, each with a leaf slice, as they established a working farm far below the Earth's surface. This species of leaf cutter had practiced the same type of agriculture for some 50 million years which showed the sustainability of their farming. The ants were growing a special fungus which met their nutritional requirements with no need for sunlight.

There was an almost magical division of labor. Farm work was arranged into specialized tasks: leaf handlers, defenders of the colony, and garden tenders, while others specialized in cutting leaves. Another group of tiny ants straddled the backs of the larger workers to defend them from carnivorous flies which, when given a chance, would lay eggs at the base of their heads where their larvae would eat into the inside of the ant and continue devouring until it died.

Those tending the garden moved about quickly and efficiently, never stopping their conscientious cultivation. Curiously, their legs and abdomens were covered with a white, downy film. Dipping their sharp claws into the downy film, they indiscriminately patted the leaf pieces. As fast as the ants wiped the film from their bodies, it reappeared as if it had never been touched, as if there were a never-ending supply. Pieces of cut leaves often carried a mold that could ravage the ant colony, except when the ant tenders applied their downy film. Within hours, the mold began to die. So potent was the white film, any mold was purged from the leaves within 24 hours.

What was the white film? Could it have been like a cotton boll of toxin, each tiny fiber containing a lethal dose of poison? Had these ants developed a new type of miraculous chemical warfare within their bodies? Had they found a way to protect themselves and their offspring from threats of the outside world? If they had, how did they discern between that which threatened and that which harmlessly crossed their paths?

3

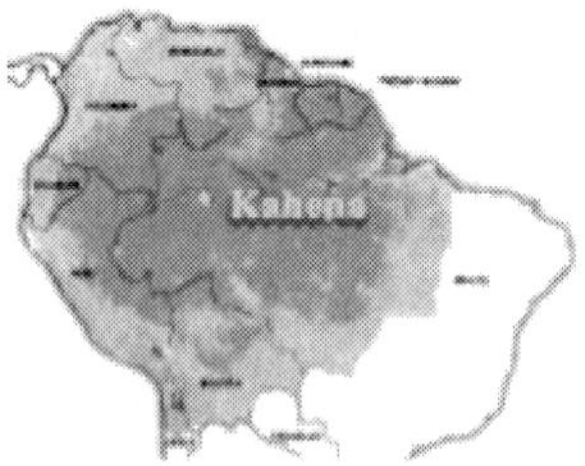

Amazon Rainforest, near Kahepa, Brazil
Hunting the mogno (mahogany) tree

The Amazon night broke peacefully, early rays of sunlight struggling to pierce the soupy layer of air saturated with the night's infusion of humidity. The sun electrified the dense tree canopy causing a gasp of carbon dioxide to bubble fresh oxygen into the hazy air gripping the unbroken weave of trees and vines and moss, each colored every imaginable shade of green and gray and brown. Hazy air, for sure, but air so pure it could be inhaled into one's lungs not only through the natural process but even through the skin, causing glorious euphoria. Sunlight pressed downward through the trees like a gentle whisper, scattering into ever smaller rays making their way past leaf after leaf until the last pinpoint of light landed on the deepest leaf in the canopy.

A sense of the advancing dawn of life emerged silently, accompanied by a steady drum roll of anticipation throughout the rainforest. New life sprang from the shadowy ground, growing, reaching up to thicken the majestic tree canopy, before dropping leaves to decay in a primeval growth cycle of raw life.

Instantly the silent drumming was joined by a cadence of laughing children chasing through their playground of amargo trees. Ever mindful of snakes, poisonous spiders, and dangerous animals, they ran and climbed as effortlessly as the monkeys who joined them in the trees overhead.

A small brown boy was being chased by two older boys down the packed dirt path, a green mesh of leaves slapping against his bare chest as he ran. Clad only in tattered gray shorts, the boy jumped over fallen logs and occasional jutting rocks as he listened for the tromping steps gaining on each of his shorter strides.

Up ahead he noticed several walking trees just off the path, their roots a mass of bars where he could hide his tiny frame. He glanced back and dove through the tangle of life-sustaining underpinnings just before his two pursuers came into sight. They sprang past and never saw him lying flat against the forest floor.

The boy covered his mouth to stifle the laughter that threatened to give him away. He waited until he heard only the sounds of the forest around him before climbing from his hiding place and brushing the dirt from his stomach and knees, stopping only when he recognized the sound of a chainsaw come to life.

The boy had known the loggers were coming. As he ran to his hiding place, he heard the call of the akaki bird's warning, *Aka. Aka. Aka-i. Aka-yhujjjjjji. Be careful. They are here.* He knew what would happen. He had watched it for the first time a moon ago. He was excited to think he might see another giant tree crash to the ground, even though the shaman had warned of the anger aroused in the heart of the god of the forest when a mighty soul was brought down...especially the great kapok because everyone knew the tree had a soul.

The boy eyed the path behind making sure the others were not returning, since he could no longer hear their footfalls with the grinding noise so close. He had listened to the saws late yesterday and knew the men had now come back to finish what they started. He began to creep off the path toward the killers when the saws fell silent. He heard a man's sharp cry and then something he could not understand. He was once again surrounded by only the noises of the forest. In another moment, the boy's attention was drawn toward a sound he did recognize, as woolly monkeys screeched an alarm.

He ran toward the commotion and, from a distance, saw the monkeys huddled together overhead in a tight, frenzied group. Below them was the shadowy outline of a man slumped at the base of a towering *mogno* tree, head leaning to one side, mouth slightly open, eyes closed. The boy could not be sure, but it appeared the man might be sleeping. *How could you fall asleep so fast*?

The boy felt no sense of danger toward strangers, so he drew closer, waiting patiently for the man to awaken. He sat on his haunches and remained quiet. The boy drew in a long breath and looked around for the source of a new, earthy smell. He noticed sawdust from a fresh tree cut scattered around the man like powder. He reached down and picked up a handful of the tree pieces and watched as they slipped through his fingers, drifting slowly back to the ground.

The boy stared at the man's face and inclined his head slightly pondering why the man was so still. *Why are you sleeping*? *Can't you hear the noise of the monkeys*? The boy regarded the man's face noticing how sharply the color contrasted with the brownish-red, crackled bark of the tree buttress.

The boy waited a few more moments for the man to wake up, as long as his young patience could tolerate, and then he reached for a stick, inching over to prod the man awake. As the tip of the stick reached the man's chest, a single drop of blood slid from his nose. The boy watched it skim over the man's lips, finally coming to rest as it dangled from his chin, leaving a slimy, ruby trail in its wake.

The monkeys jumped overhead in some nearby trees now, howling so loudly the boy covered his ears. Glancing toward the uproar, he caught a glimpse of two more men in the nearly topless trees on the hill above, their bodies hanging limp as they dangled from their tree harnesses, saws still swaying from ropes at their sides.

When the boy looked back into the face of the sitting figure, blood began to pour from the man's nose and ears like red snakes slithering down his body.

The boy fell back and scrambled to the path.

And then he ran with purpose.

4

Dr. Stephen Elmore stood at the sink drying the last of a stack of clean Petri dishes. He wasn't compulsive by any means, but sometimes during the day he felt a need to straighten and tidy up a bit while he thought through his research.

Stephen was in his early fifties, but the years had been kind to him. His face barely showed his age, and his body was lean and conditioned like a man much younger. The only telltale sign that he was passing through middle age was his mop of thinning salt and pepper hair. He was usually serious, but sometimes he found humor in unexpected places, like watching two small lizards bowing up and pouncing, one flipping the other like wrestlers in a ring, or opening the center of a bromeliad high in the canopy and finding a new kind of insect crouched inside. Those things made him sport a crooked little smile.

Trained first as a medical doctor, Stephen switched careers almost immediately after his surgical internship ended. He found his personality more suited to a life of solitude than constant contact with patients and staff. His work in the Amazon as a research scientist for a large pharmaceutical company from the US had allowed him to call the rainforest his home for more than twenty years, and Stephen couldn't have been happier with his choice. Much of that time was spent deep in the forest camping, climbing in the canopy, and collecting samples of unidentified plants. He spent months testing and tweaking, adding this and that, and then retesting. Stephen was a discoverer. His work had been fruitful, providing eleven new drugs over the years and documentation for hundreds of healing agents through his work with local shamans.

At a table nearby, Dr. Julia Cole bent over a microscope, her attention moving between the fungus she had just extracted from a dead ant and the notepad where she recorded her findings. Her fascination with insect-infecting fungi had grown out of an encounter with a tomato worm while in her second year of college. She'd found the worm on a tomato plant and was amazed when she saw a patch of knobby shoots pushing up through its back. The worm appeared to be part of the plant, as leaves grew through the skin next to what she later found out were actually fungus sprouts. It was creepy but fascinating, and she had to know more about what was going on. Two burning questions were sparked with that first encounter. First, how did a fungus get into an insect, eat the insides, and then spike out of the body to spread its spores? Secondly, what prevented the fungus from doing the same to humans?

Julia sat up and swatted a tiny mosquito threatening to bite her tanned thigh. She wore white shorts, which she just noticed were beginning to fray at the cuff, a light pink tank top, and the ever-present socks and over-the-ankle boots. Julia had tried the flip flops and sandals routine like Stephen often wore, but she preferred closed shoes because of all the tiny creatures, stickers, and other forest debris that could get into her feet. Julia flicked the dead mosquito from her skin and thought, *maybe it's time to pull out some jeans*.

Julia stretched her shoulders and turned toward Stephen. "I just need a few more minutes with this. It shouldn't be long." She knew he wanted to share some of his recent findings with her.

"Take your time. I'm just doing a little housekeeping." Stephen's strong British accent was apparent even though he'd been gone from his homeland for decades.

Lupa came in with a light snack of fruit and cheese, which he placed on the counter. "You ready for snack?"

Stephen nodded and smiled. "Yes, my friend. Thanks."

Lupa nodded back and left quietly. The small Indian had been part of Stephen's household for almost fifteen years after a chance meeting in Peru that almost cost them both their lives. Lupa had been a practicing shaman when they met. Now, he limited his practice to mostly herb and tea concoctions or light remedies for aches and pains. Mostly he kept house for Stephen and the compound in order, bossing everyone around while cooking some of the best meals imaginable.

Stephen offered Julia the plate Lupa had left.

"No thanks." Julia shook her head. "I need to wash up first."

"It can keep." Stephen laid a lid over the plate.

Julia extracted some fungus from a dead grasshopper and placed it in the dish next to the ant fungus. With a big sigh, she shrugged. "Sometimes I feel like I'm just shooting in the dark."

Stephen hung up a towel. "You think so? Why is that?"

"There are *millions* of insects with their individual fungus out there. Millions, Stephan!"

"It's quite the treasure hunt, Julia. You never know what you'll find."

"No, I guess not." Julia sighed again.

Stephen noted her frustration. "You realize that I came across my fifth drug by chance? It's mind boggling to ponder how many fungi there are that have antibiotic properties." Stephen shrugged "Could be thousands…millions. We just need to find and test as many as we can."

"You're right. Just seems like there isn't enough time, and ever since I've been coming here, I've been searching for one thing or another."

"And you have some pretty important finds," Stephen reassured.

Julia had returned to the US after her last visit with over a thousand samples of different types of fungi, and two already showed promising signs of good medicinal properties. There were three more from past trips.

For the last five years, Julia had been visiting the rainforest compound every chance she got, usually at Christmas and for spring and summer breaks. Her first trip had been her twenty-fifth birthday present to herself. She had known she wanted to spend time in the Amazon for years, and couldn't wait any longer to get here.

After that first trip, she worked on many of Stephen's projects. Once she became a professor, she gathered flora to study the microbial diversity for research assignments back at the university, and the last few years she collected fungus-filled insects for a project she was working on currently coordinated by the US Centers for Disease Control and Prevention (CDC).

A few years ago she was contacted by a doctor at the CDC when a colleague mentioned her work in the Amazon. It was the perfect place for gathering and testing fungi. The project was working towards finding the cause and treatment for a little known sickness called Morgellon's Disease, an illness where the patient feels that something is crawling, stinging, or biting under their skin. Advanced cases present with sores or rashes, and the patient feels fibers under their flesh. Other symptoms, consistent with chronic fatigue disorder and depression, may also appear.

Some doctors believed it might be an infection caused by clothing fibers, or something on the legs of mites, or a bacterium from plants. Other scientists believed the illness was a psychological condition, telling doctors their patients needed antipsychotic drugs. One group at the CDC thought it might be some kind of fungus attacking the individual.

No matter what was causing the illness, collecting the fungi was a good idea. The Amazon was one of the richest sources for organisms on the planet because of the tens of millions of different categories of insects, each under attack by its own unique parasite. Who knew what type of medicinal gem might be hiding in the fungi?

Julia helped Stephen with his work, but spent part of her time each week gathering dead insects sprouting fungus and isolating samples to take back to the CDC for testing.

Stephen cleared his throat. "Eduardo should be coming back to the village soon." He opened a cabinet and reached for the broom.

Julia nodded but didn't respond. Eduardo Tavares was a local constable of sorts. The villagers called him Delegado.

The last time Julia saw Eduardo he was blissfully married to Serena. When they met several years ago, Julia felt an instant attraction to him. His body was fit and deeply tanned. He was handsome and rugged, and when he spoke his eyes were as expressive as his words. But it was clear he belonged to Serena. He had been polite and engaging to Julia, but nothing more. Now things were different—Serena died last year.

When she arrived, Julia had learned that Eduardo had gone on what Stephen called his 'soul-searching journey.'

Julia hoped Eduardo had found some peace and comfort while being away. Julia knew people processed grief differently. Some took more time than others, and she knew that sometimes a person never got over losing the love of his life.

Julia was into the second month of her three-month sabbatical from the University of Georgia. She was supposed to have taught a class for the summer. Something was driving her, and she knew she needed a break from the classroom. She told the university this research was important, which it was, but she had been struggling with an underlying current of uneasiness.

Who am I kidding? she thought derisively. Not only was her work at the university grueling right now, but her relationship with her fiancé, Mitch, had not been going well for a while. After all, they were supposed to be married in a matter of months. It was not like she didn't love him. It was just that their personal lives were always the same, unquestionably in a rut. Mitch's indifference to most things could be tolerated, but when she felt it channeled in her direction, it made her feel unimportant.

Even though the wedding was close, Julia had nothing planned. They hadn't even secured a venue.

Mitch had said, "A civil ceremony will be sufficient, and we can celebrate anywhere."

Talk about indifference. *Maybe that's why I'm stalling.*

Julia glanced at the emerald on her left hand and considered the irony of her personal life. Last time she and Eduardo were together, she was available and he wasn't. This time, she wasn't and he was. How would Eduardo act toward her now? And more importantly, how would she react to him?

Julia placed a glass cap on top of the Petri dish. "That's the last one." She made a few more notes before standing and putting away the microscope and the rest of her equipment. She stowed the dish in the refrigerator and went to the sink to wash her hands and the last of the instruments on her work tray.

Julia smiled as Stephen handed her a towel. She felt most at home here in the Amazon with Stephen. They had a comfortable friendship, more like father and daughter than anything else. It was the same with

Lupa, except he doted on her like she was a granddaughter.

"The students will be here tomorrow," Julia reminded. "Don't forget."

"Ahh, yes. The students." Stephen often offered professors and college students his compound as a base camp, especially during the summer. Most of them were from the US, and Stephen provided a place for them to stay while they collected and studied the rainforest environment. The professors and students provided extra hands to gather new plants and insects and helped conduct experiments for Stephen's research. The arrangement was symbiotic, as each gave to the other and received something in return.

"You'll like them," Julia said.

"I usually do," Stephen countered as he took the towel from her and hung it up to dry. "I'd like to run some ideas past you as to my findings." He reached for a short stack of papers and Julia moved her stool closer.

Julia pushed the lid from the snack Lupa had brought and reached for a fresh piece of guava.

For the next couple of hours, they kept their heads together over the fresh data, their conversation and concentration so keen, they blocked out the rhythmic uproar from the forest as millions of insects outside carried on their once-in-a-lifetime courtships and inevitably deadly confrontations…some of which both Julia and Stephen were blissfully unaware.

5

Eduardo learned about the bodies when he landed his Cessna 182 at the grassy Kahepa airport. One of his men was waiting for him. Eduardo's jeep was parked inside the hanger where his plane usually sat, just as he had left it months before. He climbed in and drove off, leaving Mario, the airport overseer, to put the small plane into its place. And then the sky opened up.

Eduardo stood next to his jeep in the downpour. He pulled his collar together to keep out as much of the streaming rain as possible, even though he knew the effort was pointless. He tucked himself under a *bananeira* leaf so large even a man his size could easily stand under it without getting wet. He pulled off his hat and shook it, raking his fingers through his dark hair as he watched the water stream around him. From under his organic umbrella, Eduardo had a relatively clear view of his surroundings.

High overhead he could just make out dark silhouettes appearing like shadowy figures behind a gossamer curtain as monkeys moved from branch to branch.

Everywhere Eduardo looked was a maze of vegetation. Occasionally, even he, born not far from here, was taken aback by the immensity of the forest. Enormous trees, like massive buildings, spiraled upward more than one hundred feet, sometimes two hundred. One tree had buttresses traveling fifteen feet up its trunk, and then gently sloped outward toward the ground some twenty feet before diving into the Earth-like anchors pulled taught by a ship. Standing next to one of these mammoth trees, Eduardo felt as small as an insect.

The taller trees grew hundreds of feet into the sky, with only their massive trunks seen at ground level. Their branches high overhead reached far from the trunks for optimal use of sunlight which smothered much of the light below. Eduardo knew that high above the base of the *mogno*, the tops of the tree were swaying in the hot, often violent air currents. Here, within the underside of the canopy, no blowing wind reached so far below. Eduardo was drenched, not only from the rain but also by deep shadows. Moss hung everywhere, seeming to grow as he watched. Small plants grew out of vines clinging to trees covered with even more plants. Vines of exotic shapes and sizes knitted everything together.

Eduardo thought, *And this isn't even the densest part of the forest.*

There was still one body hanging in a tree. Water streamed down the corpse as two men struggled to lower it. Eduardo watched as his lead officer trotted to a group of local natives who emerged from the forest about twenty yards down the path. They stopped and waited.

Eduardo looked up. Rain continued to gush through the canopy overpowering almost all other sounds as it cascaded down a staircase of thousands of leaves before splashing onto the muddy ground. In another month, this land would be some twenty or thirty feet underwater, not drying again for several more months.

The irony of the weather, thought Eduardo. It hadn't rained for several days, and he wished it would have waited just one more. *Lot of good it will do to try to collect any evidence.*

There was never anything pretty about death, but given the extended time of exposure, especially in a rainforest, things became even uglier. The scene they found when they arrived was particularly disgusting. The bodies were in terrible shape. It had taken a day for locals to reach his office with the news. If Eduardo and his men had arrived here in another day, or two at the latest, muscle would have been sliding off the bones. Skin around their belts was already swollen, torn and oozing, with insects burrowing deep inside. Things decomposed quickly here. Huge fallen trees could be reduced to compost in a matter of months. It was the constant eighty degree or hotter heat and one hundred percent humidity. Perfect atmosphere for fast decay. On the other hand, the Brazilian *mogno* tree was so dense and rot resistant, a fallen tree branch could remain in pristine condition for decades, one of the reasons the tree was prized by illegal loggers. Above all, its value in foreign markets trumped all other reasons.

His officer turned from the natives and slogged back toward him. The officer slipped and almost fell before regaining his footing. "*O menino achou-os*," he yelled still sliding as he motioned behind him.

Eduardo glanced over the officer's shoulder and noticed a little boy peeking from behind a man's bare legs. The man gave no indication that the falling rain was any bother as it ran over his face and down his bare chest. The small group around him looked like sentries guarding their ruler. It was obvious they were not coming any closer. *So the boy found them.*

"*Ele disse que o homem sentando-se no chão cobras vermelhas tidas vindo do seu nariz e orelhas.*" The officer glanced at the natives and then back at Eduardo, concern etched on his face.

Eduardo looked up at the corpse. The boy's description was vivid. *Red snakes coming from his ears and nose*? *What could cause blood to stream that way*?

"*Eu sei que era sangue que ele conversava sobre. O que quer dizer*?"

The man was not dumb. Of course he knew the boy was talking about blood and not snakes. *I've never seen anything like this*, Eduardo thought. He clapped the shorter man on the shoulder and smiled confidently as he shouted, "*Não preocupe-se, meu amigo. Nós o compreender-nos-emos*." *Yes…we will figure it out*.

He would never let on, but Eduardo had no clue where to start. Every detail about these deaths was curious. There were no apparent wounds, only the tearing of swollen flesh caused after death from heat, humidity, and bugs. He expected holes from bullets, poisonous darts, spears, something. But there were none of those. Nothing. *So what did these men stumble into*?

As the last body neared the ground, the men carefully wrapped plastic around the torso and then around the head. They could hardly look at the body much less touch the skin. These men had never worn long, latex gloves, but Eduardo insisted on the precaution since, until they had autopsy results, he didn't know what they might be dealing with. Perhaps because of the protection, as one man cut the rope from the harness, he lost his grip on the corpse.

"*Vigilia*!" he shouted.

Eduardo turned in time to see the body hit the ground with a sickening pop. In all the muddy wetness, the head of the corpse had found an exposed root. Eduardo held his breath, closed his eyes, and shook his head. It was an unmistakable sound, even over the noise of the driving rain, like the sound of a melon dropping onto hard ground. The unfortunate man who lost his grip looked up, obviously wishing his boss were not standing there to witness his blunder. Eduardo had the same thought as he moved to the sheltered truck bed and pulled on his own latex gloves.

His lead officer followed, forced to yell in order to make himself heard. "*O que você pensa, Delegado*?"

For a moment Eduardo didn't know what to think. The body farthest away had been at the base of the tree. He reached for the closer corpse, pulled back the plastic, pushed one blue jean pant leg to the knee, and examined the man's skin. Eduardo pressed his thumb firmly against the flesh for about a half a minute, and then he let go, looking closely again.

The man standing next to him watched him, curious as to what Eduardo was doing.

Eduardo knew that, when a person died, the heart stopped beating and the blood stopped moving. Blood slowly started collecting in the lower part of the body. The men hanging in the harnesses should have lots of blood collected in the feet and legs. The dead man's skin was pale, and there was only a slight hint of bluing. No blood pooled in his lower body. Eduardo explained everything to the man watching him.

The man nodded his understanding and then slowly began to shake his head. "*Não parece-se há muito sangue nas suas pernas nem pés.*"

Eduardo exhaled and agreed that the legs didn't look blue. "*Não a mim, também não, meu amigo.*" The rain continued as he stared at the ground where the men had been hanging. *Where is all the blood*? The murky pool could have been mud or blood. He just couldn't know for sure because of all the water. He knew blood had seeped from the men's ears and nose because of the boy's account. Even so, there should have been a good bit left inside the body. Maybe what blood remained would help explain what had happened to the men.

Eduardo shielded his eyes from the rain as he checked the surroundings. Nothing looked unusual. Tall trunks. So many colors of green you couldn't begin to count them. Vines snaking up into the light. The calls of birds piercing the downpour. Nothing out of place. The jungle appeared as it always did.

They moved to the side of the truck as the last body slid into the bed. Eduardo finally answered the man's first question, "*De improviso, eu não posso pensar em nada que talvez tenha causado isto. Nós sabemos quem eles são*?" Not only did he not know what had killed the men, but he didn't even know who they were. Eduardo stripped off his gloves, turned them inside out, and tucked them into a small bag from his pocket. He tied it tightly closed and tossed it into a mesh trash bin on the side of the truck.

As the man shook his head and ranted in his native tongue, Eduardo became aware they had searched the truck and found nothing to identify the dead bodies. He was dismayed that there were no IDs. and no logging papers. The dead men had probably been illegal loggers. Even though they were pale from loss of blood, they looked like Brazilians. Other than those facts, Eduardo knew nothing about the men.

They might never know who these men were. Everyone knew the rules of illegal jungle loggers. If you got caught, you were on your own; no one claimed you; no one came to your defense; no one tried to help you. Most illegal loggers got away. Some got caught and were either deported or sent to jail. Occasionally, a few were killed. Eduardo agreed that the men probably thought no one would ever know they were here.

The rain slackened as if someone were turning off a faucet. Dark recesses in the sky grew lighter as more clouds moved past and the sun tried to penetrate the thick overhead foliage.

Eduardo's voice was lower as he faced the officer and asked if he had seen everything they found. "*Há algo mais eu não vi*?"

The officer answered that they had the climbing gear, the logging equipment, and the truck. They also had the rigging system off the trees.

Eduardo saw a tiny army of men looking through the forest for anything that might have been missed. With the heavy downpour,

Eduardo doubted they would find anything more.

The three bodies lay in the center of the bed of the truck, two straight and one in a sitting position.

Eduardo rewrapped the plastic on the body's legs. He needed to see a list of everything they had found. The officer assured that the list would be ready by the time he got to the village.

Eduardo shut the short tailgate and patted the top edge. "*Receba os corpos na geladeira no armazém.*" Eduardo smiled ruefully. *Ricardo doesn't like it, but he knows they're coming.* He had already called him to let him know to expect the bodies.

The man said he'd get the bodies into the cooler at Ricardo's store.

As the rain slowed to a trickle, the sound of insects increased. Their noise was almost as loud as the pounding rain had been. Eduardo crawled into the jeep and took one last look around as the men finished packing up to leave. He peered into the branches above, noticing all the shadowy figures were gone.

"*Nós vamos,*" the lead officer said as he opened the driver's door. The others packed into the front and back seats calling out similar goodbyes. No one wanted to ride in the truck bed with the bodies.

"*Veja-o num tempo,*" Eduardo said, assuring them that he would see them soon. He watched the trucks until they disappeared from view. They would have a sloppy drive back to the village maneuvering through the rain. Hopefully, when he finished his notes, the drizzle would be over.

Eduardo pulled out his notebook. There was not much to write in it. Mostly there were questions, so he began jotting them down.

As he finished, the rain ended. Looking back down at his notes, Eduardo thought, *Maybe Stephen can help answer some of my questions.*

Eduardo smiled a little remembering he sometimes referred to Stephen as "that old jungle doctor," especially if he wanted to get a rise out of him. Stephen wasn't really old, just older than Eduardo.

A couple of years ago Stephen learned of Eduardo's passion for gardening. Growing up, Eduardo had spent most of his summers tending an expansive family garden with his mother, but her death had stolen his interest for many years.

Eduardo attended the *Universidade de* São Paulo and studied economics, intending to work in international trade with a cousin. He hadn't graduated in the usual four years because he had to work to put himself through school. When he returned home at the age of twenty-four, he rekindled his childhood love with Serena, and as their relationship grew he knew there was no leaving again. Serena refused to go, and the bond they shared was too strong to allow him to leave. *Have I really been back in the jungle for twenty-two years*?

He and Serena married on a beautiful hillside where they built their home, and through her love and care, his zeal for gardening was restored.

His collection of plants and trees was expansive, spanning acre after acre behind his house. People from the area, and some from far away, were always finding a new plant or seedling and leaving an unfamiliar but welcomed edition on his porch. He spent hours, sometimes days, pouring through books and web sites trying to determine what the plant or tree might be. Several times Stephen helped him identify a specimen, and twice they discovered a plant never seen by the outside world, which they jointly named. When Stephen first saw Eduardo's garden, he was in awe. Even though he did not enjoy the tending, Stephen shared his passion for plants, and would often gather some specimens he thought Eduardo would find interesting.

It had been a while since Eduardo had seen Stephen. Three months ago, Eduardo set off on a journey to the Atlantic Ocean in his plane. He had to get away from the memories of Serena, to find a way to get past her death. He hopscotched across northern Brazil, stopping for fuel every three or four hours. The plane could probably make five and a half hours of flying time before needing refueling, but Eduardo wanted there to be no chance of running out of fuel over the jungle. He made it to São Luis and then turned southeast, flying along the coast until he found a secluded beach wide enough to land his plane and set up camp.

There was a small village several miles away, so he occasionally hiked to it for provisions and a good home-cooked meal. His favorite was *pernil,* a sandwich of pork, cheese, and pineapple that he washed down with *siriguila* juice made from a grainy fruit resembling a pear, with a similar taste combined with apple.

Several times he rented a motorboat and explored the small river that emptied into the ocean next to the village. He dove for lobster, speared tasty sea bass the locals called *merluza,* and even captured a mature octopus in the emerald, rocky shallows off shore. The variety of tasty meals were easy to cook and satisfying. Most of the time he lay in his hammock, strung between two tall palms next to the brightest white beach he had ever seen, and thought of Serena.

Serena. Would he ever get over losing his raven-haired beauty? Whether with her words or with her lovely body, she could always get him going. Whenever he angered her, her temper was hot and unrelenting. She fought him like a tiger. Just as quickly as her temper flared, she would be over it, all soft and sorry, and those times were certainly worth it all. After a wild burst of anger, her lovemaking was just as intense.

He pictured Serena standing barefoot in the kitchen kneading bread on the big wooden block in the center, a smudge of flour falling on her cheek as she tucked a wisp of hair behind her ear; Serena waiting for him on the porch as he made his way home each day, waving her apron as he rounded the bend in the narrow road; Serena holding his hand and pulling him through the valley to the waterfall swirling in mist not far from their home; Serena dropping her skirt and opening her blouse to his hands…his lips. He shook his head, trying to shake the memories away as the start of a smile faded. He must get on with his life. He had to get over her.

By the time he was ready to return to Kahepa, his soul was healing. He would always have the Serena scar, but the festering was over and the itching had begun. Life would go on, and now he knew, so would he.

Eduardo gazed up at the water dripping from the bougainvillea leaves next to the jeep. A ray of light penetrated the canopy spotlighting one leaf. Shaped like a small heart, it was a dark, rich green, in striking contrast to the plant's mass of neon purple flowers.

Eduardo thought back to the bodies. He needed autopsies as soon as possible. He'd call Stephen and see if he could meet him in the village later this afternoon. Eduardo glanced over at his travel-worn bag, and could not wait to get home. Instead, he started the jeep and headed back toward the village.

6

Charlie Felks hugged the trunk of the *andiroba* tree and pulled himself over the limb he'd been trying to reach for a good ten minutes. Standing about eighty feet at its dome, it wasn't a large tree by Amazon standards, but it was still impressive. This one had the potential to top out at 120 or so feet. As he juggled binoculars, rope, and an awkward walkie-talkie, Charlie took a moment to realize the climb had been strenuous even for him, an avid mountain biker and black belt in karate. As a sophomore in college, Charlie was not exactly sure what he wanted to do with his grown-up life but soon recognized that it wasn't this.

They were an odd group who'd arrived in the Amazon five days before. A package set with a professor, Dr. Nigel Diobelo, his graduate assistant, Drake Harris, and two lucky students, Charlie and his girlfriend, Jennifer Parnell, both chosen to accompany Nigel and Drake as they planned to explore the Amazon collecting environmental samples of soil, plants, and air for various projects back at Chapel Hill. It was not until they arrived that the students suspected their professor and his assistant had a hidden agenda.

Nigel came to be a professor late in life. He had only been in front of a classroom for eight years, and he was fifty-nine. He joked that he had been unsure of what he wanted to be when he grew up, so he had tried many career paths. He was tall and beginning to round a little through the middle, and there was always a slight smile on his face, which in itself was a little disconcerting. He had a full head of shocking black hair that could be mistaken as dyed but for a sprinkling of gray that had to be natural.

Nigel carried a satchel similar to the one Indiana Jones always carried, brown and worn soft from oily skin and perspiration. It was always slung across his chest so there was never a chance of losing it. Charlie had glimpsed all manner of professor-type stuff, a notebook with pens, various small plant and insect identification booklets, a small magnifying glass, but he never saw Nigel use them. All he ever saw the professor pull out was another box of Chiclets chewing gum. Nigel made no secret of this part of his stash, always offering them around.

I guess we all have our addictions, Charlie thought when he first saw them. He couldn't put his finger on what bothered him so much about Nigel. Maybe it was that little smile. Maybe it was the way he manipulated everyone around him. Maybe it was the sound of his voice, which had a smoothness running through it like Sir Anthony Hopkins's portrayal of Hannibal Lector in *Silence of the Lambs*. Charlie inadvertently shivered at the comparison.

Drake had a strange personality. No matter what Charlie said or did, Drake took exception to it. It was as though Drake felt threatened by him, and there was no reason. Charlie couldn't have cared less about sparring with him, and Drake could be the big dog as far as Charlie was concerned. But there was something abnormal about Drake. He would vacillate between explosive outbursts, and other times he would be quiet and introspective. Often, his excessively serious opinion sharpened into sarcasm, and he seemed to enjoy taking verbal jabs at the others.

He was small but very strong, carrying much more equipment than his thin body should allow. His light blonde hair and blue eyes made him an oddity in this part of the world, and his dark rimmed glasses reminded Charlie of the frames Harry Potter wore. He appeared to idolize Nigel, which was relatively normal for professors and their assistants, but it verged on blind adoration. He did whatever his professor asked of him. Put a gun in his hand and Charlie was certain Drake would kill someone if Nigel asked, especially if he was in one of his volatile moods. To add to this formula, he was fastidious with everything, straightening and cleaning anything he could reach out and touch. He was also constantly snacking on a seemingly never-ending supply of nutty-fruity trail mix.

Charlie looked down at Jennifer. She had found a seat on a fallen limb from this very tree, and she smiled up at him. He smiled back. His tall, thin Jennifer, with the body of a runner—and run she did almost every day—was his soul mate. Oh, they had a fuss or two now and then, but nothing that could push them apart. Her long, curly hair was held in a semblance of order by a ponytail, and she couldn't have looked prettier. Her main interest in coming to the Amazon was to see the wildlife. She was an avid animal lover. She had already declared zoology her field of study, even though she had just finished her freshman year.

Her near obsession began when she read a short journal article describing a sixteen month expedition recently completed into the Amazon River basin where thousands of new animal, insect, and reptile species had been discovered. So far, they hadn't seen as much as one monkey. They observed armies of ants and scads of mosquitoes, and the largest beetle Charlie ever saw crawled over him last night, otherwise, no mammals or reptiles except for a few lizards raced across their path.

Jennifer had taken a class with Nigel on rainforest preservation and his knowledge and seemingly gentle nature impressed her. A trip to the

Amazon fit in well with her college plans, so when he invited her along, she jumped at the prospect. It wasn't until after she made her plans that Nigel revealed a catch. She could come along if she could pay her way, and if her father would give a donation to help defray the cost of all the essentials the professor needed to acquire. As a dot com giant, her father was more than happy to send a sizable check that paid for everything they needed and more. He thought the trip would be good for his daughter. Toughen her up. Let her dodge jaguars. After all, he'd dodged a few over the years in his line of work. And he had plans of his own that didn't include a college-age daughter being under him all summer.

Charlie looked at the binoculars in his hand and knew they had taken a chunk of Mr. Parnell's donation. Jennifer also paid Charlie's way, which hurt his pride a little, but he didn't have the money and neither did his mother back home in Colorado.

Then there was the guide, Tiago, what the Amazonians called a *seringueiro*, or long-time rubber tapper, who had prowled the forest at night for decades, eking out one of the most dangerous and lonely livings on the planet. In order to make any profit, rubber tappers must tap at least a hundred trees a day, starting in the wee hours of the morning and gathering their cups by midday, before the warmth of the afternoon thickened and solidified the tree resin, and sealed off the cuts.

Once the cups were retrieved, there was more work to do. The *serengueiro* returned to his hut where he sat over a bed of burning palm nuts, the only fuel that could cure the rubber resin properly. He applied layer after layer of molten rubber until it became a ball of about one hundred pounds. At the end of this process, it was time to go back out and begin another day of cutting, collecting, and curing.

Tiago had met Nigel the year before and was happy to work for the professor—not only because he paid him so well but also because Nigel took him away from rubber tapping. Tiago was proud he no longer had to live the life of a slave of sorts, since tappers were never completely out of debt to the middlemen who provided food and supplies in exchange for the rubber.

There were times Tiago was forced to guide some unsavory characters, and if he occasionally had to look the other way when one of them broke the law, he did it because it kept him away from the drudgery life of the rubber tapper. But Tiago sensed an evil side to Nigel. He never spoke of it, nor was there anyone he could talk to without fear for his own life.

As for Nigel, Tiago had proven himself a trusted guide who never overstepped the bounds of employer and employee. Tiago knew his place, and Nigel knew it too.

Tiago was more agile than a man half his age, almost toothless, and always wore a long sleeved plaid shirt and someone's cast-off khaki pants. Since they were two sizes greater than he needed, they were held up with a rope tied in a slip knot. His feet were covered with the thinnest of shoes and his dark skin sometimes held signs of red or black stains, ceremonial leftovers from growing up in his tribe.

When the group reached the rainforest, Nigel explained there was more to this trip than their projects back home. He gave a passionate plea to the students to help save the Amazon from illegal loggers who were destroying it at an alarming rate. Drake already knew the agenda before coming here, but Charlie and Jennifer had no clue. Nigel's plea became a lecture filled with one horrific tale of devastation after another, and finally convinced by their leader, Charlie and Jennifer agreed to help.

So there was Charlie, high in a tree. He was unsure how far Nigel planned to go to stop the road crew out there, but Charlie already voiced his conviction and concern that there would be no bloodshed. He might be from the West but Charlie wasn't getting involved in any kind of show-down.

When the conversation took place, Nigel had smiled and cut his eyes toward Drake before quietly saying, "Of course not…we are here to gather information." The words rang hollow.

A recent course in cultural anthropology piqued Charlie's interest, especially in the medical practices of Indian shamans. He agreed to accompany Jennifer to the Amazon because of his interest in the indigenous people of the area, though at this point he didn't know whether he would get to see one up close on this trip. Then, after meeting Nigel and Drake, Charlie knew he could never let Jennifer make the trip without him.

A soft squelch from the walkie-talkie made him look down at the three people thirty feet below. He pushed the button on the side, "Yeees?"

"What do you see?" Nigel's level voice filled the box.

"I just got up here. Can you give me a minute?"

There was no answer.

Charlie was aware he was breathing hard from the climb, so he slowly inhaled and exhaled, willing his heart to calm so he could balance himself. He sat straddling the limb, his legs locked tightly, like a cowboy on a bull waiting to come out of its chute. Even though there was no 2,000 pound animal furious at his being on its back, Charlie felt himself in a precarious position, which, in truth, he was.

He put the binoculars to his eyes and began to focus. "Whoa…" he mumbled to himself surprised at the high resolution. "This has to be government-issue." He took a moment to examine them. Olive drab should have given it away, but he'd had no time to look at them before he'd half crawled, half been hauled up here in the makeshift harness that had surely put welts in his crotch. He adjusted the ropes in the creases of his legs and winced.

Charlie glanced back down at Nigel. *I can't stand that man. I don't even know him, and I hate him.* He would never say it aloud. *Remind me why I'm here*, he thought for the millionth time.

About a half-mile to the south, the loggers set up a crude camp next to the river. The work equipment compared to the makeshift camp looked fairly new and large. Charlie had spent five summers working for his uncle building roads, and he learned to drive almost every kind of machinery available.

"I'd love to climb onto that bad boy," he mumbled as he eyed the largest dozer. He pressed the zoom button and was shocked when he could make out the face of one man next to it who was shouting up to another man.

Charlie picked up the radio. "Okay. I see two dozers. One is an Allis Chalmer…I think it's an HD16, and the other is a Cat D8H. The Allis Chalmer has a rotohead on the front. There are two king cab three fifties and one military light truck that can carry fourteen to sixteen in the back. I count…eight men…wait…there come two more. Ten men I can see."

"Are you sure?"

Charlie looked down, and thought sarcastically to himself, *I can't see inside tents and behind trees*. He picked up the binoculars again. "So far I've seen two trucks for hauling the dozers and the others for the men. Wait, three men are walking along the perimeter around the opening of the forest with automatic weapons, so that makes thirteen. The foreman has a gun tucked in his belt at his back. Wait. Another man just stepped out from behind a tree. Looks like he was using it as a urinal." Charlie chuckled at his joke. He heard no answer. He didn't think Nigel or Drake enjoyed his humor.

The bulldozer engine died. Charlie looked back through the binoculars toward the camp and froze. Staring back at him was a man standing in the doorway of the dozer with his own pair of binoculars. He shouted to the foreman and motioned toward Charlie.

"They've spotted me!" Charlie yelled as he slid the rope and pulley over the edge and belayed toward the ground. Nigel and Drake grabbed their packs and took off running through the forest, leaving the two younger students to follow as best they could.

Jennifer motioned Charlie down. "Hurry!" Her panic rose as it took what seemed like hours for him to reach the ground. She hastily put on her backpack and looped Charlie's over her shoulder. As his feet hit the dirt, Jennifer grabbed his hand and pulled hard, propelling him forward as she began to run after the others.

Charlie jerked away while gathering the rope like a parachutist with his cords. He raced after Jennifer as the shouts grew louder behind. Shots rang out, hitting a tree near his head, and he grabbed Jennifer's hand as he moved around her. He watched Nigel and Drake dodging branches and jumping over logs. Charlie and Jennifer were the ones in the most direct line of fire.

At first he didn't feel any pain, just the forward momentum of the strike forcing him head over heels. Jennifer's hand jerked free, and she continued to run. It happened so fast, the shot barely registered. Moments later, Charlie felt searing agony in his left shoulder which almost took his breath away.

Jennifer looked behind and could just make out the men sprinting in their direction. She ran back and grabbed Charlie's hand. "Come on!" she yelled as she gritted her teeth and pulled hard. As soon as Charlie was on his feet, Jennifer pulled harder as she watched Nigel and Drake disappear from view. She hadn't seen Tiago at all.

It seemed as though Charlie was moving in slow motion. The rope was draped all around him, so Jennifer looped it several times around his neck as she propelled him forward. She sucked air through her clenched teeth as she watched the blood flow down the front of Charlie's shirt. He groaned but kept running.

Rain began to fall in sheets for the second time that afternoon, and for the next couple of minutes they continued racing headlong into the downpour. They had no idea where they were or where they were going.

Jennifer could only guess where Nigel and Drake were now. As she dragged Charlie forward, the vegetation parted, and they stopped dead when they found themselves in the middle of a road.

To their right, a truck idled. Nigel and Drake were seated in the back. The man next to the tailgate motioned for the younger students to come, and without thinking, Jennifer and Charlie raced forward and dove onto the slippery bed. Only when they slid into a seated position did they see the three plastic shrouds in the center of the truck.

Jennifer shrank away, scrambling for the corner as far away as she could get while the truck jarred forward and the gears engaged. They braced themselves as the truck worked hard to turn around. They headed back in the direction the truck had just come.

The truck moved forward as Charlie muttered, "Bodies," to no one in particular. He was irritated by the tangle of ropes rubbing against him and grimaced as he carefully lifted them over his head. He dropped them onto the shrouds covering the corpses as he groaned.

Nigel ignored Charlie's utterance and assumed an air of normalcy as he offered everyone some chewing gum. After no one accepted, he popped a few little squares into his own mouth. Motioning toward the bullet wound in Charlie's shoulder, he asked, "You all right?"

"Those are bodies, aren't they?" Charlie asked Nigel.

"Evidently," Nigel responded indifferently. "I asked...are you okay?"

The exchange roused Jennifer, and she slid closer to Charlie, dragging her backpack while rummaging for something clean to press into the seeping wound.

Charlie looked around at the group. "Where's Tiago?"

Nigel smiled and reached for the rope. He slowly wound it into a tight loop that would fit into the duffel bag he managed to snag as they raced away. "Tiago knows what he must do. He'll keep an eye on the group out there." He tossed his head toward the forest from which they had escaped.

"Oh, Charlie…Can we get this off?" Jennifer whispered as she gingerly tugged at the sleeve of his shirt.

Charlie's anger at the two men for running off and leaving them overshadowed his pain as he let Jennifer slide the sleeve from his shoulder. Bodies forgotten for the moment, he continued, "You made sure you left us between you and the loggers, didn't you? You never looked back to see if we were okay!" he spat, as he finished unbuckling the harness he'd used to get up into the tree.

Nigel smiled and clucked his tongue as he shook his head. "Charlie, Charlie, Charlie… You're a strong young man. I certainly didn't think anyone would be hit. I was trying to find a clear path, and instead, I found us a means of escape."

Jennifer ripped open a new bag of cotton socks and pushed a pair against the hole in Charlie's shoulder.

The pain was excruciating.

If there weren't three dead people between them, Charlie might have hit Nigel. Charlie yelled, "This was just one big lucky break! No one was going to get 'hit?' Guess what? You were wrong, Pro-fessor!" Charlie spit the words at him.

Jennifer tried to shush him as she slid the harness from under him.

"I won't be quiet," he flung the words at her. "There's something wrong with that man!" He spoke the words as if Nigel couldn't hear them.

Nigel lowered his head, but he raised his eyes to stare at Charlie as he placed the organized rope into the bag. "Truth be told, I've been shot. Several times." Nigel sighed heavily. "I understand your anger and your pain, this being your first trip to the jungle; and I'm supposing, your first time being shot. Each time I took a bullet, it hurt less. I willed it to hurt less, and it did. You can do that, you know."

Charlie ignored Nigel's pompous admonition, closing his eyes as the truck slid and jostled through the narrow ruts. An infuriated moan came from him, "Where are we going?"

Nigel chuckled, "I haven't the slightest idea."

Charlie opened his eyes and looked at Nigel who had not looked away. "You haven't the slightest idea…" he repeated. "Great."

Nigel uncrossed his arms and shifted his seating position. "Away from bullets, at the very least." He reached for the harness, folded it neatly, laid it atop the rope, and zipped the bag.

"Oow!" Charlie yelled as Jennifer pushed harder trying to stop the flow of blood.

"Sorry," Jennifer said quietly. "I have to stop the bleeding, Charlie." She started taking deeper breaths. "I think I might pass out."

"You push any harder, and *I* might pass out!" Charlie turned his attention back to Nigel. "Look, man, don't get smart. I've been shot. We're in the back of a hearse," he motioned toward the bodies, "with who knows what kind of men up front." Charlie didn't even try to hide his anger. "How could you jump into a truck without knowing who the men up there were? Could they possibly be the loggers? Did you think about that?" Between the pain and the anger, Charlie didn't know which was taking over.

Nigel calmly replied, "The man identified himself as a police officer of some sort. At least that is what I think he said. My Portuguese is a little rusty."

"You think?" Charlie mustered. "So first we're running from murderers, and then we end up in the back of a truck with three dead people, and you *think* he said they were police officers. That's just great. Come on," he seethed as he grabbed Jennifer's hand. He started to rise, but the pain in his shoulder surged, and he fell back against her. Hard.

"Charlie, let's just see where we end up," Jennifer whispered in his ear.

Charlie turned toward her with an incredulous look on his face, "Are you hearing yourself? We're in the middle of a jungle with parasites and snakes and all kinds of insects and animals that can kill us. I've been shot." He gestured toward the three bodies, "They may have been shot. Besides being in the company of these two madmen," he pointed at Nigel and Drake. "We're in the back of a truck with who knows who, going who knows where!" He considered their situation and laughed. "Maybe we're the crazy ones, huh, Jennifer? Are you glad you're here, now? Ready to go home yet, honey?" He sagged from the exertion.

Jennifer had enough. "Then what do you want, Charlie? You want to get out of the truck and become part of someone's target practice? This isn't helping."

"There's no reason to get angry at Jennifer," Drake spoke for the first time since they had been spotted by the loggers. "She's just trying to talk some sense into you. Were you going to fling yourself out of the back of the truck?"

Charlie glared at Drake. "Actually, that was exactly what I was going to do," he answered, grasping the absurdity as the words came out.

Drake sat next to Nigel, imitating the professor's calm demeanor. The rain stopped as quickly as it had started. Drake pulled a Ziploc bag from his pocket and removed a folded piece of cloth. He took off his glasses and dried them as he glanced in Charlie's direction. "You should be angry with yourself…." He let the words trail off.

Charlie narrowed his eyes. "What did you say?"

"You heard me." He blew hot breath on his glasses making them fog over before he resumed wiping them. "You should be angry with yourself."

"Myself."

"Yes, yourself."

"Because?"

Drake could not hide the amusement he was feeling as he finished. He carefully put his glasses back on before saying, "*You* are the one who gave us away." He grinned at Charlie as he folded the cloth, put it back in the bag, and stowed it away.

Charlie gulped in bites of air as adrenaline coursed through his body. His anger erupted. Without realizing what he was doing, he lunged across the truck, oblivious of anyone or anything as his good hand clamped around the front of Drake's throat.

Drake's glasses flew off, and before anyone could react, they were sliding precariously toward a hole in the corner of the truck bed. His eyes were wide, and the only sound coming from him was a small sucking noise as he tried to breathe.

Jennifer screamed for Charlie to stop, but he couldn't hear her.

Charlie realized Nigel's face was against his ear when he heard soft words, "Let go of him. Now."

The danger in the older man's voice wormed into Charlie's brain, and he loosened his grip on the smaller man.

The truck slipped around a corner and slowed. Charlie released Drake, who coughed as he rubbed the front of his neck. "You…will… be…sorry…" he sputtered as he crawled in the direction he had last seen his glasses. "You better hope I find…" he didn't finish as his hand closed over them. He continued to cough, and Charlie was pleased to see Drake's hands were shaking as he fumbled for another Ziploc bag with yet another clean cloth.

* * *

From the common room, Stephen looked up from reading a report when the dripping from the rain was interrupted by the sound of an approaching truck. He stayed seated, sipping a tepid cup of *pau d'arco* tea, as was his practice every day about this time. It was a special blend Lupa created from the bark of the tall canopy tree with the same name. Lupa ground the bark he gathered nearby and boiled it to extract the *bom mágica*, as he sometimes called it. Stephen guessed it was what Americans might call *mojo*, but he knew the chemicals extracted were actually quinoids and a small quantity of benzenoids and flavonoids. Lupa just knew they healed, not caring what they were called. Stephen drank the tea because he believed it killed some types of bacteria, parasites, and fungi, protected him from a variety of cancers, and mostly, kept Parkinson's disease, a curse of his family, at bay.

* * *

Charlie stifled a yell of pain as the brakes of the truck squealed.

"Maybe we're in a village," Jennifer sounded hopeful.

"Maybe we're in the logging camp," Charlie snarled, his hand again clutching the balled up socks against the front of his shoulder.

"Let me do the talking," Nigel said to everyone.

"If you can de-rust your Portuguese," Charlie countered.

Nigel smiled but made no comment.

The truck came to a final stop and two doors opened. Two men came around the back, and one pulled down the tail gate. Drake stumbled out with Nigel following. Charlie slid to the edge where one man helped him stand. He spoke to Charlie, but the words were babble. Nigel answered, and the man nodded. He turned Charlie toward the front of the truck, guiding him in the direction of a large building.

Jennifer followed, shaking from the confrontation between the men in the back of the truck. For some reason, the interaction had frightened her more than the men chasing and shooting at them. Right now, Jennifer wondered why it had been so important for her to come to the Amazon.

Stephen stood and walked to the open doorway. He recognized the men who got out of the front as working with Eduardo. *What are they doing here*?

More people appeared from the back of the truck, and Stephen saw one was bleeding. He calling over his shoulder to Lupa, "Get my medical bag!" as he hurried out to meet them.

7

The crowd of protestors below continued to grow as Arthur Livingston stood looking out the windowed wall of his office in Bettsville, Alabama, twenty-three miles from the Port of Mobile. His arms were folded over his athletic chest, his breathing not quite under control. The heavy sprinkling of silvery gray in his wavy, dark hair was more pronounced under the recessed lights above his desk, which also highlighted the glistening sweat over his upper lip.

Arthur stood tall in the window casting the illusion below of a gentle giant watching over the group. He was nowhere near gentle, and he made every effort to let anyone coming in contact with him know he was a tough man. A hard man. A man to be wary of. He ran a two billion dollar company with over 35,000 employees around the world. He had a crude tongue and didn't care whose feelings he hurt, and he was proud of his demeanor. He viewed everyone, including his family, as pawns to be used as he saw fit. Magnanimous was not a word one would use to describe Arthur Livingston.

Arthur pursed his lips, slowly shaking his head. Most signs the protesters carried had the word "rainforest" written on them and something about "workers." It was enough he had a parking lot full of unruly protesters in front of his company, but now he had problems deep in the heart of South America.

The report about the mysterious deaths from Will Thompson, his manager on the Amazon project, was disturbing. Arthur couldn't have cared less about the dead men themselves, nor could he afford to dwell on them. He always made sure he didn't know anything specific about the men he hired in other countries. Hell, he didn't even know much about the ones in this very building. He didn't need to know them. Pawns. Yes, they were all pawns.

Employees. Just another thorn in my side. Too bad everything can't be mechanized. Anyone with employees knows they are pains in the ass. Always whining about something. 'You're not fair. We want more. Don't do that.' Pains in the ass. Just like those tree-huggers waving signs outside my office.

Arthur looked at the throng down on the street and for the third time this morning wondered how much more of this his blood pressure could take. His wife made him promise that he would call for a doctor's appointment to have a physical. He wondered why she bothered. He guessed she wanted him alive long enough to finish the new house.

Arthur had been married to the same woman for over thirty years. Catherine. To Arthur, she was still a beauty, and at the maturing age of fifty-eight, she still had a girlish figure. His friends were envious. Most of them either had badgering, bossy wives who had not fared well with their looks over the years or were married to strikingly beautiful, young women who drove them crazy with worry. *It's better to have affairs with them than marry them.*

He thought of Catherine and almost smiled. Almost. He had loved her desperately all those years ago. But the passionate love he and Catherine once shared was gone, replaced with a marriage of convenience. They had two beautiful, if headstrong, daughters, who loved their mother dearly. Sometimes Arthur envied the closeness of his girls, but it was too late for him now after missing too many of their dance recitals and too many family nights, opting instead to work and pay the bills or drink and play in someone else's sandbox.

Arthur glanced back out the window. Yes, there were regrets, but there was nothing he could do to change the past.

He thought about the new house, not really a house but a pretentious mansion. How did Catherine ever convince him to even start construction? It was costing a fortune just to build it, and Arthur shied away from thinking about how much his wife was spending on new furnishings and decorating.

Arthur knew why the flame in their marriage had been extinguished. It was mostly his fault, even though he would never admit it to anyone else. As tough and strong as he was, he had a weakness. Hell, if the truth was known, he had plenty of weaknesses, but he had one in particular: a lust for young women. He had hurt Catherine, but it didn't stop him. She always had the good sense to look the other way. He often thought he should pull back, but he was not getting any younger, and at this stage of life he needed the stimulation of younger women. Arthur was afraid if he quit chasing the ladies, even older ones, he might never have the chance again, and that prospect was unthinkable.

He guessed guilt was why he let her talk him into building the mansion on Lake Minowend. This was her gift for pretending their marriage was sound, but the emerging estate was growing into a monstrosity. He'd always been told that you should plan on adding on a third of your budget to any building project, but he had to believe the plans for Happy Valley Estate, an ironic name Catherine had coined to mask their unhappy marriage, grew by over half. The interior halls had taken on the semblance of an art gallery. Hell, the dining table alone could be expanded to seat twenty-four. Arthur shook his head at the thought of the inevitable dinner parties he'd have to host.

Arthur indulged Catherine with the one speck he had of a conscience, so he turned a blind eye to the size of the project and the spending. *It is, after all, just money. If it keeps her happy and out of my hair, so be it. I'll just cut more trees to pay the bills.*

As Arthur watched through the window, he saw a woman throw something at one of his security guards. The guard didn't respond.

That's good. Keep your cool, man.

Then the guard walked back to the guard house and picked up a phone. It took a moment for Arthur to realize what the guard was doing.

"Son of a...!" Arthur yelled as he turned from the window. He grabbed the phone and pushed several buttons. The other guard lifted his radio.

"Yes, sir," the guard looked up at the side of the building.

"What the hell is he doing? Don't tell me he's calling the police!" Arthur ranted, "What do you think I pay you for? Don't you know you are playing right into their hands? That's just what they want. We get police, and they get more publicity. Get him off the damn phone! Do it now!"

Arthur threw the phone back into the cradle and fell into his chair with a thud. He covered his face and tried to calm down. He rubbed his temples with both hands and felt the blood vessel across his forehead beating like a bass drum.

I must calm down. I must calm down.

The leather squeaked as Arthur leaned back in his chair and closed his eyes. Livingston Lumber Company had been a part of his family for over a hundred years. His great-grandfather started it, focusing on hard pine for his early logging operations. During the late 1800s and the turn of the century, the company had grown enormously.

In the 1940s, his grandfather and father saw the opportunity to offer different varieties of wood and opened their first company branch outside of the United States. Livingston Lumber now sold almost sixty types of hardwoods from Central and South America, Africa, and Asia. Business was booming.

Yet, Arthur always worried. He guessed a measure of his worry had to do with those damned tree-huggers. *What is the deal with them*? They were always targeting him.

Arthur speculated how to curtail the most recent uprising from the environmentalists. He smirked as he raised his arms and put his hands behind his head. He'd put out another press release. Yes, that's just what he would do. He'd remind everyone about Livingston Lumber's forest protection certifications, its forestry college scholarships, its Protect Wildlife Foundation. After all, his company did all the right stuff when it came to their public reputation.

Arthur knew the rules, and he had pledged to act responsibly toward the management of forests through his logging practices. He'd promised to employ people ethically. He'd promised to not only protect the environment but also to enhance it. His quality control department had a paper trail tracing the origin of all of their wood from harvesting right up to selling. Of course, people had no idea the trail was bogus. His tight-lipped shipping crew could create a legal route in moments. It just took a few key strokes and *print*. They'd better make the importing look legal with what he was paying them.

Yep, Arthur had certifications out the wazoo, but certifications were only as valid as the certifier, and Arthur could bend the truth feeling no shame or guilt. Numerous lumber companies did the same thing. The public was satisfied as long as there were certificates. Who was going to check if they weren't authentic? Stupid public.

Arthur sat up and opened his eyes. The first thing he saw was a framed picture of the Earth. It was a particularly nice drawing with North and South America visible. One of his major clients brought it to him and insisted Arthur hang it in his office. Across the bottom were the words *Think Green*.

Arthur was sick and tired of hearing about deforestation and global warming. He had heard enough of that nonsense. Screw going green, unless it's green as in dollars. Let governments and churches fix the world's problems. Arthur Livingston was making money, and he'd be damned if a bunch of radical protesters were going to tell him how to run his business. And why was everyone blaming the timber companies for the shrinking Amazon anyway? It used to be the loggers, but not anymore. What about all the vegetarians in the U.S.? Didn't they know they were one of the main sources of shrinking rainforests with their rising demand for soy products?

Arthur wanted to walk outside and yell at the people below, *What is the leading cause of deforestation today? Do you know? Of course not. You're too busy blaming me. It's cattle and soybeans, you dumb asses. Not logging*. Arthur guffawed. Probably half the people down on the street in front of his building were vegetarians, directing their protest in the wrong direction. Of course, Arthur knew the vegetarians weren't the actual cause of deforestation. It was the chicken farmers who needed an endless source of soybeans to feed their chickens, although, as he thought about it, the people below probably ate a lot of chickens. They at least contributed to the destruction, or so he would like to think.

And what about the government, always sticking its nose into his business? Livingston Lumber stayed one step ahead of the law on almost every job, and even when they did get caught, the fines were laughable. Arthur sneered. Why, once one of his customers was caught with a load of illegal mahogany and was fined a whopping three thousand dollars.

Arthur chuckled for a moment and then frowned. He glanced toward the window thinking that in recent years, the Brazilian government was cracking down on the logging of mahogany trees. There was pressure coming from everywhere. Extricating and delivering the trees was getting tougher. Just recently, a competitor from an Asian company was fined almost two million dollars. Arthur wanted to steer clear of that type of fine.

Arthur, once again focused on the issue at hand: the mahogany trees. "Mogno," as the Brazilians called it, was the most valuable in the world, and it was the most beautiful. Arthur looked at his desk. It had been his grandfather's. This mahogany desk had been built when trees were felled and floated out of the Amazon on log rafts.

Arthur swiveled his chair and looked at the collection of pictures adorning the wall to his left. They were grainy, black and white pictures of the huge rafts, one after another floating through the smooth current of the giant Amazon River in what appeared to be a parade. There was one picture showing the tree trunks lashed together forming a gigantic, buoyant barge. Still another picture captured a man running across the logs as effortlessly as a gymnast preparing for a series of handsprings on a gymnasium floor.

Damn shame, Arthur thought. Very few logs came down the river today unless there was documentation showing they had been legally harvested. Of course, there weren't any significant trees still standing conveniently near a waterway. They were long gone.

Oh, how Arthur wished he could have experienced that earlier time for himself. *Now those were the days*, he thought, as he ran his hand over the smooth grain of his desk. He leaned forward and pushed a button.

"Yes, sir," Jane came on the line instantly.

"Jane, I need a strong cup of coffee." He thought a moment as he sucked in a large breath and changed his mind. "Come to think of it, maybe I've had enough coffee for today. I'll grab a bottle of water from the fridge, but would you bring me some aspirin?"

"I think that's a good idea," Jane's voice sounded thin and far away.

"Can you get Will back on the phone?"

"I'm sure I can. Just take a minute." The line clicked off.

This latest event in South America only added to Arthur's burdens. Three dead men could be a problem, even if they were over 4000 miles away. Of course, no one knew they worked for him. Arthur really had very little control of the situation from here, but he knew Will would do everything possible to make sure no one associated the dead men with Livingston Lumber.

A few minutes later Jane brought him a bottle of aspirin, gesturing toward the phone as it began to ring.

Arthur still marveled at today's technology. His men were outfitted with the best satellite phones available and were reachable in minutes.

"Give me some good news, boy." Arthur poured more than the recommended dosage into his palm and downed the pills, as he sat back and tipped the bottle of water.

"Not much info yet, Mr. Livingston. The natives are spooked. From what I can tell the deaths were kinda nasty; pretty gory."

Arthur picked up a letter and scanned it. "Well, I really am sorry," he answered distantly. "Just tell me who did it and when you'll be back on the job."

"No one has any idea who did it, sir. All I've heard is that the authorities are baffled. Nothing like anything they've ever seen before."

Arthur crumbled the paper in his hands and tossed it into the trash. He half rose and slammed his hands flat onto his desk. He knew Will heard it at the other end of the line. "That's not what I asked you!" Arthur felt his face redden as his blood pressure shot higher. Even though he knew he shouldn't be so hard on the boy, he yelled, "Frankly I don't give a rat's ass about what killed them. I only want to know when you will be cutting me some more logs!"

"Mr. Livingston, these men are scared. Hell, I'm scared! There were no outside wounds. Word has it they were bleeding from their noses. From their ears. I knew those men. I was supposed to go with them, but somethin' else came up. It could have been me!" Will breathed heavily when he finished, shocked at his outburst toward the man who paid his salary. He checked his temper and tried to calm down.

Arthur was surprised as well. He had worked with Will for some time now, and the boy never got rattled. Arthur had the presence of mind not to snap back at Will. He certainly didn't want Will to up and quit. Arthur changed his tactics. He needed Will right now, at least until he could find a good replacement. He could never let Will know he was even considering that.

He kept his voice soft and reassuring, but even so, his words came out ominous. "Look, Will. Strange things happen. I'm just glad you weren't with them. But don't let this stop you from getting some men right back out there. We've got competitors nipping at our heels. Those Chinks would love to see us out of business. I've got orders waiting to be filled. You do have some men to take their places, don't you?"

Will heard the tone in Arthur's voice and understood its meaning. When he answered his voice sounded composed. "I've got two foremen willing to take out a team. They're the only ones left with experience out in the field. I'll have to get more men from somewhere else. No one around here wants to take a chance after what they've heard. I'll send upriver for recruits."

"Well, you just do that," Arthur's voice remained cool. He cleared his throat. "I've got another chore for you, Will."

"What's that, Mr. Livingston?" Will struggled to avoid any sarcasm creeping into his voice as he wiped the perspiration from his forehead.

Arthur fingered the box sitting on his desk. He considered how to approach his next request. Arthur knew he would get no argument about what he would ask of Will, but the last time he asked the boy to take care of a similar problem, Arthur sensed a hint of reluctance. He lifted the top off the box, and slid out a sheet of tattered parchment paper. Before he could get the lid secured, a cricket jumped out of the box and onto his desk. Arthur slapped the lid back onto the box without losing another of his tiny forgers. He picked up a copy of the latest profit and loss statement and rolled it tightly into a tube. Slowly and quietly he revealed, "I found another tract of land for you to check out."

Will heard a whack through the receiver.

Arthur picked up his waste basket and thumped the lifeless insect into the trash.

Will pursed his lips and looked up as he pondered his boss's statement. He knew what he was being asked to do. *In the last year I've checked out several tracts of land for you.* Will snarled, "Just send me the coordinates, and I'll take care of it." He paused and peeled some bark from a post he was leaning against. "Got any idea how many this time?"

Arthur leered, "Does it matter?"

"Not really. I was just wonderin'."

"Don't know. Four...maybe five."

"I'll get it done, Mr. Livingston."

"Well, you just be careful, Will."

Will knew what his boss expected…demanded. He was resigned to do what Livingston asked. "Oh, and I have some more disturbin' news. Our road crew's got four or five people followin' them around. I'm afraid they're gonna be trouble. The crew chased a man out of a tree yesterday, spyin' on them with binoculars. There were several more who scattered. The foreman thinks he got a bullet into one of 'em, but the whole group got away. I had him post more guards around the equipment."

"You think they'll try and sabotage the machinery?" This was another annoyance Arthur could live without.

"Don't know. Just want to be careful."

There was a short silence on the phone as Arthur reached for another box and quickly removed another sheet of paper. "When you get the new men, let the next group go out to cut without you, just in case something else happens."

When he spoke, Will's voice was low, "Mr. Livingston these people expect me to be there with them otherwise we may start to have some trust issues here."

"Damn it Will! Just take care of it!" he insisted. "And take care of yourself." The apparent concern sounded like an afterthought. "Get back to me as soon as you have another cutting crew to go out."

Arthur opened the final box and removed its single page before cutting the connection. He picked up the first page he had removed from the box and blew off a scattering of paper dust and cricket droppings. He leaned over the wastebasket and wiped the edges with his finger, watching as shards of tattered, nibbled on paper came away. Arthur studied the deed for 1653 hectares of prime rainforest not far from where Will was working in Brazil. The name listed as purchaser was Arthur R. Livingston, Sr. ...his grandfather.

It really does look official, Arthur thought as he turned the page over and dusted the other side. The yellowing from the insects' excrements and fraying where they had been eating really made it look archaic. The document would be easily viewed as almost one hundred years old. He learned of the simple method of aging documents a long time ago from a golfing buddy, a reformed forger who had spent twelve years in prison for his work.

Arthur held the document up to the light one page at a time. This was about the best he'd ever made. His grandfather would have been proud.

Arthur scowled as he considered it: Would his grandfather have been proud? Then he snickered. He really didn't care. Arthur was proud enough for both of them. He was, after all, adding to the family estate, even if he did have to steal the land to get it, and it was easy enough to do. Send Will to eliminate the man, couple, or family unfortunate enough to be claiming the land, buy off a clerk at the closest recording office, send the deed, and then the clerk would slip it into the file. The document certainly looked authentic. It wouldn't work here in the States but it was being sent to the heart of the Amazon that was so remote no one would ever think to do any kind of scientific testing to see if the documents were real. And who really cared? No one.

Arthur pulled a large brown envelope from his desk drawer and scrawled the name and address from the list he kept locked in his filing cabinet. The name this time was Freho Silgate, the clerk in San Reho, Amazonia, Brazil. Arthur noted that his list of recording offices was growing.

As he inserted the pages into the envelope Arthur wondered aloud, "Who killed my men…?" But then he gave a nonchalant shrug as he added a one-hundred and fifty dollars, more than a year's income for most rural Brazilians, and sealed the envelope.

He stood and walked to the window. Arthur hung his head after he glanced toward the street below. All he could do was groan. Three police cars with lights flashing and a news van were parked out front.

He banged his fist against the glass. Livingston Lumber was back in the news.

8

In the pre-dawn light, Stephen smoked his pipe as he rocked in his favorite chair on the porch. He thought about the unexpected visitors who appeared from the forest yesterday. He'd extend an invitation for them to stay awhile since he could use the extra hands to help process data and perhaps perform some simple experiments. At the very least, they could help with the clean-up jobs. Charlie wasn't going anywhere until he was back on his feet, and in the meantime, the others could make themselves useful.

The group was actually delivered to the compound by mistake. When the police officer stopped to offer assistance, Nigel, in his broken Portuguese, conveyed that he was a professor researching with his students. Knowing of Stephen's work with similar groups, the officer assumed they belonged with him, so they were brought to the compound.

Smoke curled around Stephen's head as he contemplated the puzzling tale of being chased for no reason by unknown attackers. Something didn't ring true with their story.

Charlie's wound wasn't serious, but Stephen knew it was painful. Luckily, the bullet had passed through cleanly and nothing vital was damaged. Stephen flushed the wound after giving Charlie a shot of morphine to ease the pain. He packed it and applied bandages front and back. The boy needed to sleep, so Stephen sent him to bed on the cot on his back porch. The hammock in the sleeping hall would have been much too uncomfortable right now. Maybe in a day or two.

Stephen looked toward the dark, quiet buildings around the compound. About a hundred meters from his house sat the long sleeping hall for guests, eight rooms strung together, one room after another, with a roof overhead and a long porch along the front. Each room had a small open closet, a tiny window, four hooks on the walls for two hammocks, a hook on the ceiling above each hammock for mosquito netting, a rod to slide down across the door for protection and privacy, and a large machete leaning against the door frame. Not the amenities one would find in most places. They were sparse but adequate for the needs of visitors. Only Julia and Lupa had bedrooms in Stephen's house. Charlie would remain on the back porch for a while, but everyone else slept in the sleeping hall.

There were also two outdoor showers at one end, encircled with small walls for privacy but open at the top and bottom for safety. Bathers needed to be able to see around their exposed legs and feet at all times to be sure no snakes hid in corners. If someone looked toward a shower in use, there were always legs and feet at the bottom and a head above the top of the privacy walls. It was a little disconcerting when someone first climbed in and disrobed, but after a while no one considered the open showers out of the ordinary.

Between his front porch and the sleeping hall, Stephen saw Lupa puttering around in the large common room earlier than usual as he prepared for the extra guests they would have at breakfast. Screened over halfway down and all the way around, the building had great ventilation, so the scent of coffee reached him as it drifted through the darkness. It was a good-sized room with an open kitchen. Near the center was a giant mahogany table, weighing nearly a ton, cut from a confiscated, illegally-cut log many years ago. At mealtime the table held bowls and plates of food. When locals came to confer about sustainable management of their land, it became a desk. When students and professors were organizing forest harvests, it became a sorting table. For Stephen, it was an ever-present reminder of what was being lost as forest land was cut and burned.

Just inside the door nearest the sleeping hall were rows of benches, like pews in a church, for study or simply places to congregate and chat. Behind the table was a long wall with a pull-down writing board handy for instruction. Overhead fans kept things cool, if that was possible in the intense heat, while a water closet in one corner completed the space.

Stephen was proud of his compound, built from many different kinds of wood, all prized for their beauty, and all confiscated from illegal logging operations. The trees were already cut, and instead of allowing them to sit and rot, the government cut and distributed boards to build hotels and compounds in the rainforest to help educate outsiders of the value of the wood and the forest, and more importantly, discourage locals from cutting and burning as hopefully, they realized what they were losing. Visitors inevitably marveled at the beauty of the buildings that would have cost a fortune to build in another country. Stephen paid for nothing except the labor to build them. Regardless of the use, the forest paid the ultimate price.

Stephen leaned down holding his watch near the lamp on the table in front of him and saw there was still another hour until daylight. He sat back and rocked, drawing the last smoke from the pipe as the embers began to die out.

He was happy to hear from Eduardo yesterday but the phone call had been troubling. Stephen had joined Eduardo in the village and performed the autopsies and collected fluid and tissue samples. Julia offered to help, but he knew she was in the middle of a crucial piece of research, so he told her he could handle it himself. The initial findings were perplexing. There was no indication of why the three men had died.

Stephen stood and walked to the edge of the porch, tapping the ashes from his pipe and then tucking it into his shirt pocket. He thought again how odd it was that he hadn't found any noticeable wounds on the men. Maybe the body samples collected would reveal something. Stephen picked up the lamp and opened the screen door to head back upstairs to his room anxious to get ready for the day and even more eager to get into the lab.

9

They were just finishing a tasty breakfast of fruit and a delicious cheese roll called *pão de queijo* when Julia stood. “I’m getting to work.”

"I’ll be there briefly,” Stephen said.

Julia gathered up her breakfast dishes and took them to the sink.

Nigel sat across the table from Stephen. “So you work for a pharmaceutical company, right?”

Stephen nodded, “I enjoy it. Actually, I can’t imagine doing anything else. I fancy it is about the best job around,” Stephen swirled the last of his coffee.

Lupa kneaded fresh dough for a new batch of rolls as they talked. Occasionally, he looked in their direction, a scowl on his face when he saw Nigel.

Nigel noticed and smiled at Lupa.

Lupa’s eyes narrowed.

Nigel focused back on Stephen. “What drew you to this field?”

Stephen considered the question. Sunlight was beginning to beam through the canopy. A wide ray lit the doorway, streaming into the room. “I believe there’s everything we need to heal ourselves out there.”

“In the Amazon?”

“Not just the Amazon. Forests of all kinds around the world. Each forest is unique. Different animals. Different plants. Different insects. Different slimy, crusty, fuzzy creatures, with their own distinctive characteristics and chemical make-ups. We test for alkaloids, tannins, saponins…”

Nigel held up his hand, “*Anthraquinones*, *cardenolides*…I know the drill.”

“You know your medicinal plant testing.”

“A little.”

“Impressive.”

That brought a genuine smile to Nigel’s face. “I have spent a good deal of time in both the rainforests and in the lab.”

“Seems so.” Stephen packed his pipe for an after-breakfast smoke.

Nigel reached into his pocket and palmed a handful of Chiclets. He tossed them into his mouth and asked, "How do you think those men died?"

Stephen shook his head. "Could've been a lot of things. I have considered the usual, but for the life of me I believe it's most likely the unusual we must consider." Nigel chewed a moment before he spoke softly. "Most people think they'll live forever, but living beings are easy to kill off, especially humans." He noticed a small spider on the edge of the table and laid his finger in its path. The spider crawled easily onto the perch, and Nigel turned his palm up.

"How do you mean?"

The spider crept to the center of Nigel's hand. He slowly closed his fist, wanting so much to squeeze the life from it but thought it better he not show his true lack of concern for the environment in front of this old "flora and fauna" coot. He opened his hand and let the spider drop to the floor. Nigel leaned his chin on one fist and brought the heel of his boot down on the spider. He smiled as he heard a tiny pop. "Well…let's think about sodium cyanide."

"Sodium cyanide?" Stephen frowned.

Nigel lifted the spoon he had used in his coffee, slowly twirling it between his fingers. e n "A perfect killer."

"Are you saying someone could…?"

"I didn't *say* anything." Nigel fought the urge to sneer. "But all things should be considered, wouldn't you agree?

"I..."

Nigel watched the spoon. The corners of his mouth rose slightly as he continued chewing his gum. "You can mix it with liquid, mix it into your drink, a drink that you spill on the gentleman behind you. Oops"

Nigel continued watching the spoon move methodically through his fingers. He was chewing with his lips parted, as though reliving a moment of intense enjoyment. "It soaks into his clothes, his skin…his…his system.

Stephen never took his eyes off Nigel's face.

Nigel slowly blinked his eyes and continued to stare at the revolving spoon. "He's dead."

Stephen didn't move.

Nigel sucked in a breath and smiled his most winning smile at Stephen, like he was wakening from a trance. "So easy!"

Drake came through the door. "I can't believe I slept this late. Why didn't you wake me, Nigel?" He looked between the two men, each silent. "Nigel?"

Nigel laid the spoon down and stared up at Drake. "Yes?"

"Is everything okay?"

Nigel chuckled. "Of course, everything is fine. Stephen and I were just discussing a possible way to kill a person."

Drake's eyes searched Nigel's face, "Why would you want to kill someone?"

Stephen cleared his throat. "Actually, Nigel here was enlightening me with a plot for a murder mystery, weren't you Nigel?" Stephen gave him a pointed glance.

Nigel replied as he stood and pushed his chair back to leave, "Of course I was. I read about it somewhere, I'm sure." He smiled first at Stephen and then toward Lupa, who glared back at him. "At least, I think I read it, or maybe it was television. Oh, by the way, Stephen," Nigel cut off the cyanide conversation. "Drake and I plan to do some research all hours of the day and night. We might be coming and going, if that's okay. If Charlie and Jennifer could hang out here with you, at least until Charlie's wound is better, that would be a great help."

"Certainly," Stephen said. "I planned to extend the invitation. I'll put Charlie to work in the lab as soon as he's able. Jennifer can help now. Work for their supper, so to speak. They'll be fine. What kind of research are you doing?"

Nigel looked hard at Drake, who took the cue and reached into his backpack. He pulled out a small piece of equipment Stephen recognized as measuring CO2. "We're working with a friend of Nigel's from Harvard on a project about global warming." He waved a small notebook in the air. "Just collecting our first real data."

Nigel spoke up, "We'll have a long conversation about what we find when we are finished. It would be a pleasure to pick your brain."

"I look forward to the chat." Stephen gestured outside, "Be careful out there at night. Jaguars. Snakes."

Nigel nodded, "Right-o." He picked up his cup and took one last sip of coffee before sitting it back on the table. He slapped Drake on the back, "Get some coffee, boy."

Drake zipped his backpack with the CO2 measuring device secure in the back pocket.

"In Stephen's dialect, I can honestly say, 'It's bloody good brew.'" Nigel turned and walked from the building as Jennifer and Charlie were coming up the path from Stephen's house.

"Good morning you two," he cheerfully greeted them. "I pray you slept well last night, Charlie."

"Oh, yeah. Slept like the dead," Charlie mocked.

"Careful there." Nigel wagged a finger in his direction. "You could have easily been killed yesterday. Do not tempt fate." Nigel sauntered onto a path that turned abruptly, and as they watched, his form was soon enveloped by the foliage.

"He's beginning to make my skin crawl," Jennifer shivered.

"Man, it took you long enough! He's set me on edge since I first met him."

From the doorway, Stephen greeted Jennifer and Charlie and stepped aside, inviting them to help themselves to breakfast. "How's the shoulder, Charlie?"

"I'll live," he rubbed above the wound. "Thanks for the bed. Don't think I could have rested at all if I'd been in a hammock."

Stephen laughed, "No, and the morphine probably helped too."

Charlie grinned, "Oh, yeah. And thanks for that too!"

Drake had filled a plate with breakfast and walked past them and out the door, barely giving the group a nod.

"Where do you suppose he's going?" Jennifer asked.

"Who cares," Charlie answered as he closed the screened door behind them. They walked to the breakfast bar and climbed onto stools. "Man, that smells good."

Lupa gave them plates and heaped food on them. Lupa wasn't one to hide his sentiments and it was becoming obvious to even the newcomers that Lupa had "not good feeling" about that duo.

Charlie watched Lupa scowl toward the path Nigel had taken. "What do you think of our fearsome leader?" he asked Lupa.

"Hmmph." Lupa laid down the knife he was using to cut more fruit and spoke so softly, they had to lean forward to hear. "There is circle of evil you leader not know."

"Circle of evil?" Jennifer eyed Charlie and then Lupa.

Lupa nodded his head. "Sim…yes, circle of evil."

"What do you mean?" Charlie asked.

Lupa reached for two cups and pulled a kettle off the stove. As they watched, he poured each of them a cup, but before he handed them the tea, he moved his hands over each one chanting in a language they had never heard.

"Here," he ordered. "Drink this. All of it."

They took a sip. It was bitter but not unpalatable.

Lupa leaned close to them and began telling a story. "One time there was mean chief. His people want him die. One day he wake up, say, 'I no be mean. I be kind.' Then he name 'gentle chief.' One day one elder ask why chief decide be kind. He say he ride horse in forest…see dog chase coati." Lupa pointed at a poster which held pictures of many animals of the Amazon. One animal looked like a raccoon with a long snout. Under the picture was the word, 'coati.'

Lupa continued. "First look like coati be free, but dog bite…break coati leg. Chief go to village see same dog bark at man. Man pick up large stone throw at dog. Dog leg break. Man not go far…horse kick. Break man leg. Horse run…leg go in hole." Lupa put his fists together and twisted them in a breaking motion. "Ccrrk," he imitated. "Horse break leg. Chief say, 'hmmm.' He think… 'evil bring evil.' He think if he be evil, evil come for him." Lupa shrugged. "He change. That not all. Elder go away. Decide kill chief…take chief place."

Lupa shook his finger at the couple. "No good. Circle of evil go on.

Man no see long step. Man fall down...break neck."

Charlie commented, "One can only wish Nigel would fall down some stairs."

Lupa responded with a harsh curse. "No tempt circle of evil. Think protect." He gestured again. "Drink tea. Tea protect you from evil man."

They both drained their cups as Lupa poured one for himself and another for Stephen.

Charlie and Jennifer stared at each other in disbelief as they gulped the mystical tea.

* * *

Stephen held his pipe between his teeth, the flame long since extinguished. He stood outside the common room holding the cup of tea Lupa brought him and considered his discussion with Nigel about the sodium cyanide. Stephen had never considered how easily the drug could kill someone if placed on the skin. Nigel was right. It was the perfect killer. Most pathologists didn't test for cyanide in autopsies, not unless it was requested.

"What do I remember about cyanide?" Stephen mumbled as he turned and walked toward the lab. The effects of potassium and sodium cyanide were the same. If left untreated, people exposed to the toxic agents usually died in less than an hour. Entomologists used sodium cyanide in their collecting jars because insects died in seconds, which helped protect them from damaging themselves. Cyanide was produced by specific bacteria, algae, and fungi and was found in thousands of plants and also many fruits and vegetables. Although in minute amounts, it could be found in the seeds of fruits such as peach, mango, and apple. *You can even find it in our prized* manioc, *a staple for most families in Brazil.* Of course, cyanide didn't cause bleeding like the dead men experienced. But combined with another agent? Maybe from a new species not seen before? Could the men have been sprayed by something?

In the lab, Julia remarked, "We need to leave in an hour to pick up the students."

"We will take the boat."

Julia smiled. "*Tambaqui*?"

He nodded. "I have some chaps catching them even as we speak," Stephen rubbed his hands together. "Stopped by early this morning on their way out to fish."

Tambaqui was their favorite fish for roasting.

"I'll ready the boat in a few minutes," he remarked as he reached for the refrigerator door. "I need to do one thing before I go."

Stephen pulled out some tissue samples and began a new test. This time it was for sodium cyanide.

10

Lupa was at the helm of the boat, and Julia and Stephen sat near the front, as far away from the noisy motor as possible. Jennifer and Charlie stayed at the compound so Charlie could continue mending, not because there wasn't room for them to come along. The deck could have easily held twenty people. It had a covered area to avoid rain or as shelter from the sun, but today the sun felt nice.

The motor trolled on as they moved along the shoreline. Every turn brought something new. Islands dotted the center in places. They passed swirling whirlpools where submerged rocks poked through the surface or sometimes remained just below the water line. The river bottom below was over fifty feet down and suddenly would become shallow as they skimmed over submerged logs and sandbars, both visible from the boat. Each new bend in the river brought more wonder. It would become deep and wide, and often the currents pulled and pushed the boat simultaneously.

For the last three years, Julia had brought two students with her to Stephen's compound but this year Julia had arrived ahead of them due to their schedules.

"Who do we have coming today?" Stephen asked before lighting his pipe.

"Alexis and Kosey." Julia reached up and pulled her ponytail a bit tighter.

"Tell me about them."

"Let's see…"

They rounded a bend in the river and Stephen waved to the fishermen who were working their lines. "Wait," he patted Julia's shoulder as he stood. Lupa slowed, and Stephen called out in Portuguese.

The men shook their heads indicating they had not caught anything yet.

Stephen gave a thumbs-up of encouragement, and Lupa increased the speed after they passed the other boat.

Stephen settled back down and Julia continued. "They are really good students. Kosey is from Chad in Africa. Kosey Alingue is his full name. His family really had to sacrifice for him to get to America. He works hard. He's fascinating because he's always coming up with African sayings that fit situations. His grandmother kept an extensive collection of them in a journal, which Kosey remembers from his childhood. He also loves old American movies and can remember lines from them that I could never remember. I think he has a photographic memory."

"Sounds interesting."

"He's really quick picking up instructions. And so is Alexis."

"Alexis. Nice name."

Julia smiled. "Alexis Cotter. She went back to school after raising a family. Alexis is always prepared and serious about her studies. And she's easy to be around. She's comfortable in her own skin, if you know what I mean."

"Confident."

"Yes, exactly," Julia agreed. "She's confident. Alexis and Kosey work well together. They've been working with me for almost a year now. Good students and good researchers. Both are in their third year. Still so inquisitive and interested in learning everything."

"Sounds like they'll be an asset as we work through the body samples and then both of our other projects. How long will they be staying?"

"We all leave in three weeks.

"Hmm. Don't like the sound of 'we', Julia. I've been thinking. How would you feel about leaving the university and working here permanently." It was a statement rather than a question.

They'd gone over this time and time again. "Maybe one day, Stephen, but you know my work means a great deal to me." Julia sighed, remembering she was supposed to be getting married. "And of course, there's Mitch."

Stephen watched a huge crocodile slide into the water followed by two smaller ones. "Ah, yes. Mitch. Well, perhaps one day." He let the conversation drop and enjoyed his pipe while Julia's mind wandered.

She thought of her students. Alexis was a lovely woman of forty-three. She'd gone back to finish her education when her youngest child started college last year. Kosey was the age of Alexis's oldest son, so she naturally had a motherly attitude toward him. She arrived at UGA because she wanted to study and work with Julia. Alexis had her college life planned out. She would have her PhD in another four years, and she also planned, just like Julia, to divide her time between teaching and research. Alexis was sure it would happen, but Julia knew how easily plans can change as life situations evolved.

Kosey had a strong sense of commitment. He managed to juggle schoolwork, his lab responsibilities, and a second job at the university book store. He'd gotten a full scholarship because of his aptitude, so he didn't have to pay tuition, room, or board. He lived frugally and even though he didn't make much money, he still managed to send a nice sum home every month.

The timbre of the motor changed as the boat began to slow. Julia hadn't realized they were at the landing by the airfield at Kahepa already. They wouldn't be going all the way to the village. She suddenly found herself thinking about Eduardo and wondered when she would see him.

A short, heavy man, barefoot and wearing only a bright blue pair of shorts, grabbed the front of the boat and pulled it against wood decking that looked as if it could collapse at any minute. When he took Julia's hand to help her out, his face broke into a grin that was contagious. She beamed at him as she thanked him.

Stephen tied up the front of the boat, while Lupa took care of the back.

They climbed the steep steps to a long, green field. Down the center ran the airstrip. They walked over to the hanger to wait in the shade. It was more like a big shed, boards hanging askew off one side and others missing entirely, but the posts holding up the roof were strong, and the tin had recently been replaced. Two small planes were inside, and a man was working on one of the engines. Around the sides and in the back, Julia spied a collection of old trucks, tires, and spare plane parts. Large oil drums, mounds of coiled hose and storage boxes sat open and overflowing with all manner of debris. It looked a bit like a junkyard around the planes, and even from a distance, Julia had smelled the strong odor of spent grease and oil.

They heard the engine of an approaching plane before it came into sight.

"Right on time." Julia walked out into the sunshine as she shielded her eyes and watched the plane circle the field to land.

She had tried her hand at learning to fly years ago. Julia remembered the first time she reached 3,000 feet in a small 172 Cessna. Her instructor turned off the engine, and that simple exercise was almost her undoing. As the single propeller turned slowly in the wind, the plane spiraled downward in lazy circles. Julia was amazed it took almost fifteen minutes to get close to the pasture below, plenty of time to find a safe place to land. Julia practiced that and other maneuvers over and over. She was able to do it all. All, except the landing. She never became comfortable with falling from the sky, never flew solo, and watching the plane's descent reminded her why.

Kosey was the first to step off the plane followed by Alexis. Julia hugged both students before introducing them to Stephen and Lupa. Stephen took one of each of their bags as he guided them toward the boat. Lupa pulled Alexis's backpack from her shoulder even though she protested she was fine carrying it. Julia noticed almost immediately that

Stephen spoke mostly to Alexis as she followed them toward the boat.

Kosey took one look at the boat, assumed a pose of grandeur and recited, "'Nobody in Africa, but yours truly, can get a good head of steam on the old African Queen.'"

Everyone laughed except Lupa.

"She doesn't look quite like the African Queen," Stephen proclaimed, "but she sometimes sounds like her!"

Lupa turned a quizzical eye toward Kosey who explained, "It's from the movie, *The African Queen*. Katherine Hepburn? Humphrey Bogart? Surely you've seen it, man."

Lupa shook his head as he fired up the motor. "Lupa no see."

As Kosey heard the sputtering, he cried out, "Yes…the African Queen!" and they laughed again.

Stephen threw the ropes in after all were seated and pushed off. The boat moved into the flow in the center of the river, choppy with the current. Stephen balanced like a tightrope walker as he moved across the deck adjusting duffel bags and backpacks making his way back toward Alexis.

Alexis couldn't help watching ahead for something she feared, a natural fear shared by many people. Anaconda. More specifically, the giant anaconda, or *sucuriju gigante*, as the Indians of the forest called them. She researched the enormous snake when she learned she was selected for this trip and had discovered the longest actual length of anacondas was disputed, some scientists believed twenty feet, while others felt it was at least thirty. But accounts of the *sucuriju gigante* had been recounted by explorers and others for hundreds of years, some reports gave accounts of snakes up to sixty, eighty and even exceeding one hundred feet.

She asked Stephen about the snake.

"Actually, Alexis," he said as he sat down next to her, "I think people would be mad to deny there are giant snakes in these waters. I haven't seen them myself, but Lupa's father told him a story of a man from their village who saw one while he was fishing. It was almost dark when he noticed some twenty feet away in the water, a pair of blue lights about a foot apart just under the surface of the water. At that distance, a pair of anaconda eyes a foot apart implied a snake well over forty feet in length. As it grew nearer, the eyes came out of the water, and the man knew it was a *sucuriju*. The strangest thing was that it either had horns or very long teeth."

"Horns?" Alexis searched the waters in front and behind as if she expected an apparition to rise.

Stephen leaned down and reached into the water, rinsing his hands as they sped down the river. "Yes, and he's not the first to tell such a tale." He flung off the drops before wiping his hands on his pants. "Not too many years ago, a man reported seeing a *sucuriju* with horns that looked like the roots of a tree, and that snake had flashing green eyes."

Up ahead, a cluster of shacks marked a small village. Children played in the water, which horrified Alexis because of her concern over the snakes. She pointed and Stephen acknowledged.

"Can't keep them out." He shook his head. "The river is one of their main playgrounds."

"Isn't it dangerous?" she asked incredulously as the children swam toward the boat waving and laughing.

Stephen shrugged as he waved back. "I guess no more dangerous than an interstate full of cars."

Alexis shook her head. They passed before the children got into their path, and she was glad they were out of sight in a few minutes. The whole idea of children playing in snake and crocodile-infested water was terrifying. She looked again around the boat for any indication of either, scanning far ahead before checking again behind.

To distract Alexis from her anaconda watch, Julia told the students about the dead loggers. Not that the issue was any more pleasant, but it was a way to engage them in a different subject, something they would be facing back at the compound. Julia concluded by saying to Stephen, "I didn't see the bodies, but it's baffling that you have no idea how the men died."

Stephen shook his head. "I have *no* idea. What I do know is they had massive bleeding, but why it happened is the big question, and I have found no record of a similar event anywhere in the Amazon. I even tested the blood samples for cyanide this morning while you were working."

"Cyanide? Why cyanide? It doesn't cause bleeding."

"I know," Stephen said cutting her off as he crossed his arms and leaned back. "I just wanted to make sure some new parasite or some other sinister creature or plant might not have surfaced that mixed the chemical with something else." Stephen thought it was senseless, really, a seed of an idea planted by a...*by a what*? *What was Nigel*? Stephen shook his head, "No cyanide."

"We'll figure it out," Julia said with certainty. "We'll test the samples and gather the facts, and they will lead us to the answer."

"It's not the facts which concern me, Julia. It's all the questions. I have a feeling this is much larger than we suspect." Stephen had an unsettled tone in his voice.

The river had calmed somewhat, and Stephen used the moment to light his pipe again. He hadn't told them everything. When he was performing the autopsies, he noticed the linings of the blood vessels near the surface of the skin in the nose and ears had cracks in them resembling splintered mirrors. The breaks were everywhere, accounting for the bleeding. The bronchial tubes in the lungs had also shown signs of breakdown, and the lungs were filled with blood. But there was no blood in the stomachs, and the hearts were completely intact. He knew the cracks were important to the investigation, but he couldn't figure out what might have caused them.

Stephen watched Julia as she scanned the forest, eyes vivid, a slight smile on her face. He looked at Alexis, still searching the water's surface and Kosey as he stood now on the bow, a figurehead with his arms outstretched like the Christ the Redeemer statue on Corcovado Mountain overlooking Rio.

Stephen gnawed the inside of his lip as his eyes were drawn back to Julia. *Should I tell her*? He made the decision to tell her…but later, when they were alone.

"What's on your mind?" Julia asked after she turned and caught him watching her.

"Oh, just mulling over the clues," he answered turning his pipe and looking at it.

"We don't have that many clues," Julia stated as she looked back out to the passing forest.

Stephen chuckled. "That we do not, my girl." He pointed, and they all watched a flock of hoatkins erupt from the trees up ahead, their bright blue faces bejeweled with color as the sunlight spilled across their sparkling black feathers.

"Do you perform many autopsies, Stephen?" Alexis asked. "I mean, is that part of what you do here? Or is this something out of the ordinary?"

Stephen frowned slightly when he answered, "Oh, there has been an occasional animal mauling, where the villagers needed to identify the type of animal to hunt down and kill. But generally, no. Not part of the curriculum, so to speak." He smiled to keep them at ease.

Alexis wanted to continue their conversation, even if it was a little gruesome. "Are these the first murders you have autopsied?"

Stephen pointed again as the hoatkins settled into the top of a tall, sparse tree several meters inland from the riverbank, looking like bright ornaments atop a Grinch tree.

Stephen turned back to Alexis after they rounded a bend and the birds were out of sight. He explained, "There hasn't been much need for a pathologist, since there has been only one murder in this area in the last fifteen years that I know of. And we're still not sure if these were murders. They are an anomaly."

"It's hard to believe anyone has been murdered here, Stephen," Julia remarked.

"Yes, so we'll continue to unravel this mystery," was all he said.

Alexis finally relaxed and gave up her vigil as snake spotter. "This may sound a little crazy, but I worry about animals attacking more than people."

Stephen stood and walked to the front of the boat where he

straightened a corner of the overhead cover. His tanned muscles flexed as he reached up.

He is very nice looking, Alexis thought.

"The animals are fairly easy to avoid, Alexis." He caught her watching him.

Alexis blushed and looked away.

Stephen's gnarly grin flashed. "You just need to be alert, and you'll be fine." He moved past her toward Lupa. "That first murder was relatively easy to solve, since a crowd saw it happen. Two men fighting over a woman." He finished, "All three lost in the end."

They had been traveling for almost half an hour when they encountered the fishermen again. They had moved to a different place on the river that looked like the perfect place to find the fish. Tall trees hung over the river, their long branches dipping into the water.

This time one of the fishermen turned his thumb up.

"Yay!" Julia clapped her hands. "*Tambaqui* for dinner tonight!"

Lupa glided easily next to their boat, and the fishermen stopped fishing long enough to greet them and for Stephen to hand over payment for their dinner.

One man leaned out and handed Lupa three nice fish. With extra people in camp, this was a perfect catch, but it was more than they would eat since each fish weighed over ten kilos. Lupa chose one fish and handed it back, a common practice, which the men gratefully accepted.

"Is it good fish?" Kosey asked.

Julia nodded vigorously. "The best! The fish is mostly a vegetarian, feeding mainly on fruits and berries which drop into the water," Julia explained. "The meat is a succulent, white fillet with an extremely mellow flavor, not fishy tasting at all."

They traveled on for a distance without speaking.

As Lupa made the final turn heading for the compound, he called out, "Home, everyone!"

Julia gave him a quick smile that diminished as she looked down into the muddy water and thought about the men who had died in her rainforest. She glanced at Stephen. "When do you think the men died?"

"Looks like it was early morning. Not too long after sunrise."

Julia asked, "Why do you think it was early morning?"

Stephen chewed on his pipe, "Well, you know insects are attracted to death."

Julia nodded. She knew a little about forensic science, but most of it was way out of her field. She had certainly never performed an autopsy.

"As soon as ten minutes after someone dies, the body has an odor triggering a very specific and predictable pattern of behavior in some of the little buggers flying about. When they dig into flesh, it's a nasty sight. Maybe if I had to deal with it more, I might get used to it..." His voice drifted off. “Well, anyway, blowflies and flesh flies are the first insects to arrive. By observing their eggs and larvae over time, we can tell the approximate time someone died.”

“Can you really be sure?” Alexis’s curiosity was aroused.

“If you do a rearing,” Stephen lit his pipe and watched a crocodile slither into the water from the bank. “You simply recreate a similar event using beef liver and some of the original larvae. I’ll show you. Our little experiment should be finished later tonight.”

“When did you start it?” Julia asked. “I had no idea you put together the test.”

“You were busy, my dear. So absorbed in your work, you didn’t see. It only took a few minutes.”

Julia remembered seeing a box on the corner of a far table. She suddenly had a flurry of questions as the boat slid next to the dock. “Wonder what they were doing right before they died. What did they eat? What did they drink? Could someone have poisoned them? There are so many ways to poison people and so many plants filled with toxins. Is that what you were thinking when you tried the cyanide?”

“Yes, I have wondered all of that, too, and yes about the cyanide”

“Could they have been bitten or stung by something?” Julia asked.

Stephen nodded. “Yes, that too is possible. New species are found all the time, and as loggers and miners move deeper into the forests…who knows what might follow them back out. You see, Julia, every time I turn around, I have another question.” He picked up the rope as soon as the motor died. “And we’ll answer all our questions one at a time.” Stephen stepped out and tied off the boat before offering Julia his hand to follow.

Alexis looked up at Stephen. “I’ll do whatever I can to help find the answers.”

Stephen smiled down at Alexis still standing in the boat, “Do you think you’re up to it?”

Alexis gave him her hand and nodded as she climbed out next to him. “I’m ready.”

11

Nigel had just finished removing the hulls from the castor beans he collected that morning when he heard Drake's voice come over the radio. He pulled the mask and gloves off and climbed up the hillside where he could see the young man high overhead in an *acaraquara* tree. It was a beautiful tree, its deep furrows in the trunk more pronounced than others Nigel had seen.

"What is it?" Nigel asked.

"I think they might be on the move."

"You *think*?" Nigel was losing his patience with Drake prefacing everything with 'I think.' *Can't that idiot come to a conclusion*?

Tiago squatted a short distance away, appearing to ignore the conversation.

"Their tent is coming down."

"On purpose?"

"How should I know?" Drake too, was becoming disenchanted with Nigel's bullying.

Nigel held tight to his temper. He was just about tired of the boy. "Did someone begin disassembling the tent or did it just fall down?"

He waited for a minute with no response before he looked up and gestured the universal signal of "Well?" his arms outstretched and his shoulders hunched.

"I wasn't watching," a small voice squawked over the radio.

"You weren't watching." Nigel felt the vein on his temple pulsing.

"I looked away for just a minute, and then one corner of the tent was down."

Nigel's next words came out slowly, as though he were addressing an imbecile. "Look at it now, and tell me if someone is taking it down further." He saw Drake shift on the limb and put the binoculars back to his eyes. Nigel went back down the hill and put on fresh gloves and a mask while he waited for Drake to speak again.

Nigel placed the beans in the grinder and added ten ounces of acetone. He had slipped back into camp after the boat left the compound earlier and had seen Jennifer and Charlie heading onto a path Stephen said lead to a waterfall. He went to the lab and found the hand grinder, some lye, and the bottle of acetone. Along with water, that was all he needed to create the toxin. He was glad he had the covered grinder. It was much safer and a lot easier than grinding the beans with a bowl and pestle. He planned to return everything he didn't use, although there would be no need. Everyone at the compound would be dead in a matter of days.

Nigel soaked about three ounces of the beans in ten ounces of water, mixing in two tablespoons of lye. He weighted down the beans with leaves and a large rock. It would take about an hour for his concoction to ferment. He laid the beans out to dry, which took about fifteen minutes, and then he would be ready to grind.

The first time he had extracted ricin from castor beans Nigel had been surprised at how much it looked like coffee. He'd save enough to get rid of the loggers and Drake, once he was done with him, and then mix the rest in the jacu coffee Stephen loved so much.

Nigel unscrewed the jar from the bottom of the grinder and placed the lid back on top. It would sit for seventy-two more hours, and then it would be ready. He had already found a place near the compound where he would hide it—a place where no one would find it. He put everything back in his backpack and stored the jar with a towel wrapped around it so as not to risk breaking it.

"It's okay," he heard over the radio. "I think someone just tripped over one of the corner ropes. They're driving the stake back in."

"Good," Nigel growled into the radio.

Drake heard the menace in his professor's voice. He'd never heard it directed toward him before. Drake removed his glasses and took out a clean cloth. He wiped the lenses meticulously before wiping his wet forehead.

"Get down here," Nigel demanded.

When Drake came down to the camp Tiago crafted yesterday, he saw Nigel packing their backpacks. "Are we going back to the compound?"

"After we drain some oil and pour these in the engines," he held up two gallon jugs of sodium silicate, more items liberated from Stephen's lab. He looked at his watch. The men at the camp were probably settling down for dinner and shots of their cheap white *cachaça.*

"Tiago, you stay here," Nigel said to the guide. He knew the man didn't like violence, and Nigel was just as happy to keep him away from it. Maybe the old man wouldn't have to die with all the others, but then again Nigel couldn't afford any loose ends.

Nigel already had a new logging group to follow thanks to Tiago. Tiago put a tracking device on one of their pieces of equipment when he found them, and Nigel had already triangulated their whereabouts. Now he could locate them anywhere in the Amazon.

It was beginning to get dark as Nigel and Drake crept closer to the logging camp. Nigel no longer cared whether these men were cutting timber legally or not. They would die because he chose to make them die. His compulsion to kill was becoming stronger. Nigel would not be able to control himself even if he wanted to, which of course, he didn't.

Anyone watching his actions would believe he wanted to save the rainforest, but he didn't. He was there only because he chose to be there. And he chose to be there because he chose to keep his job, which required field study each year. He chose to keep his job because performing in the classroom in front of college students was gratifying. Seducing young women, a new one or two each semester, was gratifying. Being idolized by them was physically and mentally gratifying. *Everything* was to feed his gratification. Everything.

Going to the Amazon provided a perfect opportunity to satisfy his need to kill. It was so easy. Nigel could have simply poisoned everyone and been done with it, but what fun was that? He enjoyed toying with his kills. Some people might even think the killings of the illegal loggers was justified. The loggers were, after all, somewhat like rats. *Rat poisoning*. Nigel smiled to himself and felt justified.

Drake followed his leader like a puppet. Nigel wasn't sure how the boy would take to killing, but he would soon find out. Not that it mattered. Nigel had plans for his demise as well. So far, Nigel had only spoken about vandalizing equipment, which Drake was eager to follow. *A gateway crime*. Nigel amused himself with that thought.

The men in the logging camp sat by the fire in the dying light drinking from various tall bottles, turning up the 'burning water' as it was often called. They were so absorbed in their nightly routine, no one noticed the two men creeping around the heavy equipment.

There was still enough light to see without flashlights as Drake slid under the massive bulldozer and loosened the plug from the oil pan. The dark liquid slogged out just in time before it hit the ground. He let several gallons of oil drain and then replaced the plug. He brushed sand and leaves over the spilled oil hoping no one would see it before the engine seized up for good. It would only take about five minutes once they started it.

Drake moved to the second dozer and performed the same routine. Once the two were out of commission, the men would be on guard, and the games would begin. But that was a game for tomorrow.

Nigel poured the last of the sodium silicate into the second engine as Drake dusted off his pants. Nigel replaced the cap and placed the two empty bottles on the back of one of the trucks. The men would find them later, and they would realize what stopped their engines. They wouldn't know who put it there. Again, Nigel amused himself with the thought of creating chaos before the kill.

Drake strolled back down the path they took and grabbed up his backpack and some of the gear.

Nigel followed as they headed toward the compound. They had a good three hour hike to get there, and he hoped the common room would be empty by the time they arrived. He was hungry and knew Lupa would leave some good leftovers in the kitchen. If they were lucky, no one would even know they had returned.

12

She was a beauty. The DA42 Twinstar cruised at 170 miles an hour. Will loved this plane, loved the power of the engines and their dominating advantage over the rainforest. The Twinstar could climb high above the expanse of trees or glide close to the canopy top, circling a specimen tree and taunting the great Amazon. Even the risk was exhilarating. One slip and the Amazon was ready to grab its provoker like the striking jaws of a snake, pulling its catch down into the web of the forest and swallowing the powerful little plane.

While waiting for Carlos to get back with the replacement crew, Will had some extra time on his hands, so he and Paulo decided to fly. Will worried Carlos might have trouble finding enough capable men willing to venture into the jungle forest if word had already spread about the deaths of the other loggers.

"Might as well get a head start on plotting the future," Will muttered.

Scouting for the next mahogany harvest was one of Will's favorite pastimes. Soaring above the rainforest, he could relax and enjoy the longer glides and lazy turns around thinner canopies where mahoganies grew in the sun.

Will was lucky to have Paulo on board operating the GPS. The Global Positioning System made simple work of recording the location of a specimen tree for future cutting. Will had managed flying the plane and operating the tracking system several times alone, but he much preferred keeping his mind focused on his pilot duties. By mid-afternoon they had already plotted the locations of six new trees, enough to round out next year's cut. Two were really big ones, rising above the canopy to astounding heights of 150 feet, maybe higher.

That oughta make Livingston happy, Will thought as he checked his watch and then looked at the fuel gauge. They were fine, but the sun was sliding closer to the horizon, and it wouldn't be long before the Amazon dusk tucked the mahoganies into the canopy.

"Over there!" Paulo pointed under the binoculars.

Will rolled the plane into a steep bank, and there it was…the Amazon's signature tree…another giant mahogany. The massive tree peered through the canopy surface like the peak of a mountain, where a hot equatorial breeze ruffled the metallic shine of its leaves into a shimmering display of silvery, green fireworks.

The sight always reminded Will of a quaking aspen in Utah. Both trees quivered because of the type of leaves. There were no single leaves like the elm or oak. Both the mahogany leaves and quaking aspen leaves were complex, with long stems and multiple leaflets on each stalk. The color was a green—challenging to describe but unforgettable when seen from above.

Will's heart raced as he flew directly over the treetop to get the GPS location fix. This was a champion giant. Will had never seen a mahogany this tall with such a commanding canopy spread.

He watched Paulo enter the position of the GPS database. *Ah, modern technology*, Will thought. The GPS was a boon for logging crews. Until the new technology came along, plotting the precise site of a tree had been luck, at best. Even finding them was a crap shoot. If you didn't have a good map and keen sense of direction, you stood a good chance of losing them after you found them. Now, with a click of a button, you could pinpoint the location within inches. Will was thrilled with this new toy.

"That's it," Will happily remarked to Paulo.

Even though the new trees would have to wait another year to cut, he knew exactly where they would begin. The rainy season was drawing near and that would open the sky and stop heavy ground operations. The beauty below would be the jewel for next year.

As he banked the plane into a wide turn and headed back toward the landing strip, Will eyed the dying light. The sun was sinking faster than he anticipated, and he cursed under his breath because there was so much jungle between the plane and the dirt runway. The grass landing strip had no lights, and both men knew it was a death sentence if Will failed to spot it. He pushed the thought of a missed landing from his mind and revved the propellers to top speed.

Will shifted his focus to his two foremen—Paulo and Carlos. Paulo was a quiet man, while Carlos was talkative. Throughout the flight, Paulo spoke less than a handful of words. Had Carlos been beside him today, there would have been an endless chatter on board. But Will was okay with both men because they always got the job done. Will checked quickly and saw that Paulo had plotted the big mahogany precisely and effortlessly.

Will glared toward the west. The pale, pink light was rapidly turning to a deep orange. *Not much time left. Gotta get this baby down.* Will scanned the horizon.

The plane's engines roared smoothly heading deeper into the sunset. Will estimated ten more minutes of useful light left before the Earth disappeared below.

The horizon's last dim orange sliver of light began fading to a gray when Paulo blurted out, "There!"

Will saw the clearing and laughed with relief. Now, why had he worried? They reached the landing strip with time to spare. *Yeah, plenty of time.* With the last thread of light in the blackening sky, the plane flared toward the Earth and the wheels touched the ground. Will pressed the brakes. *Now we've got ground work to do.*

* * *

An hour after Will and Paulo climbed from the plane, they drove their truck up to a landing dock not far from their camp. Six men were getting out of a boat. The men laughed and talked, oblivious to the uncertainty they faced. Will watched them and scowled. He was thinking of Livingston's request—*or was it a demand*?—that he not go out on the next cut. If anyone thought that Will didn't care enough about his men to protect them from whomever was out there killing the others, no one would ever want to work for him again. He cared about his men, but he only cared enough to get the job done, and he always kept that to himself.

Thinking back to the dead men, Will kept wondering who could have killed them and why. He surprised himself when he began to question whether it was even a who. *Could it be a* what? *Now, that's a scary thought.*

Will had already planned their next trip out into the forest. Carlos would go out with the men he recruited, and that gave Paulo some time to spend at home.

Will always reminded them that it was important for everyone to spend time with their families. But the real reason for this seemingly noble suggestion was that each foreman only worked for short periods of time so he didn't get careless. Too much was at stake for anyone to become too comfortable in their roles. Will had a great deal invested in them. The working arrangement kept the foremen happy, and it suggested they had a boss who cared. It was also one reason he never had trouble finding help.

The recent deaths tarnished everything. Carlos pointed out to Will that the trip to recruit these workers had been tough. Evidently, these five had not heard about the dead men in the last crew and came willingly. But Carlos had to spend a lot of time before he found this handful of uninformed workers.

"It was long trip, Boss," Carlos admitted as he helped the men stow their gear and climb into the back of the truck. "I go almost fifty kilometers up-river to find a village with no knowing about..." His voice trailed off as he realized the men were listening. They appeared to be strong, easygoing men and three had cut logs before, which was a huge plus for Will. He was hopeful the crew's bad luck was now turning around.

Once they began driving through the night, Carlos slid the small window between the cab and the back closed and continued. "All up the river the story of the men moved, almost faster than I go. I overhear one shaman talk about it. Give me *califrio*. How you say…ummm… creeps?. Yes. Give me creeps. He say the men drip from the trees. It make me sick." He turned toward Will with a shiver. "They drip, Boss?" Concern, fear, and horror were fixed on his face.

Will only told his foremen the men had been killed. Men were killed in this line of work…a hazard of the trade. But Will never gave them any details. They assumed the men were shot.

"I didn't see them myself, Carlos." Will brushed aside the worry he felt gnawing deep in his own gut. "We'll just have to wait and see what the police find out. I got people askin' questions. You know how people talk." His voice softened to almost a whisper. He didn't dare tell Carlos about the men stalking the road crew. That would certainly put an end to this operation. He knew Carlos was loyal, but dripping bodies *and* pursuers? Everyone had their limits. He changed the subject. "How was the river?"

Carlos was off on a tale about the days of travel on the river he loved. It had taken more time traveling up the river because of the push of the current against the boat, but the return ride today was a different story.

"Man, we fly. One time, I look and see baby crock in water. Not see us. I stop motor. Little croc keep swimming, lazy like, till we get to him." Carlos leaned over and acted like his hand was dangling over the side of the boat. "One man lean out to catch." He shook his head, "Not get him, but when he touch croc's tail…" Carlos yelped with laughter. "…if a croc can have heart attack, that one did. I think he go and roll over and die—scare him so bad. Whooee! Wish you there to see! I laugh. My side hurt!"

Will found himself smiling with Carlos. The man's laughter was contagious, probably because it came from a source of pure innocence and joy; something Will had long forgotten.

Carlos continued laughing as he reached over the back seat and slid open the window he had just closed. In rapid Portuguese he reminded the men what had happened with the baby croc. Soon they were all agreeing and laughing.

Will glanced in the rearview mirror and saw a couple of men grinning at him. He smiled back and nodded with a forced smile.

"Truck come, Boss?" Carlos closed the window again.

Will shook his head as he thought about his other truck. They'd lost it to the police when the bodies were found. The new one was promised for tomorrow or the next day. He always kept at least two trucks just in case of problems. There was the carry-all for the dozer that would pull out the trees, but if the jungle patrol came, Will was out of there. Trucks could be replaced easily enough.

"We're movin' a good ways from the last site. Don't want to be too close to all the commotion." Carlos nodded and listened without comment. "Road crew is goin' out first thing in the morning and finish punching out the road to the next tree."

Will scanned the bed of the truck and saw the new rigging gear Paulo had purchased. *What a waste*. But the last equipment had been abandoned to the police too.

"Did Paulo get enough for all of us?" Will nodded toward the back.

"He say he get two set of gear for four to climb. You drive dozer, I climb with three men, and two keep watch. What kind rigging system we use?" Carlos glanced out the window as the forest passed by.

"We're just doin' it the quickest way. Like the last time. Cut out the tops of a couple of big trees nearby and set up the pulleys. Cut the tree into logs, pull them out, load up the logs, and get the hell out."

Will's way to hook up a pulley system took less than an hour to set up once the trees were topped. His method caused enormous ruts in the ground because of the repeated dragging of heavy logs over the same pathway. There were systems that were easier on the land, but they took too much time and work, both of which cost money. The ground damage was just part of the cost of doing business. So far, the system had worked just fine for them.

Paulo had two log trucks scheduled for three days from today: one for midday and one for late afternoon, and Will would make sure the tree was down and in logs for transport. While his crew cut down one tree, the road crew would make its way toward the next tree. It was an efficient system when everything went well, and generally it did.

They got to the camp, and the men settled in for the night. It was crude. Two pieces of canvas spread between trees with a wide pole holding up the center of each, but it would do. Will would sleep in the truck as usual.

Will frowned when he realized he'd forgotten to phone Livingston, probably because he was reluctant to make the call. He pulled out the phone, punched in the number, and waited on the line as it rang. It seemed to take forever before the old man answered, but then a loud laugh was the first sound from the speaker. *At least he's in a good mood*, Will thought. *Maybe this will be easier than I thought*.

"Will!" Arthur called out. "Good to hear from you, boy. I know you've got some good news for me."

"Sure do," Will smiled, caught off guard by the humor in his boss's voice. "Carlos found five new men. Three even have experience in loggin'. Just got a few more kinks to work out."

Once he started talking, he was on a roll and couldn't stop. Actually, Will was afraid to stop because he didn't want Livingston to ask him not to go with his men again. He was also aware that Carlos was listening.

Will continued giving his boss the logging plans as though nothing was on his mind but his work. "I want to practice with the men and make sure they know what they're doin' before go out. Don't want any surprises when we get to cuttin'. We'll be ready to go out in a couple of days. Meantime, the road's continuin' in tomorrow. We'll have you two truckloads of logs by the end of the week."

"Good boy." Arthur lowered his voice, "I keep hearing you say *we*. There ain't no *we* to it. You remember what I told you, Will. That's an order. You hear me?"

Will took a deep breath and scowled, his voice giving no indication of his true thoughts, "I hear you, Mr. Livingston."

"Good. Call me the first night when they get back to camp. Fill me in on everything," Arthur finished. A woman giggled in the background, and then the line went dead.

Will's smile was fading as he glanced at Carlos. Carlos smiled slightly. They both shrugged as Will snapped the phone shut and looked away.

13

In late evening, the lab was filled with the glow of warm, yellow light from low wattage bulbs and lab equipment screens. Papers were spread on a separate table piled high with folders and research books. Two computers hummed in the corner, processing data Stephen entered earlier. There were two sinks under one window, a lighted work board along the far wall above a short row of wire cages, each holding a single white rat, and three work tables in the center crowded with test tubes, microscopes, and other equipment.

Stephen and Julia worked late into the evening in the lab. Alexis and Kosey were in the common room getting to know Lupa and working through their jet lag. Jennifer was settling injured Charlie to bed on Stephen's back porch and promised to stop by the lab on her way back.

"Where do you suppose Nigel and Drake have gone?" Julia asked as she organized her work area.

Stephen picked up the box holding the rearing experiment and placed it on the table next to where Julia was working. "No one seems to know, from what I can gather. Nigel informed me at breakfast they would be coming and going for a while, collecting CO2 samples, I believe. Strange pair. It is obvious Drake worships his professor." Stephen shook his head as he took the top off the box and peered inside. "As for Nigel…there is something not right with that one."

"You think so?" Julia responded.

"Lupa believes he is evil. That tea you drank earlier with dinner was his tea of protection."

Julia frowned, "Do you think there will be trouble?"

"Oh, I doubt it," Stephen answered absently. "But following Lupa's ancient arts is never a bad thing. He's always taken good care of me. Us."

Julia went to the refrigerator and was reaching for the samples Stephen collected at the autopsies when he stopped her. "We'll save the samples for tomorrow after we prep the students on the equipment. More hands to test quicker." He turned on the microscope and pulled a short stack of slides from a drawer. "I want to see what's happened with our rearing," he said as he went to work.

Instead of the samples, Julia reached for her fungus collection. She checked for any changes in their structure and made a few notes of subtle deviations.

A few minutes later Stephen called out, "Look at this, Julia." He didn't take his eye from the microscope until he felt Julia next to him. As he slid off the stool, she settled onto his vacant seat. "See the larvae?" he asked.

Julia adjusted the eyepiece. "I see them. It's odd that I've rarely seen one. You'd think I would run into something like this more often, but I don't."

Stephen found no need to comment as he handed her a small stainless steel ruler. "How long are they?"

Julia carefully slid the ruler next to the closest. "This one is just a little over four millimeters." She checked a couple more. "The rest measure pretty much the same." She looked up. "What does it mean?"

"Well, the ones I found in the bodies were also just over four millimeters. When blow flies lay their eggs, nothing much happens in the first eight hours. The total egg stage usually lasts about twenty-four hours." Julia slid off the stool and let Stephen get back to the microscope. He rubbed his eyes and readjusted the lens. "Bad enough I'm losing my hair. Now the eyes are going."

Jennifer came in smiling when she heard Julia chuckle.

"Sounds like fun in here," she commented. She pulled up a stool and sat down to listen.

"It is fun," Julia playfully jabbed Stephen's side with her elbow. "Come on. Finish telling me about the larvae. What does four millimeters tell you?"

He included Jennifer in his explanation. "Well, forensic pathologists have determined it takes larvae one point eight days to reach five millimeters." Stephen picked up a calculator. "So if I have calculated this correctly, the larvae grow at a rate of one millimeter every six hours and forty minutes. I harvested the first ones at about 11:00 at night. When you do all the math, it tells us whatever happened to those men, happened a little after seven in the morning two days before I collected the first larvae."

"Fascinating," Julia said. "Every time I come here I learn something new. I can't wait to share your findings with Alexis. She seemed really interested on the boat ride today."

Jennifer stretched out her back and tried to stifle a yawn, "I hope we can start learning more soon. Nigel hasn't given us much instruction since we've been here." She smiled, took a deep breath and released it, puffing out her cheeks and closing her eyes as she did. She was exhausted. She had been exhausted when she finished Lupa's wonderful dinner.

The motions weren't lost on Stephen, who stood and began putting things away. "We must call it a night. My eyes are burning, and my mind is muddy. We have a big day tomorrow. Jennifer, you'll learn your way around the lab in the morning with Alexis and Kosey. Off with you now."

Jennifer nodded her thanks and walked back toward the common room to tell the others good night.

Stephen spoke quietly, "I told Eduardo to be here by nine."

"That's good. I hope he's doing better. Grief can be so debilitating."

"Indeed." Stephen finished wiping the lenses on the microscope and repositioned it on the work table. "Have you ever been to Eduardo's garden?"

"No," Julia fussed with a stack of already straightened folders.

Stephen failed to notice the level of excitement in Julia's demeanor. "Oh, you must see it, Julia," he continued cheerfully.

Julia mulled over his suggestion. "What's so special about his garden?"

"He has a spectacular collection of some of the most exquisite plantings I've ever seen. Better than the botanical garden in Rio."

Julia smiled. "You know how much I love that garden, Stephen." She put her fungus back in the refrigerator.

"Yes. I do."

"Well then I must see this treasure for myself," she said as she put her notebook back in her work drawer and slid the stool back under the table. "Perhaps you and Eduardo can give me a tour."

Stephen reached for the door but stopped and turned back. "I'm glad you're here, Julia. These deaths are puzzling and unsettling." He tapped his head and walked outside. "Yet a good mystery is healthy for the brain." He held the screen door open for her. "I haven't solved a good whodunit in a great while. Maybe we'll discover something significant."

"Maybe we will." Julia turned off the lights and followed Stephen out the door thinking about a lush garden tended by an interesting man.

14

Eduardo sat on the porch in a rocker, his long legs stretched out and crossed at the ankles. The chair barely moved as he gazed down the market street to his right watching sparse groups of locals and natives bartering their morning cache of goods. Their babbling reached him even if their words didn't.

An old woman rustled out of a small grove of *babassu* palms where she had been collecting leaves for the mats she thatched. She lowered the bundle from her head when two young men approached her. Eduardo sat up a little straighter recognizing them as young troublemakers. He was climbing from his seat when he heard the old woman's voice rise in anger while she gestured toward the forest. He smiled and relaxed as she chased them away with a broom.

Another woman sat nearby cracking open the fruit from the same palms, separating the oil-rich kernels in the center from the shells. That was just the beginning of a long process of separating the oil, grinding the pulp into flour, and then turning the shell into charcoal. It was what his people had been doing for generations, and Eduardo knew they would continue for many more.

A group of young children darted past with several small dogs barking at their heels. One boy decided to take a shortcut across the porch, oblivious to Eduardo until he was on top of him.

"*Eu sou pesaroso*! *Eu sou pesaroso*, *Delegado*," the boy yelled after he rolled over Eduardo's legs, off the porch, and out into the road. He never stopped moving as he jumped up and continued racing.

Eduardo laughed as he retrieved his hat from the ground next to the porch and called after the boy, "*Você pode dizer que você sente muito, mas toma cuidado com o velhos. Você os terá arremessou no rio se você não é cuidadoso*!" The boy might be sorry, but Eduardo wasn't in the mood to fish someone out of the river if they happened to be in the way as the boy ran past.

The boy ran backwards grinning. He saluted Eduardo before turning and sprinting down the slope.

Eduardo dusted off his hat and settled back into the rocker. The smell of fish from the river mixing with the dampness of the forest gave the air a strong, earthy scent. The rainy season was upon them, and as he surveyed the sky, Eduardo noticed dark clouds gathering. Before long the river would swell and overflow its already wide banks, climbing the hillside until it was sometimes just a few meters from where he was sitting. Other villages were forced to move higher into the forest when the river overflowed, but not here in Kahepa because it was built much higher than the river.

One of the weekly supply boats blasted its horn, announcing it was coming around the bend in the river. The boat horn had a mournful edge to it, as if it didn't quite have enough strength to blast out a strong blow, but it was a welcoming invitation that had people poking their heads from huts and gravitating toward the riverbank.

The boat appeared old and tired as it fought its way slowly against the current, its once bright white and red paint long since faded and flecked from the wooden frame. The smoke from the engine told its own tale of woe as it labored toward the dock.

Eduardo felt a little bit like the boat. He rubbed his stubby goatee realizing it had been a while since he trimmed it. He had showered last night and changed his clothes, but he hadn't looked at himself in the mirror. He looked down at his khakis and sighed, realizing how wrinkled they were from lack of care. *Yes*, he thought to himself. *I could easily be compared to the boat, all rumpled and scruffy*.

Over the last year, he had remained here at the station more often, even though his home was not far into the forest. The station was adequate, with an office, a bathroom, and a bunk room. His own house was airy and comfortable, and ladies might call it cute or quaint. But, for Eduardo, it had felt empty since Serena had gone. He would finally go home tonight. It was time. He had finally made his peace with Serena's memory.

Eduardo gazed at the river. He watched children clamoring to be the first to meet the boat, but then his thoughts were drawn back to the mysterious deaths in the forest. They were troubling. He had returned to the site yesterday to take another look around. The rain did a thorough job of washing everything away, including the blood. The crime was going to be next to impossible to solve unless Stephen found something in the body samples.

Yesterday, Stephen completed the autopsies in record time but offered Eduardo little more than grunts in response to his steady torrent of questions. He asked Eduardo to be at the compound by 9:00 a.m. today to discuss what they already knew and what he had observed during the autopsies.

Stephen told him Julia was here. Eduardo hadn't seen her in over a year. He liked Julia. She was lovely, smart, and easy to be around.

Suddenly Eduardo realized he was seeing Julia as a woman, not just Stephen's exceptional student and colleague.

Eduardo looked again at his disheveled mess and decided to change clothes and tidy himself up a bit. With the decision made, he hurried inside with a welcomed lighter step to his gait.

15

In the thick morning mist, shiny dew droplets clung to the leaves before they began to drop, and Julia opened her eyes and yawned. Stephen had let her sleep in. What a gift! Julia yawned again as the morning roar of insects crowded her ears and dominated her consciousness.

She parted the bed's mosquito netting as the forest sounds pulled her toward the open window. In the calm morning air, above the din of insect calls, Julia recognized the distant, eerie cries of mantled howler monkeys staking out the day's territories. She slid slowly onto the window seat and stretched outside, her sleepy eyes searching for a glimpse of the toucan announcing the morning high in the canopy.

Now, where are you? Julia squinted. She slowly scanned the trees until she spotted it. *There you are*. Julia saw the bird settled deep in the branches of an emergent *virola* tree, its bright plumage blending with the dark green leaves and tiny yellow flowers. The tree was in full bloom, and Julia thought she caught a whiff of its pungent, sweet scent.

The yellow-ridged toco toucan was a tall one, at least two feet high. Its bill must have been six or seven inches long, and even though it looked like it was heavy enough to tip the bird upside down, the bill was not heavy. The bird tossed something, probably a piece of *virola* fruit, a few feet higher to a smaller toucan in the next tree.

"Are you flirting or just playing a game?" Julia exclaimed. "Trying to attract a mate to your roost?" She queried in a louder voice.

The toucans looked in her direction before darting off on their small wings, bursting from tree to tree in short, fervent flights.

Julia folded her legs under her lap and closed her eyes, inhaling the scents of dark earth, damp with the dripping dew, green vegetation, and fragrant flowers. There was nothing else that smelled like the rainforest.

She opened her eyes and examined the orchid-laden tangle of vines a few yards away and noticed several hummingbirds flitting from flower to flower, jostling with each other for the richest nectar. Julia wondered how they ever managed to get enough to eat. They were constantly dipping and dancing and chasing each other like little dive bombers, wings racing in a blur.

The level of noise they generated was far beyond their tiny size. Until Julia came to the rainforest, she never knew hummingbirds could be noisy, much less so aggressive. They seemed much too small and delicate looking. Once she approached too closely to a nesting mother and was convinced the little creature was going to strike and wound her, not to mention the uproar the vigilant bird made.

Julia sat back and leaned her head against the edge of the window. She noticed a thick patch of yellow fluttering in the distance. *Butterflies.* Probably hundreds of them. Butterflies were a passion for Julia. Looking back out her window, she could see several types of swallowtails and many more brush foots.

When a blue morphos landed on the sill near her arm, Julia caught her breath. It was her favorite butterfly, with its brilliant seven or eight inch long blue wings. The morphos pulled together its wings and rested motionless. Julia gazed at the bronze colored wing spots imbedded in the brown underside. Like giant eyes, the spots were a great defense as they glared at would-be predators, scaring them away or causing them to pause, which often gave the butterfly time for escape.

She extended a finger toward it, the butterfly still didn't move. Julia wondered if it landed here for its final breaths when the butterfly suddenly lifted and floated away.

A knock at her door startled her attention to the hour. Julia jumped up, snatched her pajamas off, and reached for her jeans. "Be right down!" she called.

Stephen held open the door two minutes later as she ran down the stairs. "I presume you slept well, my dear," he said as she bounded past him scooping her hair into the ever present Amazonian pony tail and slipped on the rubber band that had been around her wrist.

"Very. Thanks for letting me sleep in."

As they strolled down the dirt path toward the common room, Julia noticed Eduardo seated near the doorway, feet stretched out in front of him, hat tipped over his eyes. Eduardo looked like he was asleep, and he also looked like he might slide out of the chair at any moment.

When their shadows reached him, Eduardo snarled, "'Bout time you got out here, old man."

It wasn't until he pushed back his hat that Eduardo saw Julia. It took a moment for her presence to register. Her face was almost in silhouette as rays of sunlight streamed behind her, illuminating her hair like a halo. Julia stepped to the side, and her face was beautifully lit.

Eduardo had forgotten how fair she was. Tall and slender, casual yet classy, stunning but not ravishing. He had never considered her as anything more than an acquaintance. He stood and faced her.

Julia looked at him with the interest of a cat meeting a stranger. Her disinterest rankled him a bit, but he didn't know why. Eduardo didn't want to want a woman. Serena was gone, and he never wanted to love like that again. It was too painful to lose it. Julia was his friend, and that was how it was going to remain.

Eduardo said matter-of-factly, "I must marvel at any woman who could live with this stubborn, old geezer for weeks at a time and return year after year for more punishment." His Brazilian-Portuguese accent gave his words a mysterious air. He couldn't resist reaching for her hand. "Julia, it is a pleasure to see you again." He bowed.

Julia blinked, holding back her sense of alarm. The way her name fell from his lips felt a little too close-up and personal, as if it had tumbled around inside his warm mouth before escaping to the open air. It was a little unnerving.

"It is good to see you too, Eduardo," her voice caught a little as she pulled her hand from his. *I can't have a personal interest in Eduardo. Who could compete with a dead spouse*? *What am I thinking*?

Eduardo gave a nod. "Now," Eduardo said to Stephen, "we must get to some food."

Inside, Lupa set out a small feast of fresh mango juice, platters of fruit including *chirimoyas*, bananas, *pepinos*, and apples, a cereal of Andean grains, yogurt, and milk.

Alexis, Kosey, Jennifer, and Charlie came in one after the other as Eduardo, Stephen, and Julia settled around the large table. They welcomed Eduardo into the group as if they had known him forever.

Alexis savored a bite of a roll and hummed her pleasure. "What is this called?" she asked Lupa.

Lupa beamed. "You like?"

"Yeees," she purred, taking another bite.

"*Pao de queijo*…cheese bread."

"I could eat my weight in these," Alexis hummed.

Kosey shook his head. "That would not be good, Alexis. 'Overeating spoils the stomach and broadens the hips.'"

Alexis scowled. "Oh, stop. Let me enjoy this wonderful morsel." She held out a warm roll toward him. "Have you eaten one of these?"

"I have not had the pleasure." He took another sip of coffee. "I have not had enough of this coffee. What kind is it?" Kosey asked.

Stephen looked down at his own cup, "It's one of my favorites."

Kosey sniffed the dark liquid as steam drifted up. "Full, but not overpowering…with a hint of molasses and, what is that…a smell of brown bread?"

Stephen drew in his breath, enjoying the aroma before chuckling, "It's *jacu* coffee."

"Mmmm. *Jacu*? " Kosey took another sip, "I have never heard of it. What does *jacu* mean?"

"Actually, it's the name of a bird that lives around the coffee plantations in southeast Brazil." Stephen pointed toward the cup, "This is very rare coffee. I have a friend who flies to Sao Paulo several times each year on business. He always buys a large bag of beans and divvies it out when he returns."

"A bird?" Charlie asked.

"Yes, a bird."

"Mmmm," Charlie took another sip.

Eduardo laughed, enjoying the conversation and what was to come, "So, as I recall, the *jacu* bird coffee beans are cured in a similar manner as the *kopi luwak* coffee beans."

"Precisely."

"What are *kopi luwak* coffee beans?" Jennifer asked taking a large gulp.

"Just the finest coffee in the world." Stephen took another sip. "It costs three hundred dollars per pound."

Jennifer put down her cup, "You're kidding!"

The students chorused their astonishment.

"No way."

"*ʔò teé*!"

"Seriously?"

Julia laughed. She'd been drinking *jacu* coffee with Stephen for years and decided long ago not to think about how it was processed.

"*Jacu* bird coffee beans are only twelve dollars per pound," Stephen explained.

Kosey stood as if to give a toast. "I care not how much it costs, those other beans can be no better than these." He downed the rest and headed back for more.

"Yes," Stephen spoke quietly so Kosey would not hear. "These beans pass right through the *jacu* bird just like the *kopi luwak* beans pass through the toddy cat in Indonesia."

Alexis, Jennifer, and Charlie laid their cups down.

"I thought it was a civet..." Eduardo mused to Stephen.

The others sat listening, looking first at the men and then at their cups.

Stephen nodded, "Same thing. Locals call it the palm toddy cat."

Kosey returned and reached for the sugar jar. "What gives it the great flavor?"

Stephen tried not to smile. He had no idea if the idea of drinking coffee which had passed through the digestive tract of a bird would bother the boy or not, but he always enjoyed sharing the story with newcomers. Everyone remained silent.

Kosey noticed the others were not drinking. "Drink up!" He cheerily stirred his coffee.

"You see, my boy, these are some of the finest beans in the world."

Kosey nodded. "Yes, yes," and encouraged Stephen to continue as he sipped.

"The *jacu* bird has a discriminating eye and only chooses the brightest, ripest of the coffee cherries to eat."

"Mmmm, I can tell." Kosey breathed deeply as he took another swallow.

"They digest the bright red fruit off the outside, and…the remaining beans pass right through them ready to be harvested." Stephen swirled a mouthful around. "I find no lingering after-taste from the rumination, just rich, robust Brazilian flavor. And how about you?" He looked up, smiling this time.

Kosey stared into the brown liquid which had been a joy to drink just moments before, a mouthful still pooching out his cheeks. He wasn't sure if he should excuse himself and spew the coffee out the door, or keep his cool demeanor and literally suck it up.

Stephen scooted his chair back a little, afraid the boy might spit it out. But with a loud gurgling sound deep in his throat, Kosey swallowed and slowly put the cup down. He coughed and wiped his mouth with the napkin Alexis handed him.

Kosey cleared his throat. "Odd how your perception can be altered through knowledge." Kosey pushed the cup toward the center of the table. "I am having a mini-paradigm shift."

Alexis began to laugh. She had never seen Kosey at a loss for words.

"What, no saying for *jacu* coffee?" she asked.

With a somber look on his face he answered, "'He who asks questions, cannot avoid the answers.'"

Julia laughed and soon the others were laughing around the table.

"Now…" Stephen stood and downed the last of his coffee, "…we must begin compiling our clues." He walked to the wall across from the table and pulled down the writing board. Everyone moved to a seat where they faced the board. There were pieces of paper with writing on them taped in various spots. "Aaahh," Stephen remarked, "I see you have brought your system with you, Eduardo."

"Couldn't waste time waiting for you this morning."

Stephen picked up the marker. "Couldn't you just use this?"

Eduardo shrugged, "I brought them with me. Didn't see any reason to write them again."

Stephen nodded and explained to the others, "We don't see many big crimes here, but Eduardo has a type of system. Uncanny, if you ask me." He glanced back at the board. "He starts out by randomly putting up notes about what he's found as to what the scene looked like, even the weather, and plants and animals nearby. Then he sits back and stares at his array of papers. It is the oddest thing I've ever seen. On the last case, I came by often enough to see him reared back in his chair just staring. Each day, he repositioned the notes. Added new ones. Somehow, they fell into place and began relating to each other. Another case solved."

Stephen picked up the marker and pulled off the cap. "We will continue with paper and tape so we can move them around easier. Now, let us talk through available facts." He opened a ream of paper, and they began.

Jennifer offered to help and taped up the clues as Stephen wrote them down.

An hour later, they didn't understand much more than when they started. Eduardo stood up and assessed the board. A few more notes had been added as they talked through the case, but the information still left them all puzzling for conclusions. Stephen lit his pipe and slowly puffed. Julia was perched on a tall stool, feet propped high on a rung, with her chin in her hands and her elbows on her knees. The four students sat at the table and contributed little. Everyone stared at the notes on the board, yet no one felt compelled to talk.

They separated the bits and pieces into categories: body condition, location, truck with inventory, witness accounts, animals, insects, and types of trees and plants nearby. As expected, there was more information in some categories than others. There wasn't much in the way of hard evidence except for the body conditions documented from the autopsy and the little boy's description. Eduardo collected samples of plants near the death site. Of those plants, only a couple showed any known poisonous effects, and that was only if they were abused and ingested beyond what was almost humanly possible. There were still more samples to be tested.

Julia remarked as she studied the wall of clues, "Now, that is a storyboard." It reminded her of the stories she told kindergarten classes that she mentored back in Athens. She was always putting pictures in a row on the dark, green-felted boards to illustrate the story she was telling. She read the words and put the pictures up for children to visualize what was happening since most of them had not yet learned to read. Julia and other mentors helped them put the pieces together so they could make sense of any words they didn't understand.

Stephen and Eduardo preferred calling the wall tablet an investigation board, as they lined up the facts like mathematical formulas.

Julia had chosen science as her career because she liked to solve mysteries, and she liked to base the findings on science…truth. Solving mysteries. She often thought she was more of a playwright instead of a scientist, but then what was a scientist if not a playwright? She was always creating new scenarios to explain events, clearing up the unknown. Maybe all scientists were playwrights in disguise.

Stephen nodded. "Somewhere up there is definitely a story."

Alexis had been studying the columns of information. She asked, "What about the insects?" Several types known to have poisonous venom were listed under the heading.

"Good point, Alexis," Stephen said looking at the board. "The most logical killer in that group is the ants. They are fascinating creatures. They carry many toxins, and some are lethal. The jumper ant and bulldog ant of Australia have caused many deaths. Two to three percent of locals are highly allergic. When stung, sensitive people go into *anaphylactic* shock and die." He finished by saying, "And ants are a smorgasbord for many other creatures." He turned to Julia. "What about the funguses you study? Surely some of them are toxic. You're still finding new ones."

"Fungus?" Jennifer finally spoke up.

Julia nodded. "Could be." She thought a moment before answering Jennifer's question. "All insects have a fungus that targets it as a vessel for procreation. I've got a great article stored in my laptop. I'll print and leave it for you all to read. It will give you a good grasp of what a fungus can do to an ant or other insect." She made a note on her pad to print it out.

Stephen bowed his head, popping the marker cap off and on as he pondered. "Back to the ants. They are very organized and structured creatures. Their lives are highly predictable, and they're extremely social. Each tiny insect specializes in a single job. They never veer from their appointed task, and they never fight amongst themselves within their individual colonies. Maybe their predictability is why they've become prey to so many."

"Prey?" Alexis asked.

"Yes. Like Julia said, fungi invade them, but there are other parasites always invading their bodies and using them to incubate and grow and metamorphose into something else."

"I had no idea," Eduardo said. "So their insides are being eaten?"

"Precisely," Stephen answered.

"What parasites exactly are we talking about?" Charlie asked as he rubbed his sore shoulder.

"Oh, too many to count. Things like flukes or wasps that lay their larvae inside ants or spiders or even roaches. They get inside and eat the little buggers up, leaving a mere shell when they're finished or get themselves and the ant shells eaten by other creatures for proliferation." Deep in thought Stephen muttered, "Nature has found very interesting ways to keep itself going."

Julia pulled out her phone and took a picture of the clues on the board. She looked at Eduardo. "I'll download this so you'll have a copy to look over."

"Stephen has my address," he responded. "And thank you. That will be most helpful," he added with a smile.

They all studied the clues on the board in silence.

Eduardo looked at Charlie. "How's the shoulder?"

"Much better. No more throbbing."

Eduardo waited until they finished brainstorming to ask the couple, "Where are Nigel and Drake?"

"I have been wondering that myself," Stephen chimed in.

"Beats me," Charlie shrugged which drew a wince.

"They've been gone since yesterday," Jennifer's face masked all emotion.

"Come here in night," Lupa said from the kitchen area.

Stephen turned to him and asked, "How do you know?"

"Fruit no here Lupa pick yesterday," he answered. "And bread and cheese no here."

Stephen looked hard at Charlie and Jennifer. "What are they up to?"

Charlie and Jennifer looked at each other.

"I don't know," Jennifer's small voice whined. "They said they were working on a project."

Eduardo searched their faces. *What were they hiding*? Aloud he asked, "What were you really doing when you got shot, Charlie?"

"Running for my life," he sounded defensive.

Stephen asked, "Why are you here in the forest?"

"To study."

"Study what?" Eduardo asked.

For Charlie, it felt like these two men were cornering him. "Look, we just came here to hike and take pictures and take back samples to study in Nigel's lab. Whatever else they're doing, I couldn't guess. Nigel was showing Drake how to use some kind of measuring gizmo."

"Yes," Stephen interjected, "I saw it. CO2 levels. He told me the same thing, but somehow, I'm not sure he was telling the whole truth."

Eduardo watched Charlie as he slowly asked, "What can you tell me about Nigel and Drake?" He folded his arms across his chest.

Jennifer put her hand on Charlie's good shoulder, her eyes imploring him to tell them about the Nigel that was now surfacing.

Charlie hoped she didn't say more. "I've only known them for a month or so, certainly not long enough to know much. He's Jennifer's professor, and he invited us to come along. It sounded like fun." He looked away. "They're an odd couple. That's all I know."

Stephen decided to let it go for now. He stood. "We need to go to the lab. We have many more samples to sort through."

Eduardo wasn't quite ready to let it drop. "On my way here, I went out to the place where my men picked you up. I tried to retrace your race for your life, and I found what appeared to be a large campsite that probably held a host of men and machinery to cut trees. Do you know anything about that?"

"No," Charlie's temper threatened to surface. "I told you, we were hiking and exploring. We just got here a few days before and hadn't started doing a lot of work, what with the jet lag and all."

Eduardo stared at the young man. He knew Charlie was leaving out some important details.

Charlie ducked his head and rubbed his shoulder again.

Jennifer glanced at Charlie and then looked away.

They are definitely hiding something, Eduardo thought.

Ever the peacemaker, Alexis tried to change the subject. "Can I ask you some questions about the loggers?"

"Sure…," Eduardo answered, his eyes not leaving Charlie and Jennifer. Then he turned his attention to Alexis.

Alexis frowned, "I know those men were loggers, but exactly what were they doing?"

"They were about to cut a gem of a tree," Stephen answered for Eduardo. "And while you explain this, Eduardo, Lupa and I are going to the garden. He has a new group of vegetables he wants me to see. Will you join all of us in the lab later?"

"Not today. I have some business to take care of in the village."

"Very well. We have much work to complete. Try to wrap this up by the time I finish with Lupa. See you all in about twenty minutes?"

"Okay," Julia said. The others agreed.

Eduardo explained as the two men left through the kitchen, "We're almost certain the men who died were part of a rigging crew, men who go out ahead of the cutting crew and saw out the tops of trees to prepare a staging area. They didn't have all the necessary equipment to begin cutting. Different loggers cut using different methods. Sometimes the same men rig and cut."

Kosey asked, "What do you mean by staging area?"

His answer came smoothly. "It's the spot where the men bring in the trucks to load logs. Most install a pulley system in the trees for pulling the logs up the hillside to the staging area. It can create quite a mess if it's not done carefully. I guess it just depends on the intent of the loggers. If they care about the land, they are careful, otherwise…." Eduardo shrugged.

When he didn't continue, Alexis asked, "What kind of trees are they after?"

Eduardo gave a low chuckle. "Mogno."

"Mogno?"

"You Americans call it mahogany."

"Mahogany? Oh, I love mahogany," Alexis said cheerfully. "The table in my hall is mahogany. It was my grandmother's."

Eduardo didn't act as if he heard her. He continued in a dull voice, "All the major stands of mahogany trees have been cut throughout the Amazon except in the most remote areas. Actually, the stands were cut in the early and middle part of the 1900s. There are only isolated trees left, no more than one per hectare…a little less than two and a half acres in your measurement. And that is only for younger, much smaller trees. That's the way they grow now, isolated and far apart."

He was lost in his own world now. "The Brazilian government has worked diligently to stop the cutting of *mogno* trees, and for a while the cutting slowed. Brazilian law says it's now illegal to cut them for any reason, but they're still cut every day." He smiled sadly, "The *mogno* trees are the reason we lost much of the Amazon early on."

"I don't understand," Alexis saw the sadness in his eyes.

"You see, *mogno* is even more valuable than heroin," he continued. "It is the only tree valuable enough to make it financially appealing to bring in the machinery to carve out a road. The Amazon Rainforest has a spider's web of roads running through it. Once the loggers get the *mogno* out, another wave of loggers comes through and cuts the next most valuable wood, like *ipê* trees. Believe it or not, behind them, another group follows, and the soft woods are cut for pulp…for pressed board…for paper…for napkins. If we can stop the *mogno* loggers, we can stop the roads, and then the others will have no access to the lesser trees. Then if we can stop the cattle ranchers and soy bean farmers and wildcat gold miners." Eduardo paused. "We might save a wealth of natural resources that are *phiado*, being *plundered*, as you would say."

Looking at Julia he said, "You know, I climbed down the hillside to the *mogno* tree the dead loggers were starting to cut."

"You did?" she asked. She heard the new smile in his voice.

"It is beautiful. Massive. The largest I have ever seen. I know the loggers were excited with their find. There aren't many like it left. Maybe they got careless."

Julia noticed green flecks in the warm brown eyes watching her. She felt a burning begin at the bottom of her neck and move up and then back down. Suddenly, she felt warm all over. His voice. The passion he had for the rainforest. It was stimulating her senses. *It's stimulating, something*! She became self-conscious and hoped her flush went unnoticed.

"At the base, the tree itself is over twelve feet across even without the buttresses, which stretched fifteen feet up the tree and over thirty feet out into the forest on all sides. The trunk rose at least seventy feet before the first branch."

Kosey whistled, "That's one big bush."

"Wow!" Alexis exclaimed. "I'd love to see it."

Julia had trouble taking in the immense size. "Me, too," she said in more of a hush.

Eduardo nodded, "You will be in awe. It is very impressive, even more are the limbs stretched out so far," he paused searching for his words, "I had to pace them off twice just to believe it. From what I could see, the top branches spanned over forty meters."

The others watched as Eduardo's eyes never left Julia. "Do you realize how large that is, Julia?"

She shook her head. She thought she was going to faint.

Kosey spoke what Julia and Alexis were thinking. "Give us something that compares to it."

Eduardo thought for a minute. "Let's see…soccer fields vary in size." He looked at the group and asked, "How wide is an American football field?"

Julia guessed, "Maybe fifty yards?"

"It's fifty-three point three yards, to be exact," Alexis asserted, "At least for a regulation field…not arena football. And it's a hundred and twenty yards deep." *Might as well throw that in*, she thought.

Julia's eyes widened in amazement.

Alexis shrugged as she explained, "My son played football."

Eduardo did some mental calculations. "Okay, that's right at one hundred and sixty feet from side to side. Imagine. The tree's limbs spread almost as wide…and it was going to be gone in a matter of days."

Julia just shook her head. "I want to see it."

"Please take all of us," Alexis pleaded.

"Yes. We will see it soon," Eduardo told her.

Julia studied Eduardo's face as his smile dissolved. He was thinking of something else.

"Do you know who buys the most mahogany?" Eduardo didn't call it *mogno*.

Julia thought she knew the answer. *It's our fault again*. "The US?"

"Yes, sixty percent of the global trade. And what does the US do with it?" He sounded exasperated and exhausted.

She tried to think. "Make furniture…" She faltered. She honestly couldn't think of anything else.

Alexis continued, "Paneling for expensive homes and buildings, framing for walls and pictures…" She wafted into silent thought.

Eduardo stood. "Yes. One of the most common pieces of furniture in the US actually is only seen for a little while. Then it is gone, forever, from sight." Julia was mystified now. *What is he talking about*?

"Do you know what the furniture is?" His voice was soft and low. He stood at the screen door looking out into the forest, his back toward them.

Alexis and Kosey looked at each other and then at Julia.

"I can't imagine," Julia reflected. She mused, "What is created from such beautiful and expensive wood and only seen for a short time?"

Eduardo turned back and looked at Julia and gave a brief but sad smile. "They are put into the ground."

Alexis gasped.

Julia stiffened.

Kosey just looked baffled.

"Oh, no. Don't tell me." Julia covered her mouth with her hand.

Eduardo nodded and didn't speak another word. He just waved goodbye.

Alexis got up and grabbed Kosey's arm, pulling him to his feet and out the door. Alexis explained about the wood as they walked toward the lab.

Julia heard Eduardo's jeep start and drive away. She knew the answer to his question even before she heard Kosey exclaim through the forest, "I cannot believe it!"

Mogno trees…mahogany trees…trees that had taken hundreds or even thousands of years to seed and birth and grow and live. Those trees were being cut and crafted into caskets…which were put back into the ground not for the living…but for the dead.

16

It is remarkably easy to kill people, especially when the attack is unexpected. Will always had ambivalence with these situations. It was almost as if he didn't accomplish his boss's wishes, he too would be DOA from a gunshot wound. Will comforted himself from his guilt: Kill or be killed. It didn't matter that these were innocent and simple people. They stood in the way of progress, and his own well-being. At least that was what he kept telling himself.

Will walked into the clearing and saw the house, if it could be called that, sitting directly in the center. A man worked in the garden in the rear, diligently holding the encroaching forest at bay with his machete. A woman stood with her back to the open door, preparing something on the table in front of her. Will pulled the revolver from his belt and screwed on a silencer. He hated the sound of a gun almost as much as the sight of blood, and the silencer kept the element of surprise for the others he would kill. He pulled the trigger only once, and the woman toppled onto the table and then fell to the floor.

A child let out a wail, and Will stepped behind a broken wagon lying on its side next to him. He hadn't noticed the woman wore a sling with a young child nestled next to her body. When the man in the garden heard the child's wails, he casually strolled around the side of the house, wiping his hands with a stained rag he pulled from a nail as he passed. He saw his wife crumpled on the floor, so he ran and knelt by her side. Will put a bullet in the back of his head. The man and woman literally never knew what hit them.

What a way to go… Will thought. He frowned as the wailing continued. *Damn.* He walked to the front door and stepped into the house. Leaning over the dead parents, he aimed and looked away as he pulled the trigger. The wailing stopped. Will felt a burn of bile creep up the back of his throat. *Shit. A baby. I had to kill a baby. This job is getting worse by the day.*

Outside, Will walked around the house and looked at the clothes hanging on a makeshift line. Hanging between the baby clothes, work pants, and skirts was one small pair of shorts and a faded red t-shirt. He guessed there was one child left. Will stuffed the gun back in his waistband as he walked to the edge of the forest where he had stored a can of gasoline. He doused the rotting wood and threw a match on the floor in the doorway. The shack burst into flames immediately.

Faintly at first, but growing louder, Will heard the calls of an excited child drawing closer. He tossed the can and retrieved his gun as he scanned the forest again.

The boy came through an opening to his left carrying a string of fish and his pole, a large smile on his face, obviously proud of his catch. He stopped and stared at his burning home, as if he wasn't sure what he was seeing. As comprehension dawned, he dropped everything and ran toward the growing blaze. He noticed the man with the gun when he was halfway across the clearing and without slowing, darted back into the underbrush.

Will reacted by putting several rounds into the flapping leaves. Had he hit him? He picked up the machete and trotted after the boy.

Will was glad it was almost over. He didn't enjoy killing people, especially children, and the young boy he was hunting down reminded him of his own innocent youth at that age.

Will's voice sounded pleasant as he hacked at the limbs and vines. "Where aaarrre you?" He moved down a small trail following the path on which he hoped the boy had continued.

The nearly completed extermination had only taken a few minutes. Will considered how odd the reality that a family can be alive one minute and wiped completely away the next. With the shack gone, he knew it would only take a month or so for the forest to reclaim the garden spot and charred remains of the only home the boy had probably ever known.

The forest was dense on this side of the homestead, and it was slower going as Will continued to hack at the foliage. He came to a large fallen tree and stooped to go under. Right in front of his face was a red smear, and Will squatted down and touched the spot. His finger came away wet and deep red. He rubbed it with his thumb before wiping it on a damp leaf. He had hit the boy after all.

Will stood and turned in a slow circle, looking for any indication the boy was near. As he ducked under the tree, he saw two small hand and knee prints. The child had fallen and yes, he had crawled further into the undergrowth. Blood drops were apparent at closer intervals as Will moved on.

The forest opened up a little. Ahead, he could see one of the sixteen giant mahogany trees he had found on this land, Livingston's land now. At first he wondered why Livingston needed to steal the land, since he stole the trees anyway.

Will asked him one day and Arthur remarked, "More land means more money, boy." And that was it. It was all about the money. More land…more money.

Will chopped a woven vine as large as his forearm and headed in that direction, following the marks the boy made as he dragged himself over the ground.

When he found him, the boy appeared to be sleeping, lying on his side, legs drawn up, hands folded and tucked neatly between the dirt and his ear. He had pulled his body into the shelter of two of the mahogany's tall, flowing buttresses before he gave out.

Will nudged the boy's bare foot with his boot to see if he would rouse. The child never moved as blood continued to ooze and pool on the ground under his chest from the hole that had been created in his back just above his heart. Will nudged him again before turning to leave. It was going to be a good hike to the truck, and he longed to chug a drink back in the saloon.

Will left the tiny body in its mahogany enclosure, an ironic open casket. It was a fit enough resting place, if the body lasted long enough. He looked back once as the sky opened and rain poured down over the little boy, blending with the deep red pool gathering beneath before washing the innocent blood deep into the ground.

17

Lupa crept across the boulders toward the back of the waterfall. The cave where he stored his shaman supplies was hidden from view by a moss encrusted protrusion of greenstone and quartz. When a ray of sunlight made its way through the small breach in the canopy above the surging water, brilliant crystals sparkled in the rock. Shamans believed the brilliant outcropping indicated a sacred place.

Vines of mature philodendron, with glossy, dark green leaves, so large they resembled elephant ears, meandered up the craggy wall of rock that stretched skyward. A thick vine of guarana intertwined in its climb toward the sunlight holding gifts of fruit Lupa collected to concoct his own version of an energy drink. Nestled around the rocky base were scatterings of caladiums, some dark pink with green striations and others bright white with fine pink and green marbling, so delicate they resembled angel's wings. Further from the spraying mist a profusion of coral and pink impatiens cascaded onto the forest floor finding pockets of soil in rocky pores.

This was Lupa's private place, the place where he kept his shaman secrets. Lupa moved around a rock and slipped into the dark recesses of the cave. The smell of dried natural compost surrounded him. Herbs and plants hung upside down in fragrant bouquets from sticks strung across the ceiling. A natural stone ledge served as his worktable where there were many jars containing extracts, saps, seeds, and crushed leaves, a bowl with pestle for grinding and mixing, and an oil lamp which Lupa lit immediately. Water dripped into pools near the back, but the surface where he worked was merely damp.

Lupa came here often to assess his plant stores, sometimes collecting fresh leaves and herbs while replacing older samples. Occasionally, he lit a fire in a small pit and cooked up a fresh brew for an ache or pain or perhaps a tonic of some sort for himself or for Stephen. Lupa rarely practiced his shamanistic talents with visitors anymore, but on occasion, he used his knowledge to help someone who was sick.

The plants were his teachers. He would drink of the *ayahuasca* and his mind would be opened to the teachers. Whatever the problem brought to him, the plant-teachers told him what to blend for healing. The plant spirits were the learned ones. Locals called him the "*vegetalista*," the human vessel used by the plant-teachers to heal.

Lupa came here today to gather what he needed to fight the evil which had entered their otherwise idyllic compound. It had been a long time since he cast out demons, and those who came to him in the past had done so of their own accord. He wondered if Nigel wanted his demon driven out. Lupa wasn't sure if it was possible to extricate it at all, but he would try.

His plan was to roll several ceremonial cigars encasing a combination of plants. He would start with natural tobacco, not like the tobacco in the cigarettes in North America but a potent blend he had planted for years, dried, and used both for pleasure and as medicine. Blowing tobacco smoke over the individual when using one of many medicinal plants purified the area and built a shield from evil spirits. Many plant-teachers were fond of tobacco and performed better when it was added to the mix.

Lupa unrolled a layer of sacred *mapacho* tobacco leaves to act as the outside casing for the cigar. He reached for a jar of shredded sassafras root to ward off evil spirits. He sprinkled a few pieces in the bowl, along with a few *anadenanthera* seeds to overcome the supernatural, some *ajo sacho* to rid any spells that might have been cast over Nigel, some leaves of the kapok for spiritual protection, and a few shavings of *chinic sanango*, which hopefully would soften the evil one's heart a bit.

Lupa picked up the pestle and began to grind. When the powder was a consistency he thought was right, he added a bit of water from the falls. He shaped the paste into a tube and rolled it in the *mapacho* leaves and then set it above the lamp to dry. He repeated the steps three more times to make sure he had enough cigars to last the night. He left the lamp burning to finish the drying process.

He reached for other jars and then scooped out shards of *angeleca* for the evil spirits. He added *datura* for cleansing, *mugwart* for dreaming, and *damiana* as a general tonic. He ground each to a fine powder and poured them into his medicine bag. Then he put extra tobacco in another bag. He was finally ready for the cleansing ceremony.

Lupa wasn't sure how the ceremony might work, especially since he could only chant in his head, and he had to do that while they were unaware. Generally one was not supposed to do any kind of ceremony without the subject's permission, but Lupa knew in his soul that something wicked was present, and it had to be removed. The patients would be asleep, but Lupa was determined to try anything to rid their bodies of the evil he knew lived there.

When the cigars were dry, Lupa added them to the last bag, turned off the lamp, and left the cave. On the way back to the compound he gathered the fruit from the *meh-nu* tree and harvested some resin from the *u-sha* berry tree for the ceremonial design he would put on his face and body.

Lupa hurried home to ready everything for the evil men's return.

18

Stephen and Julia spent the rest of the morning into early afternoon teaching the students how to use all of the equipment and the testing procedures they would use as they moved forward. Everyone worked hard for hours clearing sample after sample of plants, air, and soil, pausing only once to eat a light lunch of fruit and sandwiches Lupa had left before he disappeared into the forest.

Stephen looked at his watch and rolled his shoulders. "I need a rest." He looked at the others. "Anybody else need a break?"

The students were still tired from the trip, so they agreed. They headed off for hammocks or food.

"I'll be back in an hour," Stephen said as he left.

Alexis remarked, "I could stay and help if you'd like."

"I'm going to find the ant article I promised to print out," Julia waved her off. "Go," she said. "I might be off for a rest myself soon."

Julia couldn't find the article, so she Skyped a colleague asking specific questions about toxins the ants produce and their effects on humans. She listened to the research scientist describe a particular project he worked on related to fire ant toxins and the possibility the toxins were becoming stronger. He then promised to e-mail her, among other reports, an interesting paper written by one of his lab technicians about a particular study they were engaged in looking at the reproduction of parasites and their manipulation of multiple hosts, including ants, in the process. True to his word, the mail came almost immediately, and Julia printed out the attachments. The first one was written in a style of writing more like recording an observation. Julia found it easy to visualize what transpired.

A lab technician unscrews the lid from a jar and releases a common land snail which has been feeding on cow dung infested with fluke eggs all week and now carries lancet fluke larvae through its body. The fluke eggs hatch inside the snail's intestine where the larvae penetrate the snail's organs, eventually spawning an army of young parasites. When they break out of the organs, the parasites cause the snail to produce a delicacy.

The snail drags itself ever so slowly over the grassy terrain leaving a slimy film-trail. Before long, formica ants arrive, drawn by the scent of the glistening trail laid down by the snail. One ant follows the sticky ooze until it finds what it is looking for; it finds the delicacy. This savory treat is a slime ball, but this one is different from others the ants have found. The delicacy is teeming with hundreds of infant lancet flukes. Then another ant finds one. And another. One by one the tidbits are eaten until they are completely consumed. For the ants, this is a feast…but, unknown to the ants, it is a feast with deadly consequences.

After they are ingested, most of the flukes remain sedentary in the ants' abdomens. They seem to be content to stay in the warmth and dine with the ants. But in each of the ants, two or three scouts inevitably break away from the gang. They are on a mission, looking for the nerves below the throat controlling the ant's movements…the ant's command center.

When the scouting team eventually locates it, the ant is essentially hijacked, and the scouts perform their parasitic witchcraft on the ant's nervous system. The ant becomes a puppet. Under the direction of the primitive creature now in command of its nerve center, the ant is compelled to do things that are not part of its DNA-programmed behavior.

As night approaches, the infected ants abandon their daily routine of returning to the colony. Instead, for no apparent reason, en mass the affected ants climb up a blade of grass and clamp down on the tip to wait. Clustered together, the ants hang on for hours, inherently offering themselves to be eaten by cattle or sheep or other grazing animals.

If the ants cling the whole night without being eaten, they scurry to the ground in the morning. Conversely, if they were to tarry under the heat of the morning sun, they would bake, and the parasites would die along with the ants. The parasites are too smart for that. The flukes allow the ants to loosen their grips and resume normal ant behavior. At the next nightfall, the flukes, still in control, command the ants, again in a collective group, to climb a blade of grass to be another night offering.

Once a grazing cow finally eats the ants, the flukes settle in the cow's small intestine, and then they worm their way to its liver. The flukes live, produce eggs, and die in the liver. Left unchecked, they can decimate a herd of cattle. The eggs are excreted through the cattle feces, where newly arrived snails begin to forage. The cycle begins anew, and no one can stop it.

Julia laid down the papers and wondered…what would happen if that parasite found its way into a human? How could it get there? Would it progress in the same manner as she read there…through two hosts to get to a human? Maybe a honey bee to an orange blossom into an orange? Could that next red apple or ripe peach hold a parasite capable of controlling human brains…making humans do things at the parasite's whim…actions a human would never think to do? And if a parasite can hijack the everyday behavior of a group of ants, could they have evolved to attack the cells inside humans? Could the men who died in the forest have breathed in a new strain of parasites long hidden in the forest?

19

The new road was only a few hours old. Will's eyes beamed, pleased with the rapid progress his road crew was making. The rain stopped while he was having a quick bite of lunch and three big mugs of *chopp*. Will was still basking in the mellow glow of the Brazilian draft beer, which had been icy cold for a change.

The truck bounced over and through muddy ruts and around large, fallen trees, cut and left behind, like pick-up sticks tossed about by a child. He felt like a pioneer in the Amazon, conquering its tenacious growth with his powerful machines.

His powerful machines. Will's face dissolved into a scowl as he thought about the ruined engine in his dozer. Thank goodness the men had the sense not to start the second one until after they drained the oil and purged the system. Otherwise, he'd be down two machines. *Damn tree-huggers*. It had to be them, and he'd find them. He had his feelers out asking where they might be hiding.

Will wasn't going to let the memory of the lost dozer or the memory of the family from this morning mess up this fine day. He forced himself not to dwell on any of it. Instead, he thought about how fast this road was going in.

In the thick, gnarly growth of the Amazon basin, felling large trees with dozers made getting to the next mahogany faster, especially where the forest canopy was dense. In tight areas where the woody liana vines thrived, they wove through the canopy layer tying the forest together like fabric. Pulling down a single, huge tree cleared a gaping hole in the upper canopy larger than the space occupied by the tree itself. Tearing out the canopy began a domino effect of felling and killing nearby trees. Will could not have cared less. Only the mahogany mattered. There were other rainforest giants like the smooth kapoks that Will wished were profitable. Kapoks had little value in this line of work, except they did offer the benefit of sweeping away as many as thirty lesser trees on their way to the ground.

Will passed the trucks carrying the work crew and equipment about a mile back, so he knew the active cutting couldn't be far ahead. Around another bend was the dead dozer they would abandon. He drove another half mile before he saw a cloud of dark smoke hovering above the cab of the other dozer.

He stopped the truck high on a bluff. As he stepped into the bright sunshine, Will could hear the chainsaws gnawing. He liked to imagine the saws were the Harleys of the chainsaw world. When you held one of those big boys, its power flowed into your hands and up your arms, transforming you into half-machine, just like climbing on the back of a Harley motorcycle and feeling the rumbling between your legs. It was exhilarating. With bars almost three feet long, they needed a strong man even to be lifted. A well-maintained saw could easily last twenty or more years even in the dampness of the forest and against the size of these trees.

The day was cooler than usual, perfect weather for making good time. The smell of diesel and gasoline permeated the air. Will folded his arms and spread his feet apart. He took in a slow, deep breath as he surveyed the scene. *Ahh*, Will thought, *the smell of money.*

His mind wandered back to the crew he lost three days before. *What could have happened to those men*? *We've lost a half week of work…* There had been a lot of buzz around Kahepa, including in the saloon at his hotel. Will sniffed…*his hotel.* It was the only hotel, if you could call it that. Six rooms in all, and he had the only private bath.

The night the dead men in the forest were found, Will spent the evening in the saloon wanting to hear what people said. He heard the local police were looking into the deaths. Tavares was the head man's name. Eventually the man would get around to his hotel with questions, so it was time to move on.

Will stood with his feet planted on the hillside, watching the men working below for a long time before anyone noticed him. One of the men signaled to the foreman, who looked up and scurried over.

"We move fast, yes?" the man queried with a crooked grin as he approached.

"Better than I expected," Will answered as he continued watching. He eyed the towering kapok they were ready to cut. He couldn't see the men at its base, but Will knew they were cutting because the upper branches were trembling. It wouldn't be long now. Close to 200 feet in height, the kapok would do its duty and clear out scores of smaller trees. He wondered which way it would fall.

Reading Will's thoughts, the foreman explained, "It fall the other way, about two o'clock."

At the widest spread, the diameter of the uppermost limbs was about sixty feet. As though in a slow motion ballet, the trunk began to lean ever so slowly until those overhead limbs tipped and connected with the downward pull of gravity. All it took was one…two…three…four…

five.... Several hundred years of growth ripped open the canopy and hit the ground as lianas tangled in lesser trees grabbed adjoining limbs, held tight, and pulled. Just like an earthquake, the first powerful jolt was followed by after-jolts. Multiple crashes followed in sequence like a finale of fireworks on the Fourth of July. A hole almost as large as a soccer field opened into the sky.

Will slapped the foreman on the back and let out a hoot. He loved to see one of these old-timers come down. He couldn't have driven up at a better moment. With no use for a kapok, Will was glad to leave it for the locals to salvage for canoes.

The foreman was happy with his boss's mood. He'd seen Will plenty angry in the past few months, when delays continually set them back. He had heard the word that something awful happened to part of the cutting crew a few days ago, and some were even calling the dead ones 'dripping men.' The foreman had worked hard to convince his people not to abandon his crew after they, too, had heard. He wanted to ask Will what happened, but he was afraid. He wasn't sure if he was more afraid of how Will would react to his question or of knowing what actually happened. In all his fifty years in the rainforest, the foreman had never heard about someone dying like those men were said to have died. Next week he would be in his home village where he would ask his shaman to explain. But from all he heard, he didn't think his shaman would have any more answers than the local authorities. To make matters worse, they'd had the trouble with the man spying in the tree and the others they chased and shot at. Then, this morning, there was the useless dozer. A series of hassling and now mysterious events.

The workers were now aware Will was on the job scene. They moved at a feverish pace, casting glances at both Will and the foreman, hoping their boss would have some answers for them when they settled into camp at dark. Several were already planning to leave during the night if they did not find out what happened to the dripping men. They had families and were afraid for their wives and children, as well as themselves.

Will offered the older man a bonus for getting the road finished early so Will and his cutting crew could move in tomorrow morning. There was only about a half mile left to the mahogany, and the foreman assured Will they would be finished and out the other side by nightfall. He had the coordinates for the next tree, so they would move in its direction at first light.

Will climbed into his truck and headed back to the saloon. He stopped on the side of a bluff to admire the mahogany hovering high over the forest in the distance, dark against the late afternoon sky. *Tomorrow you are mine.*

20

The evening meal was wonderful. A delicious roast cooked with dried *aji panca* peppers, mashed yellow potatoes, *canario* beans and fresh *tumbo* juice.

Alexis commented, "I think this is the best pot roast I have ever eaten."

Lupa grinned.

"I'm almost afraid to ask," Kosey looked down at his plate, "but what kind of animal is this?"

"You like this one," Lupa said. "It not come through bowels of bird."

Alexis wrinkled her nose in disgust.

"This," Lupa held his hands framing the sliced meat on the platter, "...*paca* or *majas*, best meat in jungle."

Kosey frowned, "*Paca...majas*?"

Stephen sucked in his lips before explaining, "It is a large, nocturnal, fruit eating animal. The fruit is what makes the meat so delicious."

Kosey cocked his head to the side as he poked his fork into the meat. "Yes, but what does it look like? What family does it resemble?"

Julia leaned over and patted Kosey's hand. "Just enjoy it, Kosey. Everyone who ever eats *paca* considers it the best."

"No, I want to know." He threw out his chest, "I am here to learn and to experience the culture."

"Rodent," Stephen uttered.

Jennifer and Alexis both gasped.

Kosey stood. "I have eaten a rat," he choked out in horror.

"No, you have eaten a *paca*," Stephen was trying hard to be patient.

"Rat is rodent. *Paca* is rodent. I have eaten a rat!" Kosey proclaimed.

"Okay, so you ate a rat," Charlie reached for another helping. "Wasn't it tasty?"

Kosey contemplated the thought. "Yes, it was very tasty...a very tasty rat." And with that, he sat down, picked up another bite, and popped it into his mouth with a sigh of contentment.

The humor was not lost on anyone, and they all rolled with laughter.

Julia and Stephen rushed through the rest of the meal and took a silent tongue lashing from Lupa for their quick retreat to the lab. Lupa should be used to it by now. Stephen always ate quickly and dashed off to work when he was immersed in a project, but preparing a meal was a ritual in which Lupa took great pride.

As the others beat a hasty retreat to the lab, Julia returned to the kitchen. She knew the planning and care that was involved. "Dinner was great," she said. "I wish I could cook like you." She smiled and gave him a hasty squeeze.

Stephen looked back toward the common room and noticed Lupa watching through the screen. He gave his old friend a thumbs up, and Lupa grinned, whistling as he turned to tidy up for the day. He sensed it was going to be a long night in the lab.

Stephen was already pulling the tissue and blood samples from the refrigerator and helping the students set up their experiments when Julia entered the lab. She hopped onto a stool and watched his methodical movements as he set up the night's tasks.

"I'll make the blood slides," Julia decided.

"Perfect," Stephen concurred. "I will start with the tissue samples."

The students worked in pairs and kept up a light-hearted banter. The four had bonded easily, so conversation was relaxed. They finished their samples quickly, so Stephen excused them. They cleaned up all the equipment, left their notes easily accessible, and then went to find Lupa and, of course, more food.

Alexis held back as usual. "Would you like some help?" she asked Julia.

"No, you go ahead. I want to finish these samples, myself. I've got a good system going, and I don't want to break my rhythm." Julia barely looked up.

"Okay," Alexis said. "Give a shout if you change your mind," she called from the doorway.

"I will."

Stephen looked up and smiled at Alexis before she left. "Thanks for offering, Alexis."

She smiled back. "My pleasure." She slipped silently through the door.

Stephen went right back to work.

Julia was concentrating so hard on the slides, she never noticed the exchange.

Results of the blood samples looked fairly normal. There were some abnormalities with one of the victims obviously fighting off some sort of infection because his samples showed an elevated level of white blood cells.

Julia looked up from the microscope quizzically. "Could the cause of death be some sort of virus?"

"Why do you ask?" Stephen responded, not looking up from his own work.

She recounted finding the white cells but only in the samples from the single victim.

"So far, I haven't seen anything to indicate a virus," Stephen stated as he made another slide.

Julia stood and walked to the window. She had worked a great deal with viruses in recent years and knew what mean little creatures they could be. They weren't actually living creatures at all, yet they reproduced themselves inside other living cells. It was hard to understand exactly how a virus existed.

Julia moved back to the worktable and picked up her notebook. Mindlessly, she returned to the window as if it would help release her thoughts. Julia mulled the nature of viruses. She jotted down:

Viruses—nasty
Tiny—cause countless problems for all living matter
Virus particles develop
Host cell swells until it bursts
Releases new virus particles
White cells go in and eat the virus particles
When immune system is low, host doesn't make enough white cells
Virus can kill host

Julia nodded and pursed her lips. *Could be*, she thought to herself.

Stephen glanced up. "Maybe he was just coming down with the flu, Julia. It could be just that simple."

She took her place back down on her stool ignoring the slides, "And who taught me to look for all possibilities yet not rule out the obvious?"

Now it was Stephen's turn to stand. He stretched and leaned against the counter. "Okay, what are you thinking?"

"I was thinking about a project I worked on recently. Every year there are natural epidemics around the world which wipe out whole populations of caterpillars and other insects. We've isolated the particular viruses, or should I say baculoviruses, and have even been able to engineer them."

Stephen was interested. "How does it work?"

"Just like any other virus. It goes in, takes over cells, and grows until the cells explode. We use caterpillars, and after we infect them, they become lethargic and begin to slow down. They stop eating because their digestive tracks are disintegrating. After about a week, the caterpillars just explode in a gooey mess. The baculovirus particles infect the leaves or twigs they touch, and another caterpillar comes along, eats some of them, and the process starts all over."

Stephen recalled the cracks he had seen in the walls of the blood vessels. "Hmm," he hummed softly.

Julia continued. "One of the interesting things about the baculovirus is it targets only certain insects. It might kill cabbage loopers, or cotton bollworms, or even a diamondback moth. But, on the other hand, the same baculovirus won't harm a fly."

Stephen's eyes narrowed as he listened intently. "It doesn't harm a fly? What's different about the fly?"

Julia shrugged and shook her head. "That...we don't know. The virus must sense something about them that we don't. And it happens every time."

"Every time?"

"Yes. And, we're hoping one day it can be used as an insect killer, you know, a *natural* pesticide."

"I can understand not wanting to use chemical pesticides, but still..." Stephen wasn't sure how he felt about the viruses being created.

"It doesn't kill as quickly as the chemicals," Julia continued, "but the good thing is that it doesn't last as long in the environment."

"How is that?"

"Over time the baculovirus fades because they are inactivated, we think, by the UV rays in the sunlight."

Stephen was deep in thought. "Interesting. A virus which targets its prey..."

Julia cocked her head to one side. "The way you phrase it makes it sound like the baculovirus has a degree of intelligence, Stephen."

"How else would you explain it? Would it be programmed inside the DNA?" Stephen frowned as he contemplated the information. "I don't think so..." Then he looked directly at her. "If you can engineer a baculovirus which attacks pesky insects, what makes you think it can't mutate to attack beneficial ones? How do you explain that it only kills the bad ones?"

Julia shook her head. "We don't have an answer, but we're working on it." She pulled the slides a little closer. "We'll figure it out." Julia pondered the questions.

Stephen reached for his pipe, packed fresh, dark tobacco inside, lit it, and slowly shook the match as his mind whirled through the possibilities. "Julia, we've seen how easy it is for some species to mutate." He clenched the pipe between his teeth and spoke around it as he cleaned the lens of his microscope. "I'm tired of so many people mucking around with nature." He pulled the pipe from his mouth. "One of these days, I can just picture all of those human creations backfiring, and what a clanger it will be, attacking things not meant to be killed." Stephen put the pipe down, tossed the towel aside, and swiveled to face her. "Julia, you know as well as I do it only takes a slight change in DNA structure to make a vicious killing machine. It is conceivable right now—terrorists somewhere, very angry or greedy people, are working to create a virus meant to kill off most of mankind."

With an ironic laugh and a sigh, he continued: "It wouldn't be hard.

Create an anti-virus you save for chosen people, and the rest of us could be gone in a matter of months. Maybe weeks. Scientists come up with incredible drugs and breakthroughs which are quite wonderful, but there is the same chance they will one day create something that will, over time, take command of itself and become something no one can stop."

While Stephen verbalized his thoughts, Julia privately considered the same thing. She quietly asked, "Do you think we might be seeing that here…now, Stephen?" As she looked at the slides stacked neatly next to her arm, a shiver up her spine reminded her how close she was to them.

"I don't think so. I didn't see any virus in the tissues. But even so…" His thoughts returned to the bizarre cracks in the blood vessels.

21

Lupa crouched in the forest shadows listening for Nigel and Drake. He knew they would return soon, and he was ready. Earlier he had cleansed their sleeping room. In each corner was a small pile of ashes, a combination of tobacco and the leaves of *aire sacha*, *camé*, and coca, shavings from the bark of *rediloksi*, *pritjari*, *and jarakopi*. He added some sap from the *chicle* tree, hoping the spirit of the tree would purge any lingering evil brought in by the tiny pieces of white gum Nigel always chewed. The room held the smell of spicy smoke and burnt resin.

Lupa prepared himself beforehand in the glowing light of the evening fire. Everyone had long-since gone to bed when he sat on a stone and ground the fruit of the *meh-nu* tree into a fine paste. He mixed it with warm ashes from the dying coals and painted a snakelike figure across his forehead with the deep blue dye. He then mashed *u-sha* berries and painted the red extract in zigzag patterns down each cheek. He put on his ceremonial red loin cloth, and when he had finished the preparations, there was no sign he had even been there.

He had never done what he was about to do, and he had no idea if it would work but he had been practicing his "*lo-co-mo-jo*" for many years. He hoped he would not have to kill the men though. That would make for worse energy in the jungle, but it would be easy enough. A prick from a curare-tipped dart, and they would die quickly. Or even a boiled brew made from the *al-lah-ku-pah-ne* vine. Similar to curare, just drops of the potent blend could be slipped into their beer, and death would be painless. They would simply become very calm and be gone.

But Lupa had never killed a man, and he didn't expect to start now. He knew he would kill if someone forced him, but he hoped it would not come to that.

He heard the two men well before they entered the compound, their careless, sloppy footsteps demonstrating their arrogance and ignorance for the forest dangers that lurked everywhere.

Nigel and Drake helped themselves to leftovers and drank *cachaça* for a long time. Lupa smiled to himself. That was good. He might be able to chant a bit if they passed out.

The two men finally made their way toward their room, and as Nigel pulled open the door, he swore. "What the hell?" He waved his hand back and forth like a fan as he tumbled backward.

Drake righted him as he was about to fall to the ground.

"Where is that liddle…" Nigel's speech was slurred and his legs were like jelly, as he wavered from one foot to the other, undulating from side to side. He looked all around before he bellowed, "Where 're ya', ya' liddle…" His words were muffled as Drake pulled him inside.

Lupa heard the bar go down across the door. But that was okay. He knew how to get in and out of the room

Lupa waited another hour before stepping from the darkness into the moonlit clearing. He crossed to the sleeping house and opened the door to the room adjacent to the two men. He slipped open the panel in the closet and pulled open the other closet. Soon he was standing between the sleeping men, who reeked of rum and sweat.

Lupa opened the jar which held dried, crushed scorpions and tarantulas and poured the powder onto each man's chest. He lit his ceremonial cigar and blew the smoke across the powder. Neither man moved, so deep were they in their inebriated fog. Lupa began to quietly chant as he moved around the room. He blew more smoke across the men until Drake began to cough.

Drake bolted upright in his hammock and grabbed for his backpack. He groped and continued to cough for a moment before his fingers felt the cool steel of his flashlight. With trembling fingers, he pushed the button and for an instant couldn't remember where he was. He stumbled from the hammock and flung the latch holding the door shut. Smoke poured from the room and rolled out into the darkness. He staggered outside for fresh air and then spun around turning the light back into the room, doubling over from coughing. When he caught his breath, he swept the beam from corner to corner of the room expecting to see someone besides Nigel, who continued to snore lightly, occasionally coughing a little as the smoke cleared. Drake saw nothing else. Not even the cause of the smoke.

He turned the light back out to the darkness and backed slowly into the room. He fanned the door several times trying to let out more smoke before dropping the lock into place again and crawling back into his hammock, flashlight still searching the room.

Drake fell asleep watching the swirling mist, heart finally calming, as the air continued to clear. The flashlight winked out as daylight peeked through the window.

22

In the early morning light, Will's new brown king cab shined nearly magenta in color. Will drove alone in the truck even though the sticker touted it comfortably seated six. The five workers recruited for logging the mahogany bounced in the back bed along with the logging gear. *The hell with seating capacity*, Will thought.

Carlos followed, with the semi-flatbed trailer hauling a D7R Caterpillar dozer. If he thought it odd Will had not let the men ride inside the truck, he never voiced it.

Since neither he nor Carlos had had time to teach one of the men in back to drive, they had left the older truck at the camp. Will didn't like not having the extra truck with them, but he hated wasting time and money more.

Will could have easily let the workers ride inside the truck with him, but he didn't want to listen to any of their chatter. Even though he had spent almost a decade in Brazil, he never bothered to learn the Portuguese language, so, for the most part, he understood very little of what they were saying. For him, their endless babbling was just useless noise. Besides, he had a lot on his mind.

Will turned off the main road and thought about his own boss. *Damn Livingston*. Last night Livingston had called him again, warning him not to go out with the crew. *Damn him*. How was Will supposed to explain it to Carlos when he didn't go? If he went anyway and something happened, well, he guessed it wouldn't matter in the end. It finally came down to the fact that Will valued his life more than his reputation. He decided to watch from a safe distance to see how things went…good or bad.

He felt a bit like a coward for having formulated a plan that kept him away from the men while they started cutting, but he was resigned to keep a good distance from the potential danger—whatever it was. He stopped the truck next to a clearing the road crew left to park the semi-flatbed trailer. The workers piled out of the back, but Will motioned them back in.

Carlos drove into the clearing, jumped out, and jogged up to check where Will wanted him to set up the staging area.

"You take three men on down and get started." Will motioned to a point about 300 yards ahead. "I already marked the two trees to use for the pulley system. This is a good spot to leave the dozer and semi out of the way while we work. It'll also allow the log trucks to get in and out easier. Leave two men up here with me so they can help guide the dozer off the trailer. I want to run a double-check of the fluids. Paulo thought we might have a leak."

Carlos nodded and motioned for two men to get out. He asked Will if it would be okay for one man to go below to the mahogany tree and begin cutting the buttresses away as soon as everything was positioned at the staging area. Since they had an extra man, it would save time. This mahogany wasn't nearly as large as the one they had lost with the dead men, but it still had five fins which needed to be taken off and would require considerably more time to remove than actually cutting down the tree. Will agreed.

Carlos gave the two men he was leaving behind some instructions and climbed into the pickup truck.

Will watched them move down the slope before stepping onto the flatbed. When they got to the staging area near the mahogany, Carlos and the other three men climbed out hauling the large saws and ropes with them.

The two workers staying behind sat near the dozer while Will made a big show of checking over the big machine's engine. The men positioned themselves in a spot where they couldn't see the men working the staging area down the hill.

The mahogany was much closer to the staging area than usual, and without the small rise between the two, they might not have even needed the staging area at all.

Will took his time. He looked through the undercarriage keeping an eye on the two workers sitting nearby while directing his main attention to the others down the hill. He saw Carlos rigging the ropes, listened while the three workers started the saws to get them warmed up. They didn't want any problems with equipment not working properly once they moved up into the trees. Half an hour later, Carlos called on his radio and told Will they were ready to start cutting.

The two men by the dozer were engaged in a lively discussion, one man speaking animatedly as the other burst into gales of laughter, slapping him on the back. They were lost to any activity down the hill.

Will reached into the cab and retrieved a small pair of binoculars he had tucked away last night. He shifted out of sight of the two men and aimed the binoculars down the hill. Carlos had climbed about forty feet off the ground and was cutting a branch out of a *capirona* tree. Another worker was up about thirty feet in a ficus tree. Each tree had a nice fork which made it convenient for rigging a pulley system.

Down the hillside from where Carlos and the crew worked, Will eyed the waiting mahogany tree. The limbs were long and straight. Will grinned, realizing they would get a lot of good wood from it.

As Carlos continued to cut, Will held his breath. The work was moving along smoothly and the workers looked fine as one man was almost finished cutting his first limb. They had to cut out the upper, smaller limbs before topping the lower part of the trees. Will let out a breath of relief and relaxed a little. Everything looked normal. The men in the trees were doing well, and the men working below were operating as usual. Everything was routine.

Will watched a couple more minutes and noticed the fourth man heading for the mahogany with his saw. He heard the chainsaw burst into life and listened as the man gunned the motor a few times before laying into the mahogany. Will could see the end of the saw moving smoothly through the buttress but he would have known the man was cutting the mahogany even if he wasn't looking. Mahogany wood was much denser, the sound was different from the sound of the saws in the *capirona* and ficus trees.

The chainsaw imbedded in the mahogany sent up a cloud of sawdust, which plumed into the air and floated up toward the staging area. The man cutting the buttress bore down hard, shifting his feet farther apart for greater traction.

Will tossed the binoculars into the cab above and clapped his hands together. "It's goin' to be a fine day," he said aloud. Going back to the dozer engine, he checked it over with a vengeance. He was almost finished and anxious to join the others to hurry things along. He climbed into the cab of the dozer, checked all the controls, and started the engine. He climbed back out and continued checking the equipment as he let the engine warm enough to check the hydraulic fluid, as the roar of the dozer engine drowned out the chainsaws. Will turned and absent-mindedly glanced down at the rigging crew.

The first tree in the staging area had a larger opening on top, and Will was struck by the sight of one worker hanging from his rope. It looked like he was jumping, as though he were a puppet dancing on a stage. Will froze. The man had been high in the tree just a moment ago, hadn't he? Or was this another man climbing up the tree?

Will blinked a couple of times not grasping what he was seeing. He strained to glimpse the man at the mahogany. *Where is he*? Will couldn't see him anymore nor could he find the sawdust cloud coming from behind the buttress. He squeezed his eyes closed, blinking a few more times when he opened them. He still couldn't see the man anywhere.

Carlos was in the second tree, focused on his cutting, when he noticed his safety glasses fog over. He was having trouble seeing. He stopped the rotation of the saw's chain and let it hang on its rope. Then he took a moment to pull off his glasses and wipe them.

As he did, Carlos felt something like rain dropping on and around him, but the feeling was sharper, and he wasn't wet. Then a large black ant was on his arm. It hunched over, and before he could react, its stinger was imbedded in his skin. Carlos felt like he had been shot. He slapped it away and rubbed the red spot vigorously. His arm was on fire from the sting, but he got back to work, pushing his glasses back on, picking up the saw, and putting it back in place.

As the limb Carlos cut fell away, his glasses fogged over again. Then he felt a sting on his neck. He took a swipe at it. Another ant. He was reaching to take off his glasses for the second time when he felt the most intense pain in his chest he had ever experienced.

Carlos looked over and noticed no one was in the other tree. Then he saw the worker hanging in his harness, thrashing about, swiping at his arms and head. Then the man began to bleed. Carlos realized this wasn't ordinary bleeding. Blood fell from his nose, from his mouth, even from his eyes. The color of the blood was changing from a deep red to a light pink. As Carlos watched in horror, a scream formed in his own throat, but it never came out. The man pouring blood was the last thing Carlos saw before he fell.

Will saw Carlos as he let his saw hang and pulled off his glasses. *What is going on*? He raced back and climbed into the cab searching for the binoculars. *Where are the damn things*? He finally located them where they had fallen between the far seat and the wall of the cab. The strap was caught on a screw head, and it took another few long seconds as he frantically tugged and pulled until the handle flew over his head as he wrestled it free. With a ragged breath, Will positioned the binoculars over his eyes and focused each lens. The scene through his binoculars made his heart skip a beat…then another beat…and another beat. Then it began to flutter as if he was hitting the bottom of a long plunge on a roller coaster.

The worker in the tree next to Carlos was hanging from the rope in his harness. His whole body was convulsing. Creamy blood flowed from him like water through a garden hose. As Will watched, Carlos dropped his saw again, and this time he fell, his body quaking as he too began to vomit blood. Then blood began streaming from every orifice of his body.

The man standing on the ground below was not watching the men overhead until blood spattered down causing him to look at the warm droplets on his arms. As he looked up, Will could see the terror on his face. The man panicked and began to scream. Will could not hear him over the roar of the dozer, but he could see his mouth moving in utter despair. Still screaming, the man began to run, swiping at his arms as he ran. Will watched with fixed eyes as the man fell to the ground, his body jerking as he lay prone.

Will looked back at the mahogany and noticed smoke from the saw rising from behind the buttress, where a deep gouge had been cut. He could picture the man twitching on the ground, blood pouring from his body.

Will tossed the binoculars. He left the dozer engine running and yanked the last two workers to their feet as he passed them. He motioned them inside the semi's cab with him. Wildly gesturing, he convinced them to roll up their window. An intense heat settled around them in the closed cab as though they had stepped into an oven. The two men looked at each other puzzled as Will raced the semi engine and negotiated the turn around. Then they were speeding back along the road they had driven in on earlier, pulling the trailer still loaded with the rocking dozer.

Will saw the workers were confused, and he knew they wanted to know why they were leaving the job site. He couldn't answer them. They struggled to see the men they were leaving behind, but they were already out of sight.

Hell, I can barely breathe, Will thought. He kept checking his rearview mirror, expecting…what was he expecting? Will drove as if he were possessed by a demon or being chased by one, which made the two workers more nervous. They spoke in hushed tones, their prattling irritating Will.

"Shut up!" he growled over the noise of the truck.

The men continued to speak anxiously to each other.

"I said, 'shut up!'" Will screamed.

Not understanding the words, the men certainly recognized Will's tone.

They went quiet.

What just happened? Will had witnessed the most horrific sight he could have ever…no never, have imagined, yet there appeared to be no cause. The new men were dead. Carlos was dead.

Will continued racing for a few minutes, and then, skidding the truck onto the main road, he slammed the brakes causing the two men to slide part way to the floor. Will threw the gears into park, jumped from the truck, and staggered to the back. He leaned over and vomited, terrified to see if he too was vomiting blood. He looked back down the road and began to tremble. Leaning back against the hot steel of the trailer, he swiped his mouth with the back of his hand. *Get a grip, man.*

Will breathed hard as he climbed up into the dozer to shut off the engine. He sat there in a stupor drawing in deep breaths. Even in the sweltering heat, he continued to shiver uncontrollably.

Will rolled his head and saw the two men standing outside the truck. They were looking back in the direction of Carlos and the other workers, and their expressions told Will they did not want this job anymore.

13

Julia spent a long restless night tossing and turning. Her dreams were filled with caterpillars and ants, and one time she found herself stuck in a huge pile of green goo that had her thrashing until she awoke. She finally threw back the sheet and netting and dressed to escape the wild imaginings in her dreams.

Lupa was busy preparing breakfast when Julia wandered into the common room. It was barely dawn, and no one else had arrived. She sat at the counter watching him slice a ripe yellow pineapple onto a small red plate. On the counter next to the sink were six ripe *cupauçu*.

"Mmmmm. Please tell me you are making sorbet."

Lupa grinned, nodding quickly. "Yes, Miss Julia. I make it for this night. I know it you favorite."

"Thank you, Lupa. The others will like it too."

"I pick fruit just this morning. Okay?"

"I can't wait."

Lupa sat the red plate in front of her, and Julia picked up some pineapple with her fingers, popping it enthusiastically into her mouth. The flavor was what Julia described as loud; even though Stephen insisted one couldn't use a word like 'loud' to explain taste. She had missed the intensity of the taste of cold, fresh pineapple and smiled at Lupa as she chewed.

"Is good?" his grin sought her approval.

"Gooood," Julia crooned, wiping a drop that had squeezed from the corner of her mouth. "And loud." She nodded.

They both laughed.

"We have company today, Miss Julia."

"Company? We don't have room for much more company," she chuckled.

"Eduardo come this day to bring samples for you and Stephen to look with him. He call last night while you and Stephen work in lab." He reached for a large knife and sliced through one of the *cupauçu*. The green and brown skin reminded Julia of a large fig not yet ripened; it smelled great. Her mouth was watering.

Cupauçu sorbet is a heavenly taste, Julia thought. *It's a bit like a piña colada, a cool and fruity concoction. And the seeds? Delicious.* Lupa made a thin wafer cookie, tasting much like a pretzel, which they used to scoop out the white buttery filling, a wonderful, white chocolate flavor Julia found irresistible.

"I'm ready to get to work," Stephen said as he came into the room and noticed the pineapple. "What about you?"

Julia saw him look at the fruit.

Lupa frowned. "But you no eat, Stephen."

Julia loaded a plate with fruit and added some rolls and a few slices of cheese.

"Your cooking is the best, my friend," Stephen said to Lupa. "I ate so much last night, I am still full." He rubbed his stomach and took the plate from Julia. "But I'm never too full for some of your rolls." He smiled as he picked one up and took a bite. Plate in hand, he and Julia headed for the lab.

Lupa finished putting out the food for the others and went out back to work in the garden.

In a little while, the students streamed into the common room and helped themselves to the breakfast Lupa laid out on the counter. Just as they were finishing, Nigel came through the door with Drake in tow. The room grew quiet.

Nigel purred softly, "Did anyone miss us?" as he poured a cup of coffee.

Jennifer shivered. She pictured a crocodile stealthily moving in to snatch its prey. If he'd had a tail, it would probably have just flicked.

"Sure," Charlie declared, "we *all* missed you." He scowled. "What have you been doing?"

Nigel turned to the foursome at the table. "Oh, a little of this and a little of that." He blew over the hot mug and set it on the table to cool. "Today we are going out to gather some plant samples. Would anyone like to join us?"

Kosey rose and put his plate into the sink. "I am in the middle of my own samples right now…or I would love to join you."

"Me, too." Alexis quickly added her plate on top of Kosey's. "Let us get to the lab. We are burning daylight."

"Burning daylight. That is a good one, Alexis. I have not heard that one before. Can I use it?" They were walking out the door and heading for the path to the lab. "That reminds me of one of my grandmother's sayings…" Kosey's voice faded as they got further away.

When they were out of earshot, Nigel reached for a fork and was about to pick up a plate when Charlie exploded, "Where the hell have you been?"

Drake looked at Nigel to see how he would react to Charlie's disrespectful attitude.

The silverware Nigel was holding clattered to the floor as he grabbed the front of Charlie's shirt and hauled him from his chair, which fell over backwards.

Charlie winced as fresh pain shot through his now reopened wound.

Nigel's voice seethed between clenched teeth, "Don't you ever speak to me like that again. Do you understand?"

Charlie pushed Nigel away. "They're asking questions." He pulled down on his shirt hard and smoothed the front. A small patch of blood rose to the surface of the fabric. "Damn, that hurt." He rubbed his shoulder. "You didn't have to grab me like that."

In a calmer tone, Nigel spoke soothingly, "I say again…do not speak to me that way. Ever. Do you understand?"

"Yes, I understand." Charlie's bravado was gone.

"And how did you answer their questions?" Nigel retrieved the fork he dropped as his temper flared. *Who does the little prick think he is anyway*? He'd take great pleasure in Charlie's death. "Answer my question," Nigel scowled at Jennifer, who shrank to the other end of the table.

She relayed the conversation before adding. "It just doesn't look good that you leave for a day and a half and don't come back. Do you even have any notes on CO2 levels with you? That is, after all, what you told them you were doing. I know they will ask when they see you."

"That's why we are going out again right away. We have a few things to take care of. A new illegal logging crew to check on, and then we will gather plant samples. Drake will have CO2 notes ready when we return. You could come along, but," he gestured toward Charlie, "it is obvious he isn't up to it."

Jennifer cringed. "Umm. Lupa is taking us out to gather herbs for dinner, and I was hoping to learn more about the edible plants from him. How about I go out with you tomorrow?"

He dismissed her with no concern. "Do what you want," he said indifferently, so as not to raise any suspicion as to their plans. *She would only be in the way*, he thought.

Drake looked worried. "We need to get out of here before Stephen gets wind we're here." He motioned toward the lab.

Nigel had already grabbed a bag behind the counter and was filling it with fruit and bread when he saw Lupa watching him through the screen. He smiled and waved his fingers at him.

Drake was busy cutting up fruit and bagging a variety of nuts for his trail mix. He dashed from behind the counter when he saw Lupa coming.

Lupa scowled and mumbled in his language. He came around the building and moved into his kitchen, arms laden with roots for the noon meal. He unceremoniously dumped the vegetables into the sink and moved to the pantry.

Nigel ignored him as he continued gathering food and tying up the bundles.

Lupa set out a kettle, slamming it down on the stove with a clank, and filling it with water before pouring in a mixture of dried herbs and leaves. He was brewing his evil spirit concoction. When he lit some dried ginseng root, another evil spirit deterrent, the room soon filled with pungent smoke.

"What the…" Nigel snarled as he fanned the strong cloud from around him. "What are you doing, old man?" He looked hard at Lupa, who looked just as fiercely in his direction. Nigel grabbed up the bundles, his voice sardonic. "Come on, Drake. Let's get out of this crazy man's kitchen." He took a long drink of the coffee he had all but forgotten and with that, they were gone.

Stephen strode deliberately down the path toward the common room just as Nigel and Drake disappeared into the forest. He was disappointed when he found they weren't there. He raced back out the door and several steps toward the forest before deciding it wasn't worth a battle alone, so he turned back.

Jennifer was shaken. "I'm glad you came back when you did, Lupa," she said. "I don't want to be with them any longer. Do you think Stephen and Julia will let us stay here with you instead of going with Nigel and Drake?"

"You stay." He patted his chest. "Lupa say." He noticed the blood on Charlie's shirt.

Stephen peeked back into the door asking, "Did they say when they were coming back?"

"No," Lupa answered as he motioned toward Charlie. "Wound bleed more."

"Did Nigel hit you?" Stephen asked.

"No. I just moved too quickly." Charlie waved him off. "I'm okay."

Stephen regarded him sternly. "Nigel has an air about him that's rather disconcerting. You'll tell me if he is dodgy won't you?"

Charlie nodded. "Sure…"

Stephen held open the door. "Come with me. We'll patch you up again. You must be more careful from now on."

Before leaving Charlie asked Lupa, "Did you really mean you would take us out to gather herbs, and you'd tell us about some of the plants you use as medicines?"

"Yes," Lupa said.

"Come," Stephen motioned him out.

The door slapped shut. Lupa called through the screen, "Stephen fix shoulder. Then we go."

Charlie lifted his hand in confirmation.

Jennifer tried to help Lupa get ready, but he would have none of it. She decided to see if Kosey and Alexis were at a stopping point allowing them to go on an herbal expedition.

Twenty minutes later, Lupa and the four students trekked off into the forest with baskets and nippers in hand. They would stay for hours, returning only when it was time for Lupa to fix lunch.

The morning was passing quickly. At one point Stephen looked up from his microscope and asked, "Is Alexis married?"

Julia sucked in a smile and quietly said, "Divorced."

That was all of the conversation about Alexis. They continued on as if no one had spoken. Julia and Stephen were so absorbed in their work they looked up only when their concentration was interrupted by a noisy truck engine.

The engine coughed once as it shut off.

"He's here," Stephen remarked as he continued working.

Eduardo's broad body filled the door opening as he stepped in carrying a large box of plant samples. Julia moved over to check them. As she glanced up at Eduardo's face, he gave a slow smile. Julia smiled back.

His eyes clung to her face then he turned to speak to Stephen. "Might not be a bad idea for you to go back out there with me, jungle doctor. You know more about which toxic plants to look for than I do," Eduardo commented as he positioned himself on the closest stool.

The exchange between the two had not been missed. Stephen turned away as he spoke, "Me? You are the one who was raised here. All someone needs to do is walk around your garden to see you are the expert, my friend. But, you make a point. Actually, I would like to get out there to check the plants myself, look around and get a feel for the site. I'd like to see if anything looks out of place."

"Let's go later today, if we have time," Eduardo suggested.

"We'll make time," Julia stated. She couldn't wait to get into the canopy.

Stephen agreed. "We must finish up first." Samples were spread all over the work tables. "It shouldn't take long, especially with Eduardo here to help."

"I'm ready." Eduardo squeezed his hands together with enthusiasm, happy to be in the company of this interesting woman.

They set to work in the lab. Stephen showed Eduardo how to calibrate and use several pieces of equipment and put him to work. Eduardo labored as diligently as Julia and Stephen. They had never worked together in his lab, and Stephen was surprised how easily Eduardo took to the testing routine. The three of them spent the next couple of hours meticulously working through and cataloging the samples.

At one point Stephen told Eduardo about the visit by Nigel and Drake.

Eduardo shook his head. “Charlie didn’t tell you much. What about Jennifer?”

“Tight lipped as Charlie. I like the kids, but I know they’re hiding something.”

Julia looked up from the microscope. “I believe they’re afraid.”

Stephen nodded. “That might account for their silence. I can certainly imagine Nigel threatening them.”

“With a little time, they might get comfortable enough to open up,” Julia noted.

Eduardo grumbled, “Or scared enough.”

They continued working on tests for all types of poisons, looking for anything resembling venom. They shot X-rays for metals, even checked the pH of the soil, which was more alkaline than anticipated but still fell within a high-normal range. Nothing was out of the ordinary, including the air samples.

At last Julia sat with the final slide before her. She adjusted the microscope, making notes off to the side.

Stephen was cleaning a large stack of slides.

Eduardo was finished and was in his characteristic pose…leaning back in his chair, feet crossed at the ankles, this time propped up on the adjacent table, hands clasped behind his head. His eyelids were closed.

“Hungry?” Lupa beckoned from the doorway.

“What time is it?” Stephen asked. His stomach told him it needed feeding.

“Time for late lunch,” Lupa called from the doorway.

Julia pulled the slide from her microscope and handed it to Stephen to clean. “Thank you, Lupa. That might be just the trick. The aroma drifted in ahead of you and threw my stomach in a tear.”

Stephen asked, “Where is everyone?”

Lupa stepped close to Stephen. “Lupa keep everyone busy collecting herbs.” Lupa dropped his voice to a whisper, “They clean and help cook.”

“You let them cook?” Stephen didn’t even try to hide his astonishment.

“Lupa like them. Much…” he searched for the right word, “…much… like?” Lupa looked questioningly at Stephen.

“Interest?” Stephen asked. “Are you saying they are interested?”

“Sim. Yes. Interested in forest and shaman ways.”

“They really do show greater interest than some of the students that visit.” Stephen hung the drying towel over a rod. “Let’s get to lunch everyone. Yes, a great meal prepared by my good friend and his companions is just what we need.”

Lupa exclaimed, “Come! Soon no hot.”

Julia replied, “Real soon, Lupa,” as she put the microscope away.

Lupa hurried back to the common room.

Stephen stared at the empty sample bottles and slides and shook his head, "For the life of me, I'm drawing a total blank on this."

"You aren't alone, jungle doctor." Eduardo had not moved nor even opened his eyes.

"I thought you were asleep." Stephen slapped Eduardo's feet off the table as he walked over to wash his hands at the sink.

Eduardo scrambled to catch himself.

Trying to stifle a laugh, Julia giggled. She couldn't help herself. It was automatic and couldn't be controlled. Her laughter was light, playful, and infectious.

Caught off guard, Eduardo steadied his weight. He watched as Julia threw back her head trying to catch her breath. He wanted to reach out and stroke her long, slender neck. He watched her laugh and a smile pulled at his own lips. He too began laughing, big rolls of laughter. Eduardo laughed as he hadn't in a long, long time. And then he couldn't stop.

It was a laughter of joy. A laughter of relief. A laughter of release. As easily as the laughter began, it subsided. They watched each other as both wiped the corners of their eyes where moisture collected. A self-conscious silence fell over the lab.

Stephen looked again between the two. It hadn't been *that* funny. He had seen Julia laugh heartily, her buoyant personality always looking for humor. But he had never seen Eduardo like this. He couldn't help but wonder if his boisterous behavior had something to do with Julia.

Stephen silently shook his head. It was about Serena and Julia. As he thought about it, Eduardo had not shown more than a partial smile in all these months. He laid his arm over the younger man's shoulder and pulled him outside. "Come on. Lupa is waiting. And soon we shoot our ropes into the canopy. It will be a fine afternoon for climbing."

24

Arthur Livingston sat at his desk with a smug grin on his face. He had just greased the palm of another agent to get his next shipment of mahogany past inspection in Talago, Brazil, and he wanted to celebrate. To top it off, it cost less than he expected. The new guy wasn't as knowledgeable as the last.

Give him time, Arthur thought, leaning back against his tall chair, satisfied with his good day's work. He learned early on from his father that if you pay enough money, you get what you want. It always came down to the money.

Arthur was born with a silver spoon in his mouth, and he was savvy enough to be thankful. The fortune his grandfather made had been multiplied by his shrewd father. Arthur was doing his best to enhance it even more. But who would take it from here? Arthur wasn't sure. His daughters cared less about the business. Oh, they wanted the money, all right. Like father, like daughters. *Why, oh, why didn't I have a son*?

Lately, Arthur had been thinking a great deal about the future of his company, with no heir to introduce to the suppliers and customers as his replacement, as his father had done with him. There was no one he was grooming to perform all the day-to-day legal, and not so legal, dealings to get the job done, to get the lumber needed to increase the family fortune.

The last confrontation with the environmentalists cost him dearly. He couldn't stand any more publicity right now. The picketers had left him alone for over two days now, and he guessed the chaos they created this time would keep them happy for a while. Luckily, the protest made only the local newspapers and television news. Had the news been picked up nationally or worse, internationally, it could have been a disastrous situation.

He needed to talk to Will and find out what was happening in the Amazon. He had to get the next couple of trees out clean. Arthur's customers were getting nervous, and they were all into this "green" thing. The news was filled with green this and green that. Who the hell cared about green? Ironically, all of his customers did, and they wanted assurances his wood was legally obtained.

Hell, the only legal Brazilian mahogany was farmed wood, and it wasn't nearly as valuable. Arthur was shocked and pleasantly surprised at the average customer's knowledge, or rather lack of knowledge, about Brazilian laws and environmental practices. They had no idea most lumber coming from mahogany trees was illegal. Either that or they were just pretending ignorance to appease their consciences. The only thing he knew for sure was Livingston Lumber was getting negative press, and Arthur was determined to put an end to any more bad coverage because it had a way of affecting profit, and not in a good way. People's opinions were unimportant. The bottom line was everything.

Arthur was concerned he wasn't able to contact Will. He knew Will scheduled a crew to go out earlier to prep for the next cut, and he should have been able to reach him.

Arthur sat forward and rang for Jane.

"Yes."

"Have you tried to get Will lately?"

"I keep trying every hour." Her voice carried what Arthur interpreted as a hint of anxiety. "Do you think something is wrong?"

"Naaah." He tried to keep his own concern to himself. "He's probably just having phone problems. You know how unreliable communication can be down there."

"I suppose so…" She wasn't convinced.

"Since I know you're on top of this, I'll stop wor…asking." He almost spoke *worrying* instead of *asking*. He didn't want her to know he was uneasy.

He need not have bothered. Jane had been around long enough to know, and she was worried too.

25

“Hang on to your knickers,” Stephen called when Julia climbed into the jeep.

“Don’t worry,” Jennifer stood outside Stephen’s side of the truck, “we'll have the last of the ants identified by the time you get back,” she promised.

“I know you’ll do your best.” Stephen moved the gear shift into first, pressed the accelerator, let off the clutch, and he, Julia, and her students raced down the narrow rutted lane.

“Be careful!” Charlie shouted behind them.

“We will!” they chorused.

Alexis and Kosey sat in the back holding onto the roll bar dodging undergrowth as the jeep wound in wide arcs around trees so large they could almost be hollowed out for houses. When Stephen built his compound, he removed select trees for the narrow road very carefully so as not to disturb the forest any more than necessary.

Julia looked around at the denseness of tree trunks as they bounced along. The trees were so thick here they rode mostly in shadows. Every return visit she would remember she had forgotten the sheer immensity of the trees and the incredible multiplicity of vegetation. There were trees rivaling skyscrapers with leaves the size of umbrellas. More vines than she could decipher knitted the whole forest together, snaking up trees, crossing and crisscrossing in the canopy above.

They rode along for a while admiring the forest. The jeep was climbing up the trail at a precarious angle when it was illuminated in full sunlight. Julia shielded her eyes. She was deep in thought and didn’t realize where they were. If she had, she would have braced for the brightness. Stephen pulled to a stop at the crest of the ridge and turned off the engine. He leaned his forearms on the steering wheel and gazed out over the landscape.

The expansive view was spectacular. Two mountains flanked the valley on either side. Clouds capped the upper peaks and melted into the forest. Far below, the powerful Amazon River undulated through a lush needlepoint of greens. To the left was a high waterfall, crashing more than a hundred feet into a broad, azure pool below. Even from this great distance, its roar could be heard over the background of forest sounds. A large flock of *uruba* glided down the far ridge heading for the village and the day's cast-off from early fishermen.

"Lovely, isn't it?" Stephen asked. The awe he saw on Alexis's face in the rearview mirror made him smile.

"Magnificent," breathed Alexis before she caught him watching her in the narrow frame. She smiled before averting her eyes.

"Beauty beyond words," nodded Kosey.

"When you're away, you lose the beauty of it all," Julia spoke quietly, feeling somehow the mere presence of a human voice was an intrusion.

"Indeed," was Stephen's only comment as he restarted the engine.

Julia spent the rest of the ride pointing out fauna and flora to Alexis and Kosey. A half hour later, they were unloading their gear. Julia looked up at the trees on the hillside, their uppermost branches mangled from the loggers menacing saws. All that was left on each was about a twenty foot trunk with some five feet of branches on top forming a shape like a Y.

Inquisitive Alexis asked, "Why did they choose those trees?"

Stephen explained as he uncoiled rope. "The staging area must be flat in order for the trucks to be loaded with the logs from the mahogany. The trees chosen had been nearly sixty feet tall, certainly not the giants of the forest. The loggers need younger, smaller trees so their trunks were stronger and their branches lower. Lower branches mean greater efficiency of time when attaching the pulley system and less likelihood the heavy logs being pulled up the hill would topple the staging trees." He motioned with his hands parallel to the ground. "They give a lower center of gravity. Too tall, and they would go right over with the weight of the logs."

Kosey began straightening the harnesses making ready to climb. Alexis went over to give him a hand.

Two ropes left as markers by Eduardo's men still hung in the trees where the men had been found hanging, so any investigator would know precisely where the bodies had been.

Stephen chose the closest tree to the hanging rope. It was a young rosewood, completely encased by a strangler fig. He pulled out his crossbow with its 300 foot length of thin fish-type line and attached a weighted arrow. Aiming just above a branch some forty feet high, he shot, sending the whirling shaft sailing over before it looped back down toward them. Julia ducked behind the trunk of a tree as Stephen reached for the swinging line.

"That was easy." He turned to Julia. "How often does that happen on the first shot?" He attached some parachute cord to the thin line, pulling it over the limb, and then he tied the climbing rope to the cord and dragged it into place.

"Well, I'm ready to climb," he nonchalantly handed the crossbow to Julia before starting to ready the other lines.

"Let's see you do it again." She handed back the bow. "Actually," she pointed toward the others and reminded, "You've got several more to get into the canopy. Do you think you can do it?"

Stephen chuckled. "I take it as a challenge. You…" he motioned to the tree, "will climb in the *cobaiba*."

"Sounds good to me," Julia said.

"Alexis, you will climb with Julia," Stephen called to her.

"Right," Alexis called back, surprised that she was a little disappointed she wasn't climbing with Stephen. Was she misreading his signals?

"Just watch this," Stephen said to Julia.

He checked the line, held his breath, aimed, and pulled the trigger. This shot was not as clean as the first one. The line hung up part way down the other side of the tree in a cluster of tight branches. Stephen and Julia worked for long minutes untangling and reloading the bow.

The next shot never made it over the target branch. Several more attempts were also unsuccessful. Stephen was frustrated. He tried not to show his impatience, but Julia noticed and stayed quiet and out of his way. It took another half hour before Stephen secured the last rope in place.

"Wonder where Eduardo is," Julia mused, turning her head slightly to listen for his engine.

Stephen looked at his watch before mopping his face with his handkerchief. "I would have thought he would be here by now." He eyed the roadway. "He likes to use his own harness, so he went home to grab his climbing gear."

Stephen looked from his tree to Julia's. "I think Eduardo should work in the *copaiba* with you and Alexis, Julia. There is more surface area to comb through."

"Okaay…" Julia wondered if that was the real reason Stephen wanted Eduardo in her tree.

Kosey asked, "What about me?"

"You will climb with me," Stephen answered matter-of-factly as he gathered his climbing equipment.

Julia matched her pace to Stephen's and the others duplicated her actions. They had practiced climbing almost every weekend for the last three months in the cliffs of north Georgia, so they were prepared. Of course, Julia had climbed many times with Stephen, so her actions were almost automatic. She reached for her canvas sack filled with plastic zipper bags and secured it to her belt, added a set of snips, a small screwdriver, a couple of collection jars with holes already punched in the lids, a pair of rubber gloves, and a pocket knife. Julia looked around to make sure everyone gathered all their supplies.

Stephen stepped into his harness and gave his rope a final test. The others followed suit.

Julia swept her hair to the top of her head, encircling it with a bright red scrunchie, and with a last big gulp from the water jug, began pulling herself up the rope. *Stand. Slide up the hitch. Pick up your foot. Tighten the foot loop. Stand. Slide up the hitch. Pick up your leg. Tighten the foot loop*. She felt a kinship with an inchworm.

As she climbed higher, more light penetrated the treetops. Julia looked around and thought about what a mysterious place the canopy was, especially the uppermost layer, not unlike the ocean depths before the invention of scuba gear and submarines. So many mysteries left to be unearthed. All throughout the forest there were exotic plants not yet seen by humans. Insects still undiscovered. Creatures waiting to be revealed and named. There could be something new uncovered every day for hundreds of years to come. Maybe thousands. Perhaps even longer, if mankind didn't destroy it all.

As they reached some twenty feet above the ground, Eduardo drove up, pulled out his gear without a word, and started his climb routine. He checked his lines thoroughly, and soon, he too, was drawing himself upward into the canopy.

"Thanks for setting my line," he yelled up to Stephen.

Stephen saluted him but said nothing.

Julia gasped as two spiny tree rats raced down her rope and across her arm. With athletic balance and confidence, they leapt a full six feet to another branch before sailing to the next tree and continuing their racing. She marveled at their bold courage.

"You okay?" Eduardo shot up in her direction. He watched her intently.

"Yes. Just a couple of furry little friends hurrying past. They startled me. That's all."

Stephen positioned himself in one of the clefts of the strangler-encased-rosewood. "Aaah, how are you, Old Chap," Stephen mused as he stroked the strong arms of the clinging vine-turned-tree. The fig was huge, spanning up and over its host and sucking up the sunshine above with its parasol of leaves. It wouldn't be too many years before the rosewood would die, decay, and leave the strangler a hollow monument to its host.

"Kosey, this one particular vine is extremely important to the forest ecosystem."

"I have heard of the strangler fig, but I did not know it was a vine," Kosey stared up the latticed bark.

"Yes," Stephen said. He patted the intertwining vines. "This outside wood is the strangler fig. It is encasing a rosewood tree. Eventually, the strangler will kill the rosewood."

"So it just cuts off the rosewood's circulation?"

"Basically."

"I believe it is the fruit that makes it important. Yes?" Kosey rubbed an exposed surface of smooth wood.

Stephen nodded. "There are many different kinds of fig trees in the Amazon. Each fig tree randomly fruits several times a year. Animals can always find fruit in the jungle because there's always some type of ripened fig."

The fig's branches were filled with tropical orchids and multiple types of ferns and other epiphytes. Stephen loved poking around in all the nooks and crannies. As Kosey watched, Stephen stuck out a finger and a tiny gecko climbed aboard.

Alexis pointed to a branch over Stephen's head, "Look, Julia, Eduardo." They counted seven parrots. Their vivid orange, blue, and yellow feathers contrasted with the browns and greens surrounding them. They were making quite a ruckus, obviously objecting to having company so close, and they continued squawking until, at last, they gave up and flew off to find less crowded accommodations.

Climbing into her tree, Julia looped the daisy rope around the closest limb and secured it back to her harness. She had once forgotten to secure her line and barely missed falling eighty feet to the forest floor below. It was a lesson she did not plan to repeat. She pushed aside a mass of epiphytes clinging to and covering almost all the bark near where she sat.

Stephen shouted across the way, "Julia, make sure all of you do a weight check."

"We will," she called back. To Alexis she said, "Do what I do when you get on your branch."

"Okay." Alexis threw her leg over a limb and watched.

Julia added, "Eduardo, don't forget."

"All right." He smiled to himself knowing that Julia was aware that he was no amateur at this, and Eduardo was pleased at her concern.

Julia crept out onto the limb and jumped a little, touching the branch above for balance. She moved a little further bouncing some more. Branches are sometimes weakened, and break from the constant weight of plants clinging to almost every inch of their surfaces, their added weight putting too much stress on the limbs. This one felt solid.

She watched Alexis imitate her actions and then got to work.

There were so many varieties of plants Julia wasn't quite sure where to start. She began by pulling out some of her tools. She watched as Eduardo reached his branch. He left his safety line a bit longer than she would have liked. If he slipped, he wouldn't fall too far, but a ten foot drop could easily break or injure something. Julia was about to mention the long line when Eduardo pulled it in about half way.

Stephen reminded from his perch, "Everyone, be sure to take a moment and look around. You don't want any nasty surprises."

The forest canopy presented an obstacle course of challenges. Large and small dangers were everywhere. Once while Julia and Stephen spent a dawn-to-dusk day collecting samples, they encountered poisonous reptiles, stinging insects, razor-edged leaves, prickly plants, lightning, unexpected and powerful gusts of wind, rain so cold it surprised both of them, and insufferable heat…all during that one climb. Julia took another moment to look around. She saw nothing moving or staring out at her from cover.

The first plant she examined was situated in a deep crevice where the branch met the tree. Julia was surprised to see it there since it was usually found on the ground. She guessed there was enough organic matter in the small indentation to germinate the seed and sustain the plant. It was a beautiful heliconia. The locals called it lobster claw because its long red stems held bright red cones shaped like the crustacean appendage. The tips at the ends of each claw looked as if they had been dipped in bright yellow paint.

Julia moved on. She plundered through philodendrons with leaves the size of dinner plates and ferns as long as the blades of a ceiling fan. "I see lots of ants," she called to Stephen. "Should I collect some?"

"I already have some, but they could be different in any case. Come to think of it, I'm seeing more ants than usual." Stephen drew out a new bag and snipped a tiny fern fiddle.

"I've got various ants too," Alexis chimed in.

"Ants can be very mean, but I do not think they make people bleed from their nose and eyes." Kosey looked toward Stephen. "Do they?"

"I have learned not to be surprised by new findings in the forest, Kosey. I wouldn't think they could cause bleeding, but maybe they have evolved to cause more intense reactions. Some ants let off a scent, a gas of sorts. It is conceivable that a mass of ants might be able to spray some sort of cloud that could settle around people. Combine that with a new kind of toxin…"

Kosey tilted his head, a baffled look on his face, "Is that possible?"

Stephen shrugged. "Just throwing out options. Remember, we are learning more new science every day. Just last month, scientists found a whole new species of monkey in the Columbian Amazon. They are a type of *titi* monkey. Scientists had heard about them decades ago but were unable to confirm and study them because of dangerous insurgent groups in the remote areas where they were located. With deforestation moving deeper and deeper into the forest, the little creatures finally surfaced…I'm sorry to say."

In the other tree Julia said, "I was reading a few months ago about a species of ants recently found in Peru. They actually use their formic acid as a natural herbicide to poison unwanted plants."

"Unwanted plants?" Eduardo reached into a thick cluster of green, plucked out a small purple flower and noticed about a dozen ants running out and down his hand. He quickly put the flower into a plastic bag and shook as many of the ants inside as he could before brushing off the others and sealing the bag. He dusted his hand on his pants, searching for any stray insects ready to bury their stingers.

"Yes. They create something the natives call a devil's garden."

"What in the world is a devil's garden?" Alexis asked looking over her shoulder.

"That is what the local people call them. They believe the gardens are cultivated by evil spirits." Julia pulled herself along the underside of the limb.

"I know what you're speaking of, Julia. I have seen one for myself," Eduardo said. "It was eerie to climb out of thick forest into a large sunny spot clear of vegetation except for a group of large bushes in the center of the sunshine. I saw it many years ago. We didn't go close because of all the ants. The ground was swarming with them."

Julia moved steadily forward. "The gardens basically have only one species of flora, a hollow stemmed plant the ants use for nesting purposes. Believe it or not, a single ant colony on this particular plant can exist more than eight hundred years."

"Wow," Alexis said.

Julia went on, "When scientists first came upon the site, they were baffled. How could there be this large open spot in this random area of dense forest? The only thing they could conclude was that the ants kept the area clean." She reached a fork in the limb and pulled a smaller branch. "They used their formic acid to poison any plant trying to sprout around their colony. The scientists could only speculate the ants were protecting their home."

Eduardo watched Julia move out further, wondering how far she would go before returning to a more stable area. Just as he began to speak, she turned and retraced her route back toward the trunk of the tree.

Julia continued, "To test their theories about the ants, the scientists planted a couple of small saplings in the sunny areas. Worker ants immediately attacked the trees, injecting formic acid into the leaves. The leaves began to die within twenty-four hours." She finished speaking as she was tucking away another sample.

Alexis contemplated, "True wonder of nature."

Julia sounded mildly distracted when she said, "The devil's gardens are a remarkable example of how effectively ants can manipulate their environment in order to ensure their own survival." She hoisted herself up and straddled the limb thinking about the ants and wondering if plants were the only thing they would poison. She turned and called to Stephen, "Could we be looking for a poison? Maybe from something like ants?"

Stephen nodded and pursed his lips. He said loudly, "I've considered that, myself. Get a few samples of each of the different types of ants you find. Did everyone hear that?" He moved back to where he started and pulled out more bags.

A muttering of affirmative came from the group.

After checking over the same area she had previously examined, Julia climbed to another massive branch. She tested her weight, moving out and bouncing a few times and then returned to the trunk. She gave her safety rope another once over and then climbed under the closest cluster of bromeliads, moving along slowly under the limb while inspecting deep inside its foliage.

Folding back the leaves of an orchid, Julia saw a glossy green color. It was a small frog unlike any she had seen before. It had a creamy yellow stripe extending up its back, over its face and onto its stomach.

"Whoa, little one," she uttered. "I am going to take you for a ride." Ever so slowly she pulled out one of her small jars. Carefully unscrewing the lid, she held the jar over the little frog, and with a slight hop he was inside. Julie replaced the top of the jar and held it to the light. "What a marvelous find." She whispered to herself.

"What do you have, Julia?" Alexis had been watching her.

"The cutest little frog. I've never seen one like it. What if no one has ever found one before? Hey, maybe I get to name her." Julia flashed a smile.

Alexis looked down and saw Eduardo intently scraping a piece of bark. "What have you found?" she asked.

Without looking up, he answered, "Some sort of larvae next to some lichen. It has a silk tube and…" He stopped as he peered closer at what he was holding. "It looks like…wood fragments. I'm just not sure." He repeated Julia's action opening a jar to capture *his* find.

They spent the next hour intent on their collecting but found nothing else remarkable.

Stephen was the first to begin his descent. He was a little disappointed when he reached the ground only to find a few additional varieties of ants near the base of the tree.

As Julia and Eduardo climbed down, Eduardo asked, "Are you ready to see the mahogany?"

"I can't wait." Julia smiled at him as she removed her harness, with Alexis and Kosey trailing right behind them.

Stephen called back the students. To Julia and Eduardo he said, "Just leave your gear, both of you. Alexis, Kosey, and I will stow the gear and then meet you at the tree."

Eduardo and Julia climbed down the hillside and moved toward the gigantic tree. They had seen it from the ridge, but that was a considerable distance away, and Julia was anxious to see it up close.

Coming to an opening, Eduardo held up his hand to stop. He pointed to where the hillside began to rise again, and there it was: a magnificent sight.

The mahogany's canopy was broken here and there, and its shape was not at all like Julia imagined. Somehow she had expected it to look like the oak trees of Georgia, but instead of the mushroom shape of the foliage, it was more asymmetrical, with the branches reaching out in random patterns.

Just as Eduardo had said, the mahogany was massive. They moved closer, and as she stepped next to the base, Julia felt like one of the ants she had just placed in her bags. She walked between two of the tall buttresses anchoring the tree, running her hand lightly over the deeply furrowed, reddish-black bark. Julia looked up at the canopy of the tree, realizing why she couldn't see the outside edges of the limbs Eduardo had described as almost the width of a football field. On closer inspection Julia discovered hints of green, and gold, and grey from fungi and moss nurtured by their damp habitat.

Julia walked in and out of the tall blades, while Eduardo followed her around the tree at a distance. She continued touching the surface as she circled.

For Eduardo, it was intriguing to watch her interact with the tree.

Julia stopped moving when she found the cut that went almost all the way through one of the buttresses. She ran her hand across the splintered surface, with its hardened sap-encrusted edges.

Seeing the look on her face, Eduardo ached to put the deep tissue that had been ripped away back, and make it whole again.

Julia squatted to the ground and cupped her hands scooping up the dust from the cut before slowly pouring it back to the Earth. She stood and turned her face toward the sky peering up the straight, bean-stalk trunk. Moving closer and closer she gently leaned her cheek against the bark and closed her eyes.

Resting against this centuries-old monarch was comforting for Julia. She wanted to feel a part it. She reached out as far as she could, her palms flat on the surface in oneness as she and the tree breathed in tandem…connected. Julia felt that the mahogany knew she was there.

She pictured the tiny seed the tree had once been. At the end of a flowering spring many hundreds of years ago, millions of seeds spiraled across the sky, never putting down roots. Yet, this one had. It was special. And for all these years, it had climbed toward the heavens, spreading its arms and offering itself as home to millions of plants and animals and insects. Then along came an obliterator…annihilator… exterminator…a man. Ruthless and greedy.

As he stood there watching from the distance, Eduardo felt a tenderness he had forgotten. A sensation grew inside him and his chest tightened. It was a piercing that took his breath away. Slowly he withdrew from his vantage point, leaving Julia to have her private moment. Eduardo climbed the hillside and sat down at the top. He could no longer see Julia's prone figure against the tree, just the outline of the mahogany's crown. Its bright, green leaves quaked in the sunlight giving the illusion of a shiver, and Eduardo felt his own kinship with the tree.

It was as if time had been suspended as Julia stood motionless against the majestic figure.

* * *

An hour later, Julia returned to the climb site with Alexis and Kosey and moved about through the ground cover, turning over leaves and twigs and looking below the thin undergrowth.

Stephen put the last of the samples into a box that Eduardo hefted into the jeep. Stephen dusted off his hands, pulled off his handkerchief, poured water on it, and hung the thin cloth around his neck. "We have done all we can here, I believe, Eduardo. Are you having Julia for dinner?"

The question caught Eduardo off guard. Not only had he not expected it, but the way Stephen phrased it made his mouth water. *Julia for dinner*? The hunger and ache were back. He shook his head to clear the image from his mind, like an *etch-a-sketch* erasing a child's scribbling. He watched Stephen wipe his face and raise his eyebrows inquiring an answer. "I'm not certain that is what I should do just yet," he said as he glanced at Julia who was far enough away not to hear their conversation.

Stephen waved off his objection. "Paahh. Share your garden and a glass of wine. Two friends having dinner. You've been without companionship for too long."

Eduardo continued to watch Julia as she made her way toward them. "I've seen the ring on her finger and heard her talking to someone named Mitch earlier. Isn't she engaged?"

"She says so," Stephen said, adjusting the gear in the back of the jeep. "But somehow she doesn't seem completely happy with the man."

"Do you think she'll accept my invitation?" Eduardo was warming to the idea of dinner with Julia.

"Of course she will," was all Stephen said as he secured the boxes with one of his bungee cords.

"She will what?" Julia asked as she and the students came close enough to hear them talking.

Stephen was climbing into the jeep as he answered. "Alexis," he patted the seat next to him, "you can ride up here with me. Kosey can sit in the back by himself."

Kosey vaulted into the backseat just as Stephen started the engine.

"But what about me?" Julia asked.

"You, my dear, are dining with Eduardo and walking in his garden. He'll bring you home, and *I* will not wait up." Before Julia could stop him, Stephen drove off. As he moved out of sight, they saw him wave without looking back.

Julia faced Eduardo with her hands on her hips and gave him an accusing glare.

"What?" Eduardo turned his palms up and raised his shoulders a little. "He didn't give me much of a choice."

Julia shook her head and grunted.

"Not a becoming sound, Julia." Eduardo smiled at her girlish behavior as he chastised her.

With a determined look she replied: "I don't like being manipulated. It's one of my pet peeves." Julia folded her arms and let out another unladylike growl.

Eduardo pulled the edges of his lips down and ducked his head. He didn't want to push her any further. He walked over to Julia's side of the truck, and even though there was no door to open, he pretended to open it anyway. He held out his hand to help her in and bowed in submission.

Sighing, Julia let her arms drop, calmly walked over, took his hand, and climbed into the jeep.

Eduardo pretended to shut and lock the door. He ran back around to the other side and bounded into the driver's seat.

Starting the engine, he smiled at her. "Put on your seatbelt. We must keep you safe," he said in a playful voice and began to drive.

Julia didn't reach for the belt.

Eduardo continued his conversation even though Julia had not said a word. "And where would you like to dine, tonight? Rio? Or, we could fly to Rome. Oh, I've got the perfect place. You'll think it is divine. It's a wonderful, little restaurant in the jungle. That's where we'll go. It's called…Eduardo's, and I hear he has some wonderful wine chilling as we speak."

He glanced sideways at the silent and beautiful, young woman next to him. His smile faded a little, and he thought, *I don't think the wine is the only thing chilling at the moment.*

26

Julia sat on the porch listening to Eduardo fumbling in the kitchen. She had chosen a straight chair instead of the swing because she didn't want the comfort of the swaying.

She was irritated. Not only had she been taken here without being consulted, but she'd just tried to call Mitch and couldn't get him to answer. Where was he? It was after five in Georgia and he should have been in the car heading home. And why didn't he call her more often? He'd only called twice since she had been here. 'Out of sight, out of mind' had a ring of truth.

She finally let out a big sigh, resigning herself to the evening. She heard a pot hit the floor, followed by muffled grumbling and a bustling of activity and then the tinkling of silverware clattering into the sink. She couldn't resist a tight smile. *A little trouble in the kitchen? Serves him right. What was he thinking? What was Stephen thinking?*

She had not made the trip to Eduardo's home easy. She couldn't help it, she told herself. Julia rode in silence and sat defensively with her arms crossed, staring out the open door the entire drive. She hadn't spoken a word to him since they left, even though he tried to make light conversation. This really wasn't like her. It was completely out of character for her to be so cool to anyone. *What is wrong with me?*

When he helped her into the jeep, his hand had enveloped hers. His clasp lingered a moment longer than necessary, as if the contact was something he needed. She could still feel the warmth of his fingers, which brushed ever so slightly over the back of her hand.

Julia's thoughts flashed back to Mitch at home. She stared at the ring she was twisting on her finger again. She thought of Mitch's hand in hers. When she thought of how it felt, she only remembered coolness. She thought of Eduardo's warm skin against her palm. Cool. Warm. The contrast was obvious and unsettling.

From the kitchen, she heard Eduardo call her name. She went inside and was amazed at how neat and orderly everything was. She could tell Eduardo lived alone, but he still kept a clean house. *Where's the maid?* She found her way to the kitchen and saw Eduardo stooping to retrieve two wine glasses from under a counter.

He straightened and asked, "How about a tour out back?"

Julia didn't know quite how to react. He didn't seem at all upset about how she had behaved an hour earlier, and what was he cooking? She could smell a tantalizing aroma coming from the oven.

When she raised an eyebrow and motioned toward the stove, Eduardo said, "I put in a chicken to roast." He shrugged, "It was the only tame thing I could find. Is chicken okay with you?"

She gave a small smile. "Sounds perfect. And…it smells wonderful."

He gave her a slow smile and wagged his finger in her direction, "I think someone's feeling better."

Julia's shoulders sagged. When she spoke, the words came out quickly sounding like she wanted the confession to be over. "I'm sorry, Eduardo. I acted like a spoiled brat the whole way here. I don't know what came over me. I don't like someone dictating to me. I like to be in control of my decisions. In this case I wasn't given a choice, and it put me off, which for the most part is not at all like me." Her face showed sincere regret. "And that followed such a profound experience at the mahogany…."

Eduardo laughed. "You are so funny, Julia." He walked toward her and brushed the tip of her nose with his finger. "Now that you mention it, I can see you acted like a petulant child."

Julia started to say something when he touched her lips for silence. The touch was a surprise, and Julia took a tiny breath.

"You are forgiven for being human." Eduardo did not wait for a response. Instead, he turned, opened the refrigerator, and pulled out a bottle of wine. Uncorking it, he poured a glass for each of them.

Julia inclined her head, gave a shy smile, and took the glass thinking some wine might be nice and probably necessary for her to actually relax. After the warm day in the trees, a cool drink was more than refreshing. Julia had not realized how thirsty she was. She downed the glass, and without comment, Eduardo refilled it. He returned the bottle to chill some more before he opened the back door.

"Come," Eduardo said. "Let us visit my garden before the sun goes down."

Julia let him guide her onto the terrace. The smell of roasting chicken, smothered in wonderful spices followed them.

As they moved through the back door, Julia gasped. She was engulfed in a spectacular scene she could not have imagined. From the wide, top step, she saw they were high on a mountain slope. A lush valley stretched below in the distance, complete with a gigantic cascading waterfall.

"Please tell me I can go there," Julia said to Eduardo as he cupped her elbow and led her down the steps.

"If it's your pleasure," he said, sounding a bit sad as they continued walking.

She made him pause so she could bathe in the ambiance. Spread out before her was a vista unlike any she had ever seen. Not only did the waterfall crown the beauty in the distance, but terraced before her was a garden that could have come from a fairy tale.

Julia turned to him and said, "This garden looks like it could have been lifted right out of *Southern Living Magazine* or *National Geographic*. There is no way you do both your job and keep this so beautiful."

Eduardo quickly grinned down into her face. "I have seen the *Southern Living Magazine* and *National Geographic*, and I am humbled at your comparison. And yes, you are very observant, Julia. You are correct. I have people who come here every day or two and work. I give them a place to live down the valley, and they help me keep everything in good shape."

He surveyed the scene in front of them and continued, "I have beautiful flowers for my home, fresh fruits and vegetables for my table, and all kinds of goods made from plants harvested here. I have more than enough for myself, and I'm able to share most of it with others. It works well for everyone."

Julia now understood his spotless home.

As though she had spoken aloud, Eduardo clarified, "Of course, I usually keep up most of the house by myself. I don't like others going through my things. Once a month, a woman comes in and dusts, sweeps—all those types of chores. And I also take my laundry to a woman in the village. Otherwise, I do the rest."

They had descended several steps when Julia stopped by a grouping of a variety of palms. The first one she noticed was a *tucum* palm. It had a heavily spined trunk, was about ten feet tall, and thick with its clusters of fruit.

Julia decided to humor Eduardo. She had studied all the fruits and vegetables in and around this area, but somehow she felt it was important to Eduardo that he shared this with her. Besides, she was curious about how much he really knew. "What kind of palm is this?" she asked as she reached to touch a frond hanging within reach.

"That is what we call a *tucum* palm." If Eduardo wondered why she didn't know its name, he never showed it. He reached up and plucked a ripe orb from one of the clusters. He walked over and laid it on a rock. He picked up another rock and hit the fruit several times. Taking out his pocket knife, Eduardo gently pried the broken pieces apart.

"Taste this," he offered half of the fruit to her. The way he broke it apart made a perfect little cup.

Julia sipped the clear, sweet liquid. "Wow. It's as sweet as the wine."

"And very good for you. It is filled with Vitamin A, three times more than carrots." He stood and stroked one of the long slender leaves. "The hammock you saw on my front porch is made from these leaves."

Julia pointed toward another palm. "And that one?"

She had forgotten how much she loved the taste of peach palm. Even from here, she could see deep under the long needle-like fronds a mass of orange and red fruit. *Yummy. One of my favorites.*

Eduardo took her elbow and guided her forward. "The indigenous locals plant these around their homes. They call it a peach palm. Each tree can yield up to a dozen of these bunches each year. I have several simmering in salty water on the stove right now. We will eat them with our chicken." Eduardo was studying her again.

"How would you describe their taste?"

"Well. I would describe them as a mix between a chestnut and a potato, but much better than either by itself. If you have ever bought heart-of-palm in a jar, it was probably from this type of tree." Eduardo edged her further down the path. "I am surprised you do not know these fruits. Surely, Lupa has cooked them for you."

Julia smiled to herself. She couldn't have described the taste better. "I'm sure I'll remember when I taste them again."

They strolled past purple hibiscus, bright yellow clematis, and various banana trees laden with fruit. A little further down the path was a low growing bush. It was a *fittonia* with deep dark green leaves having bright pinkish-red veins eight to ten inches across. It was so shiny Julia thought she should be able to see her reflection.

"Ahh…*fittonia*." Eduardo rubbed his fingers over the glossy leaf. "The leaves can be crushed and used to relieve a headache. Local people use it as a hallucinogen." He chuckled as he looked at her, "They say…" he pretended to be a spooky character, "it produces visions of eyeballs."

Julia laughed at his playfulness.

They came to a rambling stream winding down the hillside. On the bank was the most spectacular acacia Julia had ever seen. It had large, silvery-blue fronds exceeding a foot long and wide. It was at least twenty feet high, enormous for this type of plant. She looked toward Eduardo. She didn't have to ask.

He had seen her face light up when the tree came into view. He knew she would like it. He was looking straight into her eyes when she turned to ask him.

"An elephant ear," was all he said, using the name given to the plant by the locals.

"Oh…" Julia was following his mouth.

They stood like that for a moment before she looked away. Julia walked to a large boulder next to the stream and sat down. She trailed her fingers in the cool, clear water, inhaling the drift of a sweet scent that was strong but soothing. She looked to her left and saw a *costus*. It had long, thin leaves stiff to the touch. Its white flower with its yellow center had a lovely bell shape, while the petals were frayed at the ends. Julia turned the bell up toward her face and smelled. The scent enveloped her.

Eduardo stood next to her, watching. Quietly, he said, "You've found my *costus*. To me it has a spicy-sweet scent."

Julia agreed. She asked in a reverent tone as she held the bell in her hands, "Does the local shaman use it for anything?"

"I've been told the stalks can be boiled into a tea and used to subdue a cough. I haven't tried it. I just choose to enjoy its beauty." Eduardo stood looking down at her.

Julia didn't notice the look nor did she catch the double meaning of his words. She had been distracted across the way by the most elegant bird-of-paradise she had ever seen. It reached ten feet in height and was in full bloom, covered with brilliant white flowers. Her senses reeled from the mass of beauty and proliferation of perfumes surrounding her.

A late afternoon breeze arose from the east, coming from the direction of the waterfall. The air had cooled considerably since they first came outside.

Eduardo watched as the wind blew through Julia's hair. He wanted to reach out and touch it, but he didn't dare. Unconsciously, he tucked his hands into his pockets. He knew if he ever opened that gate, he might not be able to reel himself back in, and he wasn't sure whether she would accept him. He looked off into the distance and waited for her to move.

Julia also fought the desire she felt for Eduardo. She once told Stephen her career came first, but did it really? Julia wasn't sure about anything anymore. She could tell Eduardo was interested in her, but he wasn't ready for a relationship with another woman since losing his wife. Of course, she was making an assumption. *Maybe he is ready.*

Then there was Mitch. How could she cheat on him with another man? If she broke the engagement with Mitch, could she have a lasting relationship with Eduardo? Did she want that? The headiness from the plants and the scenery just added to her confusion.

And what about Serena? What a beautiful name. Serena. What had she been like? Was she beautiful? Julia wanted to know how Serena died, but she could never ask Eduardo. She would remember to speak to Stephen about it, thinking it a bid odd that the subject had never come up before.

The sun was dropping below the mountain ridge when Julia finally rose from the rock beside the stream. As Eduardo turned toward her, he saw her shiver. He wondered if it was from the evening wind or if something else had passed between them.

She wrapped her hands around herself and rubbed up and down her arms. "I didn't realize it was getting so cool."

"Come," Eduardo said as he gently placed his arm around her. "Let's check on dinner. It should be just about ready."

The next hour was punctuated with appreciative complements as Julia savored an exquisite meal with Eduardo. She continued with a pretense of leading Eduardo to believe he was introducing her to new foods for the first time. It seemed to give him a great deal of pleasure, and Julia hoped it would make up for her rude behavior earlier in the day,

After dinner they sat in the porch swing, Eduardo's leg pressing lightly against Julia's when he pushed against the floor. Each time Julia felt the warmth against her own leg, she also felt the tingling in her stomach. Eduardo was the first man since Mitch who caused a quivering in the pit of her stomach when the warmth from his body was near her. Sadly she realized she hadn't experienced this feeling with Mitch for a long time.

With nothing to do with her hands, Julia began to feel a bit awkward. She spoke hastily, "I know I brought it up during dinner, but I can't believe how great your peach palm fruits were. Do you call them peaches? I'm from Georgia, the Peach State, so I know a good peach when I eat one."

Eduardo noticed Julia seemed uneasy. "I've had Georgia peaches, and they're quite good. You know I'm not going to bite you, Julia. You can relax."

Julia gave a quick laugh, "I don't know why I'm so jumpy. But it was an impressive day." She smiled and continued, "I didn't know it showed."

"Just a little," he stood and extended his hand. "It's time for me to get you home."

"Yes," Julia agreed. "We have a busy day tomorrow." She placed her hand in his, the warm contact moving up her arm toward her chest. Julia gently pulled her hand free as soon as she rose.

When they pulled up to Stephen's house, Eduardo let the engine continue to run as he quietly said, "I enjoyed having you for dinner, Julia."

"I enjoyed it, too." Julia smiled. "It was truly delicious. And I can't tell you how impressed I am with the garden. Would you invite me back? There is so much more to see." She looked him straight in the face as she asked.

Eduardo smiled. He so wanted to kiss her lips. Instead, he picked up her hand and kissed it. "You have an open invitation."

He watched as Julia licked those lips he had just thought of kissing. That simple act was almost his undoing.

There was an awkward silence before he said, "Good night, Julia."

They smiled at each other.

Julia could have easily melted into his arms. Instead, she said, "Good night," and slowly climbed from the jeep.

Eduardo watched as she stepped onto the porch. Julia turned as she opened the door and waved. He held up his hand. It stayed there until after she closed the door.

27

The team, minus Julia, had worked the rest of the afternoon and into the evening in the lab buoyed by the thought they might have retrieved a sample during today's climb that could possibly help with the case. They paused for a quick dinner and then went immediately back to the lab. The students continued with their experiments, while Stephen moved to some of the more complicated testing.

Stephen searched all the science data bases he could access without any luck identifying Julia's frog or the larvae Eduardo stumbled onto. He circulated several photos of each among scientists he knew around the world and then placed the larvae and frog in separate holding cases. Julia could swab and test her frog for toxins tomorrow before returning the frog to the area where it was found. He would wait to hear any responses or professional opinions from his inquiries, a day at the most. Most importantly, he was keeping the larvae safely contained until it emerged. Something this unique could be very dangerous.

The ants might be another story. Stephen knew it might take a while to identify all of them. He was sure most of them had a certain amount of toxins, but he didn't want to test them until he figured out exactly what type of ants they were.

Kosey appeared to be finished with his experiments and was cleaning up his work area when Stephen walked over and clapped him on the shoulder. "How would you like to start trying to identify some of the ants?"

"That would be my pleasure," Kosey said. He held up his finger, "'Send a boy where he wants to go, and you will see his best pace.'"

Stephen smiled, "Thank you. I'm glad you are an eager researcher."

Kosey finished wiping the counter, "Is that not what I am here for?"

Julia called from the door, "Hey. I thought you weren't going to wait up for me." She came in and climbed onto the stool at her work station reaching for her frog as the students greeted her.

"I did not wait up for you," Stephen teased. "Our students were clamoring to see if we found anything of interest today. I am merely coddling them."

"Riiight," Julia snickered. She knew Stephen was the one driven to see what they found, and the truth be known, he would probably have waited up for her anyway. Julia held up the jar with the frog, "Did anyone figure out who this little guy might be?"

Stephen shook his head, "Not yet, but I'm working on it." He told her about sending out the pictures and waiting for a response. He noted she kept a slight smile on her face, so he hoped that was a sign she enjoyed her evening. He would not ask but instead said, "Kosey is going to identify as many of our ants as he can."

Alexis joined them. "I can help." She and Kosey moved to where the ants were waiting.

Julia looked at the jars and bags of ants. "So far we have collected, I believe, nineteen different types of ants, although some of them look so much alike, it's hard to tell them apart. But maybe it won't take too long to zero in on any suspicious toxins."

Julia checked on the progress of her insect fungi experiments and then busied herself with cleanup. It was amazing how messy the lab could get so quickly.

An hour later Stephen glanced up at the sound of an approaching engine outside. Looking at his watch, he noted it was almost midnight. *Who could that be*? He went to the door and saw Eduardo pulling to a stop. He got an uneasy *something's wrong* feeling.

Julia was busy putting slides into soapy water in the sink, and the clattering and sound of running water shielded her from hearing Eduardo's arrival. The students were huddled around the ants, now all four involved with their identifications. Without disturbing any of them, Stephen opened the screened door and went outside.

Julia heard the door slam and turned expecting to see Lupa bringing a snack. Instead, she saw Stephen leaving. When he returned, she was surprised to see Eduardo with him.

How odd for Eduardo to have come back…and so late. She knew immediately something had to be wrong. It only took one look at both Eduardo's and Stephen's faces.

Stephen stood motionless. "We have more bodies, Julia," he said quietly.

"What?" Alexis's head jerked up.

The room grew quiet.

Reaching for the towel to dry her hands, Julia said, "Let's go."

Stephen and Eduardo looked at each other, and then Eduardo stepped forward clearing his throat. She looked up into his face and knew what he was going to say. She held up her hands in an attempt to change his mind.

Eduardo took both of her hands in his and said, "We need for you to stay here, Julia. You and the others need to finish the identifications and testing. We'll be back soon."

"Oh, no you don't," her temper flashed. She jerked her hands from his. "You aren't leaving me out of this. We're almost finished here, and I'm just as much a part of this as you are."

Kosey and Charlie stepped forward, both volunteering to go.

Stephen held up his hand, "No, thank you for the offer, but you all stay here and continue working. Finish up and get some rest. We have others going with us." He moved toward Julia. Eduardo didn't know her well enough to know how determined she could be.

"Alright," Stephen said. "Here is the truth."

Eduardo stepped aside.

Julia looked hard at Stephen and scowled, "What is it?"

He exhaled slowly and said, "The bodies are different this time."

"Different?" She looked toward Eduardo. "What does he mean different? You've seen the bodies?" The questions tumbled out. "How could you have time? You just left a couple of hours ago." She tried to clear her head. "What is different about the bodies?"

"Unfortunately, I have seen them, Julia. I got a call just after I left you here. I went straight to the site. It's not good." Eduardo was no longer making eye contact.

Julia angled her head to the side and narrowed her eyes as if she were trying to see something very small in the tiny lines of his face. What was that look? Was it sadness? Confusion? Then it dawned on her. Julia's eyes widened. She was stunned to see fear on Eduardo's face. Maybe his expression held a mixture of both sadness and confusion, but Julia definitely saw fear.

From the corner of his eye Eduardo saw her watching him, and it made him uncomfortable. He could tell she was reading him. Without sounding exasperated, Eduardo addressed her questions: "Look, Julia, the bodies are a mess. They look as though someone stuck a pin in a balloon, and all the air came out." Eduardo shook his head vigorously. "They actually look much worse than that. Nothing human killed these men. The blood. The condition of the bodies. Plus they're covered with welts. They look like something stung them repeatedly. If I didn't know better, I would have thought they were punctured and beaten before they died. It is the most gruesome sight I have ever seen. And in the jungle where we found them…" his voice faded "…not very far from here…" He gestured toward the door. Eduardo looked at Julia trying to convey the horror he had seen. His voice rose as he moved in front of her and grasped both of her forearms. "At the spot where they died, Julia, there is blood everywhere…everywhere… everywhere…" he repeated the word several times as it drifted out the door and into the forest. As he said the words, he dropped his arms to his side like a man who had just been defeated. He could no longer look in her direction, as he cast his glance toward the floor.

Julia looked back and forth between the two men. There was Stephen, the man she considered a father figure. How could she let him go out there? The thought that there was something loose that could kill him was intolerable, and Julia began to feel sick to her stomach. She couldn't bear it if anything happened to him.

The other man standing there who…*who what*? she thought. What was Eduardo to her? He was a man she once pitied because he had lost his beautiful Serena. But today they had crossed an invisible line of...*what*? *What, is going on*? How could she have feelings for someone she was just getting to know? But somehow, somewhere inside, she felt as if she did know him, and that he too had a sense of who she really was.

"If it isn't safe for me out there, then it won't be safe for either of you," Julia's voice strengthened. She was starting to panic. These two men were determined to go it alone, and she knew already she couldn't win this battle of wills.

"It's really important for you to stay here and finish. We will have many more samples for you after we get back. Have you identified all the ants we collected on our climb?" Eduardo asked in an attempt to distract her.

From the other side of the room, Alexis said, "We've only identified five so far. We have many more to go."

Eduardo looked back at Julia, "With all the welts I just saw on the bodies," he pointed to the ants, "those just may be the key."

Stephen was no longer listening. He reached for his notebook and pencil and video camera. He stuffed them in a small duffel bag and retrieved the sampling kit already loaded with jars, zipper bags and gloves, and tossed in a box of masks.

Eduardo sounded firm. "I don't want you there, Julia. It's dark and we don't know what might be out there. I'd rather do it in the morning, but I'm worried about the rain. My men are taking pictures right now, but we need to get as many samples as possible before everything is washed away. We'll be back as soon as Stephen can film the site and autopsy the bodies."

Over his shoulder he said to Stephen, "Don't forget the video camera. We need to get a film to save for later."

"I have it already," Stephen patted the bag on the table.

Stephen stepped across the room to get another video card that he slid into his pocket. He watched Julia's hands go onto her hips as she faced Eduardo.

Julia raised an eyebrow, "What do you mean you don't want me there?" Here they were, controlling her again.

Stephen knew what might be coming. He turned Julia to face him and said, "I know it maddens you to be told what to do, but, Julia, this is important. If anything happens to one or both of us, you're the one who knows everything that has happened and what we've done so far. That's the main reason we need you to stay. Plus," he nodded toward the students, "you are responsible for their safety." Stephen's voice softened, "We'll be back soon…I promise."

Julia stopped protesting. It did make sense for her to stay here and work. She glanced toward the students. She *was* responsible for them…at least two of them. She would only be an observer out there, but it irked her being left behind and not having a choice. As much as she hated to agree with them, it seemed like a sensible precaution. She shut her eyes and willed herself back under control.

A few minutes later they stood next to the jeep. Lupa hurried from the kitchen and handed Eduardo two thermoses filled with his special tea. "Drink. Both. Keep you safe," he said.

"How did you know we were going?" Eduardo asked.

"Lupa know," he said with finality.

"We'll drink it on the way, my friend," Stephen said as Eduardo put the bottles between the seats.

Julia stood silently nearby.

Stephen went to her and put an arm around her shoulder. "We'll be fine, Julia," his voice was almost inaudible.

"Do you promise?"

Stephen's eyes met Eduardo's over her head.

Eduardo just shrugged.

Stephen tried to sound confident when he replied, "We *will* be fine."

28

Jennifer lay in her hammock next to Charlie's. He was feeling well enough to move out to the sleeping hall, which was a relief to her. She had been frightened without him.

What a day it had been. The exhilaration of the climb in the canopy, collecting samples, testing in the lab; then the bombshell dropped when Eduardo returned with news of the deaths. The initial exhilaration-mutating-to-horror experience had taken a toll on them.

Julia sent them all to bed after they identified most of the ants, saying she knew they were tired. Jennifer thought Julia just wanted some alone-time to get herself together. It was obvious she was shaken when Stephen and Eduardo left.

Another worry was Nigel and Drake. Jennifer and Charlie had planned to follow the duo if they came and went from the camp tonight. Now she just hoped she would sleep lightly, if she slept at all, questioning whether anyone in the compound would get much sleep that night.

Charlie's breathing told her that he was sound asleep when she heard the rattle of dishes in the common room. Nigel and Drake were back. Jennifer reached over and shook Charlie into a groan, as he moved clumsily with his shoulder still stinging

"Whaaat?" he asked in a groggy voice.

"Shhh…Nigel and Drake are back. We need to know what they're doing."

Charlie began to protest: "I'm sore and there's who-knows-what out there killing people. You're nuts."

Jennifer lashed back in an annoyed whisper: "Nuts? Well, how do we know *they* aren't the killers and they're going to come back here and kill all of us? I'd rather take my chances in the jungle than be a sitting duck. Now get your clothes on!" She hissed as she threw his forest clothes at him. "And don't forget the machete!" Jennifer's head was reeling as she tried to think back as to why in the hell she came on this trip in the first place.

After changing their clothes, they inched open their door and waited until they saw the two dark figures leaving. As quietly as possible, they slipped out into the night.

Nigel and Drake moved quickly through the forest, and Jennifer and Charlie struggled to keep up. Jennifer stumbled several times when her boots caught on roots erupting from the path.

It was a dark night filled with so many insect and animal voices that Jennifer was unable to differentiate any single individual sound. As they moved forward, she listened to a chorus of murmuring mixed with raucous shouts and croaks and most disconcerting of all, the rustling of mysterious creatures crawling through the darkness. When she had been safely resting in her sleeping room with Charlie and her trusty machete, the voices of the night seemed to lull her to sleep. But while out amongst them, the same voices became menacing—or was it the human element that seemed so threatening?

Every so often, Charlie paused to check his GPS to be sure they had a satellite signal. By using the 'track' function, they were laying a virtual 'bread crumb' trail. It would be easy to find their way back to camp unless they lost their signal. *So far so good*, he thought as he looked at the bright green meandering line indicating the route they were taking.

An hour later Charlie stopped short and Jennifer bumped into him from behind.

"What is it?" she whispered.

He pointed ahead; they could barely make out Nigel and Drake with another person. Charlie put a finger to his lips, and they stepped off the path and settled beside a fallen tree where they could see the small fire the men sat around.

"What do we do now?" Drake asked, rubbing his hands together over the fire. It was surprising how cool it got near the equator when the sun went down.

"We eat," Nigel said as he dropped the bag in front of Tiago, who quietly and efficiently began unpacking the food. There was soon the aroma of warmed meat and yams along with toasted bread and goat cheese.

Jennifer leaned close to Charlie's ear and asked, "What are we doing?"

"Waiting."

"For what?"

A "shhh" came out of Charlie, perhaps a bit too abruptly.

Nigel's head jerked in their direction. "Did you hear something?"

Drake wrinkled his face, "Are you kidding? Above that racket?" He waved his hand in the air.

Nigel shook his head. "I'm not referring to the forest noises," he resisted adding 'stupid.' "I was referring to a human-type noise. Like a shushing."

"Tiago check," Tiago said as he picked up the machete and strolled into the dark forest.

Jennifer and Charlie lay facing each other under the log. Fortunately for them they were average size people because Tiago never saw them in the shadow as he climbed over their hiding place, his feet tramping close enough to Jennifer's head that he caught and pulled her hair. Jennifer stifled a scream of pain and knew the man must have heard her heart thudding out of her chest, like the tell-tale heart in Poe's story. *Thud. Thud. Thud.*

They heard Drake ask, "Why are we waiting here? Shouldn't we be doing something?"

"We are doing something," Nigel replied, still trying to differentiate the night sounds. "We are sitting beside the fire."

"That's obvious. I'm not stupid," Drake said sarcastically.

Nigel looked hard at him thinking that the word "stupid" was exactly what he was. "We wait for the logging camp to settle for the night…Drake."

Drake gave him an annoyed nod with a twisted grimace as his reply.

Jennifer and Charlie lay under the tree until they heard Tiago speak to Nigel. It had taken over a half hour for him to make his way back into the campsite from the other side.

Nigel flicked his lighter off and on watching the tiny flame come and go. He loved fire. He loved how it danced and consumed itself.

"What's the plan for later?" Drake asked. "Are we going to slit some tires or something like that?"

Nigel laughed quietly, "Something like that…"

Why did Nigel always have to be so mysterious? thought Drake. It was as though Nigel didn't trust him or something. Drake was getting sick of being left out of the planning. What was he, just a fetcher? Nigel's lackey? Professor or not, Nigel needed to give Drake some respect. Ask his opinion. Let him offer some input.

Drake stood up and flailed his arms, "Are you going to keep it a secret like you always do? I'm tired of you always being so tight-lipped. I've got some ideas too. Ever think of that?" He continued muttering to himself, his tone all sulky and whiny. "Everything has to be a surpriiise…" he whined. Then he stood over Nigel, "I'm tired of it."

At first Nigel acted as though he hadn't heard Drake's outburst. The silence between the two men was long enough that Drake began to be uncomfortable. Finally, Nigel rasped, "Sit down and be quiet. I am tired…of you." He didn't stop watching the little flame pop up and down as the menacing tone flowed from his mouth.

The color drained from Drake's face as he settled back down where he had been before his little tirade. The simple words held a definite threat.

"You can be quite tiring, Drake."

Nigel pulled out his blanket, used his backpack as a pillow, and turned away from the fire.

Drake silently lay down facing the fire and his professor, his mentor, realizing that this man had most likely become his adversary.

"We leave in two hours," Nigel spoke toward the forest. "Set your watch."

Two hours later they were up and moving. Jennifer drifted out of her fog of near-sleep and nudged Charlie awake, this time holding her hand over his mouth in case he spoke. She worried the whole time they had leaned against the log that a giant spider or some other insect might get on her, so she had cocooned herself in a light sheet she brought along. Charlie, on the other hand, had fallen into a deep sleep as soon as the others quieted.

They followed the trio for a mile or so until they saw another camp in the distance. Charlie left the path and circled closer. He could still see Nigel and the others moving in tandem with them. He wasn't sure what Nigel planned to do, but he knew he was up to some kind of sabotage. Charlie just hoped there wouldn't be any violence toward the men in the camp.

He and Jennifer climbed up into a strangler fig and settled into a cleft ten feet above the ground. It was a great vantage point. Jennifer burrowed her back on his chest and leaned against him. He moved her head to his good shoulder, afraid she might inadvertently bump his injury which could have resulted in a painful outcry. That would certainly bring them the attention they didn't want.

It took a few minutes for Charlie to recognize one of the men guarding the camp. This was the same group they had encountered when he was shot. The camp had two large tents, and each was dark and silent.

"Guess they're in for the night," Charlie whispered in Jennifer's ear.

Two men sat by a fire, guns at their sides. Their hushed voices wafting into the trees.

Charlie asked, "Where's Nigel?"

Jennifer turned her head toward him and answered quietly, "Don't know." Her eyes were beginning to droop.

Suddenly, one of the tents erupted in flames as one man came running out, his back and arms on fire.

Jennifer stifled a scream and almost fell out of the tree but regained her balance as they scurried back to the ground, both crouching as they ran back up the path.

"Come on," Nigel motioned impatiently. Tiago took the lead, and luckily for Jennifer and Charlie, they left in the opposite direction.

Jennifer and Charlie heard the screaming man for a long way as they jogged back toward the safety of the compound. When they were closer to safety Jennifer said, "We need to tell Stephen or Eduardo what Nigel and Drake are up to."

Charlie slowed their trot to a walk and considered before he shook his head. “No. I need to think about what to do. How much we want them to know. I’m afraid we might be in trouble because…” he threw his head back in the direction from which they had come, “…Eduardo might find out what just happened back there and that Nigel and Drake were responsible. We came with them, and he might believe we had a part in it. Have you ever seen *locked up abroad*? I don’t think I want to get locked up in Brazil. It could take months before they realize we’re not involved.”

Jennifer shivered. “You’re right...but…” as she had another thought. She grabbed his arm and forced him to stop and face her. With wide eyes she asked, “What about Nigel? Would he do something to *us*?”

Charlie looked back down the path they had just taken and shook his head. “Nah. He’s scary, but he’s not stupid. We are of no threat to him…at least I don’t think so.”

Even though she felt more secure when they got back to the compound, Jennifer was unsettled by the doubt she heard in Charlie’s voice. If Nigel could set a total stranger on fire, what other evil things was he capable of? She pledged to sleep lightly…if she could sleep at all.

29

Julia spent the night cleaning in the lab, having long since sent the students to bed. She went back to Stephen's house but couldn't sleep in her room. She waited on the front porch.

When Lupa saw she intended to stay up until the men returned, he helped her drape some mosquito netting around the swing. So far this year, the tiny pests had not come out in full force, but Julia was leery of falling asleep and being bitten all over.

Julia drifted in and out of sleep shrouded in the white netting. It was 5:30 a.m. when Stephen and Eduardo finally returned to the compound. When they drove into the clearing and the headlights hit her, she resembled a large cocoon. Having seen so many bizarre things during the night, the men's imaginations were running wild. As tired as they were, both men recoiled at the sight.

Julia threw open the netting, startling them again, as she raced out to meet them. She flew into Stephen's arms. Then she reached for Eduardo, who embraced her just as tightly in return. Lupa joined them and herded everyone into the kitchen.

Lupa set breakfast foods around the table, but they all ate sparingly.

Julia was anxious to hear the details of their night. In a half desperate, half quizzical tone she blurted, "Ok guys. I can't wait any longer, what did you find out there?"

Stephen nodded in agreement. "I know, I know." He patted her hand with one hand while he took a long drink from his coffee. "We found a mess. It was extraordinary and not in a good way. I have never encountered anything like it…" Stephen shook his head and eyed the faint light of morning through the kitchen window.

"I can hardly begin to describe it," Eduardo said, pale even with his olive complexion.

"Well, somebody had better start," Julia began helping Lupa clear the table, but he shooed her back to her seat in protest. Julia sat back down and crossed her arms before muttering indignantly, "Leave me home, worrying about whether you'll ever come back…" She finished in a sing-song manner, "…and then you come waltzing in expecting me to just let you keep it all to yourselves." She spoke firmly, "I don't think so. Spill it." And she slammed her hand on the table causing both Stephen and Eduardo to jump nervously.

Stephen took another sip of his coffee and licked his lips. He set the cup down, crossed his legs, locked his fingers together, and laid the tight fist in his lap. "Okay. Let me be brief and to the point. There were four men. Two were hanging in harnesses in the trees at a new staging area, and one was lying on the ground under them. We found a fourth man a little ways away where he had just started to cut the first buttress off a *mogno* tree. As I said before, they were a mess…actually gruesome…and when I cut them open...their internal organs were not there."

"Not there?" Julia's expression was incredulous.

Stephen nodded, looking away from her, "I should have said, 'not intact.' Not one organ was intact. Everything inside was like a bloody soup…what was left inside them. The men were…" he paused, trying to search for words to explain the condition of the men. "I'm not sure how to describe it…almost hollow…and…shrunken…" He thought for a moment and then nodded, "Yes, hollow and shrunken is the most accurate description I can think of."

"Yes, like mummies I've seen in museums," Eduardo added.

Stephen flexed his hands open a couple of times and nodded in Eduardo's direction, rocking a finger in agreement. "That is exactly how they looked. It also makes it a little easier to think of them as being long dead."

"Okay, okay. What else?" Julia was anxious for more information.

Stephen rose from the table and reached for his pipe. "I've never seen or imagined anything like it."

Julia irritably tapped her foot on the floor. "You already said that, Stephen."

"Yes, I suppose I did," he said absently. "But Julia, we didn't just find blood. These men expelled some of their body fluids."

"…and the smell…" Eduardo spoke softly. "It was like nothing I've ever smelled before."

Stephen filled the pipe with tobacco and took advantage of the pause to light it. He shook out the match and tossed it into the dish that served as an ashtray, and he sat again.

Julia tried hard to pull more information out of them. She couldn't get it fast enough. "Before you left you said there were some sort of stings on them. Do you know what stung them? Could it have been the ants?"

Stephen shook his head. "It could have been ants, but we need to keep our minds open to the possibility that one thing caused the stings and something different caused their deaths. I would rather not get our hypothesis stuck on ants alone. The stings could be from almost anything. Think of it as a tiny hole with severe swelling. I brought sample tissue with several bites from each man, so we should be able to isolate what type of insect it could be." Stephen sat back down crossing his legs. "I have never seen anything…" he caught himself, realizing he was repeating the same phrase.

"I thought about bees," Julia temporarily changed the conversation away from ants. "Bees have been known to kill. They can swarm by the hundreds. Killer bees, maybe?"

Stephen looked toward Eduardo, who neither looked up nor offered a reply. "I didn't see any indication of bees, no stingers left behind, but it doesn't mean there weren't any. What do you think, Eduardo?" Stephen asked as he chewed on his pipe.

Eduardo didn't look up from where he was staring. "I was thinking about other creatures which might be shrunken after being attacked."

Julia and Stephen looked puzzled. They looked at each other and then back at Eduardo. Neither had any idea what he was referring to.

"Spiders," Eduardo offered.

Stephen looked up and to the right in thought. "Spiders?" he echoed. "That would be highly unusual…but so are these circumstances."

Eduardo leaned forward and looked directly at him. "Think about how some spiders kill and eat their prey. A bug gets caught in a web or the spider chases it down. The spider grabs the prey and injects it with...with...something…?"

"Enzymes," Julia filled in.

"That's it," he snapped toward her, "enzymes." He frowned, "Then the spider just sucks the insides out. Correct?"

"Yes," Julia nodded. "Like the enzymes in our stomachs help dissolve the food we eat…" her words began to slow as they came out, "…spider enzymes dissolve the insides of the spider's prey."

Eduardo reached for his coffee cup and downed the last swallow, satisfied he might have contributed a clue to the mystery.

Stephen was deep in thought. "Did you see any evidence of spiders at the scene?"

Eduardo shook his head vigorously and put his cup back on the table. "I'm not saying it *was* spiders. Just offering some other ideas."

Julia picked up his train of thought. "I think I see where you're going with this." She moved to the edge of her seat facing Stephen, who sat back, content for her to continue since the science of it was not his forte. Julia was excited. "Let's follow through on your autopsy findings and think about nature." She patted Eduardo's leg, "That was good thinking, Eduardo. I hadn't thought of that before."

He looked at the hand patting his leg.

Julia withdrew it as the flicker of physical contact added to her tension. "We both know man has scarcely touched on all the creatures we have out there."

Eduardo thought, *speaking of touched…* He said aloud, “This could be something entirely new we haven’t encountered before, or maybe something evolving into something new. If spiders have the ability to dissolve their preys’ insides before eating them, what makes us think there isn’t something else out there that can do something similar?”

“Actually, it’s more than spiders with their soup trick. Spiders are arachnids. Most arachnids, eight legged invertebrate animals, around the world, inject enzymes or other toxins into their prey to turn the preys’ insides into mush. And it’s not just arachnids. Other bugs do the same.

“Bugs like…?”

“Oh, some types of water bugs, assassin bugs, which in America we call wheel bugs, robber bugs in Thailand, even the gentle lady bugs treat aphids the same way. The list goes on and on.”

Stephen took his pipe from his mouth and stood. “Quite. Let’s go to the common room and work on our board.”

Stephen was the first out, and Eduardo held the door open with one arm as Julia slipped on her shoes. She looked up at him when she passed through the door, blushing at the thought of her hand on his leg.

“Come, come,” Stephen threw back their way as he moved decisively down the path.

“Coming,” Julia’s retort rang out as she trotted to catch up with him.

Eduardo’s long legs played catch-up. He was almost even with them when Charlie and Jennifer emerged from their room looking as if neither had any sleep. Alexis emerged from her door as they passed, and the group of six came together like a deck of cards being shuffled.

Kosey was just finishing an early morning shower. “I will be right there,” he called as he toweled off.

Lupa was already inside preparing breakfast.

“Has anyone seen anything of our wayward pair?” Stephen asked, referring to Nigel and Drake as the students gathered plates of food and settled around the table.

Everyone shook their heads but no one commented.

Stephen looked pointedly at Charlie and Jennifer. “Anything you two want to tell us?”

They looked up and then shook their heads.

“Very well.” Stephen thought he caught a sideways glace between them, but then faced the board and scanned the clues as Kosey slipped into the room.

Eduardo resolved not to ask any more questions right now. They had more important things to do than worry about the absent professor and his assistant. People were dying.

As Stephen explained the second set of deaths, the students were taken aback. He went over the earlier discussion with Julia and Eduardo so everyone had the same information before the group started their brainstorming session.

"Okay, let's see what we can do about solving this mystery." Stephen handed Kosey and Alexis each a stack of paper and a marker

"Okay, let's start with 'shrunken,' Alexis. Write it big," he pointed down to the paper.

She wrote the word on the paper, picked it up, and turned.

Jennifer jumped up, took the paper from Alexis and taped it on the board with the other clues.

"Kosey, write 'spider.' Alexis, 'digestive enzyme.'" He looked to Julia and Eduardo, "What else?"

Julia prompted, "Stings."

Alexis wrote and handed it to Jennifer.

They wrote more and handed the pages to Jennifer as the ideas flowed.

The group started throwing words:

"Ant."

"Bee."

"Mosquito."

"Wasp."

The ideas were coming fast. Jennifer had trouble keeping up until the barrage had slowed. Finally she stood back, and they looked at the list.

Stephen cleared his throat and pointed at the board. "Okay, let's go back to the bees. The more I think about it, this could have been some of the killer bees."

"Yes, but you said there were no stingers left in the wounds," Julia reminded him.

Stephen thought a moment before nodding, "Perhaps I should do another check."

"I don't have much knowledge of killer bees. Does anyone know if their poison causes blood cells to explode and internal organs to go to mush?" Julia asked looking around the room.

Only Stephen responded. "I don't think so, but remember what Eduardo said. Think nature, not what man already knows. Nature mutates and evolves. Something could have changed drastically."

"Cross a killer bee with a spider and what do you get?" Eduardo pondered.

"Precisely. Or cross a killer bee with another type of injecting creature." Stephen said.

"You've got to be kidding." Charlie tossed a smirk in their direction.

Stephen was serious. "Think about it. We know our forests are changing more rapidly now than throughout all history, even in the old, untouched rainforests. Carbon dioxide gas levels are rising faster than ever. And no one really knows how deeply those changes are affecting our atmosphere, oceans, and land. Those changes, by mankind *and* the natural order are affecting all organisms of the rainforests."

Julia interrupted as an aside, “For that matter, we haven’t put much thought into how it’s affecting the human race either.”

“You’re right, my dear. Only yesterday, you said as you’ve gotten older, you have developed more allergies. Perhaps it has nothing to do with getting older.”

“Yeah. Maybe what’s been triggering my allergies has gotten stronger.”

Stephen nodded, “Quite possible. Strange things could be going on which haven’t yet been detected. Things which might not manifest themselves for some time.”

Julia looked at Stephen. “Maybe those higher CO2 levels are affecting some of the insects. Making them stronger. Deadlier.”

Stephen nodded. “Could be,” was all he said. “What else?”

Alexis muttered, “Maybe it’s our immune systems which are changing.”

“Our immune systems?” Stephen angled his head to one side as he evaluated the thought.

“I don’t mean building up immunities. I mean maybe our immune systems are somehow turning against us.” Alexis was becoming more vocal and involved.

Stephen agreed, “Well, it certainly could be a possibility. It happens with things like AIDS and HIV. Nasty happenings when the immune system turns against itself.”

“Turns against itself?” Kosey looked startled.

“Yes. Our immune system tries to do the right thing. You get a cold, and it kicks into action trying to overcome the virus. But in trying to do the right thing, sometimes it overreacts. It can make your life miserable. With something like AIDS you literally become allergic to yourself. Your immune system turns against you.”

“It is hard for *me* to avoid *me*!” Kosey spoke wide-eyed.

“Exactly. That is an interesting premise, Alexis,” Stephen said. “Write that down please.” *Could our immune system be reacting differently to stings that otherwise might not be lethal*? Stephen needed to think about it.

Julia opened her mouth to speak but then stopped.

Stephen noticed. “What were you thinking, Julia?”

“I was thinking of a study I read about just the other day. One of my colleagues was concentrating on a theory of incremental exposure to environmental toxins which build to a deadly threshold. Some scientists theorized the critical threshold then resulted in an explosive disease. Could that have killed the loggers?”

“But why didn’t it kill the boy playing nearby who found them?” Alexis asked. “According to the boy, he went over right after the saw went silent.”

"Exposure over time," Julia reminded. "Maybe the men had never been exposed to…whatever it is…and maybe the boy was exposed over time so he built up immunity."

Stephen wasn't sure they were on the right path, but he would consider the theory. "Write it down, Kosey. We'll consider everything until we rule it out." He stood and began to pace. "It is possible the mechanism could be a toxin isolated to the forest canopy environment and either was injected by insects or airborne for short distances by spores. That might explain why only the loggers were affected. Write down spores, Kosey."

"But what about us?" Julia asked. "We were out there yesterday climbing in the same spot as the first men who died. Nothing happened to us."

Stephen shrugged, "No. Not yet. Maybe spores are expelled at certain times and not at others. Perhaps we should not climb in the canopy until we have some more answers." He frowned and stared at the paper that held the clue 'critical threshold toxin' and began to shake his head. "You can take that one down, Kosey." He pointed at the clue.

"Why is that?" Julia asked.

"I don't believe that could be the case. What about the animals? We haven't found any dead animals, and they live in the canopy," Stephen said.

"Maybe they are immune." Kosey felt protective of Julia's theory.

"I would think it unlikely everything out there would be immune except man," Stephen said. "Just take it down for now, Kosey. Set it aside, and keep it for later in case we decide the idea is credible."

That seemed to satisfy Kosey, who started a back-up pile, happy to put that self-destruction theory aside.

They started evaluating one item after another, adding details as they went, taking down others as they discounted them. When they got to the ants, they slowed down.

Stephen sat in a rocker next to the table. "Ants," he said as he gently moved back and forth, "are certainly an obvious insect to sting those men. And there are so many different kinds."

"Yes. And new species are being found all the time." Julia nodded.

Stephen reached for his pipe and then put it back. He stood instead, reached for Kosey's marker and wrote 'deadly toxin' on a sheet of paper and put it under 'ant' before he settled again.

Julia continued the ant discussion, "Some of the worst toxins known come from ants. The most deadly ant in this area of the world is the bullet ant. It's said they have the most painful sting of any insect in the world and one of the most toxic venoms. The bullet ant has been known to kill, but I have never heard of people bleeding out as they died. It would take probably a hundred stings or more to kill the men."

Eduardo nodded, "Those men easily had over a hundred stings."

Stephen added, "But the first men did not."

Kosey interjected: "I have read about jack jumper ants in Australia, and I know of *siafu* ants in Africa. Both can kill people, but the *siafu* ants go even further. They eat people!"

"You have *got* to be kidding." *How many times have I said that*! "What's with you people?" Charlie's sarcasm easily came through. He was well on his way to total disgust with the entire trip. Getting shot, sneaking in the jungle, and now trying to solve a bunch of murders. *Take this one off the Frommer's Guide to Exotic Vacations list.*

"Wow," Jennifer attempted to soften Charlie's comment. She gave him a stern look of disapproval. "I never even heard of them."

Charlie raised an eyebrow at her but said nothing. It was all he could do to sit there without screaming, *Just get me the hell out of here*!

Eduardo let out a loud yawn and stretched his long arms skyward. "I've had it. I'm beat."

Julia knew both men needed some sleep. For that matter, so did she. She had dozed in the swing shortly before they arrived, but the thought of lying in her own bed was drawing her like a magnet toward the house.

"Mind if I grab a few hours of sleep on the cot in the lab?" Eduardo asked.

"Help yourself. The students are going into the forest with Lupa, so they should be gone for quite a while," Stephen replied as he pushed himself up from the rocker. "I find it hard to sleep in the daytime, but today, I doubt I'll have any trouble at all."

They all looked at the scattering of notes on the board. It resembled a display of third grade students' work, with their scribbling and papers hanging haphazardly. Somewhere among the notes might be the answer to these deaths; giant puzzle pieces waiting to take form.

Julia, Stephen and Eduardo walked back up the path toward the house and lab, and each headed off for bed.

Immune system, was on Stephen's mind as he drifted into sleep.

Julia couldn't fall asleep. It could have been the earlier nap or the daylight, but more than anything, she was obsessed with the thought of ants. She kept visualizing ants crawling in the canopy where they collected specimens at the first death site.

Her thoughts drifted to a study she recently reviewed documenting stink ant behavior in an African rainforest in Cameroon. Ants have been a part of rainforests for as long as they have been on Earth, and that extended timeframe had allowed many unusual and complex relationships to develop among its inhabitants.

Details of the study were coming back to her, as fresh as if she had actually observed the ants herself. *Maybe it is still on my hard drive…* Julia pulled her computer onto her lap and searched for several minutes before she found the report.

Like the last report she read, this one was also written as an observation. Julia pictured the researcher hiking through the rainforest to a location she had visited every day for several weeks.

The woman winds along the path and stops at the same spot she has been observing each day. She finds the scene set as expected. There is a large, black ant hanging high on a blade of grass, the same as yesterday. She knew it would still be in the same spot and position. She unpacks her magnifying panel, settles onto her stool and focuses her attention on the ground below the ant.

She scatters tiny shavings from an apple over the ground below the hanging ant and waits. It doesn't take long for a stink ant to arrive, its name derived from the strong odor it emits, even stronger if it is smashed. It is among a handful of ants on Earth which makes a cry audible to the human ear.

The ant lives by foraging for food among the fallen leaves and undergrowth. This ant searches at an agitated pace. The woman watches as it finds the apple and eats it. Her eyes shift to the ant hanging on the grass. The ant moving about does not look up and doesn't see the mirrored image of itself hanging lifeless above.

Then it happens. The woman sees a quick orange puff spurt into the air above the hanging ant. The orange cloud settles around the ant dining below. The woman has previously documented what is now happening once again. The ant on the ground is breathing in the tiny orange spores. Now, it is infected.

The woman knows a single spore will travel to the ant's tiny brain. It sets up its home there and gets to work. The spore begins growing into a fungus. Within a short period of time, the fungus causes changes in the ant's behavior, causing the ant to become troubled and confused. For the first time in its life, the ant leaves the forest floor and begins to climb.

The woman has observed that occasionally, an infected ant will embark on a long and exhausting climb. It might climb a tall tree, reaching a great height. Most times, like this ant, it merely climbs a tall blade of grass and clamps its mandible into the soft tissue. Then the ant waits. Unknowingly, it is waiting to die. This way of dying is common in some sections of the forest. For the fungus, it is the stink ant's reason for existing.

The fungus continues to grow. It first feeds on the nerve cells, and then it moves on to the soft tissue remaining within the ant. It consumes the ant until the ant is hollow…useless…dead.

The woman checks on the ant each day. On the fourteenth day, she arrives at the spot early. She waits and watches. Then she notices a change in the top of the ant's head. It is cracking open. Within a few hours, there is a bright orange tip protruding. The next day the prong is over an inch long and laden with spores.

Again, the woman has settled onto her stool with her magnifying panel. She sprinkles tiny shavings of apple on the ground next to the spot. She watches and waits. It does not take long for another ant to come. It too is a stink ant. She watches as a tiny orange colored puff is emitted from the prong in the head of the dead ant high on the blade of grass. Falling spores slowly settle around the unsuspecting ant below, and it breathes in an orange spore.

Julia gently closed the laptop and laid it on the floor next to the bed. Climbing under the sheet, she thought about the orange spores. She knew the human immune system kept the spores from growing in her own body. But they were there, nonetheless. What might happen should her immune system change? Could she one day have an orange spike protruding from her head?

In her mind Julia pictured her body…its nerve center gone…her zombie eyes staring at nothing…a ravaged, hollow body hanging from the branch of a tree…an orange halo of spores raining around her.

These were her lingering thoughts as Julia drifted off to an unsettling sleep.

30

Damn my head hurts! Actually, it felt like it was going to explode. Will placed his hands on each side of his head and pressed tightly before opening his eyes. Slowly the fog began to lift, and then he remembered. As the memories of what he had seen in the forest yesterday flooded back, Will felt he might be sick. Again.

After their wild ride out of the forest, Will dropped off the two confused and frightened men at the base camp. He knew they would be long gone by now, and he didn't care. All he was sure of was he had to block out the gruesome image of the horror he witnessed.

Will spent the afternoon and most of the night drinking in the canteen downstairs. He remembered ordering a bottle of *cacique*, a strong Venezuelan brand of rum which most Brazilians considered a national treasure. He poured the first glass and drank it straight. He drank another. Before he realized it, the bottle was near empty.

Will couldn't recall whether he finished the bottle or how he got to his room. The last thing he remembered was a beautiful woman pressing her warm body next to his at the bar. At least he thought she was beautiful. She could have been like a country song he had once heard. How did it go? At ten she was a two. By two she was a ten. Will grimaced. He could only guess what must have happened.

He glanced at the bedside table and swore under his breath. His wallet was gone. He felt under the back of the headboard and found the package taped securely. At least she only got some cash. All the important stuff was still there.

With that thought in mind, he climbed out of bed and headed for the shower, hoping there was hot water. As fate would have it, there wasn't. Regardless, he stayed under the cold spray a long time. He didn't have the energy to pull himself out. He looked down his body, half expecting to see blood flowing over it. He closed his eyes, trying to block out the forest memory, but quickly opened them when he realized closing them was worse.

Getting out of the shower, Will caught sight of the clothes he had worn yesterday. He never wanted to touch them again. He pulled a clean t-shirt and some shorts out of the battered chest of drawers at the foot of his bed and slipped slowly into them while he thought about his boss.

What was he going to tell Livingston? He hadn't called him yet. *Hell*, Will thought, *I don't even know what killed my men. It definitely wasn't a who.* All Will knew for sure was he didn't want to go back out there. He was ready to hang it up, and nothing Livingston could say would make him change his mind. He was finished with the logging business, legal or otherwise. After what he had seen, it wasn't worth it. He had enough money stashed away. And he'd tell Livingston that. Livingston Lumber didn't own him. *I have to find something safer to do for a livin'! For a livin'…livin' for what? What was out there livin' and causin' horrific death like he had seen?*

Safer to…. Was anything safe now? Will wasn't sure. He needed to know what happened out there, had to know because he wanted to make sure it didn't happen to him.

Then he thought of the jobs he had "taken care of" for Arthur. Why had the deaths he had witnessed of his men affected him so much worse than what he had done to all those families? Those children. How had they felt when they knew they were going to die? The idea of "Karma" was a joke to him before. Could he be weakening? He shrugged off the idea.

And what about Carlos? Damn shame losing him. Not only was Carlos a hard worker, but he had a wife and six kids. Will wasn't going to tell them their daddy was dead. He'd leave that to the authorities. Hopefully, the authorities would never make an identification. Even with a photo, Will knew Carlos didn't look like himself. Will had seen his face changing right before his eyes. His family might never know what happened to him.

He licked his dry and wrinkled lips, which felt like they were ready to crack in several places. He was thirstier than he could ever remember. He went to the closet and pulled out a gallon of water, turned it up and chugged it. He drank until the plastic sucked into itself and was half empty. Water dripped from his chin, and he wiped it with the bottom of his shirt, As he was putting the cap back on, the sound of yelling in the streets below drew him toward the window. He pulled the curtain to the side and looked out the dingy glass. At his knees, the small air conditioner hummed loudly and gave an occasional sputter. The coolness was the only reason worth coming to this hell-hole of a room.

Out the window he saw several women hanging out their wash on makeshift clothes lines. Dressed in bright colors with full skirts and low cut blouses, they looked pretty from here.

Three young children chased each other in and out of the hanging clothes, squealing laughter following them. One boy of about eight caught the legs of a pair of long pants on his upraised arms, pulling them free from the line as they flew past him to the ground.

One of the women grabbed them up, giving the child a stern rebuke. The boy ducked his head and fled up the narrow street. The other two, larger boys were clearly delighted it was not them getting into trouble. They made fun of the smaller boy, jumping and taunting, as the youngster fisted air around them.

Will smiled, but as quickly as the smile came, it was gone. The carefree moment was over in a heartbeat as he recalled the horror. He wanted to throw the window up and lean out. He wanted to shout an alarm for everyone to hear. *Get your children in the house. Lock your doors. Don't go out unless it's a matter of life and death.* The truth in Will's mind right now was that this *was* a matter of life and death, including his own.

He stood at the window unsure what he should do from here. He looked around the room and knew this was not where he wanted to be. His head was throbbing. He was still thirsty. More importantly, he was afraid to go out.

Will turned from the window and squeezed his eyes shut. He tried to convince himself that his head didn't hurt. He could make the pain go away. He took deep breaths telling the pain in his brain to leave. He pushed and rubbed against his temples. He opened his eyes and lowered his hands. His head still felt like it was coming off. *Is it just the alcohol, or is somethin' more sinister goin' on*?

He let out a long sigh and lowered his head. He needed to check on the men. Instead, he spoke aloud, "I need a drink."

Will took some tape out of a bag in the closet. He peeled the package off the back of the bed, pulled out some cash, and reattached the package.

As he opened the door to leave the room, he saw the phone. He really needed to call Livingston. For a long minute he considered making the call. Then he shook his head. Not now. He closed the door and locked it, not caring if it was late morning. Will needed a drink.

31

It was almost noon when Julia awoke. When she realized how late it was, she leaped out of bed and went to find Stephen. He was still sound asleep. She gave a tentative knock on his door and told him she would meet him in the lab.

Then she went out to wake Eduardo. His cot was empty, and Julia was surprised at how much it disappointed her for him not to be there.

That thought threw her attention back to the States, and Mitch. She'd finally contacted him yesterday, but he had been distracted. He was having a dinner meeting with an out-of-town client, and her conversation with him had been friendly but not warm as she had wished. Julia hung up the phone feeling dismissed and neglected. Oddly, she didn't feel disappointed. This was becoming the norm in their relationship, distant and detached.

The students were out with Lupa learning more about plants and herbs and roots, so Julia went to work. Alexis had put their storyboard into a spreadsheet and e-mailed it to Bill Miller, a statistician friend of Julia's. He planned to crunch some numbers and circulate the information among other members of his team for feedback. Maybe all the information would help them come up with a plausible theory as to what was happening.

Alexis had left a Post-it telling her Bill would call this afternoon. Julia needed to take the next few minutes to get her thoughts together, so she plugged in her laptop to review her notes.

She was on the phone a half hour later when Stephen arrived and quietly started working without interrupting her. Julia listened to Bill's interpretation of the data as she opened the refrigerator and pulled out the leftover fruit salad Lupa had made. She spooned out a plate for herself and Stephen. In another few minutes, she was finished with her call.

"And how is Bill?" Stephen asked without looking up.

Julia thought for a moment. "I think he's beginning to be a little worried. He mentioned contacting the CDC to send a team down here to help figure this out."

"Please stop him from doing that. E-mail him right now, please.

When we know more information, we'll reconsider. The last thing I want is more people in my lab. Relay that to Bill, and then get back to work, young lady," he said as he pointed to the door. "We have an abundance of work to do here."

The students returned from their outdoor excursion a solemn group. This new set of deaths had them all a bit anxious about being in the forest at all, so they stayed close to the compound on this outing.

Everyone was beginning to feel a sense of urgency now. A need to find an answer quickly. The killings were much too close.

Julia finished setting her microscope, and then she turned her attention to the testing that needed to be run. When Stephen and Eduardo made it back home earlier this morning, they had stuffed everything into the refrigerator. Julia tugged open the heavy door. Cool air spilled out around her legs as she lifted one of the boxes and placed it on the work table. It took a while for her to sift through all the new specimens.

"What's this?" Julia stared in bewilderment. She was holding up a vial.

"I told you when I opened the bodies for the autopsies there was not much there, but what was there was essentially a bloody soup. You're looking at what I drew out of one of them. That," Stephen raised an eyebrow toward the vial, "is their internal organs mixed with blood and body fluids and who knows what else." He answered in a quiet voice sounding as though he really didn't want to speak the words out loud.

"Nasty looking stuff," Charlie said over her shoulder.

Kosey looked over the other shoulder. "Like tomato soup, with swirls of cream in it."

"We can skip the menu metaphors if you don't mind," Julia said as she examined it.

One vial after another was pulled from the cooler and placed in four plastic vial trays, one for each man. The samples all looked basically the same. Julia and Stephen drew out test samples from each vial. They prepared slide after slide, passing them back and forth between each other, labeling each as to vial number, time of day, and cataloguing anything recognizable. Even though there wasn't much to record, they methodically recorded each individual sample.

Julia cast a glance toward the outside. Lengthening afternoon shadows fell across the windows as darkness came early under the dense rainforest canopy. Equipment screens around the room glowed in deep Earth tones and the lab felt eerie, giving Julia a chill.

In a low voice so Jennifer and Charlie couldn't hear, Julia said, "What do you think has happened to Nigel and Drake? Do you suppose they're okay?"

"Eduardo is checking around. We both believe they're into mischief."

"Huh. Interesting. I wonder what it could be," she looked

quizzically.

"We shall see. Have you noticed anything significant in the body samples?"

Julia sat back and reflected as Stephen stood and went to the sink to wash his hands. "It's hard to believe," she said where the others *could* hear. "I'm not finding much of anything. Certainly little identifiable as human."

She stretched her shoulders and stood, thinking about her work back in Georgia. Her work. Back there she was testing this and testing that. Mixing this and mixing that. Teaching classes. Grading papers. Sure it was exciting…sometimes, but all the things waiting for her attention at home right now seemed straightforward and structured compared to the mysteries down here. These were real lives impacted. Natural. And, events were uncontrollable.

"I can't think of anything comparable to what we've got here," Julia said gesturing toward the slides.

Stephen stood and wiped his hands on a clean, white towel. "There is much to consider. Sometimes I feel a little daft trying to think of all the possibilities."

He finished drying his hands and placed the towel back on the rack, straightening it neatly before he continued as much to himself as to Julia, "Maybe they got stung by an insect we don't know about. We know they were stung, but maybe they also ate a poisonous plant they thought was edible. Perhaps there are new parasites that have taken on the traits of spiders...there are so many combinations of possibilities and even more considerations we know nothing about."

He went to the window and stared out. "There is so much unknown in nature, Julia. Even in places where man has searched and searched, someone is always finding a new species of insect. A new epiphyte. A new frog or lizard. It could be anything." Stephen pondered the endless prospects.

For a few minutes no one spoke. The students had been listening intently to the discussion.

"Maybe it's something airborne?" Alexis speculated out loud.

Stephen shook his head. "I doubt it. Just think about it. There is the first little boy who found them. According to his account, blood started dripping from the bodies after he got there. They couldn't possibly have been dead long; otherwise, the bleeding would have happened earlier and subsided. No blood pooled in the legs of the men in the harnesses, even at that first site, so they must have bled extensively. Were it airborne, why was the little boy not affected?" Stephen asked matter-of-factly. "And then we have the villagers who saw the next group of bodies. No one was hurt."

"Yeah, you're right. Sort of a no brainer, isn't it?" Alexis sighed. "So much for my logical reasoning." Slightly embarrassed, she slumped and continued to work.

"No, please, keep giving your ideas. It's how we zero in on the answer. One question leads to another. One idea leads to another. We'll get there. Keep going. What else are you thinking?" Stephen was trying to be encouraging as he jotted down notes while they discussed the circumstances.

"I can't help but believe that it has a lot to do with the stings on their bodies. I just can't get it out of my mind." Julia sat back down before she bent back over the microscope.

Stephen nodded. "It is possible. I don't know if any of you know this, but a while back, a scientist discovered a single tree in Peru which was home to forty-three different species of ants. By all accounts, it's approximately the total number of ant species in my entire homeland."

Julia looked up. "Forty-three species," she muttered.

Charlie whistled while the others shook their heads.

Stephen turned again to gaze at the forest outside. "We'll make another trip to the site in the morning. Julia, you're welcomed to accompany us."

"What about us?" Kosey queried.

"You'll stay and continue testing. There isn't room for everyone in my jeep. Maybe Lupa can entertain you some more, if you finish. I'll speak to him about it. Just stay close to the compound."

"Don't worry. There's plenty to keep us busy," Alexis replied feeling a bit more confident that Stephen would allow them to stay behind unsupervised.

Stephen finished by saying, "And now you can all tidy up and head to the common room. Julia and I will finish up here."

Alexis, ever the adult of the students, offered, "I'll be happy to stay and work a while."

"No," Julia said. "We've got it covered, but thanks. Catch up on your e-mails."

Alexis nodded, "I have tons. The kids have been asking so many questions about my trip."

Julia and Stephen checked more slides while the students finished. In a matter of minutes, their areas were clean, and they were out the door.

After they left, Stephen said, "I do hope the rain holds off so we can wrap up our investigation."

"I want to see where it happened, and I also want to see the men." She said the words even though she wasn't certain it was actually true.

"I'll call Eduardo on the radio shortly and ask him to meet us out there if it's all clear. Seriously Julia, I don't want any of us to be in harm's way."

"Sounds good to me," Julia said as she guided another slide onto the stand.

Stephen picked up his half empty vials and carried them to the sink, where he ran hot water along with soap. He secured several samples from each man and put them back into the refrigerator before he glanced at Julia.

She stared intently through the microscope. She dipped her head even closer to the lens as though she was trying to force her eye deeper while turning the focus knob back and forth. Then her shoulders went down, and she grew very still.

Stephen watched and could tell she had found something. Her back grew straighter, and her eye squinted as she focused the lenses further. He leaned back against a counter in anticipation.

Then, Julia looked up at him. “Take a look at this slide, Stephen, and tell me if you see anything?”

Julia slid off the stool, and Stephen took her place. He adjusted both lenses so that he could see. “What am I looking for?”

“I don’t want to say. Just tell me if you see something.”

Stephen rubbed his eyes before readjusting the lenses back and forth. Then he saw it, and he became very still. *There you are. What are you*? A tiny blip pulsed to the left of the slide. He rubbed his eyes a second time and fixed them on it, again. He sat up and looked at Julia. “What can that be?”

Julia shrugged her shoulders and raised her eyebrows. “I don’t know. I was hoping you might recognize it.”

Positioning himself back over the microscope, Stephen looked again. Since this was a stereomicroscope with a mounted camera, he took a picture of…whatever it was. He’d blow it up for everyone to see. He’d also have to call some of his scientist friends and pass the word, or rather picture, around. But not quite yet. He wanted to know more before he let something like this out. He isolated it. Holding up the photograph, Stephen stared at it as he said, “Have you thought of a name, Julia?”

Julia frowned as she looked over his shoulder first at the picture and then at his profile. She watched as he nodded.

“We must give it a name, Julia. That’s our tradition when we discover something new.”

“A name?” She gave him a puzzled look.

“Face it, Julia. In all likelihood, you *have* discovered something new. I didn’t see it first. You saw it. So, what do you want to call it?”

Julia stared up toward the ceiling. Then she looked down. Naming something that could be so horrific wasn’t exactly something she wanted to be in charge of.

Stephen persisted. “I would bet my last quid if we sent this to every scientist on the internet, no one would have ever seen anything like it.” Stephen continued to move the picture around looking at it from every angle possible. He wished he had a confocal microscope, and then he could look at it three dimensionally. He would check around and see who might have one. "We need a logical name. Even a number will do…or perhaps a combination of the two."

Stephen looked over at his table of laboratory rats and had an idea. "Let's see if we can find another one. I want to see what happens if we inject it into one of those." He pointed to the rats and then began looking through more slides, while Julia tried to come up with a name. She wrote combinations of possibilities, crossing out one after the other. One by one she bounced off ideas, while Stephen offered his own suggestions.

It took an hour and a half before Stephen found another one. He isolated it for further study and then took the first one Julia found over to the cages. He already had a syringe ready and no qualms about testing with rats. Stephen told Julia a long time ago it was his belief that animal testing was why rats were put on Earth. What else could be their reason for being?

"Want me to film it?" she asked just as Stephen was about to make the injection.

He stopped and grimaced, "Yes. I should have thought of it myself. Try to remind me to film everything we do from now on, even those activities which seem mundane. Let's take the video and still cameras everywhere we go."

Julia was already grabbing the video camera, checking the batteries, and popping a fresh, mini DVD disk into it.

Stephen reached into one of the cages and grasped a rat. He held it by the neck as he waited for Julia to finish setting up the camera. "I have a feeling this is an extraordinary find, Julia." When Julia was ready, Stephen bent over the rat with the syringe. "Okay, little vessel," he said to the rat. "Here comes…" he paused and looked back at Julia. "Have we settled on a name?"

"We have," Julia replied. "Pulsating Anomaly Life-force." Julia bobbed her head once for emphasis. "PAL."

"PAL," Stephen repeated to himself. "Good name. Easy to remember. Ironic. Okay, little vessel, here comes your PAL."

Stephen injected the small rodent, put him back into his cage, and secured the door. Within moments, the rat began to move. First, it was a twitch. Then its legs began to tremble. Then, its eyes rolled back in its head, and it began to shake uncontrollably. The rat cried out only once before it began to bleed from its mouth. It continued like it would never stop.

Stephen couldn't find his voice. *Who could imagine an animal so small could have so much blood*? The red fluid gushed, turned into a milky substance, and in front of their eyes, the little animal deflated. *Where's all the liquid coming from*?

Julia stepped back in horror. Stephen followed suit. In less than fifteen seconds, the small rodent was still. Before them lay a fur-covered skeleton. Most of the rat's blood and body fluids were in the bottom of the cage. Neither Stephen nor Julia could move. The whole process had been quick, violent, and final.

Julia was shaken. "Stephen…what…what…" She thought she would faint. She had never experienced something so brutal in her life.

Stephen reached for her with the pretense of helping her to a chair. Actually, he needed some steadying himself. Watching the rat die had been the most gruesome thing he had ever seen. *Is that what happened to the men in the jungle*?

Stephen went to his desk in the corner and grabbed a bottle of cognac. Before he poured a small glass for Julia, he poured one for himself and downed it. He steadied Julia's hands as she cupped the glass. He rubbed her back, as she began puffing for air. Stephen took the glass from her and poured another, but she brushed it away.

As for Julia, she was working hard to control herself. She fought the urge to scream. Her mind was whirling. *How contagious is it*? *What if it has gotten into us*? *Where has it come from*? *How did it get into those men*? *Is it a mutation*? The questions churned through her mind, but she was too shaken to find her voice. Her voice was almost inaudible when she spoke, "PAL is out there, Stephen."

Then she swung her gaze all around. "No…maybe it's in here." She was shuddering and beginning to sweat.

She rushed to the sink, dousing her arms with liquid soap and scrubbed hard. "We don't know what it is or where it comes from or where it will go next! We don't know anything except it kills in less than a minute, and it's awful! There's no time to get help!"

She halted abruptly and faced him, hands in the air, water and soap streaming down and dripping from her elbows. "There is no antivenin..." She looked toward the door, "What can it be, Stephen?! What?" She was on the verge of panic.

Stephen reached for a towel and quickly dried her. He knew the words held little comfort for either of them, but he said them anyway, "We are safe, Julia." In truth, he was still unnerved.

Julia acted as though she hadn't heard him. She pulled away and wrung her hands. Each sentence coming out in exaggerated breaths. "One minute you're here, and the next minute you're gone. No time to think. No time to call out." She halted openmouthed, "What are we going to do?" She stood like a child with her hands on her hips trying to calm herself before coming to a decision. "We must warn people…" She grabbed Stephen's shoulders, her voice rising in desperation. "Call Eduardo! Get the students and Lupa away from here! We have to get *everyone* away!" She frantically looked around. "But where? Where will we be safe?" Julia began to back away.

Stephen caught her and sat her back down. He shook her gently but firmly. "Calm down, Julia. Don't be frightened. We're all safe. If not, we would already be dead. Think about it. We handled the serum without gloves. We breathed around it for hours. It…will…not…harm us."

The cage was only a few feet away. Julia straightened her back and pointed a shaky finger toward the white rat lying in the red pool. "It will not harm us? How can you say that after what just happened? It will not harm us?" She jerked toward Stephen and hissed just inches from his face. "I don't believe you!" Julia was becoming unglued.

Stephen continued trying to reassure her. "We will be more careful from now on, but trust me. It's not airborne. It's not highly contagious. Stop and think about it. I injected it directly into the blood stream. As a precaution, we'll wear gloves and masks when handling the serum from now on. We won't let the students handle any of the body fluids."

Julia began to take deep breaths, blowing them out hard, trying not to hyperventilate although unconsciousness seemed like a better place to be.

Stephen put his arms around her.

Julia leaned against him. A tear started streaming down her cheek. "Will we really be fine?"

For the second time in twenty-four hours, Stephen reassured Julia with the words, "We will be fine," hoping he was right both times.

32

Julia and Stephen sat outside in silence on the porch steps. Their thoughts were still reeling from what they just witnessed.

Eduardo drove up, catching sight of the two sitting side by side. They barely looked up and neither one greeted or even acknowledged him.

Eduardo joked as he climbed out of the jeep. "If I remember correctly, there is an American saying which goes something like, 'You both look like you just lost your best friend.' Did I get it right, Julia?"

Julia looked away.

Stephen coughed a little. "You might say we found something major, Eduardo, but," he held his breath as he looked back toward the lab, "we're not quite sure what we found."

"Oooo, you are sounding mysterious, jungle doctor," quipped Eduardo, trying to lighten the mood. His banter was lost on the two sitting on the steps. As Julia reached to run her hand through her hair, he noticed her fingers were trembling.

"Say," he squatted in front of her. "What is it?" He took her hands in his and looked at her intently. Without thinking he pulled her into his arms and held her tightly.

It was almost too much for Julia. She buried her face in his shoulder but didn't cry. Instead, she drew in long deep breaths, determined not to lose control. As she breathed in the scent of Eduardo, she quivered.

Eduardo thought she was going to cry. "Shhh. It's okay." He nudged her away from him and waited for her to tell him what happened.

"We found something," was all she said in a thin childlike voice.

Eduardo looked up at Stephen, who had risen to his feet and climbed into a rocker so Eduardo could sit next to Julia. Stephen nodded in agreement as he pulled out his pipe and filled it.

"Well, what did you find?" Eduardo's mood shifted as he sensed the anxiety.

Stephen and Julia each waited for the other to say something. Neither did. The only sound was the whirling of insects, an occasional screech of a monkey, and several macaws calling out from a tree nearby.

Finally, Julia said, "We found what must have caused those men to be…'shrunken'…as you called it."

"Well…?" He looked from Julia to Stephen, who was puffing his pipe and rocking gently, looking for all practical purposes like a kindly grandfather with not a care in the world.

"We call it PAL," Stephen replied around his pipe. "Short for Pulsating Anomaly Life-force," he explained as he stood. "I will be right back," he said as he stepped down the stairs between the two. He headed for the lab, returning almost immediately with the video camera. He fumbled with it a minute before he got the side panel open and turned it on.

"See for yourself." Stephen handed the camera to Eduardo and climbed the steps, settling back into his rocker.

Eduardo adjusted the volume as loud as it would go and then watched the tiny screen. He could hear Julia in the background as she adjusted the lens. He watched as objects went in and out of focus, and then Stephen's face filled the frame. The camera zoomed out, and he could see a rat's cage on a table next to Stephen, who was patiently waiting for her to finish with the camera settings.

Eduardo listened to Julia's voice fill with laughter as she said, 'Okay, I'm ready.' He was still smiling as he watched Stephen hold the rat. "What are you injecting?"

"Watch," was all Stephen said. He drew in on the pipe and blew a large cloud toward the ceiling.

Eduardo impatiently waited for something to happen, moving his face closer to see more detail. And then it happened. His eyes widened as the rat violently shook, and he pulled back when he saw the small rodent spewing blood. When the screen went black, Eduardo handed the camera to Julia. She turned it off and closed the panel.

"*Maldição…*" Eduardo said softly. He shook his head and looked out into the forest as he repeated, "*Maldição…mas que diabos*?" He took the camera back from her. "Where do I turn it on?" he asked.

Julia showed him, and then she got up and walked over to the swing.

Eduardo watched it again. When the tiny animal was finished, he hit the pause button. He turned the camera a little sideways like he was trying to see around the rat.

"You can see it in the lab. I haven't moved it yet," Stephen said. "I needed a little air."

Eduardo was still looking at the screen. "This is from the blood samples?"

"Indeed," Stephen nodded.

"That PAL you found and what it did to the rat must have been the same thing that happened to the men," Eduardo muttered as he scrutinized Stephen.

Stephen muttered, "It is precisely what happened to them. Did you see how the rat looked at the end?"

Julia looked up at Stephen, "Like a furry mummy?"

Stephen nodded in agreement, "Like a furry mummy." He sat pensively for a moment, and then continued. "Whatever this is…" Stephen peered into the jungle, "…it is evolving."

"Evolving?" both Julia and Eduardo asked at the same time.

Stephen murmured. "Yes, evolving."

He described the cracked vessels he saw with the first victims. He held up his hand to Julia when she started to protest because he had not revealed this detail to her before. "Look, love, since I did not know what was going on, I saw no point in bringing up a detail that may not have been relevant," he said gently.

Julia appeared to have something to say but kept it to herself.

Stephen continued, "The first bodies still had all the internal organs intact, but some had cracks in the linings. In the latest men, the linings of all the internal organs were completely gone, so the cracks progressed exploding the cells and the linings. It has been less than a week between deaths. Whatever is out there is apparently changing at an incredible rate of speed."

"I find it curious," Julia spoke when he finished. "This PAL has only affected those two groups of people. They are all native people. There are plenty of others around who could also have been in the same area." She was much more composed now, shaking off the earlier shock of watching the rat die so violently.

Eduardo puffed out a long, low breath. *Man*, he thought, *I don't like what I have to tell them*. From far away, he heard the cry of a jaguar. It sounded lonely…like it was looking for company. Eduardo felt a little sorry for it, understanding that he and the big cat had something in common. As he stood he shoved his hands in his pockets and faced Stephen and Julia. He appeared to have something else on his mind.

An anticipated silence filled the porch as they waited for him to speak.

"I got a call today," hesitating he bit his lower lip as he glanced from one to the other. "The closest police patrol is a little over two hundred kilometers away. My friend Juan is one of two officers watching over that area." He walked over next to the porch and leaned against the railing. He brushed a small ant off the top of the rail before he placed his palm on it. "We have more bodies."

Julia bolted upright, about to leap off the swing, "How many? In what condition?"

Stephen was on his feet. "When did it happen?"

Eduardo answered their questions in rapid succession. "Juan and his men have the three bodies in a cooler in their village. From his description, it sounds like they died the same way our men died. You know, shrunken and all. It also seems they died at about the same time as our latest group." There. It was out.

Julia had risen from the swing, "I'll get the sampling bags ready."

Stephen automatically reached for the door, "We need to get there. I'll grab…"

"Wait a minute," Eduardo's voice stopped him before he went inside. With a sternness that was not his ordinary style, he caught Julia's arm and held it before she could move down the steps. "Both of you. Stop." Their eyes locked. "I've already scheduled to fly us there first thing in the morning. We don't have enough daylight left today, and there are no landing lights at the airport. It can wait through the night. We'll go tomorrow."

Stephen closed the door and lowered himself back into his seat. Ever so quietly he mumbled, "More… than… two hundred… kilometers… away."

Julia looked down at Eduardo's hand still touching her bare skin.

Lupa came onto the porch carrying a tray filled with *linguica*, Eduardo's favorite sausage dish. "We eat on porch tonight. Lupa tell others in afternoon." He carried it to the far corner of the table and set it down. "Lupa make fried polenta cakes. You stay, Eduardo."

Eduardo released Julia, who moved back to the swing.

"Thank you, Lupa. I think I will…" Eduardo eyed Julia as Lupa turned and went back into the house.

The students strode up the path.

Lupa came out a moment later with an oil lantern and another tray. He hung the lantern above the table, lit it, and finished setting out the plates and food.

"Just one more," he said moving past Stephen. Lupa stopped and looked at him. "You okay, Stephen?" he asked, a look of concern on his face.

Neither Julia nor Eduardo had been paying attention to Stephen the last few moments. When they turned toward him, even in the pale light, it almost looked as if he were in pain.

Julia was next to Stephen at once. "The news of the new deaths is troubling, but is there something more you haven't told us?"

"What new deaths?" Charlie asked as the group came closer. They stood at the base of the stairs listening.

The seconds ticked by as Stephen slowly turned to face Julia. His face melted a little as he looked at her. "You do realize what this means, my dear."

Julia's eyebrows pulled together in thought. "The new deaths?"

He nodded his head.

She pondered what he meant. "Do you mean because they are two hundred kilometers away?"

He nodded again.

Julia looked away. What was the coincidence of both deaths happening at the same time? Her head reeled back toward Stephen, who continued to nod but still said nothing, as her eyes grew large at the realization. The PALs had not only evolved…they were spreading.

33

Will was staggering. It had been fifty-six hours since the nightmare in the forest, but as far as he was concerned, time stood still. He opened the door to his room and stumbled toward the bed. He sat down and then fell backward onto the mattress, springs squeaking loudly as he hit. He lay there a few minutes, almost drifting off to sleep before he heard voices in the hallway and turned his head toward the sound. The door was wide open.

"Whoops," he said as he snorted and pulled himself upright. Well, he wasn't exactly straight. Actually, he was listing, like a ship taking on water. He thought he might capsize before he could make it to the door. He fell hard against the wall and leaned against it for a while before deciding his head had stopped spinning enough to move again. He reached around and took hold of the knob.

Just as he was about to shut the door, a beautiful woman put her hand against it. Will's eyes were drawn to the front of her blouse which was open so he could see mounds around cleavage. There was pink lace slightly exposed, and he smelled a light scent like flowers. Another time he may have been taken in by her appearance, but even after a day and a half of drinking he still couldn't rid himself of the image of Carlos and the others dying their horrible deaths. He had no interest in the woman's company.

Will looked at her face. He tried to decide if she could be the woman from last night. *Hell, never mind*, he thought. He just couldn't remember. *She is a little pretty*, he told himself. But he put the thought out of his mind. Will made a conscious decision, which for him right now was a miracle in itself. He wasn't going to have anything to do with the woman standing before him.

He opened his mouth as the woman asked in very good English, "Would you like some company?"

He stared at her for a moment. He peered closer and frowned. *What is it about her mouth*? He noticed her lipstick wasn't on straight. He blinked and tried to clear his mind by shaking his head. As he squinted and tipped a little closer trying to focus better, the woman took this as an invitation.

"Well, are you going to let a lady in?" She asked the question with a slight pout on her face. She put her hands on her hips and shook her breasts a little. "Or am I more woman than you can handle?"

For the first time, Will noticed her make-up was thick and looked as if it had been painted on. *How old is she*? Will thought, as revulsion raced through him. "You gotta be kiddin'," Will said as he started to shut the door.

She caught it with her foot and tried to push the door back open. "Please, sir," her voice rasping as she pleaded desperately, "I need money." She glanced down the corridor as though she were expecting someone else.

Will stuck out his head looking back and forth with her. There was no one in sight. Will moved back in and tried to shut the door again. "Look, I'm not interested. Find someone else to get your money." His head was still pounding as though it was about to explode. Will thought, *I think I might be havin' a stroke*.

"But sir..." This time she tried to force herself inside.

"I said, 'No!" Will shouted as he slammed the door. He leaned his ear against it so he could hear her leave.

She rattled the handle and then slapped the door hard as she cursed in Portuguese.

Will waited until her angry footsteps receded down the hall. He stared at the desk and saw the bag with his overseas phone. He looked blearily at his watch and realized Livingston might still be in his office, since he sometimes stayed long after his employees departed. Between the pain and the *cacique* he had been drinking, he had enough courage to make the call.

Will was sure Livingston would be angry and had probably been calling all day. He walked over and picked up the case. He sat back down on the bed, pulled out the phone, and laid it on his lap. Powering up the phone, he punched key number one, drawing in a deep breath as he pressed 'call'.

Maybe he won't be there. It rang once. Twice.

On the third ring, Livingston answered, "Will, is that you?"

At first Will couldn't answer.

"Will? Are you there?"

He cleared his throat. "Mr. Livingston?" He sounded goofy, and he knew it but he didn't care.

"What the hell is going on, Will? Where have you been?" Livingston sounding agitated.

Yep, Livingston's angry. Will giggled.

Arthur's speech then slightly restrained: "Hey, Will. Are you there?"

"Yeah, I'm here."

This time, Arthur shouted, "Well, what the hell is happening?"

Will ran his hand through his wiry, brown hair as he tried to concentrate. He had to pick his words carefully. He snickered again. "I don't even know where to start."

Arthur cocked his head. "Have you been drinking, boy?" He looked at his watch. "Hell, boy. It's not even six o'clock there. Don't tell me you've been drinking *and* working. How does that look to your men? And don't tell me they're drinking with you!" Arthur's anger boiled over.

Will couldn't stop himself. Everything he had been through in the last couple of days had bottled up into an explosion of words tumbling out, "Look, Mr. Livingston, I'm not with my men, but hell, yes, I've been drinkin'. And I'm gonna go back down in a few minutes and drink some more. I might never stop. And I'll tell you another thing," his voice rose as he stood, as if by standing, he could show this opponent he was ready to fight, "I am finished. You hear me? I'm not goin' back out there. You got it?"

Arthur pulled his head away from the phone almost as if he had been slapped.

As for Will, he was ready, his confidence stoked by fear and booze. Livingston had no idea what he'd been going through. He was sitting there in his nice posh office, and he had no idea of the horror happening below the equator. And even if he knew, Will knew his boss wouldn't care.

Arthur had never heard Will like this. Their last call had been difficult, but this was worse. *Who does the little pip-squeak think he's talking to anyway*?

"Let me tell you something, Will Thompson," Arthur growled into the phone, his voice holding a hint of menace. "I don't know what the hell is going on, but I'll give you ten seconds to get yourself under control, and then we'll start this conversation over."

Arthur's tone took Will by surprise. He stood up a little straighter sobering slightly. Maybe he should rethink the things he wanted to say to his boss or at least his delivery. Livingston was not a nice man, and he had people everywhere.

Will carried the phone with him to the window. Looking outside, he saw the children from yesterday playing in the alley. Everything looked normal. *Yeah, I remember thinkin' the same thing before all hell broke loose.*

"Okay…" Will spoke back into the phone, this time a little more controlled. He blinked and stared at nothing as he said, "I've lost Carlos and three other men."

"Lost them?" Livingston sounded confused.

"Yeah…"

"What do you mean, you lost them?" Arthur was having trouble understanding what the boy was talking about.

"They're all dead."

34

No one had seen Nigel or Drake for two days. Jennifer and Charlie huddled together in one hammock listening to the night sounds, waiting to hear the two fumbling around in the common room. This time it was Charlie who picked up on a noise that was not of the jungle. The light touch of metal on metal had him pulling his good arm out from under Jennifer and making his way to the cracked door. He had made sure the hinges were well lubricated earlier so they would give no sound when he opened it. *Why the hell am I here*? *And with these damn psychos*? was becoming his theme song. He moved alone, down low toward the common room.

Nigel and Drake were indeed home, although it looked like not for long. Charlie crept across the path and ducked under the low wooden wall of the common room. He could easily hear them whispering through the screen above.

"Don't forget the ricin," Drake said.

"Shut up," Nigel snarled. "What if someone hears you, you imbecile?"

"Who's going to hear me? They're all asleep. And soon, it will be permanent. And stop calling me stupid."

Nigel grabbed Drake and snatched his arm hard. "I told you to shut up!" his voice and grip getting tighter with each word.

Drake jerked his arm away. "That hurt, Nigel." He rubbed where he knew a bruise would appear.

"Oh boo-hoo. I'm sooo sorry," mewed Nigel. "Now, where's the coffee?" He was reaching into his backpack for the jar of poison.

Earlier today, Nigel finished making the ricin. After three days of waiting for the poison to be ready, he used a coffee filter and removed as much of the acetone as possible. He repeated the filtering process five times with a new one. When he was finished, he had the perfect poison to kill everyone in the compound, the loggers, and anyone else in his way. It was such a sport to him.

Drake handed him the ricin can, and Nigel found a small bowl. He poured out some of the coffee and sprinkled the ricin over the dark flakes.

He handed the poison back to Drake, "Put the top back on and be careful. We wouldn't want anything to happen to you, now would we?" The sarcasm wasn't lost on Drake.

Drake glanced at Nigel in the dark. Before he replaced the lid he quickly poured a little into a plastic bag. He was getting tired of being treated like an idiot and a flunky. Drake handed him back the jar of poison.

Nigel returned the ricin to his bag and picked up the other bag filled with food.

"You have the explosives?" Drake asked.

Nigel stared at the younger man and his thoughts grew darker than the night. *When can I kill you*?

Drake knew he was mad. "Sorry," he whispered.

Nigel shoved him toward the door.

Drake held onto the zipper bag that contained the ricin. After another heated exchange with Nigel yesterday he decided that he might be in trouble with his mentor. Even the thought of Nigel trying to kill him entered his mind, so he'd started being very careful with his food and water, making sure Nigel never had access to it. Drake knew he had been pushing the professor's buttons, and he didn't know exactly how far the old man would go. He could kill a stranger with little regard, so why not him too? Drake shoved the bag into his jeans' pocket and grabbed his backpack and the other bag of food.

They were out the door and headed back into the jungle.

Jennifer crouched and ran to where Charlie was squatting.

He told her to wait and he scurried around the corner.

"Where are you…?

He waved her quiet. He returned in a moment and grabbed Jennifer's hand as they ran to follow the two men, now enclosed in the dark foliage. One of the men had turned on a flashlight, so it was easier to follow them this time. It was apparent they were getting more brazen in their travels, since no one had accosted them in their movements up to this point.

They walked for over an hour when Charlie realized they were headed for the same camp as before. He turned back to Jennifer who had trouble keeping up. She was breathing hard, so he stopped for a moment, "They're going to the same camp."

Jennifer stood still trying hard to catch her breath, "How…do you…know?"

"I recognize the path. I know it sounds crazy, but I recognize some of the downed trees and that last big chunk of rocks I stumbled over was the same one as last time. Besides," he showed her the GPS, "this tells me we are on the same path. Come on." He grabbed her hand and pulled her forward.

They walked silently along the trail until they heard low voices. Nigel and Drake were just up ahead. Charlie drew Jennifer off the trail when he saw a banyan tree, its stilt-roots easy to grasp and climb. He boosted Jennifer as high as he could, and she was soon settled about five feet off the ground in a crevice large enough for both of them. Charlie shimmied up after her and handed her a bottle of water from his backpack.

Charlie noticed there was movement in the camp just a short distance away. Obviously, they were planning to get an early start as several men were moving around the equipment.

Jennifer was exhausted and fought the urge to sleep. At that point she didn't care about spiders or other insects. Charlie motioned with his finger on his lips and then pointed that he was going to get a closer look. He saw that Nigel and Drake stopped to rest before their next assault on the loggers.

Charlie returned to the banyan and settled in next to Jennifer. His shoulder ached from the climbing, so he popped one of the pain pills Stephen had given him, took a long drink of water, and closed his eyes.

* * *

The explosion almost threw them out of the tree. Jennifer clutched at the limb under her and started screaming. Charlie shook her vigorously until she stopped.

"Be quiet!" he shushed.

Jennifer oriented herself and remembered what they were doing. "I'm so sorry," she said, truly upset by her outburst.

She looked toward the source of the explosion and saw a bulldozer was on fire, appearing like a giant torch in the darkness. A man hung halfway out of the cab, flaming bright gold and blue. At least part of him was there. Jennifer let out a gasp loud enough to be heard.

* * *

On the ground, Nigel's head snapped around. "What the…" He turned toward the noise but saw nothing. He grabbed his binoculars and focused on the trees that reflected in the glow, and he spotted Jennifer and Charlie. *What are they doing here*? He squinted toward the camp and noticed that the foreman stood on top of a truck bed looking toward the forest with his own binoculars. He watched as the man pointed toward the students. Nigel looked back at the pair and saw that Charlie had seen the foreman also. The two were scrambling down from the tree.

Nigel broke into a fiendish grin. He might be off the hook again. This might be easier than he expected.

"What?" Drake asked. He could see the expression on Nigel's face.

"Seems we have two heroes today."

"Who?" Drake had no idea what he was talking about.

"Doesn't matter," was all Nigel said. "Come on." Nigel grabbed his backpack and moved away from the devastation.

They crouched behind a bank of ferns as the loggers chased past them. When they were several hundred yards ahead, Nigel stepped out, looked toward the burning bulldozer, and felt pride. The piece of man hanging from the cab was dark and crispy. Nigel led the way following the crowd as the loggers trailed Charlie and Jennifer.

* * *

They ran for their lives, moving off the trail in what Charlie thought was the general direction of the compound. He checked his GPS often, knowing from their previous trek that he was heading toward their sanctuary.

Soon, the loggers were completely lost, and with the dark shadows everywhere, they had no idea where their attackers had gone.

* * *

The foreman finally called a halt to their fruitless hunting. Early morning light was barely visible under the dense canopy. "Come on," he said. "We'll get help from the *Catawishi*."

The *Catawishi* were a local indigenous tribe with whom he had made friends recently. The foreman had been a god to them, giving them extra knives and machetes along with food and trinkets. Tomorrow, he'd give them a rifle and promise to teach them how to use it as soon as they tracked down the man and woman who attacked his people. By tonight, he would know where those people were staying, and he would finally take care of them.

35

Julia sat staring at the story board. She, Stephen, and the students had stayed up working on it after Eduardo left late last night.

What time is it anyway? Julia realized she was punchy, probably because she had only slept a few hours, so anxious was she to make their trip. She sat in the common room in the predawn hours staring at the white pieces of paper she could barely make out in the dimness of the morning. Even though the beans and pot had beckoned her, Julia delayed brewing coffee, worried the aroma would snake through the darkness awakening everyone. Instead, she curled in Stephen's rocker and swayed back and forth scrutinizing the clues on the board.

What were the facts? She perused the evidence. They knew three different groups of men were dead. At least two of the groups were illegal loggers. They would find out about the third later today. It seemed two sets of deaths were related because of how the bodies looked after death. It also looked like whatever was causing the deaths was evolving because the first set of deaths had cracks in the linings of the walls of some vessels, which had caused some loss of blood, but *their* organs remained intact. The second corpses had no internal organs…they had completely disintegrated into a bloody soup…as though a giant spider had injected its digestive enzymes into their organ cavity.

The cracks were certainly a forerunner for the second and third deaths which had major bleed-outs, a breakdown of organ linings, and an incredible loss of internal fluids. Julia couldn't be sure about the men they would autopsy later today, but from the description Eduardo was given, it surely seemed to be the same. If there was a way to make the whole experience even more surreal, the catalyst of death was either spreading or moving. But, if it were simply moving instead of spreading, how could anyone explain the second set of deaths and the ones two hundred kilometers away occurring at approximately the same time?

Julia shook her head trying to keep everything straight. *No. It's spreading*. It had to be. Nothing known in nature could move such a great distance in such a short period of time. Of course, the important variable of the equation was 'nothing known in nature.'

The Amazon Rainforest had an infinite quantity of unknown aspects. There were innumerable discoveries waiting there just as there were mysteries in the depths of the ocean yet to be encountered. But these deaths were not just something out there waiting to be revealed. They were happening now, and the event was new because if it had ever happened before, someone would have reported it.

Juan told Eduardo there were an unusual number of dead insects where the latest bodies were found. What could that mean? As Eduardo recounted this information, he reflected how he hadn't thought much about it at the time, but there were also dead insects on the ground around the second site. Not a great many, but there were enough that he noticed them even with all the gore. The large number of dead insects began to stand out like an important piece of the puzzle.

Question after question ran through Julia's mind. There were still so many, and with little answers, it was beginning to frustrate her. Usually, she could reason out theories from information she was working with, but this information was uniquely different. Not only were things happening so quickly she couldn't reason them out, but too many clues didn't make sense. Time was of the essence because people were dying for no apparent reason other than the fact they were illegally cutting trees in the rainforest.

Julia bit back the fear. She was more than scared, and she had certainly shown her fear when the rat churned out its insides

Julia mulled the words scrawled across the board. What else was there? She locked her hands behind her head and leaned back staring at the rafters. Each back and forth motion of the chair gave a little squeak while the sound of the night-into-morning insects was nearly deafening. She heard the background musicians as Stephen liked to call them. Having been back long enough, she was able to tune them out especially when she was deep in thought.

She heard one of the doors open from the sleeping hall and noticed Alexis coming toward the common room. Julia called out quietly to let her know she was there so as not to scare her. "Alexis, it's Julia."

Alexis jumped as she heard Julia's voice. "You scared the wits out of me!" She held her hand to her chest. She hadn't dressed yet and still wore short sleeping pants and a t-shirt, but she had taken time to slip on her shoes. "Why are you up so early?" she asked as she went to get a drink of water in the kitchen. She lifted another glass and Julia nodded.

"Just couldn't sleep. Can't wait to have coffee, but I didn't want to take a chance on waking everyone."

Alexis grabbed a fresh glass and filled it with water handing it to Julia as she sat down beside her.

Alexis looked at the wall of papers with Julia. " Geeze…I have so many questions."

"Me too."

Alexis scanned the notes and stopped at PAL. "What do we know about your Pulsating Anomaly Life-forces?"

"Let's see." Julia said. "It kills with lightning speed. It seems to be selective in its prey because it didn't harm the child who found the first men."

Alexis opened her computer she'd left on the table earlier in the evening and it winked on quickly. She began to type notes. "You and Stephen both handled the body fluids containing PAL. Neither of you were wearing gloves, and you were breathing all around it, so that would show it wasn't airborne, right?"

Julia shivered a "Yes" thinking about how they handled the samples so casually. "I'll never forget the sight of that rat dying like it did."

Alexis had seen the video and shook her head. "The only puncture marks on the men were stings. Had whatever stung them injected them with a PAL?"

That has to be it. Julia turned abruptly. "We may need to take another look at the stings on the bodies."

Alexis continued to type her questions. "And what about those stings? Were they caused by the ants? Did the type of ants in those trees cause the deaths? If so, why hadn't the investigators and we, who all climbed in the same canopy where the men died, been attacked?" Alexis took a deep breath and paused as she looked down the list of notes under Ants on the board. Softly she suggested, "All the ants encountered on our sampling climb looked to me like they were going about the routine business of ants, at least from what I know."

Julia's head popped around, and she stared at Alexis. "What did you say?"

Alexis turned to look at her. "I was thinking that the ants seemed so normal. Not threatening to us. They were scurrying around like they normally do for all I could see."

"Hhmmm," Julia hummed. "The business of ants." *What do we know about the business of ants? Could there be times their business is different from what we expect?* She thought about the parasites which took over the nerve centers of the ants and made them do things they wouldn't ordinarily do. Julia tossed the questions around in her head, recalling curious insect behaviors from rainforests around the world.

Julia reached for her glass and took a swallow of water. She set the glass back on the table and transformed into Professor Julia Cole. "When thinking about ants going about their business, most of the time the ants are fixated on building and maintaining their nests, nurturing and feeding their larva and young, or tending to the colony as a whole…but ants do much more than that."

"Really? Like what?"

"There is a green caterpillar deep in the western Amazon, in Peru, where it lives in a striking relationship, feeding each night on a small *caryocar* tree. Shortly after hatching, the caterpillar inches its way down the stem of the tree vibrating its body as a signal for a protector to come. And it doesn't take long before its bodyguard quickly comes to protect it."

Julia continued. "The caterpillar has a voracious appetite, actually the fastest feeding rate of any known creature. In less than three weeks, its weight will increase by as much as ten thousand times. It's a virtual eating machine. To grow that fast, the caterpillar sheds its skin five or six times over a three-week growing period. Then it spins a cocoon and waits for its transformation."

Without thinking, Alexis raised her hand before speaking, "Go back to the part about the vibration call. How does the caterpillar know to do that to get a protector?

Julia stood and crossed to the storyboard, "It has to be built into its DNA since the little creature doesn't live long enough to teach the behavior to new caterpillar generations."

"What is the protector?"

Julia looked back over her shoulder, "A large orange and black colored ant. The ant guards the caterpillar from the early stages of life until it becomes a fully developed butterfly. It's really quite simple. When a potential predator nears the caterpillar, the ant attacks and kills it."

Alexis laid down the computer, walked past Julia and began straightening the notes on the wall.

Julia wasn't finished. "Not only does the ant protect the caterpillar but it builds a separate sleeping chamber apart from the ant nest. Sometimes it's built into the hollow stem of the tree where the caterpillar feeds or a hollow branch lying on the ground. It could even be below the surface of the ground next to the feeding tree. It's large enough for the caterpillar to sleep in, yet small enough to be easily guarded. Essentially, the ant is farming the green caterpillar. Sometimes there are more bodyguard ants, and they might be protecting several caterpillars at once. A team of ants with a herd of caterpillars."

Alexis finished and stepped back beside Julia. "How do the ants protect the caterpillars from birds? Seems like a bird could easily grab one away from even a large group of ants."

"Good question," Julia replied. "This type of ant is nocturnal and trains the caterpillars to adapt and live the same way. The ants build a silky pathway from the sleeping chambers up into the treetops. At nightfall the ants rouse the caterpillars from their sleeping chambers and hurry them up the silky lane where they graze throughout the night. That's when they are easier to protect because of the darkness. After a night of nonstop eating, the ants guide all the caterpillars back to their sleeping chambers."

"That's really incredible, Julia. Seriously. A whole different world. But one thing I don't understand. Why would the ants protect the caterpillars in the first place? What do they get out of it? Surely there is something the caterpillars give in return."

Feeling like she was actually teaching someone something Julia continued. "After the caterpillars are safe in their sleeping chambers, the ants become excited…and that's," she held up a finger, "when they get their reward." Julia moved her fingers like she was typing, "They begin crawling over and around each caterpillar in a frenzy of activity. Using their antennae, the ants massage the backs of their growing, green pets. The massaging causes small liquid drops, called honeydew, to ooze out of special pores on the backs of the caterpillars. The ants consume the nectar until they are full."

"So the caterpillars have developed a sort of martini for the ants?"

Julia smiled, "That's a good way to describe it."

"What an odd arrangement."

"Very odd…and very mysterious."

"So after they drink their fill, the ants settle down and protect the sleeping caterpillars all day."

"Exactly."

"Do we know what's in the honeydew?"

"One study I read about states the drops contain carbohydrates and enzymes the ants need for just the right nourishment."

Alexis shook her head still taking in the new information. "What a phenomenal working relationship," she said.

"Yes," Julia agreed. "I can't help but wonder which one might have taken the first step along the path toward the relationship. How many others in nature have established something similar that haven't been discovered? It's almost hard to believe the bond between such disparate living things and how they work together to fulfill each other's needs so completely without a moment of conflict."

Alexis sighed. "What a lesson for the human race."

Both women stood quiet while scrutinizing the storyboard.

Alexis started to speak but held back.

"What?"

"I was just wondering…"

Julia waited.

"I know it's going to sound a bit crazy, but if the caterpillars have developed honeydew for their protective ants…could they evolve to create PAL as a protecting agent against humans?"

Julia stared at her. "What an interesting idea, Alexis." She grabbed a marker off the table and began to write. The morning was getting lighter and while Julia wrote, Alexis excused herself to change for the day.

When she finished, Julia added another piece of paper under 'ant.'

Picking up her pad lying on the table Julia sat down and began to list more questions. She would ask Eduardo and Stephen about them while they were flying later this morning. Julia jumped when she heard the phone ring in the main house and ran as hard as she could to answer it, but as she reached inside the door, Lupa grabbed it first.

"Yes?" Lupa said. His brow furrowed as he looked at Julia already dressed for the day.

"Okay," he said as he hung up. He stood there a moment. Except for her change of clothing, she didn't look as though she had gone to bed. He raised one eyebrow.

She shrugged. "I couldn't sleep." She nodded back to the common room, "I'm trying to sort out the clues on the board."

Lupa shook his head and walked past her, muttering as he moved outside toward the common room kitchen.

"Well?" Julia followed in his wake.

Lupa turned back to face her in the dim morning light.

"Do you want to tell me who that was this early in the morning?" she asked more briskly than she felt.

"Eduardo say you and Stephen go to airstrip at nine. He meet you there. He go to village." As he turned to continue on his way, he said, "And Julia need sleep."

"He did not say that," Julia called after him.

"No," Lupa say. "And Lupa late."

What was with everyone dismissing her? She jogged after him. "You don't look like you've slept either,"

He never turned around. He just flapped a dish towel over his shoulder and continued into the common room, turning on lights as he moved into the kitchen.

Julia wondered if he was angry. *Nah.* She followed him inside and walked back to her rocking chair as he filled the coffee pot. She heard him plop the pot onto the stove talking to himself in his Portuguese dialect.

Well, I guess I really have been dismissed. Sitting down into the rocker she leaned back and looked at the notes again. What else was there that she hadn't seen? She spent the next ten minutes reviewing the clues. She came up with nothing.

"Miss Julia like coffee while you think?"

Lupa stood next to her looking at the board.

Julia knew he wasn't angry with her. Maybe he was just tired.

"I'd love some," she smiled, rising and giving him a hug.

She felt him pat her once on the back. "Right-O, Miss Julia."

Julia pursed her lips and sighed. She wanted him to call her *Julia*, not *Miss* Julia. But all the times she had been here, she could not get him to change. In her mind she felt it put him in the position of being a servant, and he was nothing near that. He was her friend, part of the team.

Lupa returned carrying a steaming cup of coffee, with cream and sugar, just the way she liked it.

"I take students in forest again today," he said.

Julia nodded. "They are looking forward to it. You're good with them, Lupa."

Lupa smiled, "They good with me…"

"Will you sit with me a while?" she asked.

Lupa sat next to her as she continued rocking.

They didn't speak for a few minutes. Julia sipped the steaming cup while both of them gazed at the board. Julia kept silent as she watched Lupa study it. She could see him laboring over the words. She knew he could read English, but she knew from experience how hard it was to comprehend another language. She gave him time to process what was written.

After a few minutes he asked, "Miss Julia?"

"Yes."

"Lupa no know treehoppers?"

Julia had to stop and think. "They are a kind of insect which bores into the bark of a tree and drinks the sap. They are bright and shiny, sometimes with many colors."

Lupa nodded. "Here we say tree jewel. They beautiful. Children collect for high color," he turned toward her, "like you butterflies, but no big." He made several attempts to add something and always stopped himself. Finally he spoke, again, "Lupa not tell you work, Miss Julia, but Lupa see…treehoppers…." Lupa searched for the word. Finally he said, "big deal…"

He moved to leave, but Julia put her hand on his arm. He sat back down.

"What do you mean?" Julia looked at the notes.

"Lupa no push in, Miss Julia, but listen Eduardo last night he talk. Lupa hear him talk of insects on dirt, at far away deaths, and he say insects under second men. Treehoppers at both. What does mean?"

Julia felt he had a valid point which had somehow evaded all of them.

Looking back at the board, Julia considered the question. "I'm not sure what it means."

Julia thought about what Lupa said. He never commented on much of what she and Stephen were working on. She turned and looked at the older man.

The look on Lupa's face showed he was concerned. "People at these places, Miss Julia. Lupa worry." His face showed he was unsure what he should do.

Looking back at the board, Julia considered all the facts. "You should be concerned, Lupa. But at this moment, I'm not sure about what," was all she could say.

Lupa stood. "When you know, Miss Julia, tell Lupa, so Lupa do what need do?"

It was spoken in a voice which told her Lupa was confident he could believe in her. For Julia, it was an uncomfortable feeling that he was putting his trust in her. She had no idea what they were facing. Lupa evidently decided he could trust her to make things work out. It made her feel like a protector of sorts, like an ant with a caterpillar. At this moment, however, Julia doubted the ant could even protect herself.

36

It was very early when Eduardo entered the hotel in Kahepa, but Pepe was already at the counter. He worked there for many years, and Eduardo had known him as long as he could remember. After exchanging pleasantries, Eduardo asked to see who recently checked in.

There were seven people registered. Four were regulars: entomologists studying the canopy in the local area forest. The group always stayed at the hotel for a few days becoming acclimated and planning where they would go and how long they would stay out. Eduardo remembered them because they always left an itinerary and contact information with him so he could search for them if they failed to return as scheduled. So far, there had never been any incidents, but there were different circumstances plaguing the area right now. He needed to caution and advise them about what was going on out there, even though he himself didn't know exactly what to tell them. He then made a mental note to try and talk to them about the insects dying with the men. Maybe they could help make a connection.

There was also a writer who was doing research for a book about the wonders of the rainforest, and he had a traveling companion.

Finally, there was a young American who went out sometimes for days or weeks at a time keeping a room here for the last couple of months. Pepe said he hadn't seen him often, and the man had specifically asked that no one clean his room.

Eduardo wondered why he hadn't seen the man around the village. Surely he would have noticed him.

"He come at odd hour," Pepe told him. "It has been strange though…about the American…" he drifted off in thought.

"Strange?" Eduardo asked.

"Yes. He is not leaving building for almost two day now. He drinking much and stay little in his room." Pepe nodded thoughtfully.

"So, he was in the canteen, yesterday?"

Pepe nodded. "Much of the day. I see him go in yesterday about, don't know…maybe lunch. I go over later before I retire for night, and he still at bar. He way drunk when he leave maybe five. He almost fall upstair. I try to help." He shoved the air with both hands. "He push me away. Yell something at me I no understand."

That's probably a good thing, Eduardo thought but did not say. "Did you ever see him with anyone else? Any other men?"

Pepe shook his head. "I see no one in hotel with him. I no go to canteen much. You ask Senhor Pantoja about man."

Eduardo glanced toward the canteen. The room was just to the right of the counter. If anyone left with the American while Pepe was here, he would have seen them.

"Can you get a message to the science group to please make sure they see me before they go into the forest?"

Pepe nodded.

"*Grazie. Tchau*, Pepe," he said as he headed for the doorway to the canteen.

Pepe grabbed a piece of paper to write a short note. The men were staying in the back section of the hotel, and this was the perfect time for Pepe to slip back and give them the message before he got busy. He would be back in less than five minutes.

It was still early morning and the canteen was empty. When Eduardo's eyes adjusted to the dim lighting, he saw a man arranging fresh liquor bottles behind the bar. Short and heavy, the man had to stand on a stool to reach the top shelf.

"Senhor Pantoja," Eduardo called from the doorway.

The older man looked up and grinned. "Eduardo. Come in. Come in." He motioned for Eduardo to come to the bar as he stepped down to the floor. "You have been a stranger, Eduardo. You should come by some day and see the fellows. They ask about you. We miss taking your money in our poker game," he laughed.

Eduardo smiled. It had been a long time since he had played cards, not since just before losing Serena. Senhor Pantoja caught a wistful look crossing Eduardo's face, and then it evaporated.

"Yes, and I miss those times. Maybe I will come again soon." Eduardo climbed onto the barstool as Senhor Pantoja poured two small drinks.

He fluttered his hand indicating Eduardo should drink up. "A little rum is good for cleansing the pallet and a little help to think," he winked and shrugged his shoulders before downing the drink and banging the empty glass on the counter.

"Are you here about the men in the trees, my friend?" Senhor Pantoja asked.

Eduardo nodded. "I was wondering what you could tell me about the American staying here. Pepe said he had been drinking quite a bit the last couple of days."

Senhor Pantoja pursed his lips and nodded.

"Did you ever see him with anyone?" Eduardo prodded.

For a few moments Senhor Pantoja said nothing, twirling his empty glass around on the bar. It was as though he were trying to decide what to say.

"Only Magdela," he looked reluctant as he said it.

"Magdela San Richo," Eduardo repeated.

"Yes."

Eduardo took another sip of his drink as he thought of Magdela. He had known her since he was a kid. She was almost twenty years older than him and had been tempting men for a long time.

"You find out what killed men in forest?

"No. We aren't sure what killed the men," Eduardo admitted without thinking. The alarm on the older man's face made him wince as he watched the man make the sign of the cross over his chest.

Pouring himself another drink, Senhor Pantoja pulled up a stool and lowered his voice, "I worry about the American."

Eduardo resisted the temptation to take another sip of the fiery liquid. He reminded himself that he would be flying a plane in a short time, and he would have some very important cargo with him.

"What about the American?" Eduardo asked again.

"He have some deep trouble. I see him some before, but two day ago, he come in and drink. He drink most all day since." Senhor Pantoja had a grave look on his face.

"Could you tell what was bothering him?"

Senhor Pantoja shook his head. "I ask. I tell him nicelike sometime it help to talk about things." He smirked as he finished. "He tell me to mind my own business. I do not think he is nice man."

Eduardo smiled. "You were always a good judge of character, Senhor Pantoja. You are probably right. Did you ever see him with anyone else?"

Senhor Pantoja thought for a minute. Then he shook his head. "No. He keep to self."

The conversation turned to the town and fishing and the poker game, which was coming up on the weekend. Eduardo listened to Senhor Pantoja talk glowingly about his grandchildren and his vegetable garden behind his house. Eduardo nodded as on cue and answered when appropriate, but his thoughts were of the men who had died and the mystery surrounding their deaths. When the conversation was over, they both sat in silence, one sipping and one drinking, both lost in their own thoughts.

37

Last night after Will revealed Carlos's and the other men's deaths, he and Arthur had gotten into it again. The conversation got so heated the old man threatened Will's life if he didn't get back in the forest and cut his timber. *So much for loyalty*. Somehow, Will thought he meant more to the old man, but he should have known better. Why would anything other than money interest that blowhard? But the threats didn't scare Will. He had enough money socked away to disappear for a long, long time, and he threw that at Livingston during their turbulent discussion.

If the men Will hired knew the kind of money their boss was paid, they would be shocked. Oh, he paid his foremen well enough, but the others…they got what they got, and it wasn't much.

Will spent little of his money over ten years. He wasn't even sure how much he had. Each month it was wired to an off-shore account in the Cayman Islands, and his banker would call after each transaction to let him know his money had arrived. Will hadn't bothered to inquire about the balance in years. When he needed money, the banker wired it. Otherwise, it just sat there waiting for the day he would need it, and he was going to need it soon. The last thing he'd said to Livingston before hanging up on him the night before was that he was gone! Done. Finished.

Will forgot to turn the phone off and could have kicked himself when it rang at 6:00 a.m.. There was only one person who could be calling him so early, and he felt like throwing the phone out the window when it rang. He staggered over to the desk and answered it.

Instead of Livingston yelling and cursing like he did last night, he sounded syrupy smooth. Will pulled the phone away from his ear and looked at it as if someone was speaking a language he had never heard before from an object he didn't recognize. Nope, it was his phone, and it was Livingston's voice.

Livingston must have been awake all night thinking, and now he had a proposition for Will, and it was one he couldn't pass up. Livingston explained that he was out on a limb with this one, no pun intended, then forced a laugh. He had promised a very influential man, a very powerful man with many connections, two truckloads of mahogany. Will knew some of the men Livingston rubbed shoulders with, and they were seldom upstanding people.

Instead of more threats, Livingston offered him a bonus, a very considerable bonus, to go back to the first tree and harvest it.

At first Will argued. "But three men died at that tree. I really don't want to be the fourth." Will was ready to stand up for himself if it was needed. *Bring it on, old man.*

"Think about it, Will," Livingston responded gently. "Look at all the investigators who were out there. Didn't you tell me a small boy found the men? Nothing happened to him, right?"

Will put his hand over his mouth and wiped off the sweat that was collecting there. He peered out into the dim morning light.

The old man sensed Will was wavering. "Whatever was there is long gone. Let me ask you, did Carlos and the others die anywhere close to the first tree?"

Will did some quick mental calculations. "No. They were at least thirty five miles away as a bird flies, maybe more. Whatever was there mighta gone deeper into the jungle." Will had to admit, Livingston made a lot of sense especially with this new sizeable offer.

Arthur could hear it in his voice. "Look," he said. "Don't you worry. After this tree, you take some time off. And don't worry about leaving me shorthanded. I got to thinking about it, and you've been down there a long time, boy. I've got some feelers out for a relief project manager for you."

Will narrowed his eyes in thought. The old man was being unusually accommodating. *What is he up to*?

"You deserve some time away," his voice rang out. "Take a year. Hell, take five years. When you get bored, get back in touch with me. I'll put you back to work. There will always be trees to cut somewhere, and you've got a place to work until you die with Livingston Lumber."

Will didn't know if there'd always be trees to cut. Mahoganies were getting harder and harder to find. Livingston was kidding himself. In five years, there might not be many left. He kept his thoughts to himself, while the words "until you die" made him very uneasy.

"Go to Paulo's village. Maybe he hasn't found out about the deaths. Offer him a nice bonus to help you get the tree out. You name it. I'll pay it. Hell, everything's ready. Didn't you tell me the trees for the pulleys are already topped?"

"Yes." Will's mind was racing.

Arthur said the next sentence slowly and quietly, trying his best to hide his rage under the surface. "All you gotta do is cut the damn tree."

"Yeah…" Will's voice fell away. He didn't need the money, but hell…it was a *lot* of dough.

Arthur thought, *How dare you quit on me*! *How dare you hang up on me*? Nobody hung up on Arthur Livingston without some serious consequences. *I'll make you pay. Maybe not this minute, but I'm working on it.* Arthur picked up the paper he'd printed from an e-mail a few minutes earlier. One of his IT fellows had tracked their company wire trail to Will's bank. Arthur knew exactly how much money the boy had, and frankly it flabbergasted him. He hadn't realized he'd paid him so much. The boy's point was well taken last night. He could disappear for a long, long time.

"Alright," Will finally broke the silence. "But this is the end. And I want my money wired before I go out. All of it." Arthur realized that the boy no longer trusted him, but it made no difference. He needed that damn tree. Arthur kept the cheer in his voice. "Okay, okay. Have it your way. Now, you call me when those logs are on their way, alright, boy?"

Will showered, grabbed a few clothes, and hastily threw the maps and other papers into his backpack, along with the phone tucked neatly into its pouch.

When he was ready, he walked to the closet and looked inside. It was nearly empty. He stood at the door and scanned the room. Everything looked fine.

Downstairs a few moments later, a shadow darkened the doorway of the canteen and moved on, leaving the hotel as Will passed outside unseen by either Eduardo or Senhor Pantoja or the watchful eye of Pepe, who was absent from his post on his errand for Eduardo.

Will crept to the old Jeep in the alley, his backpack slung over his shoulder. He would be back in a day or two to get the rest of his things, but right now he had to find Paulo, and it would take most of the day to get to his house.

Slamming his foot down on the accelerator Will laughed as he raced the Jeep out of town. He thought back to the end of their conversation when Livingston asked him to call when the logs were out. Right. "Yeah, I'll call," he said and hit the off button before Arthur responded. Tapping his fingers on the steering wheel, he imagined a livid Livingston hanging on the other end of the line. "Bastard."

* * *

Arthur sat down at his desk. He had been the first one here this morning, which wasn't unusual, but this morning felt different. He was tired—thinking maybe he was getting too old for this shit.

He went back to reading the e-mail he had been looking at earlier when he was on the phone with Will. Arthur still couldn't get over how much money Will had socked away. He put his palms flat on the arms of the chair and rocked. He thought about Will and the work the boy had done for him all these years. How could he have possibly overpaid him?

And how had that boy saved all that money? Hell, the more he thought about it, he wasn't sure Will had been worth it, but now he knew he wasn't worth it anymore. *Quit on me…hang up on me…twice*! *Oh yeah, Will…you go get that mahogany*, *and then you'll remember who's the boss*.

Arthur sat up and grabbed the e-mail he had printed. He searched for the contact information, found the name and number he was searching for, picked up the phone, and dialed.

An hour later, Arthur softly laid the receiver back on the phone. *That was reeeal easy*. He was surprised when the bank official answered the phone because of the early hour. He figured he would have to get a call back, but the man answered on the first ring. Arthur was going to get his money back, and he would have Will begging for his job.

Arthur laughed out loud thinking how easy it was to pay off the bank official. *Now*, *that was fun*.

38

"*Hucunda*," the *Catawishi* pointed toward the common room in the distance where the students were gathered with Stephen and Julia eating breakfast. Wearing a painted mask of black dye made from the fruit of the *genipapo* tree, the Indian resembled a small, nearly naked Zorro.

The foreman scanned the group. "I don't see them," he said.

"No matter," said another logger. "I get them all. Easy shot." He raised the rifle, but the foreman pulled the barrel down toward the ground.

"No, we wait until we talk to Will," said the foreman. He had no problem killing all of the people, but he wanted to check with his boss first.

"They not leave. We know where they stay. We wait."

One hundred yards to their left, Nigel, Drake, and Tiago crouched behind a large stand of *brugmansia* bushes, beautiful plants with their long bell shaped yellow and pink flowers hanging down all around them. Nigel and Drake noticed neither the beauty nor the perfume that washed over them as they watched the loggers watching the compound.

Tiago stroked a flower, "A plant to chase away evil…"

"What?" asked Nigel distractedly, glancing quickly at the guide.

Tiago didn't answer and looked away.

Nigel turned his attention back to the loggers. He gave a sinister grin as he waited for the men to open fire. When they didn't, he felt deflated. He was primed and ready to watch Stephen and the others die from gunshots instead of the ricin he had put in the coffee. He could almost savor the salty, iron taste of the blood, see the dark splashes, feel the warmth, smell the coppery scent. He was sorry he would not be able to stand over them and watch their eyes dilate. He especially enjoyed that, believing he could actually see a soul leave a body. It was probably the thing he loved most about killing.

"When are they going to do it?" Drake asked as he dug in his backpack.

"How the hell should I know?" Nigel grimaced, angered his daydream had been interrupted by the pest. He'd been a fool to bring him along.

"I'm hungry," Drake said as he slapped at a mosquito next to his ear.

Nigel turned and stared hard at him.

Drake noticed the look and asked, "What? I was just thinking out loud." He took a handful of trail mix and chewed loudly.

Nigel continued to stare, his eyes almost black as they bore into Drake's. *It will be such a pleasure getting rid of you.* The look on his face made Drake so queasy he had to sit down.

Nigel turned to Tiago and asked, "What do you think? What are they waiting for?"

Tiago was a man of few words. He had been drawing in the dirt with a stick as he waited. Dropping the stick, he looked at the men across the way. "They wait for leader."

Nigel hadn't considered that. He nodded as he caught a glimpse of the logger's heads moving away. It appeared they were heading back to their camp.

Tiago led the way, and they followed the other group.

The pleasure of spilling blood in the compound would not happen today, but soon…very soon, everyone drinking the tasty morning brew of coffee would begin feeling sick…very sick, indeed.

39

The road sloped down steeply on the last turn to the grass air strip. Julia and Stephen pulled to a stop next to the hanger while Mario was bringing Eduardo's plane from under the roof. Julia had forgotten how small it was until she witnessed it being pulled by hand. Of course, much larger planes could easily be pulled by hand, so she shouldn't have been caught off guard. As Julia and Stephen watched, Mario brought the plane toward the center of the field and aligned it facing the long, grassy lane serving as a runway.

Stephen reached into the back of the Jeep and pulled out two duffel bags containing sampling supplies and autopsy tools. He wasn't sure exactly what to bring, so he had probably over-packed

Julia grabbed her backpack and searched for her phone. Now was the perfect time to call Mitch. She dialed his number at the office. No answer. She didn't leave a message. She dialed his cell phone. It rang six times before his voicemail picked up.

"Just wanted to let you know I'm still alive," Julia said, a forced smile on her face. "Hope you are doing well." *How lame was that*? She couldn't think of anything else to say. Then clearing her throat she added, "We're flying to another village where more people have been found dead. Guess I'll talk to you later." She bit her top lip and considered how to finish the message. She hung up without even saying goodbye. *Awkward. Why did that feel so awkward*? Shrugging off the feeling, she saw Eduardo's truck burst from the forest and swing to a stop near her. Almost instantly, Julia was bowled over by a cloud of dust. Closing her eyes and covering her mouth and nose, she fanned the air to try to inhale without huffing in a ball of dirt.

Eduardo was often amused by Julia's reactions. Even under these horrific circumstances he realized she could easily put a smile on his face. He noticed the band of sweat around the top of her shirt forming a V, creating an image he found appealing. He imagined tiny beads of sweat sliding down between two firm breasts, and the power of the image caused him to look away. He took a deep breath and blew it out loudly. He looked back at her. *What is it about this woman that captures my attention and imagination*?

She grinned back at him. "Thanks for the dirt shower. It really adds to the nice water shower I had just an hour ago. Maybe I can make you some mud pies." Julia was finally beginning to relax around him, even though there was an underlying bit of restlessness. Mitch became a darkened fog when her thoughts wandered in his direction.

Eduardo closed his eyes again, cleared his throat, and climbed out.

Julia saw his reaction. "What?" she asked. She saw his jaw flexing and then noticed his shirt had shorter sleeves than normal. The muscle in his arm was large, and as he opened the tool box near the back and rummaged around, his bicep bulged and flexed. Julia caught herself wanting to run her hand over it. *Oh those thoughts*! *What the heck is going on with my mind*? *Maybe I'm losing it in the heat.*

Eduardo abruptly stopped moving and was staring directly at her. He saw her watching his arm, and it made him self-conscious. But then warmness started in the pit of his stomach that ran up to his chest and then back down. He looked away again. *What is this woman doing to me*? He shook his head trying to release the thoughts.

Julia was embarrassed to realize he saw her studying him so closely. She was about to ask him what he was looking for when he turned and walked toward the plane. She watched him. *What was that all about*?

Eduardo opened the small door and leaned in, pulling out the small laminated sheet that held the flight checklist. A good pilot never took off without checking everything about the plane. He'd done it hundreds of times, but Eduardo always followed the typed list even though he had it memorized.

Stephen joined Eduardo as he performed a 'walk-around' on the plane, testing the flaps, kicking the tires, and pulling on the guy wires. Eduardo climbed up and looked into the fuel tank. He knew Mario would have topped it off, but he had to check for himself anyway–he had to be sure everything was secure and safe.

Eduardo climbed in and started the plane. Stephen motioned for Julia to climb into the back seat. She was still mulling over what had just happened between her and Eduardo. At first he looked happy to see her when he drove up, but then something changed. He became a little distant. Perhaps he was just focusing on the task at hand. *But still…*

Eduardo finished off the checklist, and accelerated toward the trees standing at the far end of the clearing. In less than ten seconds from when he pushed the throttle up to full speed, the trees loomed large in front of them. Finally, the wheels lifted off the ground, and they arced steeply over the treetops.

For a few moments, Julia felt queasy. She pulled a cool bottle of water from her bag and drank several swallows. The sick feeling passed. She waited until the plane leveled off, and they settled into flight altitude at 2,000 feet above the ground before she pulled out her notepad and started asking her list of questions. It took a couple of hours to get to their destination, so they spent the time adding and scratching out ideas.

Eduardo's friend, Juan, met them at the plane where he guided them to an open-topped truck that looked like an old amusement ride. It was battered and dirty with the remnants of a wild paint job. The pattern looked like a combination of army camouflage and zebra stripes. It had a railing around the top with faded, yellow beaded fringe hanging down. And right in the center of the tire on the back was the tail end of what looked like a donkey.

"You like my truck?" he asked, amused as they gawked at their transportation.

"I like it," Julia smiled warmly. "I feel like I'm on safari."

"It was used in an old movie, maybe 25 years ago. I won it playing cards. I thought the fellow might kill me, but he let me live." He rubbed the side of the truck. "She is my baby." He stroked the fringe that ringed the top as he climbed in

It took only minutes to get to a village much smaller than Kahepa. There were huts scattered along the road as they bumped and dodged deep potholes. Only a handful of residents were seen as they passed. Juan pulled to a stop in front of the largest of six buildings marking the center of the village.

Inside was dark. The counter was stacked with goods. There were cans of food that looked like they had been left out in the sun for a while, with faded colors instead of the bright ones Julia was used to seeing in supermarkets back home. There was an old ice box with the words *Coca Cola* emblazoned across the front, dripping with condensation but still humming away against the wall. It appeared as if it had been lifted out of a store from the 50s.

The man and woman behind the counter were somber faced. It was obvious they felt the same as Ricardo back in Kahepa about storing bodies in the cooler in the back of their store. This situation made the couple very uneasy. Not a good sign from the heavens. The man walked to the front door after everyone was inside. The woman picked up a toddler behind the counter and hurried after him. They moved outside, leaving the horrible doings for Juan and his friends.

Eduardo helped Juan clear a place on the end of the counter close to the window and large enough to work. They hung the two lanterns Juan had brought, turned them as bright as possible, and then went inside the cooler to get the first body.

Eduardo's eyes darted toward Juan when they lifted the corpse. "So light."

"Yes. It was a surprise to me too," Juan commented, holding the feet.

Each put on a pair of gloves and surgical masks, and Julia and Stephen selected their tools and supplies and prepared for the autopsies while Eduardo and Juan unwrapped the plastic around the bodies.

If the others looked like the first man, these deaths were undeniably related to those at Kahepa. The man in front of them was even more shrunken than the last. His skin was pulled tightly across his bones with what appeared to be even less muscle mass than the men in Kahepa. It was hard to imagine they had been alive three days ago.

"What do you see, Julia, besides the deflated body?" Stephen asked.

Julia stepped closer. Even with the tightness of the skin, she knew what he was talking about. "Stings."

"Yes. Stings."

Julia had to turn away while Stephen made the opening incision. She was suddenly not feeling well again and felt like she might be sick.

Stephen saw her movement. "Are you okay?"

"I'm fine." She swallowed the bile that had just raced up her throat as she grabbed for her water bottle. "Keep going. I'll look when I can."

"Are you really okay?" Eduardo asked.

Julia tried to smile while not looking at the body. "I haven't felt great today. Maybe it's the flying. It sometimes makes me a little ill."

Eduardo pulled a package of mints out of his shirt pocket. He dropped several in her hand. "Suck on these. Mint sometimes makes me feel better."

She thanked him and did feel better after a few minutes.

Stephen took samples of tissue, searched for and finally found a small amount of body fluid in a couple of places, and then excised several sting spots from the corpse's skin.

Getting comfortable enough to watch him work, Julia stood next to him and opened and closed small collection jars for his samples, labeling them one after the other.

Eduardo stood back looking at what remained of the man and then glanced toward the cooler. *There are two more in there just like this one.* He thought back to all the clues discussed in the plane and about Stephen's realization that whatever it was, it was spreading. Juan told him these men were illegally cutting trees in the rainforest, which was one thing they all had in common. Julia had broached a subject in the plane earlier. *Could it be possible? Was the Pulsating Anomaly Life-force Julia discovered being selective with its prey? If so, how?*

It took less than an hour for Stephen to finish. The procedure was performed as quickly as possible. Everyone was uneasy handling the bodies. They weren't real autopsies he was performing: just open one up, grab a few samples, and close him…quickly. Snip some skin with stings and bag it. The procedure reminded Eduardo of a clip from a horror movie where aliens crash and the humans are examining them. *Yes, it's rather alien indeed.*

Eduardo and Juan returned the last body to the cooler and turned to leave.

Juan reached behind the door and picked up a bucket secured tightly with a lid. "Oh, one last thing," he placed it on the counter, "I told you about these, Eduardo." He pulled out his knife and pried open the lid.

Stephen reached in with a gloved hand

Juan continued, "The insects. I washed them as much as I could and laid them out to dry. It was like nothing I have ever smelled before. It would have driven you from the plane!" trying to lighten up the anxiety in the room.

"Why insects?" Julia pondered aloud. "For the life of me, I can't figure out why the PALs are attacking insects?" It sounded crazy.

Juan shrugged his shoulders. "I do not know. But there were many more. We brought these for you to take with you."

"I recognize some of the treehoppers. Several different kinds," Stephen said.

Julia was standing beside him. "And look at all the different kinds of ants."

She and Stephen traded a glance. It made no sense to anyone. Why would treehoppers die? Why ants? What did they have in common? Why no birds? Why no monkeys? Why no frogs? What was there about these insects? And what could they possibly have in common with the men?

"How about some lunch, my friend?" Juan interjected, hoping to get a small break from the dead.

Julia felt like she might throw up when he mentioned food.

The day was passing and Eduardo wanted to make sure they flew back with plenty of daylight. Lunch would have to wait until their return home, and no one had much of an appetite at this point.

Juan drove them back to the plane and waved them off.

No one spoke for several minutes, so preoccupied were they with their own thoughts. The flight was another unexpectedly smooth ride, and they skimmed above the tree canopy watching large flocks of birds soaring from one roost to another.

Julia drank her water again, trying to keep her stomach settled.

Eduardo watched her in the mirror and without saying anything, he handed her the container of mints.

She smiled and took them without comment.

He finally pushed his headset down around his neck. Eduardo's voice projected above the sound of the engine, "They are all illegal loggers."

"I know," Stephen returned. "I was thinking the same thing. But what do they have in common with the insects?"

"I was just wondering that myself..." Eduardo couldn't answer the question either.

Julia sat back, popped another mint into her mouth, opened her notebook, and began writing.

40

Lupa stood at the edge of the forest giving new instructions to the students. "We go now to place Lupa see *queixadas*. Be ready all time. Watch for easy climb tree. One in sight all time."

"You're scaring me, Lupa," Alexis said. "What is a *queixadas*?"

"White-lipped peccary…like pig. Mean animal. Go in family. *Big* family." Lupa searched for the words to describe how large the families could be. "I see *cinqüenta…*"

"Fifty?" asked Charlie.

"Yes." said Lupa "Fifty. One time Lupa see cem…100. Some say group be…" he held up two fingers, "*…mil….*"

"*Mil* means thousand," Alexis recollected and as she regarded Lupa's two raised fingers, her eyes grew wide, "*Two thousand*?"

"Sim," Lupa nodded enthusiastically, not because of the great number of animals in the herd but because he was excited that they understood some of his language.

"Does it look like a regular pig?" Charlie asked, turning the handle of the machete he was carrying.

Lupa's eyes darted back and forth. "Like little pig." He nodded again. "*Sim*, little pig."

"If they're so small, why are they so dangerous?" Charlie asked, his eyes glancing around expecting to be trampled at any minute.

Kosey climbed up into a strangler fig to scout their surroundings.

Lupa drew his middle fingers from each corner of his mouth upward toward the outside corners of his eyes. "Peccary have sharp, flat teeth strong to cut bone. Whaakkk," Lupa sliced his flattened hand through the air.

Jennifer's face was grave. "I don't think I want to go in there."

Lupa tried to reassure her, "Lupa tell so you on guard. Much good fruit and herbs there. There *is ak-kah-nah-pah-to-do-to-do*," he rubbed his stomach. "Lupa say best fruit of forest. There is *ku-mu*. Lupa need oil to cook. Lupa need *curare* fruit, but no eat. You eat; you fall down and not move for much time. But you awake. You see and hear all. And in there is much foxglove," he patted his chest, "for Lupa heart."

The students looked at each other knowing they could not go back without whatever the older man needed for his heart. Each in turn had similar thoughts. *It is* his *jungle*, *so he probably*, hopefully, *knows what he is doing*.

Lupa moved forward. He stopped as soon as he started and cautioned, "Lesson on peccary." He motioned to the machete Charlie held. "Hurt one, all come to rescue. They bite, slash feet right here," he indicated his Achilles tendon. "Know weak place on man."

Jennifer huddled closer to Charlie. She pointed at a tree up ahead. "I'm claiming that one."

They each in turn declared their tree and climbed like monkeys to get off the ground.

Lupa laughed. "No worry now. No *queixadas*."

Kosey climbed down and the others followed his example. "We just needed a practice run." Kosey held up his hand. "'Be on the alert, like the red ant that moves with its claws wide open.'"

"Anything else we need to know about the little devils?" Alexis ignored Kosey's attempt at humor as she watched the forest around them.

Lupa nodded. "Noisy jaws." He snapped his teeth together several times. "Hear far away. Herd loud. Smell bad. Have time get in tree." He designated a height of about three feet. He instructed as he cupped his ear. "Listen." Then he touched his nose. "Smell."

The group followed Lupa reluctantly as they moved forward.

In his broken English, Lupa distracted the students with information about the plants surrounding them and they continued their gathering finding mangoes, some gooseberries, and even a black walnut tree that had just begun to drop its nuts. Their bags and baskets were overloaded with food that would last for days.

Kosey put his bag down and leaned against a tall tree as he wiped the sweat running from his forehead. He noticed a large section of bark had been stripped off. "Lupa? Why is the bark gone from this tree?"

Lupa shook his head and clicked his tongue. "Village people kill tree slow. Not know they kill tree."

Alexis asked, "What do you mean?"

Lupa touched the bare space and ran his hand lightly over it chanting under his breath. Then he answered as he looked straight up the trunk, "This *kwatta kama*...spider monkey bed."

"Spider monkey bed?" Jennifer was getting her fill of the flora and fauna.

Lupa nodded. "Yes. Look high." He pointed to the crown. "See? Flat top. Spider monkey sleep there."

Kosey asked, "But why do the villagers take the bark?"

"Tea of bark heal here." He rubbed his stomach.

"Really?" Charlie asked.

"Yes," Lupa answered.

Kosey reached for the branch of a young tree on the other side of the trail and Lupa yelled.

"No, no! No touch, Kosey!" Lupa rushed forward pulling him aside before moving back to the tree. He picked up a stick and touched a single leaf. "*Kanahyeh* tree," he said gently.

Hundreds of ants swarmed down the small branch onto the leaves at the end. They dripped off the tips like hot tar, plopping to the ground only to run back up the trunk.

"Wow! Julia warned us about that tree! Don't you remember, Kosey?" Alexis questioned.

Slightly stunned he nodded. "I remember the name, but so many of the trees look alike."

Charlie sneered. "Of course, our dear professor never mentioned it to us."

"Stop…" Jennifer cut him off. She knew Charlie was not thrilled with any part of this trip, and the new developments with Nigel made him more irritable.

"Well, the genius professor didn't. There are a lot of things he failed to mention."

Trying to change the subject, Jennifer motioned to the ants still flowing off the leaves. "Why do the ants do that?"

Lupa spoke softly, "Tree give hollow stem for ant to live and sweet oil to eat. Ant give protection from danger.

"What is up with the ants?" Charlie was about to blow his cool again.

"I must thank you, Lupa," Kosey grinned. "You saved me from a very unpleasant encounter."

Lupa smiled and beckoned them to gather their bags and baskets to move on. They came to a place where there was less vegetation and saw a tree covered in thirty or more twisting, yellowish-green vines meandering skyward and then looping back over limbs like kudzu gone wild over a pine tree. The end of one vine swayed back toward the ground and was covered with large, dark heart-shaped leaves, their yellow tips giving the impression they were dipped in paint.

"What is that?" Alexis pointed to the leaves.

Lupa stopped and laid down his basket. "This *caapi*." His gaze followed the vines upward. "Plant teacher."

"Plant teacher?" she echoed.

"Yes. Shaman chop *caapi* vine. Make *ayahuasca*. Window to soul. People drink. See vision. Shaman tell what mean." Lupa stood with his hands clasped in front of him. His seriousness spilled over the others.

Alexis was intrigued. "You mean the shaman interprets the visions?"

Lupa shook his head. "Lupa not know word in...*trepet*."

"Interpret," Alexis corrected. "It means 'tell what mean,'" she explained using his own phrasing.

Lupa nodded. "*Sim*. In-ter-pret. Say what vision mean."

"Can I touch it?" she asked.

"*Sim*. No ant. Okay to touch."

Alexis pulled down the vine allowing the leaves to flow through her hands. "Are they happy visions? Sad? Scary?"

Lupa stood very still, "Sometime one. Sometime all three. *Ayahuasca* heal all thing. Spirit know what need and fix."

"Really…" Alexis crooned. "Is it dangerous?"

Lupa nodded. "Sometime yes…most time no."

"Does it taste good?" Jennifer asked.

Lupa shook his head. "No. Bitter." He pointed the ends of his fingers toward the middle of his chest. "But help look in soul. Give what need. Come," he picked up his basket. "We go back."

He took them down a different path back to the compound, and they came to the waterfall visited by Nigel. They took off their shoes and sat on the rocks, cooling their feet and legs.

"Can we swim here?" Kosey asked out of the blue. He knew his family could never imagine the sensation of the cool water on their bodies. His siblings had never felt such water.

"*Sim*. Safe to swim," Lupa gestured.

Alexis regarded the *acia* palms across the pool, their feathery fronds sparkling with waterfall mist. "What a beautiful place," she murmured.

Lupa agreed. "Yes. Is sacred place." No one except Lupa knew that his secret cave was so near.

"Sacred?" Alexis asked.

Lupa pointed to the crystals in the quartz. "Jewels, say sacred." His face saddened. "Lose much sacred all time."

Kosey added, "My country has lost much…most of our forest."

"I know,"Alexis addressed both of them. "I wish we could stop it."

Jennifer and Charlie looked at each other. Jennifer nodded in agreement while Charlie shook his head. He took her hand, and his fingers closed tightly around hers. He whispered close against her ear, "Don't. Don't say anything."

Jennifer jerked her hand from his. "I have to!" Jennifer blurted out with defiance. "Nigel and Drake are environmentalists. *Scary* environmentalists. Nigel really is a professor, and Drake really is his assistant, but they've been out every night causing problems for some of the loggers…and not just problems. All sorts of terrible things!" The words tore out of her before she could lose her courage and before Charlie could stop her. She took a deep breath and began to tell them what they had witnessed. She told them about the poison Nigel put in the coffee, which Charlie had confided in her once they settled in the tree to wait. How Charlie had taken the tainted can and stowed it safely out of use in his backpack. Then she disclosed the horror of the burning man running from the tent fire from two nights before and the man Nigel killed last night.

"Lupa think Nigel take coffee. He poison coffee?"

"Yes," Charlie finally spoke up. "I don't know where they got it, but he definitely said it was ricin he was mixing in the coffee."

Kosey's eyes were huge. "To come so close to dying. Praise be to God you two were following them!"

Lupa raised his arms and began chanting.

No one spoke until he finished.

When he stopped he looked at Jennifer. "You come to stop loggers?"

Jennifer shook her head. "At first I came because I wanted to see all of the wildlife, but now that I see what the loggers are doing…yes," she nodded briskly. "I want to stop them from cutting the forest. Someone has to do something. We are losing so much so fast. The animals and trees and plants and insects. We're killing them all. Burning them up. Bulldozing them away. We humans are like little pests to the natural world. But killing men? That is not what we came here to do. It's hideous!" She was out of breath.

Everyone was silent from the shock of what Jennifer had told them.

"I never thought Nigel was dangerous. He's the best instructor I've ever had. He seemed to have passion and knowledge and was always a powerful presence. I thought he'd be the perfect leader for our jungle excursion. But now that we're here, he's turned into something evil. …a cold blooded killer."

Lupa's next words surprised them. "No worry. *El Tunchi* take care of forest."

"*El Tunchi*?" Alexis could not imagine trying to comprehend one more thing.

Lupa nodded calmly: "*El Tunchi* is great protector of forest. Find everyone in forest. Some no believe. Lupa see *El Tunchi*."

"Is he dangerous?" Alexis asked, now feeling light headed.

Lupa nodded. "He kill easy. But…" he held up his hand, "only kill man who kill land…animals…insects…trees."

"How would we recognize him?" Alexis was hoping for a reasonable answer.

Lupa cupped his hand at his ear, "First, hear *El Tunchi*."

"Hear?"

"He whistle. Always same whistle." Lupa shook his head. "Do not whistle with him. You whistle with *El Tunchi*, and he scare you. You kill forest, he kill you." He looked out at the forest. "All man kill forest die. Not die easy." He nodded. "That is curse of *El Tunchi*."

"*Ewe Mola tuepushe na mahasidi*," Kosey mumbled.

Lupa nodded, not knowing what the words meant, yet understanding the tone.

Alexis cocked her head. "And that means?"

Kosey gave her a solemn look. "'Oh, God, save us from the evil ones.'"

41

Julia slid forward on the seat as they neared the end of their flight and leaned between Eduardo and Stephen. "How does PAL do it?"

"That is the question, isn't it?" Stephen turned and gave her a sad smile. "The logging is the only thing I see that the three groups of men have in common, plus the fact they all seem to be native people. Of course, native people are hired by all logging groups, legal or not. These people take work anywhere they can find it. Even though they don't pay much, logging jobs are relatively easy to fill."

"The loggers don't get paid much?" Julia asked incredulously. She had always thought the illegal loggers made a great deal of money cutting the giant trees.

Eduardo gave a wry smile. "You would think so, but *they* don't. Not the men doing the actual cutting of the trees. The only ones making a lot of money are the ones near the end of the tree's journey. As you say 'the men at the top,' and we don't mean the canopy of the tree. And they're getting rich. Very, very rich. The foremen and managers over the crews do fairly well, but the men of the forest..." he shrugged. "They are helping destroy our land for almost nothing. It's a very sad situation. Many are poor and need money to buy food for their families…shoes for their feet…everyday items we take for granted."

So much destruction, Julia thought. *Little pay. Loss of forest. Loss of plants, animals, and insects. Changing weather patterns.* She lowered her head. "What about the insects?" Julia asked as she eyed the bucket sitting on the floor next to her. Thankfully, they had covered them, but she still moved her feet a little further away. "Have either of you come up with a credible theory where they might fit into the puzzle?"

Stephen could only shake his head. "It's way beyond me. First thing we have to do, my dear, is some more research. Right now, I have no idea why they died along with the men."

Julia looked out the window and saw a small rainbow in the distance. *Must be a waterfall over there.* Flying over the beautiful landscape it was hard to imagine the gruesome things that were occurring below.

The drone of the engines was lulling Stephen to sleep. It had been an exhausting day.

Julia watched Stephen's head slowly rest against the window and heard him snore once, obviously napping. Her eyes were pulled to Eduardo, headset in place, checking gauges, guiding them safely back to Kahepa. Again, she noticed the muscles in his arm, and she could see their definition. The skin was smooth and tanned. She focused on the side of his face. *He really is beautiful.* She tried shaking the thoughts from her head, fearing that somehow Eduardo could read her mind

With that, he turned and looked at her, his eyes holding a longing she had been trying to ignore. Julia was taken aback with her thoughts running to: *He can't possibly know what I'm thinking*! But the longing she was also feeling was undeniable. Without a word or even changing expression, Eduardo turned back to the instruments with the soft feeling of contentment—something that had been a void for such a long time.

After they landed and were gathering the samples and gear from the plane, Stephen asked Eduardo, "Why not follow us and have dinner? I am sure there is plenty."

"Thank you. I could help you sort everything and clean up the lab so you will be ready to start working on these samples." Eduardo handed the airplane keys to Mario.

"Great. It will probably take a couple hours to get everything ready," Stephen placed the sample bags in the truck.

Eduardo turned to Julia. "Are you feeling better?"

She nodded. "Maybe all the excitement with the flight, but yes…I am feeling fine. Thanks for the mints."

"You are welcome."

Julia tossed her backpack in Stephen's Jeep and climbed in. She would have ridden with Eduardo if he had asked. But he didn't.

He simply put the bucket of insects in the back of Stephen's Jeep and then walked to his truck and climbed in.

Julia didn't like the way that felt. Always having the upper hand on her emotions, this time it was different. She was avoiding the feeling of rejection. *Rejection from what? He has no idea how I feel. Even I have no idea how I feel*! Settling into her seat, she moved her thoughts to the tasks that lay ahead as they drove toward Stephen's compound.

42

From the cover of the forest, the *Catawishi* Indian guide motioned to the logging foreman who turned and watched Lupa and his silent followers returning from the forest. The group at the compound went into the common room and unpacked their jungle booty unaware they were being watched.

The foreman turned on his satellite phone and called Will's number again. Still no answer. "What do you think we should do?"

"Why don't we turn the Indians loose on them? We could tell them these people are their enemies," the man next to him said.

"That won't work. They're not stupid." He pushed his thumb toward the compound, "What did those people do to them?"

"Do you think the Indians would help us kill them?" The man looked at the two Indians in front and two in back, all with identical masks of dye around their eyes. "We could take the compound easy with the extra hands."

The foreman shook his head. "No, we wait." He motioned for everyone to get comfortable. The Indians became guards, ever watchful of the compound. The foreman picked up the phone and dialed again. Will still didn't answer.

* * *

Lupa stood outside by the fire stirring the pot of *ayahuasca* he was secretly preparing. He needed the *ayahuasca* for the plant teachers to tell him what to do about the evil surrounding the compound. The drink was ready. As the students worked in the lab, he brewed the strong elixir.

Without warning, Lupa jerked his head and looked toward the forest. He stared directly at the Indians standing vigil as he moved the pot from the fire. Even though he couldn't see them, he sensed they were there.

They saw him stare in their direction, and they too felt that he knew they were there. Movement would betray them, so they waited in stillness to see what the man would do next.

Lupa walked into the common room and went behind the counter.

He pulled out a dark, heavy box holding a pouch and several jars. He turned his back to the forest for only a moment before turning back. He opened the first jar and stuck his index finger into it. He stared at the Indians' hiding place as he painted a zigzag of blue across his forehead. He opened the other jar and repeated the motion. This time making red diagonal stripes across each cheek. Again, he did not take his eyes from the rainforest. He drew the danger symbols on his face as he had been taught by his father. He pulled off his khaki shorts and t-shirt and tied on his bright red loin cloth.

Lupa walked back outside and dipped a cup into the *ayahuasca* and drank. He crouched behind the blazing fire and waited. Several times he threw more wood on the fire until he had an inferno. It did not take long for the effects of the *ayahuasca* to center his spirit. The plant teachers were speaking to him.

Lupa stood and raised his arms as evening slid into darkness. He began to chant and dance around the roaring logs. The sound of his voice reached the students in the lab and the others in the forest.

The loggers watched in amusement at the clowning antics the little man was displaying. None of them were believers in shaman powers. The foreman smoked his last cigarette, throwing the crumbled package in the undergrowth. One of the Indians beside him leaned down and picked it up, his eyes meeting another Indian's eyes as he held onto the white man's trash.

The students stood at the corner of the common room, mesmerized by the fearsome sight of the man they had known for the past week as fun-loving and gentle.

As for the Indians, they paid close attention to Lupa as he continued chanting and dancing. Sweat ran down his back, and the red paint was beginning to shift a bit. The blue dye on his forehead would remain for a long time, eventually wearing off as the skin cells were purged.

As the fire began to die, Lupa stood behind it, facing the hiding place with raised arms. From their vantage point, the loggers and Indians could barely see him through the chimney of smoke. Lupa let out the scream of a jaguar before reaching into his pouch and throwing a handful of his purging mix onto the fire. The explosion was instant, and the fire burned larger than ever. Smoke glistened in a kaleidoscope of colors. Sparks shot toward the sky, and Lupa appeared consumed. He could have been a phoenix rising from the flames or a demon sinking into the inferno.

Jennifer gave a muffled gasp and the students huddled together, unsure of what to do.

Lupa was standing and swaying, still with his arms raised. His voice rose and fell like swells in the ocean. Lupa roared again and fell to his knees. As he fell, the fire extinguished. Completely out. No coals. No glowing embers. Nothing. Darkness.

The loggers were astounded by what they witnessed and strangely aware that their surroundings were different. A flood of cold swept across them causing a rippling of chills. Then came another realization.

The Indians who had guided them to this place…the Indians who could help them return to their camp…the Indians who were there to protect them…were gone.

The foreman with his band of men turned and, as a group, they ran chaotically down the vanishing trail just as Stephen, Julia, and Eduardo drove into the compound.

43

Even though Lupa had assured him he was fine, Stephen was still worried about his long-time friend. He knew Lupa had been concerned about Nigel and Drake, but he had not been aware that Lupa was planning to try to purge the evil spirits he believed were waiting to attack.

After witnessing Lupa's ritual, the students were reminded how exotic and dangerous this place was. They all drank a special tea Lupa prepared, and when they finished, everyone was a bit more composed. Lupa seemed to be the only one who thought nothing of his ceremony and went about preparing dinner.

Eduardo helped to clear the room for more tests, and Julia busied herself by remaining a comfortable distance from him. Stephen could sense the familiar tension between the two. It was the first time he'd witnessed either of them acting like school children, and it was the most amusement he'd had in a while. The feeling they gave Stephen was in complete juxtaposition to the awful things happening in the forest.

Lupa beckoned everyone to dinner, and most ate in silence. It had been a long, strange day.

As he was leaving, Eduardo took the coffee can with him, after Stephen tested and confirmed that ricin was, indeed, mixed inside. Stephen explained to everyone the dangers of the poison, and, again, they were grateful for Charlie's quick thinking. Had Lupa made their morning coffee as usual—from the familiar can Nigel had poisoned—right now, they would all be dead or dying.

* * *

Stephen and Julia were up before dawn, both anxious to get to the lab. They decided to let the students sleep in and told Lupa to delay breakfast a couple of hours. That way, Stephen knew Lupa would rest a while longer.

He also decided they had better be more cautious in their work since he was now convinced the PALs were evolving into a more dangerous form. This time, he and Julia pulled on gloves, masks, and smocks to test the newest samples.

Stephen opened the lid on the bucket of insects brought back from the last death site. As he poured some onto the table, one slid a little distance from the others. It was a tiny treehopper, glistening in a profusion of color. Stephen picked it up and gazed at the shiny surface. It was orange-faced, and its back was striped like a zebra except instead of black and white, the stripes were black and yellow. Mixed here and there were thin lines of brilliant blue. Stephen saw several more with the same coloring on the table. He picked up a different one. It had something on its back, shaped like half a dinner plate, much like a sail. There was a big white spot in the middle and light orange, yellow, and black stripes before and behind the sail.

Stephen shuffled the insects around on the table. *What is that*? He leaned closer. He wasn't sure. He rummaged in the drawer to his right and pulled out a small magnifying glass. It looked like a large thorn from a bush. *Why, it's an insect. Another treehopper*? *No, it's a scale insect.*

"Look at that one," Julia said with more than a trace of awe as she reached around Stephen to pick another up. "It's a beauty!" The treehopper shone as though it were made of silver, highly polished and reflective. Julia picked it up and placed it in the palm of her hand before turning her hand over and putting it on her fourth finger like a ring. "Look Stephen," she said holding it under the light. "It could be a jewel!"

"It's lovely." Stephen reached out and turned Julia's hand back and forth to catch the light. "You know," he said, "I have been so engrossed in the plants I have rarely taken time to carefully look at many of the insects. More often than not, they have just been a nuisance. Of course, there are never so many together at one time." He held his hands cupped around the mound. "All these years…look what I have been missing."

In such a massive collection, the insects were a sparkling spectacle. "I could spend hours…no…days looking at these," Julia said faintly.

"We do not have the time, my dear. How about pulling out the blood or tissue samples and getting them ready for us to go through. It does not matter which we start with."

Julia put the shiny jewel back with the others and crossed to the refrigerator.

Stephen followed her and tightened her mask from behind.

Julia's smile was hidden. "Thank you, Stephen."

He patted both shoulders. "Can't be too cautious."

Julia opened the refrigerator and looked toward the vials with the body fluids. *PALs have to be in there*. She reached for the tissue samples. Julia pulled out slides and began wiping them to be sure they were dry.

Stephen continued sorting the insects. He wouldn't sort the whole bucket, but he needed a good sampling. He didn't know what he was looking for, so he ran a standard discovery exercise.

The scale insects were a sharp contrast to the treehoppers. There weren't as many of them, and they had none of the stunning colors. Instead, many of them looked like nothing more than little scabs of bark. They were all drab looking, spotted with browns and grays and black and white. Only occasionally was there any indication of color, and when color was there, it was faint. Drab, but good at camouflage.

And then there were the ants. The students had identified twenty-nine different types so far, one very large fellow, with most of the others a good bit smaller.

Gazing at the lot, Stephen asked himself, *What do they have in common besides being insects? And what possible connection could they have with the dead loggers?* He stared at the pile before picking up a handful and letting them trickle back to the table through his fingers. *One thing's for sure, they are all definitely dead.*

Julia had the tissue slides ready when Stephen finished with the insects. He stood up, stretched, and walked to the sink. He peeled off his gloves, unlaced the mask, and let it hang on his chest. He tucked the ends into his shirt before pushing back the sleeves of his smock, turning the tap, and cupping his hands under the stream. He leaned over and buried his face in the water, blowing out any stray drops from his nose before rubbing both his face and neck. Then he rinsed his arms up to his elbows and reached for a clean towel.

He pulled on another pair of gloves, went to where Julia had stacked the slides, turned on the light in the microscope at his workstation, and retied his mask as he climbed onto the stool. They looked at slide after slide and Julia continued to scribble in her notebook.

It was still very early. Lupa brought breakfast but neither touched it. He came back a half hour later, clucking to them that they must eat, but he left them alone, taking the untouched food back to the kitchen.

"Well, what do you think?" Stephen asked Julia after Lupa left. It was time to compare notes.

Julia loosed the ties of her mask and responded, "I know those men died quickly,"

"I agree with you, and I must say, they probably experienced a great deal of pain as they died. Actually, it had to be worse than torture. The way the muscle tissues look, the cells appear to have almost exploded." Stephen was pensive as he uttered in a flat voice, "I would think the men must have felt like their insides were on fire."

Julia was not surprised. It only took seeing the bodies to know these men had suffered quick but tortuous deaths. "Thank goodness it was quick."

Stephen nodded as he brooded over the clues. "How did the PALs learn to inflict this type of punishment?"

Julia cocked her head repeating, "Punishment?"

Stephen said nothing. *Punishment? Why did I use that word?* He felt a need to rinse off again.

His description caused Julia to break into another cold sweat. "Stephen, what about the sting areas?"

"It appears all of the men were stung by several types of ants. We can only assume, since we didn't take that many samples, that each man had at least two or three different types of stings. I also saw a couple of bite marks on one man. Since some of the ants we found normally don't sting, I can only assume, for whatever reason, they bit him."

"Curious…" Julia was staring at the insects lying on the table with a bewildered expression. She had watched as Stephen opened several earlier to see if they contained their organs.

Stephen studied her expression. "Penny for your thoughts?" he asked.

"I was thinking about most of the fluids being expelled from all of our human victims," Julia answered. "Why didn't it affect them the same way?" She motioned toward the insects on the table.

Stephen shook his head, "Just another thing I can't explain." He pulled off his gloves and picked up his pipe. "I had the same thought. Their insides were dried, probably from Juan putting them in the sun, but they were intact." He filled the tobacco as he watched Julia move back to the refrigerator.

Julia stood in the open door looking at the vials of body fluids. She knew somewhere in there was something that could kill her…could kill both of them. Could kill all of them. She pursed her lips and looked over her shoulder at Stephen. He was lighting his pipe.

Oh, well. It has to be done, Julia thought. She picked up the plastic holder and carried the upright glass tubes to the table. She set them down gingerly and reached for a stack of slides.

"Mask," Stephen said.

"Right." Julia grumbled more to herself than to him, but she tied the mask up over her mouth and nose.

As she was securing it in place, Stephen felt a sudden chill. He looked at the vials in front of Julia. He looked toward the forest. *She's probably safer out there than in here*, Stephen thought. *I can look at the fluid slides alone. That way, if anything happens…*Stephen's voice sounded abrupt when he said, "Julia!"

Julia's head shot up. It was almost as though he shouted her name.

Stephen softened his voice, "Let's step outside for a moment and talk." He guided her to the doorway before she had a chance to loosen the mask.

"Okaaay," she said.

"Hear me out," he said after he shut the door.

Julia nodded but said nothing.

"We didn't notice any insects at the first death site, did we?"

"No, but we weren't looking for them."

Stephen cleared his throat again and looked toward the window. "I was thinking. I'd like for you to go back out there to the first tree and take another look around. Just at the ground. Do you mind?" He was afraid she might see through his ploy to get her out of the lab so *he* could go through the samples. Stephen continued before she could speak, "I can look at the body fluids. We know there will be some of them in there, and I will isolate them for study later. Besides, I need to stay here to make some calls. It's time we let more of the outside world know what's going on down here."

She eyed the door. "Do you think it's safe out there?"

Stephen nodded. "Whatever was there is gone, Julia. Look at all the people who tramped around. We were in the trees ourselves. And the site is on a trail between villages. I'm sure more of the locals have passed by the place." Stephen shrugged his shoulders. "Nothing else has happened, has it?" He hoped it didn't sound like he was trying to convince her.

She turned and looked back at Stephen. He wouldn't send her out there if he had any cause to think it might not be safe. "I'm probably safer out here than in there." She pointed to the lab and gave a nervous laugh, repeating almost word for word what Stephen was thinking. "You're right, of course, and if I can find some insects on the ground, it might help us look at the evolution of this PAL…whatever-it-is."

Stephen nodded in agreement. "Yes, Julia. That would be of great help. You will go?" He tried not to sound too pushy.

Julia never suspected. "Yes," she rubbed up and down her arms. "Besides I want to stay out of this lab for a while. I've got the heebie-jeebies." Julia went back inside, tossed the mask into the trash, and peeled off the gloves. She hung her smock near the door and picked up her backpack.

Stephen forced a smile. "Enjoy the ride. You remember how to get there?" He had showed her on a map on the wall of the common room.

"Yes. You sure you'll be okay?" Julia glanced at the vials sitting on the table. "The students should be out soon."

Stephen saw where she was looking. "Yes, yes," he motioned. "I'll put them to work when they get here. Now, go. It's not far. Take this." He picked up a radio, and switched it on, handing it to her. Then he added, "I know it's early, but just in case…" He pushed a flashlight into her bag. "Call me when you get there, do you hear?"

Julia nodded and gave him a smile. Her voice crackled through the other radio sitting in the corner as she squeezed the talk button, "Cheerio." Now that she was going, she couldn't wait to be gone. She moved out the screened door at a brisk walk.

She was almost around the corner when Stephen called out after her,

"Take Lupa with you!"

Julia turned and held her bag in the air in response. She stepped backwards one step and blew him a kiss.

Stephen waved back with a smile that faded as he turned away. He walked straight to the radio and took it to his work station.

Julia went into the house to find Lupa. She searched all the rooms, but he wasn't there. She looked in the vegetable garden. Not there. Then she saw his slight figure coming from the forest with an armload of roots.

"Let's go for an outing, Lupa," Julia said, holding the door open as he bustled the roots over to the sink.

"Field trip?" Lupa asked. They had talked about field trips many times.

"Yes," she laughed. "Field trip."

Lupa frowned. "But breakfast for students?"

Julia waved her hand toward him. "Let them raid the kitchen for once. There's enough fruit out already. Grab a couple of buckets and a shovel and meet me at the Jeep, okay?" She called over her shoulder.

"You got it," Lupa imitated what she'd said to him often.

Julia wanted to make sure Stephen was okay before she left, so she retraced her steps to the lab. She looked through the screened door, and Stephen sat with his back toward her. *He's fine*, she said to herself. *Don't bother him*. She walked back to the house and picked up two fresh bananas as she headed out the front door.

Lupa sat in the Jeep waiting for her. She tossed her pack in the back seat and dropped the radio and bananas next to it. "Ready to go?" she asked.

"Field trip! Field trip!" he chanted pumping his fists up and down in the air and bouncing like a second grader on a school bus heading toward the zoo.

Julia's laughter rang out, and off they went.

Stephen heard the Jeep drive off and was smiled to himself when he heard Lupa's chanting from the Jeep. He sat on the stool in front of the microscope looking at the vials in front of him. Picking up his pipe, his eyes traveled to the worktable with the insects. He could wait no longer. He laid down his pipe, tied up his mask, opened one of the vials, and made a slide. Positioning it under the light, Stephen focused both eye pieces as he considered…*Treehoppers. Scale insects. Ants. Illegal loggers. What do you all have in common*? For the life of him, Stephen could not think of anything. He tossed around various theories in his head.

He recalled a visit to the US outside Lexington, Kentucky in 2001, where dead foals were discovered across many of the large horse farms. After much research the scientists across the country finally theorized that a heavy outbreak of tent caterpillars had caused the deaths.

An experiment was set up on one farm to show what happened. Wild cherries were planted in large containers spread out over the farm on half an acre of land. They were placed in rows, their tree branches separated from each other by several feet and isolated at root level by the containers. The head groundskeeper placed tent caterpillars onto the first row of wild cherry trees.

That day the caterpillars were ravenously eating the cherry leaves and in one day's time, the caterpillars made significant inroads of stripping the leaves off the first row of trees.

For her experiment, the groundskeeper carried a basket through the wild cherry trees, stopping at the first row with the caterpillars. There she picked several leaves, stuffed them into a plastic zip bag and then documented the tree ID on the bag. She repeated this for several trees moving to different rows further and further from the foraging caterpillars.

After the samples had been collected and labeled, the groundskeeper started with the bag holding leaves collected from the first tree with the caterpillars. She crumbled and crushed each leaf and dumped them into a test tube. She then took dried filter paper strips, which she had previously dipped into a mixture of sodium carbonate and picric acid, and stuck the strip into the test tube of leaves and added a few drops of chloroform. The procedure turned the leaves a bright, brick red color, which she said indicated a high concentration of cyanide in the leaves.

She followed the same procedure for each bag, in an order going from the leaves collected closest to the tent caterpillars to succeeding bags collected farther and farther away. As the tree distance increased, the test color that emerged was less bright, until the last sample barely turned red, yet still indicated a slight trace of cyanide.

The groundskeeper's explanation of the results, based upon research, repeated trials, and consulting with scientists was that evidence showed there was a type of signal or communication passed through the air from tree to tree that a predator was eating the first row of trees. In jest, she called it 'wireless communication,' and began working to identify the trigger mechanism and signaling technique used by the trees. Somehow, trees half an acre away, were receiving a message from a tree under attack alerting them that predators were coming. Consequently the trees began to manufacture cyanide poison to protect the leaves. She was confident because prior to placing caterpillars on the branches she had tested samples and the results showed no traces of cyanide in any tree leaf.

After running the test procedures, she went back to the first row and shook the caterpillars off the branches. Remarkably the caterpillars developed systems to maintain the cyanide within their bodies, immune from its poisoning effect. If left to feed, these caterpillars would themselves become poisonous to birds and other prey that might inadvertently eat them. The caterpillars had become little killing machines themselves, storing the poison to ward off predators.

Whether it was their excrement or the caterpillars themselves falling onto the grass for the mother horses to eat, it was the caterpillars' cyanide that killed the foals. The mothers were large enough not to be adversely affected by the poison, but the foals were not.

Stephen pulled his thoughts back to the slide in front of him. Positioning it under the light, he focused both eye pieces. He thought back to the groundskeeper and her research.

Stephen took in a sharp breath as it hit him…

44

Nigel and Drake were on the move for good. The night before when they mixed the ricin with the coffee, they collected their belongings and confiscated an extra machete and more food. There were no plans to return. Ever.

Nigel was almost finished tying up loose ends. It was time for him to change professions and create a new identity. He couldn't go back to the school once the bodies of Jennifer and Charlie were found, and Drake was never going to return. He'd see to that as well. Yes, it was time to become someone else again. The beginning of a new adventure.

He and Drake sat next to a clear rushing stream eating breakfast. Drake downed the last of his water and walked three quick steps to the edge, stooped down, and filled his canteen. It took less than ten seconds. He never saw Nigel toss a handful of ricin into his trail mix. One quick shake of the bag and it was back in the exact place Drake left it.

Drake looked quickly back at his open baggy while Nigel had both hands around his coffee cup watching him. Drake knelt and closed the bag, stuffing it back in its usual handy spot.

"Where to now?" Drake asked as he zipped his pack and hoisted it onto his back.

Nigel smiled. "How about we go home?"

"Fine by me," Drake said. "Let's get started then. It's a long trip."

Not as long as you might think. Nigel enjoyed his thoughts and suppressed a smile.

45

Eduardo's truck bounced into another pothole as he continued to think of Julia. She had been in and out of his thoughts ever since he met her and now, this morning, she was all he could think about.

The look that had passed between them on the flight home yesterday had been potent. He wanted her so badly he was unsure what might happen the next time they were alone. After Serena, Eduardo thought he could never want another woman. But he wanted Julia, and it wasn't just a physical wanting. There were many things about Julia which drew him to her.

He pulled to a stop on the ridge above the village and turned off the engine as Kahepa lay before him in the early morning light. Here and there Eduardo could see smoke rising from morning breakfast fires. The river shimmered to the left, and four small boats were setting out for the early catches of fish for the day. He checked his watch. Shortly, one of the weekly supply boats would be rounding the bend, and at that moment, he heard the whistle announcing its arrival though the boat was not yet in sight.

Eduardo leaned across the steering wheel, his thoughts returning to Julia. He wondered if she would consider living here. He wondered if she wanted children. He had always wanted them, and he and Serena planned to start a family soon. Then he stopped himself, realizing he had no idea what Julia thought.

Had it only been a little over a year since Serena had gone? It seemed like a lifetime. He hadn't been back to the waterfall behind his house since. He could close his eyes and see her lifeless body on the rocks at the base…her dark hair wavering in the water…her beautiful face untouched yet the back of her head crushed. He shuddered remembering.

Then he thought of Julia. He was drawn to her. He felt like she was drawn to him. But was she? Could he bear the pain of loss again if he surrendered to his feelings and she rejected him? His mind was in a state of confusion. *Too much to think about.*

As if she heard his thoughts, Julia's voice crackled over his radio.

"Eduardo?"

Her voice was music. He picked up the radio and answered, "Yes, Julia."

"Lupa and I are going on a field trip. Would you like to join us?"

He could barely make out her words for the static.

Eduardo frowned. "Where are you going, Julia? Can you hear me?"

"Yes, I can hear you. We are going to the mahogany. The one where the first men died." The words became a little clearer.

Lupa leaned toward the radio and shouted after Julia, "Miss Julia take Lupa on field trip!"

Eduardo smiled. "I think I could use a field trip," he agreed. "I'll be an hour, maybe less. You be careful. Okay?"

"Roger and out," Julia's voice was barely audible again.

Eduardo rummaged around looking for the spare batteries he usually kept close at hand. No batteries. *Oh well. I know where you're going.* He started the truck, and as he drove down the rutted lane he wondered what he even knew about Julia. She was educated, she was smart, and she was beautiful. Not like Serena, but different. And her hair. More than anything, he wanted to bury his face in her hair. He came close to doing it just yesterday.

Julia had been walking in front of him toward the plane when they were leaving to fly home. She stopped abruptly, and he almost bumped into her. And there was that molten layer of hair flowing below his chin. He had almost reached down and gathered it into his hands to inhale. The thought aroused him then, and it did even now. One day, he would get lost in Julia—at least he hoped he would.

But what about the man back home? Mitch. Julia rarely spoke of him. Eduardo had seen the ring, had watched her turning it around her finger on more than one occasion. Would she really marry him?

Eduardo was pleased when she ran out to his truck late last night and asked to see his garden again. *Of course*, he told her. *Let's have dinner at my house tomorrow night.* She seemed pleased with the invitation. Tonight, he would find a way to take her into his arms.

Eduardo parked in front of the hotel and went inside. Pepe waved to him from the desk. He walked over and asked, "Is our young American in?"

Pepe shook his head. "No, and I did not see him in the canteen at all yesterday. I ask Senhor Pantoja this morning, and he say the man not there last night. I keep up with him for you, Eduardo."

Eduardo put his hand on the smaller man's shoulder. "You are a good man, Pepe. Are we sure he has not left for good?" Pepe looked from side to side to be certain no one could hear him. He leaned toward Eduardo. "I hear him moving around early this morning. I hear his phone ring. He go out, but I sneak in his room. His things still in closet."

"Excellent." Eduardo was glad to know the American was still here. "I need the key, Pepe." Eduardo held out his hand and Pepe complied. As Eduardo went up the stairs he whispered, "Ring the bell if the man comes back in."

Eduardo slipped inside and turned on the light. He had to admit, the man was tidy. The room was straight, and it was apparent the floor had been swept. He pushed the door open into the bathroom and saw it was clean also, except for some wadded up clothing in the corner. On the counter was a razor and shaving cream and a can of Lysol disinfectant.

The closet held two duffel bags and a broom. Eduardo pulled out the bags and emptied one on the bed. Clothes. Underwear. Bug spray. Just the usual things a vacationer might bring. He looked in the other bag and saw three gallons of clean water in sealed containers and a six-pack of tonic water with quinine.

Eduardo put his hands on his hips and turned around. He lifted the mattress and looked under it. Nothing. He saw the desk and sat down. He opened all the drawers. Nothing. He pulled them all the way out and felt around them and inside their openings. Nothing. He looked behind the desk and glimpsed the corner of a paper lodged under it.

Eduardo pulled out the flimsy piece of furniture and picked up the paper. It was a crude drawing of a map, like someone was distracted and doodling while in thought. *What is that*? Longitude and latitude, kind of like a GPS system would give.

Written in pencil it said,

Livingston
jerk
get tree
tomorrow
10/11

Livingston? *Maybe a logging company*? *Which tree*? *Was this the map to a tree*? *And what was 10/11*? Eduardo looked up toward the ceiling. His eyes darted around as he thought. A date? What was today? Today was October 11th. 10-11.

Whatever was happening, it was happening today. He went downstairs, tossing the key to Pepe as he left. When he got in the truck, he laid the map on the seat next to him and pulled out a book of maps of the area. He began flipping pages. There it was. The coordinates on the paper were the same as for the first death site. This man was going after the first mahogany tree.

Eduardo's head jerked up. "Julia!"

46

The road Julia drove was in fair condition. She and Lupa were making good time. They came around a bend and stopped. The scene in front of them made them laugh out loud. There in the middle of the road was a small group of spider monkeys.

"Field trip!" Lupa shouted as he pointed to the group.

They did indeed look like a kindergarten class out for a field trip. Two lone females were trying to settle the youngsters down with little success.

Julia counted five young ones. She shut off the engine and enjoyed their frolicking. The youngsters raced across nearby branches, tagging the adults as they darted back into the road. As for the older ones, they were grabbing and screaming at the top of their lungs, mouths wide open, lips curled as they tried to calm the children. One of the young ones spied Julia and Lupa and came running. In a flash it bounced over her into the back seat.

And then it was a free-for-all. Julia felt like she was in a scene from *Jumanji*. Monkeys were everywhere. Julia held her arms over her head as they ran back and forth across her. Her laughter added to the pandemonium of wild screeching and chattering. The adults held back from the Jeep, taking up positions in the tree next to Julia, jumping up and down in a fury urging the youngsters to come with them.

Julia still had her head covered and her face protected from all the playfulness while Lupa crouched on the floor in front of his seat. They never noticed one of the jumping imps bump the button on the radio. The green light went off as it powered down.

* * *

A few seconds later Eduardo grabbed his radio, held down the button and yelled, "Julia! Julia!"

She didn't answer.

He shook the radio, not sure if it was working. He tried channel after channel. Still no response. He threw the radio down and started the engine. He spun the tires in the dirt of the street as he raced through the village. If there had been anyone in his way, he may not have seen them.

All he could imagine was Julia driving into danger. Even with Lupa at her side, both were in jeopardy. They were almost certain to be driving toward their deaths, and this time it was not something mysterious in the forest. It would be from a man. A man going after a tree.

* * *

The monkeys settled just a bit, and Julia peeked out from her fingers looking over Lupa and into the back seat. Two still tussled next to the smallest behind her, and two more used her head like a stepping stone as they climbed over her onto the hood. As Julia watched, the smallest monkey grabbed a banana in each hand.

"Hey, that's our breakfast!" she yelled as she tried to snatch them back.

"Is it safe to come out, Miss Julia?" Lupa still had his head covered as he crouched on the floor.

"Yes, Lupa. It's safe." She giggled at the expression on his face. After his fierce display the students described at the fire last night, this show of timidity was comical.

"Lupa brave most time, Miss Julia," he said as he climbed back into the seat. "But monkey bite Lupa as child, and Lupa no like monkey on me…no like." He waved both hands.

* * *

Eduardo drove faster than he would have ever thought possible. These roads were treacherous on good days, even when driving slowly, but Eduardo was racing. *I cannot lose her after I have just found her*, he thought. He was almost frantic.

* * *

Julia concentrated on her driving. The road was narrowing and becoming rougher. She turned onto the newly cut logging road. It had been cut no more than a couple of weeks ago. Trees lay haphazardly in the forest, just clear of the winding path. She slowed down as the Jeep climbed over low stumps and fallen branches.

The Jeep rounded a corner and there were the two trees in the staging area, their tops bedraggled and torn, fatally damaged by the saws from days before. Down the steep slope, Julia knew the mahogany waited. She turned off the Jeep and started to get out. Lupa stopped her.

"Lupa come here before, Miss Julia."

"You have been here?"

"Many time. Drive to tree. There." He pointed to a cluster of boulders to their left.

"Are you sure?" The rocks appeared to block any possible way down.

"Lupa sure."

"Okay," Julia said. "Let's go."

Sure enough, just as Julia pulled even with the outcropping, she saw a wide path, wide enough for the Jeep to make a sharp descent to the mahogany.

When the tree came into view, Lupa exclaimed, "Yes. Is place!"

Julia parked the Jeep on the far side of the tree. She sat staring up at the tall, wide trunk, marveling at the huge buttresses. "We could put a roof between those two, and we could live there easily."

"Lupa live in real house." He frowned. "Lupa live in jungle many year. No fun."

"No, I guess it wasn't," Julia agreed. She stepped out of the Jeep and went around to the back. As she pulled out a bucket, she remarked, "Oh, good. You brought two." She pulled out the two shovels and leaned them against the tire. "I don't know if we'll need these, but we'll see."

"Lupa help."

"Let's get started, then," Julia said as she handed her bucket to Lupa and grabbed the other. "We are looking for dead insects. I really don't think we will find many, since it rained so much the day the men died, but it's worth a try."

They walked around the tree and found several handfuls of treehoppers, thanks mostly to their metallic colors, which glittered through the dried mud when the scattered sunrays bounced off them. "How do you know this place, Lupa?" Julia asked as she squatted to pick up several more insects.

Lupa stood from his gathering spot and pointed to a hill just behind Julia. "Just there. Not far," his face held a look of joy and contentment, "sweetest cassava roots ever found."

"Really?" Julia perked up at the thought of some fresh *farofa amureta*. She took his bucket from his hands poured his insects into her bucket, "Go!"

Lupa was confused. "Go?"

"Yes, please go and get some."

"Lupa no leave Miss Julia." He shook his head as she held out his bucket. Lupa took it, but continued to shake his head, "Lupa no leave Miss Julia."

"Don't be silly. We aren't finding that many insects. Let's at least go home with some sweet roots to make some fresh cassava flour. I'd love some to go on our rice tomorrow. I haven't had any in a long time. My mouth is watering just thinking about it. Please, Lupa?" she pleaded.

"Pretty please?"

"Lupa no think good." It was obvious he didn't want to leave her.

"I'll be fine. Look around. There's nothing here to hurt me. Just me and the dead insects. Besides, if I have any problem, I'll yell. You can be back in a flash."

Lupa continued to shake his head. "No, Miss Julia. I wait. We go together."

Julia retrieved one of the shovels from where it had been leaning against the Jeep. She posed in a batter's stance holding the handle of the shovel preparing to swing the blade towards an imaginary ball. "If anything comes after me…" she swung, "…I'll bash in its head!"

Lupa laughed. "You funny, Miss Julia." He sobered. "No."

"Come on, Lupa," Julia rested the shovel back against the Jeep. "Think how happy Stephen will be with some fresh *farofa amureta*. The seasoning is one of his favorites."

Lupa rubbed his chin as he considered. "Stephen love *farofa amureta*. Miss Julia love *farofa amureta*. Eduardo love *farofa amureta*. Lupa love *farofa amureta*." He eyed Julia closely and hesitated. "You okay, Miss Julia?"

Julia held up both palms for emphasis. "I'll be fine, Lupa. Just go. Take your nice, empty bucket…" she said grabbing one shovel and forcing it into his hand. "…and this shovel and go. Get us some fresh cassava roots. You'll be back before I finish looking around."

"Yell loud?" he asked.

"I'll yell loud," Julia confirmed.

"Okay, Lupa back quick like jaguar." He grinned as he trotted up the hill behind the Jeep. "Lupa quick like snake strike." He continued to talk as he made his way over the top. "Like hungry hawk…like banana-stealing monkey…"

Julia grinned after him. She knelt back down envisioning fall outings, where she picked up pecans on cool autumn afternoons. Between the two sheltering buttresses, she felt snug and safe. Their massive arms along with the sounds of the forest muffled the sound of a new brown truck pulling up behind the two mangled trees at the top of the slope. Julia never heard the engine or the two men who climbed out with their gear.

* * *

"I have never done this with just the two of us, Boss Man," Paulo said as he shot the rope over the Y of the first tree. "I would not have thought we could."

Will slapped him on the back as he passed. "Think about it. The hardest part is already done." He looked up at the two trees. "All we gotta do is get the pulley system in place, and we're ready to get logs up this hill. I got trucks comin' in a few hours. We got it all covered."

"You right, Boss Man."

"Can you handle this on your own?"

Paulo was gathering all the ropes and pulleys to set up the system at the staging area, "I got it. Go, have you fun," Paulo motioned down the slope.

Will needed no encouragement. "I'm on it." He pulled his chainsaw from the back of the truck topped off the oil and gas tank. He leaned into the truck and pulled out his .44, positioning it snuggly behind his back in his belt. He trudged down the slope with his equipment, calculating as he went how long he thought it might take to cut the tree. Too bad they didn't have the rest of the crew. This would take longer than he liked with just the two of them. But he had to get it done.

There it was. The mahogany tree. Will had to marvel. The tree was a gem. He sucked in a breath to let out a whoop when he stopped. What had he just seen? Could it have been a person's head? He held his breath. Who in the hell could it be? Will lowered the chainsaw to the ground and pulled out the pistol. It felt warm and comfortable in his hand. He made his way down toward the tree, the sound of his steps blending with the forest sounds.

* * *

Julia dropped another treehopper into the bucket and looked inside. She could still see the bottom in places. There wasn't an abundance of treehoppers or ants, and she hadn't found any of the bland little scale insects. She stood and picked up the bucket intending to move further around the tree. Julia saw a flash out of the corner of her eye and fell in a heap at the base of the tree, blood oozing from a gash that opened over her eye. Everything went black.

* * *

"Damn!" Will shouted. *What the hell is a woman doing out here*? He looked around and saw the Jeep. *Is there anyone with her*? He turned all the way around looking. He walked back to where the woman lay prone on the ground, noticing for the first time the bucket that had toppled next to her. He knelt and scooped up the dead bugs. *Shit*!

He stared at the woman and looked at his gun. He stood and aimed at her head. Then he looked back toward Paulo and decided to leave her where she lay. Paulo didn't have the stomach for killing. He'd start cutting from the other side anyway, so she could just lie there. With any luck, the tree would shift and fall on her. He hit her again just to make sure she stayed down.

Will retrieved the chainsaw. It would take a while to get off all of the buttresses before he could begin cutting the trunk. He pulled down his safety glasses and hit the choke. A loud roar pierced the air as he started the saw. The noise sent birds into flight and monkeys scurrying.

Will caught sight of a sloth holding onto one of the branches above him in a nearby tree. *I guess you'll go with the tree.* The little animal slowly began to move higher. *I always wanted to get me a sloth. Maybe I'll have you mounted.* Will grinned and nodded.

The smoke from the engine puffed and gathered around Will. He walked over and started hacking at some smaller trees so he could start his work. He'd start cutting the strong buttresses after he got himself a good spot to work from.

* * *

A short distance away, Lupa scooped out another cassava root. They were just where he remembered, and more plentiful than he could have hoped. They would have flour for a long time. Lupa stopped mid-scoop as he dug in the moist dirt when he thought he heard an unusual sound. Something that wasn't from the forest. He stood up and listened to the insects and animal calls. He dug another shovelful and paused. He turned his head slightly to hone in on the sound. *There*! *What is it*? *No*! His mind screamed. Lupa held tight to the shovel and ran toward Julia…and the sound of a chainsaw.

* * *

Just a few more minutes! Eduardo was nearly out of his mind with worry. He rushed onto the side road where the trees had recently been cut. He knew the staging area was close. He rounded the last corner and slid to a halt just behind the brown truck parked beside the two topless trees. He could see the pulley system already rigged and ready to go. He rushed toward the slope half sliding as he raced toward the roar of a chainsaw.

* * *

Paulo stopped dead in his tracks and then ducked behind a tree when he heard a truck come into the clearing. He saw a man jump from the truck and race in the direction of the mahogany. The man did not see him, and Paulo heard his plodding steps as he went down the hillside. *Why was the big man here*? *Were there more men coming*? Paulo made his way down the slope trying to get to Will, but he knew he would never get there before the big man.

* * *

A fog surrounded Julia. She could hear something but she couldn't make out what she was hearing. *Buzzing…like bees? One bee? A large bee. Were killer bees coming for her?* Her head throbbed, and she reached up to touch a spot on her forehead that hurt. She turned onto her back and opened her eyes. Above her she saw the wavering outline of the canopy as she tried to bring it into focus. The bee sputtered, and she realized it was not a bee at all. It was a chainsaw, and it was very close. She could smell the fuel and realized the fog wasn't fog. It was smoke from the exhaust. Someone was cutting the mahogany.

Trying not to panic, Julia twisted onto her stomach and climbed to her knees. She saw a pool of blood where she had been lying and paused staring at the dark, sticky spot. She wiped her mouth and looked at her hand. Had she vomited that? There was blood on her hand. *What happened to me?* she wondered. She listened as the chainsaw went into the idle mode.

* * *

Will let off the gas and lowered the saw to his side. He grabbed the bottom of his shirt and wiped his face, already dripping with sweat. Gauging the best place to start, Will set the saw on the ground where it continued its loud grumbling. He pulled at the scrubby trees he had just taken down, dragging them out of the way so he could get started. He found a spot about three feet off the ground and laid the chainsaw against the buttress. Pulling the trigger, Will pressed into the tree, the blades of the chain biting into the bark and making their way into the deep tissue, severing the veins, flinging resin-soaked sawdust all around.

* * *

Julia reached for the tree for support as she walked her hands up the coarse, dark bark until she was on her feet. Sawdust floated over and around her, and she could smell the sweet scent of the freshly cut wood. Julia laid her cheek against the tree and closed her eyes. She heard the chainsaw's gnawing sound change, and she knew enough about cutting wood to know the man had taken his finger off the trigger. He was not cutting now.

* * *

Paulo was moving at a quick pace, making sure he kept cover behind and beside him. He couldn't see the big man. *Just a little further.*

* * *

Eduardo was now close enough to the tree to see Will at the base and raced toward him. He saw Julia coming from behind one of the tall fins in the back. Blood ran down her face, and she half walked, half crawled, leaning heavily on the buttress for support. He watched as she slid back to the ground. She didn't move.

"Julia!" he screamed. Eduardo had never wanted to kill anyone, had never thought he could. Now, he knew it was possible. He wanted to kill this man.

* * *

Will got back to it and was starting to put his weight into his work when he felt something on the back of his hand. It was an ant, but it wasn't just any ant. It was a bullet ant, and Will knew how badly they hurt. The ant's body arched up, and Will knew it was going to sting him. He was setting the saw down to slap it away when he felt rain falling on and around him. *Damn rain.* But it wasn't rain. It was insects. *Falling from the tree like they had with Carlos and the others…* He swatted the ant off before it sank its toxic barb into his flesh.

Will dropped the saw and began to run.

* * *

The surreal sight caused Eduardo to halt abruptly. He watched as the man withdrew the saw from the buttress. Then he saw the sky open up like a cornucopia as insects fell from the mahogany tree. Eduardo watched the man run to the Jeep and knew he could never get there in time to stop him. He instinctively ran toward Julia.

* * *

Will had no time to get to his own truck. He raced to the Jeep and turned the key. He threw it into reverse and flew back up the hill never realizing that Eduardo was there.

* * *

Paulo saw his boss run to the Jeep and take off. At first he was puzzled. Nothing made sense. Then he saw Julia lying next to the tree. *Is that woman*? He craned his neck to see her clearly. *Is that blood*? *Did Will hurt woman*? *Is she dead*? He turned and saw the big man race toward the woman. He peered back up the hill expecting others, but no one came. *Where is Will go? He leave me here?*

Paulo thought about going back up the hill for the truck but decided it would be best to leave it. He would leave everything. Paulo took off in the opposite direction and ran as he had never run before. He had to get away from the bleeding woman. He had to get away from the place where he had been abandoned by his boss, his friend. He had to get away from the terror he saw on the big man's face…on Will's face. The place was evil. Paulo knew in that moment he could not cut the trees anymore. He would find another way to feed his family.

* * *

Julia lay as still as death. Eduardo could barely breathe. The insects stopped falling but were thick on and around her. He saw several ants on her arms, one a bullet ant hunched to sting, and he swiped it from her skin. He quickly brushed all the insects he could find from her.

Eduardo thought back to the corpses he had watched Stephen and Julia autopsy. He remembered their shrunken appearance because of the lack of body fluids. He thought of all the insects gathered from under the mahogany tree at that other, far-away place.

Lupa sprinted from the forest and stood over Eduardo, breathing hard, his shovel raised at the ready for trouble. He stared down at Julia in disbelief. The grief on his face was overwhelming. Lupa didn't speak or attempt to touch Julia. Instead, he squatted down and scooped up a handful of tiny, bejeweled treehoppers…then the shaman stood…began to chant…and then to dance.

Eduardo leaned down and softly kissed Julia's cheek before he pulled off his shirt and balled it like a pillow, gently placing it under her head. He kissed her other cheek and her eyes and then he kissed her mouth. He sat up then and looked around at his beautiful Amazon Rainforest, a place where he had always felt safe. And now? *What will happen now?*

47

A quick glance at Eduardo's kitchen was proof enough dinner had been planned for this evening. Vegetables sat on the counter waiting to be cut, peeled, and cooked. The table was set for two, with a pair of wine glasses sparkling in the afternoon sunlight spiking through the window. There were even candles ready to be lit. A check of the refrigerator revealed a bottle of red Chilean wine, along with a fresh fruit salad, chilled and waiting.

The back step also waited in solitude for someone to stand and soak in the captivating view. A gentle breeze brushed the hillside overlooking the garden, lifting the palm fronds, making them wave to each other with their slender leaves. The path still wound down toward the stream, and bees buzzed along the slope, dipping in and out of open flowers lining the pathway.

The stream was still cool as it bubbled and danced gently over stones, a testimony at day's end that nature's calmness and beauty endured.

The powerful perfume of the *costas* wafted about as Julia trailed her hand in the water. Eduardo sat behind her. She was resting against him, her hair draped across his shoulder and flowing down his back. Occasionally, he felt a tickling on his opposite cheek by a single hair lifting in the breeze. When it did, he would smile, not wanting to place it back. It was a tender reminder she was here. They were here. The horrific day was behind them.

They had been sitting like this for over an hour, when Julia realized her right foot was asleep. She shifted, causing Eduardo to turn. When he did, their faces were close, and Julia didn't move away. Eduardo tilted his head and softly kissed her.

She kissed him back. "I know I'm a sight," Julia murmured, smoothing her hair to the side.

Eduardo smiled as he looked from the top of her head down to her feet. She wore a new, bright blue t-shirt he dug out of the back of his closet tied in a knot at her waist. He had dressed her wound as best he could, and now she had a clean, white patch of gauze taped to her forehead. Her slim jeans slid smoothly into high, black work boots.

"You're lovely, Julia," he said as he kissed her again.

They rose and strolled back to the house holding hands. Eduardo opened the door, and Julia brushed past him. A few minutes later she sat admiring his strong back as he worked to finish their early dinner…or was it a late lunch?

"Eduardo?" Julia asked.

He turned and leaned against the counter.

"Are you hungry?"

He knew she meant for food, but for a moment he fantasized she meant for something else. He turned to look out the window. "Not really."

"I'm not very hungry either. Why don't we just have some wine and fruit on the back step?"

"I like that idea." He took the bowl of fruit salad from the refrigerator and grabbed two forks in the other hand, while Julia picked up the wine and the glasses.

They moved onto the patio and sat comfortably on the top step. Eduardo placed the fruit between them, and they sat and ate from the same bowl. The breeze still stirred. A flock of birds skimmed the tree tops. The waterfall in the distance was white against a deep, green backdrop. They ate in silence. It was enough just to be here. Both forks clattered into the bowl in unison.

Julia poured more wine, and they watched the sun slide toward the mountain crest across the horizon. She swirled the last of the mellow liquid in her glass, took a deep breath and put the glass down, trying to think of words to start a conversation. Nothing came. Anxious to break the silence, she finally said, "I can't think of anything meaningful to say." She leaned both elbows on her knees and rested her chin in her hands. Still resting her head in her palms, she turned her head to look at him. "It's as though words don't belong in this moment," she heard herself saying.

Eduardo understood and nodded, knowing what she meant. He felt a raw exhaustion inside. Raw from chasing after Julia thinking she was headed for certain death at the tree site. Raw from struggling to get to her; raw from racing down that long slope toward the mahogany tree while blood ran down her face and dripped onto her chest; raw from believing, if only momentarily, he would never be allowed to caress the beautiful woman he watched slide to the ground at the base of a *mogno* tree. No…Eduardo had no words either.

The incident in the forest this morning would take time to digest. After Eduardo knelt beside Julia, convinced she was dead and that both he and Lupa were going to die with her, they simply waited. The saw sputtered into silence. They listened to the symphony of insect sounds, punctuated by the roar of a big cat in the distance, by monkeys chattering in the trees, and by melodic bird calls overhead. They were frozen in time, waiting for what was to come. When it didn't come, they looked around confused and stunned. Life existed as it had before. But before what?

"Let's not dwell on this right now, okay?" Eduardo spoke softly as he stood up. "Come. We have to get you home. Lupa called just as you went into the garden. He said there was something important he had to tell us."

"And I wonder what that can be?" Julia smiled in spite of the melancholy mood that gripped her. "Probably Stephen with a new revelation about the PALs."

"I don't know. He sounded mysterious to me." Eduardo reached for her hand.

"Mysterious?" Julia asked looking down at their clasped hands. "Haven't we had enough of mysterious events lately?"

Eduardo traced the lines around the bandage on her forehead. "Hurt?" he asked.

She grimaced, "Only if someone touches it."

He drew his hand away fearing he had caused her pain when he noticed she was smiling. He touched the end of her nose. "You were joking with me, right?"

She laughed softly. "Yes…and no. It does hurt but…"

They stood close for a moment. Eduardo searched Julia's face for any indication of what she was thinking. Finally, he asked, "Must you go home, Julia?"

He was thinking of Mitch and the unwelcome thought of Julia being in another man's arms. He reached to brush her hair behind her ear. He took his finger and then traced it along her cheek to her mouth.

"I don't know," she whispered a groan. "I really don't know."

He watched her for a moment longer and then smiled. "Okay. Then we must go."

Eduardo took his time, driving slower than usual, not wanting the afternoon to end.

48

Will couldn't believe his luck. Not only had he managed to get away alive, but his plane was ready when he reached the airstrip. It was the same DA42 Twinstar he flew to plot the mahoganies, and, as he looked down onto the jungle below, he spotted one of the trees above the canopy in the distance. *Damn tree*!

He'd been flying now for about an hour, and the setting sun hurried him to the next airstrip. He probably had an hour of good daylight left, which should be enough to get him safely there. Even so, he pushed the throttle to the limit to get all the speed he could.

He looked around at the sleek interior of the plane. He'd decided earlier to keep it. *Screw Livingtson*. He didn't care how much the plane was worth. He'd earned it. Will vowed to never step foot inside a rainforest again. He was leaving behind too many murders that he hadn't committed himself, and he couldn't explain them either. Whatever killed Carlos and the other men in the forest would not get to him on a sunny beach in South Florida. *But what about the Everglades*? *Almost a rainforest*? *Probably a little too much wildlife and not the kind of 'wild' I am looking for*. Maybe he'd go to the Mediterranean; just someplace far away from any jungle.

He leaned his head from side to side to stretch his tired neck muscles. As he did, he noticed some flakes of sawdust trickle down from his hair. He reached up and dusted them off, blinking a few times as he noticed something black sitting just above his knee.

Damn bullet ant! He brushed the insect to the floor and crushed it under his foot. The squeal it let out caused a tremble down his spine.

Will's right eye began to itch and as he looked down at the remains of the ant, blood began to run from his nose...and eyes...and ears...and...

One minute and six seconds later the Amazon Rainforest consumed its nemesis, its taunter...forever.

49

When the house came into sight, Lupa was on the porch. The lamp above the table emitted a soft greenish glow. Julia had a flash of memory of her father hanging the gas lantern next to her tent during their hiking vacations on the Appalachian Trail when she was a child. A small swarm of moths dipped around the light looking like electrons and protons swirling around the nucleus of an atom. It was an ironic metaphor. Julia realized that this place had become the nucleus of her life. A cribbage game was in front of Lupa where he sat studying it. No one sat across from him. The long porch held only empty furniture.

Before the Jeep stopped, Julia jumped out and ran up the steps. Lupa enveloped her in his arms, both needing a reassuring hug.

Lupa winced in anticipation as he touched the bandage on the side of her head. "Lupa sorry not protect Miss Julia." He looked her up and down and felt her shoulders and arms making sure she was not injured anywhere else. "Lupa sorry he leave. You give big fear."

"No, Lupa, I insisted. And I know how much you wanted to please me and Stephen. It's more my fault for trying to be so courageous," she tried to reassure him. "I'm glad you weren't there. He might have killed both of us instead of just knocking out a woman." It rankled her that the man had caught her off guard. *Sometimes I'm just too overconfident. Maybe that's what's bugging Mitch. Mitch.* She hadn't thought of him at all, not even during her assault.

"Maybe," Lupa conceded.

Eduardo walked to the swing and sat down. Julia continued to watch Lupa. Was there something he wasn't telling her? *Where is Stephen*?

Lupa busied himself moving chairs around. He had driven the chainsaw man's brown truck to the compound while Eduardo took Julia back to his house. When he found Stephen, he was pale with concern.

"What, no hug for me?" Stephen stood in the doorway.

She threw her arms around him in a big bear hug. Pipe tobacco. She never thought she could love that scent as much as she did right now.

"I was worried. You weren't out here to greet us. I thought maybe..."

He patted her back. "I am fine, Julia. I told you I would be. And now…you are home."

As he said the words Julia thought of Eduardo's question, *Must you go home, Julia*?

Julia moved next to Eduardo on the swing. Lupa was on the step, and Stephen headed for his rocking chair. Stephen reached for his pipe, packed it, and then struck a match. With a few draws, smoke drifted up from it. Stephen shook out the match and laid it on the table.

As the students appeared on the path, Alexis was the first up the stairs. "Julia, are you okay?"

Julia motioned them to sit down. "Yes, I'm fine. We are about to pull all of the pieces together." Julia had taken the time needed to gather her wits and thoughts while she and Eduardo sat in the garden. "I'm curious, Stephen. What did you find in the samples after we left?"

Stephen took a draw on his pipe. "I only made one slide. Based on that, there was not any reason to make more. The first one had six PALs in it, and the little blokes were no longer tiny and hard to find. When I saw them, I had a revelation; an idea hit me as to what might be happening."

Stephen rocked slowly as he puffed on his pipe, listening to the insect and animal sounds rising from the forest. The chorus rose and subsided, like a pulse, reminding them it was alive.

Stephen raised an eyebrow as he gestured toward the common room. "Most of the clues were there. We simply had not fully connected them. We know the trees themselves have evolved over millions of years. They are stationary and cannot move to escape danger, so they find other ways to protect themselves."

Eduardo spoke up, "Yes. Some trees have become able to deplete their leaves of nutrition when predators begin munching on them. Others make their leaves taste bad. There are many trees with many toxins."

Stephen drew several puffs from his pipe. "Now, you are seeing it."

Alexis was convinced ants were the cause of the deaths. "What about the insects? The ants? What do they all have in common? Why did they die with the men?"

"After Julia left this morning, I made a couple of phone calls to research scientists I know in America. I sent the data we gathered and asked them to find a connection and to get back to me within a few hours, which they did. I asked them to try to determine what treehoppers, scale insects, ants, and illegal loggers have in common."

Alexis pressed. "Okay, okay. What did you all find?"

Stephen rocked and chewed on the end of his pipe. "Trees."

"Trees?" Alexis echoed.

Stephen nodded. "The dead men, dead treehoppers, scale insects, and ants had trees, mahogany trees to be more precise, in common. Specifically, all four…were *preying* on the mahogany trees." He allowed a moment for his statement to be mulled over and sink in.

Not letting go of her ant theory, Alexis pressed. "What about the ants? They don't prey on trees."

"Yes. Indirectly they do,"

"How so?" Jennifer asked.

Stephen laid his pipe down, about to go on.

The full discovery hit Julia. Her eyes widened and she put her hand on Stephen's arm as she nodded emphatically. Stephen allowed her to continue the explanation. "Treehoppers and scale insects pierce plant stems with their beaks and feed on their sap. But it is not just plants they prey on. Many trees host them, too. The insects cause further damage to the trees when the females cut into the bark with their saw-like mouths and deposit eggs. The egg slits allow molds and other predators deeper access to the trees' inner tissues. Even large trees can be overwhelmed and killed by tiny insects if there are too many of them."

"I follow you on the treehoppers and scale insects drinking from the trees. How does that relate to the ants?" Alexis needed to make a better connection.

"Bear with me, Alexis. I am getting to them," Julia said. "The treehoppers and scale insects naturally have excess sap in their systems. Their bodies have developed glands which create and excrete a liquid scientists call 'honeydew.' This honeydew liquid attracts ants, who naturally love to drink it. We are not sure, but they act as though it might be some sort of drug. It makes them settle down, a bit sluggish even."

"Like the green caterpillar you told me about?" Alexis asked.

Julia nodded. "Exactly."

"Maaaybee they're drunk," Charlie slurred the words as he said them.

"Perhaps they are," Julia smiled in agreement. "Actually, the treehoppers and scale insects have a symbiotic relationship with the ants."

"Symbi…what Julia say, Stephen?" Lupa asked.

"Symbiotic relationships." Stephen helped him with the foreign word. "You know them but just do not know the term, Lupa. It is when two different types of organisms work together, with each benefiting from the other. Like this…" he reached into the pile of science magazines until he found the picture he was looking for. He handed the open pages to Lupa. "You see the bird on top of the zebra?"

Lupa studied the picture. "I see."

"It is, I believe, called an oxpecker."

"I know them well," Kosey interjected. "The bird eats ticks and other parasites off the zebra, so it gets food, and the zebra gets free pest control."

Understanding dawned for Lupa. "Bees and flowers have this." He did know the concept, just not the word.

"Exactly. Bees fly from flower to flower collecting food, and the flowers get pollinated by the bees," Stephen acknowledged.

Julia went on. "The treehoppers and scale insects give the ants the nectar they love, and in return, the ants give them protection from predators."

Eduardo was nodding, the breakthrough coming together for him as well. "So, you're saying the trees reached a level of damage just before they were completely destroyed, and they developed the PALs, a new defense mechanism, in order to survive."

Stephen shrugged. "I know it sounds crazy, but it's what I believe."

Having lived in the jungle most of his life, it was easy for Eduardo to recognize the theory. "It does make sense. Plants and trees create defenses all the time. The PALs are in the sap. The sap is in the insects. The tree arms itself by injecting the PALs into the layer that carries the resin. The chainsaws create sawdust laden with the PALs. The insects breathe them in and they die. The men breathe them in and they die."

Alexis inclined her head in confusion. "Stephen, I know many plants exhibit behaviors that botanists are just starting to study. Do you mean to say the mahogany trees, in their own sort of tree knowledge, knew all this, could sense this…and they knew any man cutting them was also a predator?"

Stephen looked toward her and wrinkled his brow. "Alexis, the men were cutting into the tree's inner bark. They were severing the part of the tree carrying its lifeblood. If a tree knows or can sense things, how could it not know at the very least, when it is in peril? I know it's hard to imagine a tree 'thinking' but it goes down to the nucleus of instinct…something we still can't quite quantify.

When she spoke, Alexis sounded skeptical. "The probability of all this happening at the same time is very difficult to grasp, Stephen."

His voice was gentle. "I agree, my dear. I have been struggling with it all afternoon. I could only come to one conclusion. In the realm of science, it might not be highly probable, but given all the evidence, it does become scientifically possible."

Stephen watched Alexis's face move from incredulity to thoughtful reflection.

"I have friends in California who are studying plant behavior," Julia spoke so quietly that the others were forced to concentrate to hear her voice over the forest. "They recently traveled to Florence, Italy, for meetings on what they called plant neurobiology."

Eduardo's eyes narrowed. "Plant neurobiology? Neuro? Nerve?"

Julia smiled, "Exactly." She absentmindedly patted him on the leg.

He looked down at the hand she left on his thigh. He enjoyed it there and decided not to ask for more explanation for fear she would take it away. Instead he smiled at her and let her continue.

Jennifer elbowed Charlie and nodded toward the hand. The others saw it too.

So lost was she in her own thoughts, Julia didn't realize she had left her hand where it was. "When you said it's possible but not probable, I was thinking that just a decade ago most scientists would have thought it impossible for plants to have behaviors. But with new methods of discovering neurobiology, it is becoming an interesting study."

Stephen decided to help Eduardo out by continuing the distraction. "I was recently reading an article about this in one of my other magazines. Continue, Julia."

"Well, they really believe that plants have a type of intelligence. They are even looking for a form of brain function in plants."

Lupa reached for the plant closest to him off the porch. "Brain? Think like we think?"

Julia shook her head. "No, I don't see how they can think like we do, but the cutting edge of study in botany deals with adaptations, or decisions, that plants make to survive in a hostile environment."

Kosey thought back to his homeland. "I hadn't ever considered the plants having a hostile environment, but I suppose that everything we are doing to the planet we might be creating one enormously hostile environment."

Stephen was reminded again of the article he had just mentioned. "The study I read talked about volatiles, or chemicals, plants release. When researchers snip the leaves of some plants, they release a blend of volatiles scientists have not been able to identify yet. What is interesting is that some volatiles give off an aroma, a scent, if you will. For instance, when a plant is being attacked by caterpillars, it gives off a slightly different aroma than usual. Insects that prey on caterpillars recognize the new scent and come to the aid of the plant. They eat the caterpillars. It is a way the plant signals, 'Come and get it!'"

Julia remembered similar information she had seen. "Even more interesting is the fact that the same attacking insects will not come to the plant's aid if the diners are not something they want to eat. That proves that the plant knows what aroma to send out by what is attacking it. If the plant sends out the wrong aroma, the wrong insect comes but won't eat."

"Lupa no understand," Lupa said.

"Let me give you an example, my friend," Stephen said. "Wasps are mean insects. They need to deposit their larva into another insect in order for the offspring to have food to grow and mature. A small wasp can only manage to inject its eggs into a young caterpillar, where the larvae will eat and grow until the caterpillar dies. A plant gives off one aroma for young caterpillars and a different one for adult caterpillars. The small wasps don't come to the plant when it is being attacked by the adults…only when the young ones are there. Other insects interested in the adults as a meal come with the adult aroma. The plant is very selective in the volatiles it releases. Somehow, it is making a decision."

Lupa nodded. "I not know this but see in forest when some insects eat some leaf but not others."

Eduardo interjected. "All my years of study and the years I have been gardening, I never knew either or even suspected it. We have little idea as to what is happening all around us. "

"Some scientists say it is rubbish," Stephen said. "But the evidence is overwhelming that plants have memories and make decisions on their own behalf."

Julia looked down at her hand on Eduardo's leg. Eduardo did not look at her, but he could see her. He waited for her hand to move away. It didn't.

Lupa peered out into the night. "Plant teachers…" he said. As Lupa spoke a rare breeze began to blow high in the treetops. The rustling of the forest canopy rose like a crescendo in a symphony. As quickly as it rose, it was gone. The trees were still again, and the night sounds returned to their usual level.

Kosey thought of the men 200 kilometers away. "How do you explain the men found so far away?"

Stephen picked up his pipe again. "I did some research and come to find out, not only do plants and trees arm themselves with protection from predators, but they also communicate the coming harm to others so they can arm themselves."

"This I gotta hear, psychic trees?" Charlie had about all he could take of this trip.

Stephen regaled them with the study on the wild cherry trees he'd thought about in the lab earlier. When he finished he said, "The groundskeeper offered me her thoughts on what we had witnessed. She wondered how long it had taken for that species of wild cherry trees to develop a mechanism to protect itself from predators. How long had it taken the trees to develop a method for communicating an alarm to other trees? Had it taken a million years? Ten thousand? A hundred? She wondered if the trees could now be working on new defenses against the caterpillar and other predators? Might the trees one day be able to protect themselves from all predators?"

Stephen paused to draw on his pipe. He rocked and continued, "She confessed that she was alarmed at the prospect that the day could come when the trees decided that she, herself, was one of their predators and arm themselves against her. After all, she did tear off their leaves. She did prune them back each year. She cut them with no regard for what it might mean to the trees. What if the wild cherry decided that she was, indeed, a predator? What might they do to protect themselves?"

"This all seems so far-fetched…but the study…wow." Alexis wasn't sure what to think.

So," Julia said with a flourish, "our trees in the rainforest have evidently developed the same ability to 'talk.' That's why the trees so far away were able to kill the men. They were told to arm themselves, and they did." She said it matter-of-factly, as if it should have been obvious, portraying herself as the Doctor Doolittle of the forest.

"As incredible as it seems, it does make sense," Kosey conceded.

Jennifer posed the question, "Do you think insects like the treehoppers and scale insects are doomed? I mean, if the tree carries something that can kill them, what else can the insects eat?"

Stephen shook his head. "I think the chainsaw is what pushed the tree over the edge, so to speak. The tree can tolerate some of its sap being taken. Only when its very life is being threatened would it react so violently. And…the word will get out about the deaths caused by the trees, and when it does, I definitely think the mahogany loggers will run out of luck hiring locals." He was very pleased with that idea.

"What about us?" Eduardo posed. "Why were we not killed? And the children, and the others?"

"Now, that is a harder one." Stephen leaned forward waving his pipe for emphasis. "I've put some thought toward that, myself. Somehow, I can only theorize…the tree was able to perceive you were not predators."

Charlie was making a 'you've-got-to-be-kidding expression.' "Stephen, that's a stretch. It's hard enough to accept a tree can kill people, but being selective about it? Seriously, dude. That's a hard one."

Stephen thought about Charlie's question and turned to Eduardo and Lupa. "Were there birds in the trees after the insects died today?"

Eduardo nodded, "And, I remember hearing other insect noises, actually, very loud insects."

Lupa added, "Call of toucans. Monkeys in trees."

"You see, many creatures were not killed, yet they were in and all around the tree. Only the predators died. So how, indeed, did the tree knowingly target its kill?" Stephen asked.

"Lupa see many thing not understand there," he said pointing to the forest. "Maybe *mogno* know good people and bad people."

Stephen contemplated the wise words from his old friend. Even though there was no scientific basis—at least not yet—Lupa had an unusual relationship with the jungle and its rituals. He probably understood it more than he knew. "You could be right, Lupa. You could be right."

"What about the man who got away?" Julia asked.

Stephen shook his head. "Maybe he left before the PALs made it to him. I just don't know."

"But…" Jennifer pushed. "…I understand about the trees putting poison into their leaves to kill the insects attacking their leaves, but it doesn't make sense about killing the men."

Julia smiled and turned her face toward the forest. "What is the difference between the insects preying on the tree and the men cutting them down?" She looked from one to the other. "Somehow it has the ability to recognize the difference. Neurobiology may be where we find these answers."

The uninterrupted night sounds filled the air around them. The evening sky glittered with stars.

Stephen spoke again. "There is a tree in Southeast Asia so poisonous even its sawdust can kill most people." Smoke hovered around him, glowing in the light of the lantern. No one questioned his information now. "And if the same people stand under its branches when it rains and the water drips on their skin, they can die."

"Incredible," Kosey marveled. "What kind of tree is it?"

Stephen pursed his lips in thought. "For the life of me, I can't recall the exact name of it. I do know it's in the family of flowering plants known as *anacardiaceae*. There are many common trees and bushes in that family." Stephen searched his memory.

Julia assisted. "I know the family. Down here there are cashews and mangos and lots more. In America there are sumacs and poison ivy. I hadn't thought of it before, but that family might shed even more light on what happened to those men. Consider poison ivy. The oil in the vines and leaves contains a chemical absorbed by skin cells. People who are sensitive to the oil, which is probably eighty to eighty-five percent of all humans, will develop blisters on the skin. The reaction ends only when all the contaminated cells have been shed. Heaven help the poor guy who inhales the smoke when it is being burned." Julia's mind was whirling. "The same blistering effect takes place in the lungs. It can cause extreme pain," her voice grew quieter, "…and is sometimes even fatal."

Stephen stared at Julia. "I see where you are going, my dear. If the mahogany tree in the forest filled its sap with PALs and the sap carried it through the trunk, the sawdust would have drifted throughout the air as the tree was being cut. When the men breathed it in, as potent as the little buggers were, it makes sense that as it spread from their lungs to their blood stream and throughout their bodies…"

Julia was getting edgy, "…the contaminated cells had to be shed. But still...no one else died, and there was sawdust all over. Some got on me as well."

The sounds of the night engulfed them. Something shuffled near them in the underbrush. They heard some scratching, likely one of the night birds looking for a snack. An owl hooted.

Stephen rocked and took another draw on his pipe. "Yes. That is the mystery we have yet to unravel." After blowing out the smoke he quietly said, "I now believe…the trees might win."

50

Dawn of the next morning found Drake lying not far from the surging Amazon River writhing in pain. He vomited twice as his diarrhea turned bloody. He'd realized during the night that Nigel must have put the ricin into his trail mix yesterday when he turned away to get water. But how could he have done it so fast? It didn't matter. It was done, and so was he.

Nigel looked down on the boy. "It's a good enough place to die, son. You can hear the water rushing past." He looked around as he commented, "The forest is beautiful here." He squatted down next to Drake and offered him a drink of water.

Drake shook his head.

Nigel instinctively pulled out his box of Chiclets and palmed some. He popped the gum into his mouth and began to chew, a slight smile at the corners of his lips as he peered down at Drake. "Sorry, kid," he said as he stood. "I must move on. I've still got three days of hiking to get to a village. You'll be out of your misery soon enough. I'd say '*Hasta La Vista*,' but I know that isn't going to happen."

Drake voice was scratchy. "You never know what's out there, man. We all get what's due us at some point, ya' know?" Beginning to feel intense remorse for everything he took part in, he coughed hard and grasped his stomach, doubling into a fetal position.

Nigel pushed the trail mix closer to Drake with his foot. "In case you need a little energy…and thanks for the help, kid." As he turned and walked away Nigel looked over his shoulder just before he was out of sight. Drake raised his middle finger, grinning as he gestured.

Nigel laughed and called out, "Well, you've got spunk! I have to give you that!"

Nigel spent the next six hours trudging through the undergrowth, thankful he had both his and Drake's machetes. It wouldn't be long before his was dull, and he couldn't wait to get out of this god-forsaken place.

He sat down on a tall boulder overlooking the river. His stomach turned over and for a moment, Nigel felt like he might be sick. *Hope I haven't gotten a bug.*

He pulled out the box of gum and poured the last of the little nuggets into his palm. He popped them into his mouth and began to chew. Maybe he could get the unpleasant feeling to go away with a little fresh mint. He went to toss the empty container away and happened to look inside.

It wasn't empty. In the bottom…was a tiny black fleck. Nigel spat the partly chewed gum into his hand. There, nestled throughout the sticky nugget were dozens of tiny flecks of ricin.

Nigel chuckled acknowledging the irony of Drake's action and tossed the box into the raging river. "The little shit…"

51

For ten days, Julia and the students relaxed into forest life. There were no more bodies. No more shrunken men next to chainsaws or hanging from trees. Not surprisingly, the chainsaws in their area of the forest were silent. Word of the dead men spread like the fires that once consumed the forest.

Julia wished she could stay longer, but she was soon due back for a seminar, which she couldn't change. She spent four days with Stephen, Lupa, and the students upriver, climbing and collecting plant specimens and fungus-infected insects, then returned and spent the rest of her time testing and retesting for medicinal characteristics and cataloguing the findings.

On their return to the compound, she and Stephen played cribbage at night, and when she was not playing, Lupa was.

As the days went on they spoke little of the PALs. At one point, Stephen quietly remarked, "I can only speculate, Julia, whether we will see more deaths. The PALs are not gone. They are waiting."

And then there was Eduardo. He did not offer to travel with them upriver, and Julia was disappointed, worried he was avoiding her.

In truth he was avoiding her because he knew she was struggling with her feelings for Mitch. He asked for one final dinner and walk in his garden, and she had willingly agreed this time.

Last evening, she sat with Eduardo on his back step and watched the sun drop behind the waterfall. He had kissed her again, and Julia had melted into his arms. They stayed there until the stars were cloaked in clouds and rain began to fall. That was all. He brought her home, and along with Stephen and Lupa, the four friends sat on Stephen's porch laughing and talking late into the night.

It was not until later as she readied for bed that she thought of Mitch. Thoughts of Mitch no longer held the same feelings they had in the past. Julia slid the ring up and down her finger, almost off, all the way back on. Almost off. All the way back on. She thought again of Eduardo's words, *Must you go home*, *Julia*? She supposed she must…at least for a while.

* * *

The Amazon morning peaked in perfection, a farewell gift to Julia and the students leaving today. There had been a steady rain during the night, and the coolness beneath the forest canopy summoned Julia, Stephen, and Lupa to step outside after breakfast.

Jennifer and Charlie had left the day before promising an e-mail as soon as they got home. So far, Alexis and Kosey had not climbed from their hammocks, and Nigel and Drake had not been seen again.

Almost ceremoniously, the three strolled down to the misty waterfall watching its foggy spray rise to join the next rainfall. Their meager conversation held an emptiness, almost a sadness, as though Julia were already gone. They tarried for a long while to delay the parting. Toucans were buffing their bright, oversized beaks against tree limbs, the loud tapping shaking down rain droplets from the leaves overhead.

Stephen checked his watch and cleared this throat. No one spoke as they turned back together, strolling toward the house arm-in-arm.

"I won't stay away long."

"Get back soon, Miss Julia," Lupa urged. "Stephen like jaguar with thorn in foot for many day."

"Hey, hey," Stephen protested. "Who did not want to cook for a week when she left last time? Was it me? I think not."

"All right you two. Don't make me feel any worse than I already feel." For a moment, Julia was overcome with tremendous sadness.

Alexis and Kosey were waiting for them when they got to the compound. All five of them piled into the Jeep clasping duffel bags and backpacks. For a moment it looked as if they might topple over. Lupa stood in the center and held onto the roll bar, since there was nowhere for him to sit. Kosey offered, but Lupa declined.

The ride through the forest was particularly beautiful on this new defining day for Julia. She had come to a decision for her future, and she told no one. When they crested onto the ridge, she put her hand on Stephen's shoulder as if holding him back. He knew what she wanted, so he stopped the truck and turned off the engine giving everyone a moment to absorb the beauty one more time.

"I can never look at the trees the same," Alexis said from behind. "They are more than living. Now, they are making decisions."

Stephen's eyes caught hers in the rearview mirror, "They always have. We just didn't notice it." He started the engine, and they made their way toward the airfield.

It was a perfect day for flying. Julia saw Eduardo standing beside the plane when they rounded the corner to the landing strip. Stephen pulled next to the Cessna.

Alexis and Kosey gave goodbye hugs to Stephen, Eduardo, and Lupa. Alexis lingered a moment when she got to Stephen. They held each other briefly before separating. Kosey finished loading their bags into the plane before Alexis joined him, and they climbed in behind the pilot.

Julia still sat in the front seat of the Jeep regarding the three men who had come to mean so much in her life. She blinked back tears as her gaze lingered on Eduardo. He smiled at her, but his eyes were heartbreaking. He was not hiding his misery very well. Julia smiled back as she stood. Eduardo reached for her hand and held it after she climbed down.

"Lupa forget, Miss Julia." Lupa went to the back of the Jeep and pulled out two small boxes. "Here. Surprise!" He handed a box to each of them.

Julia looked at the box. "A gift?" She smiled up at Eduardo's equally perplexed expression.

"Lupa people have custom. Miss Julia know Stephen and Lupa face death together not know each other much. Eduardo, you not know, but many, many year back, Lupa with people take Stephen deep in forest to gather plants for experiment. We come to place thick with brush where Indian attack. We not know tribe. Lupa see cannibal body paint, and it make Lupa sad at fate of people. Lupa lead ahead with Stephen when Indian surround behind. We run. We run so long, Lupa think might not breathe. Come to river. Swim. Float part day. Get out. For three day hide…run…hide…swim until safe. Lupa and Stephen bound together forever. It is way it is."

Lupa wasn't finished. He pulled a cord from around his neck. A beautiful carving that looked like ivory hung from the bottom. Stephen pulled out a similar necklace. The pieces were almost identical except one was inverted from the other. When the two men put them together, they made a perfect circle.

"Face death together, something happen. Bond. Two now part of whole. Circle not complete without two." Lupa motioned for them to open their boxes.

Each one pulled out a necklace. They laid the boxes in the Jeep. Julia lovingly held her pendant and traced the carving with her finger.

"Made from seed of ivory-nut palm. Lupa gather trip to Peru. Lupa spend time make for today. Julia and Eduardo face death together safe. Share with each other. Now two piece of one. One complete other." Lupa stopped talking then, his hands clasp in front. He stepped back bashfully after his oration, lowering his head.

Julia didn't know what to say. She was afraid to look up at Eduardo.

Eduardo put the necklace over his head. In a voice filled with emotion, he fingered the carving below his neck. "This is perfect, Lupa. It is a gift I will cherish."

Julia turned to Lupa. She put the necklace around her neck and hugged him. "It is beautiful, Lupa. I will always wear it." Julia gave him a quick squeeze and then reached back for her last bag.

Eduardo took it from her and put in on the ground as he turned her to face him. Julia did not look up. They stood very close. Around them they could hear the sounds of the forest, all wild and comforting at the same time. Eduardo laid his fingers under Julia's chin and lifted her face toward his. As he watched, a single tear slid down her cheek toward her slender neck. He closed his eyes and leaned down, placing his cheek against hers. He stood back up, and she could see the wetness on his face. "Whatever happens to you, it happens to me, Julia. Don't forget that."

Julia held her breath.

He was not finished. "I once read somewhere that people come into your life, and then they leave. When they are gone…they leave nothing behind."

Julia gazed at his face waiting for something she knew would follow.

Eduardo's finger gently stroked back and forth across the salty, wet path that lingered as he traced her cheek to her jaw and then back up to her lips before he continued, "But every once in a while, someone comes into your life and when they leave…they leave a part of themselves in your heart." As he said the word "heart," Eduardo touched the skin above her breast. The contact was electric, and Julia felt weak. Then he smiled a large smile and wrapped her into his arms, again.

Julia stayed there, leaving the remnants of her tears on his shirt.

The plane engine coughed into life. "All right, all right. No crying allowed," Stephen said brushing at his own eyes as he said it. He picked up her bag and walked over to load it in back. He lingered in the doorway of the front and spoke to Alexis. Alexis smiled and nodded. Stephen slapped the side of the plane and strode back to them grinning all the way.

Julia followed Eduardo to the door of the plane. She looked up and returned his smile. She held up her necklace symbol. Eduardo slid his piece around hers, and hers fit snugly into his. Together they made a perfect circle.

The plane was loud and the wind from the propeller whipped at their clothes. Eduardo held her firmly against him as he kissed her. He hugged her tightly one more time, and with his lips in her hair, he murmured, "When will you come back, Julia Cole?"

She waited for him to release her, and then Julia beamed up at him, her eyes clear and wide. She raised her eyebrow and playfully answered, "Maybe sooner than you think."

She turned to climb into her seat, and Eduardo gave her a swat on her backside. "Hurry back," he said.

Julia jumped. She had not expected that. She turned and grinned at him as she climbed into the plane. The little Cessna was taxiing down the field before she even got her seatbelt buckled.

For the first time, Julia's usual panic about flying didn't surface. She leaned back into the seat considering the possibilities of her future. She fingered the necklace around her neck before reaching to twist her ring.

Julia looked down at her left hand, now bare, the ring safely buried in her backpack. She was never really one for jewelry and it felt good to have her hands free. *Now, how do I break it to Mitch*? She had over 3,000 miles to figure it out.

Julia looked back and saw Kosey and Alexis watching the forest below. Up ahead was a break in the jungle. No one spoke as they came upon flames of gold and orange leaping high into the sky, brilliant shades of green turning grey and black as an inferno engulfed thriving, rich vegetation. The pilot banked the plane to the right to avoid flying over the burning forest.

Julia leaned her head against the cool window and closed her eyes. The sight of burning Amazon Rainforest always caused a tightening in her chest. *What are we losing now*?

From behind, Kosey said, "*Itunze arthi vyema*; *hukupewa ni wazazi*; *bali umekopeshwa ni wazao wako*."

Julia opened her eyes and turned toward him. "Translation, please?"

Kosey couldn't look at the fire to the south. His face tightened and a vein pulsed on his forehead. "'You must treat the Earth well. It was not given to you by your parents. It is loaned to you by your children.'"

Julia contemplated the expanse of green treetops to the west which stretched to the horizon before glancing back toward the fire below.

Kosey asked no one in particular, "We are not doing a very good job for our children, are we?"

No one felt a need to comment.

* * *

As Eduardo jumped into his Jeep, his walkie-talkie crackled with a menacing message. "Boss, we got more trouble. Fire in north from a small plane crash and two dead bodies near river. Don't know what cause dead bodies. You come quick."

Eduardo headed to his office to get the coordinates as to where exactly these two bodies were found, dreading what might be ahead. This was most definitely going to be a very bad day. Eduardo feared the loggers were beginning a new rape on the forest and with two more dead bodies, he would have his hands full.

The area where the fire was spotted was too far into the jungle for his Jeep, requiring him to do a fly-by in his plane. He would do that as soon as he investigated the new deaths. Eduardo shook his head recognizing that whoever was piloting that plane was probably the cause of his own demise.

But now there were two more bodies to investigate. "*Let's pray this is just a simple murder, or simply two fools who got lost in the jungle. This should keep me busy for a while until…until what*?" He was trying not to think about the next time he would see Julia.

52

At the cutting edge of a rainforest…

…a platoon of ants came and went to an underground nest. The steady frenzy has created a furrow in the ground as wide as the palm of someone's hand.

There a man squatted down close, fascinated by the fluttering parade of green leaves carried by ants heading for the entrance hole into their underworld. As though on a busy two-lane highway, ants without leaves raced away from the entrance on one side of the furrow, while ants carrying leaf pieces systematically march toward the nest on the other side, climbing over any exiting ant that might wander into the incoming lane.

This was not the first time the man has seen the particular group of ants. He'd been watching them every day for a month now. He had even set up a table with battery operated camera equipment so he could monitor the ants underground.

When he encountered this ant colony a month ago, he inserted a cord with his lighted camera down into the entrance hole, and then navigated over eighteen feet below the surface of the ground where the tiny eye reached the ants' base nest. Since then, he has learned a great deal about the culture of this species of leafcutters.

Following the trail, he determined these ants practiced a type of sustainable leaf harvest, slicing off only part of a leaf from a variety of plants and trees in order to avoid exhausting any vegetation. Ants were hauling pieces of leaf ten times their own size, the equivalent of a man carrying two full-grown horses above his head.

The camera showed the ants descending deeper below the surface, each with their leaf slice. After a month he was still amazed to see that the ants had established a working farm far below the Earth's surface. His research told him the species of ants must have been farmers for some fifty million years such was the sustainability of their farming.

Retrieving a sample of the crop, he learned that without the need for sunlight, the ants were growing a special fungus which met their nutritional requirements.

The man was struck by the division of labor. Farm labor was arranged into specialized tasks: leaf handlers, defenders of the colony, garden tenders, while others were leaf cutters. One group of tiny ants straddled the backs of the larger worker ants to defend them from carnivorous flies, that given a chance would lay eggs at the base of an ant's head where their larvae would eat the inside of the ant until it died.

The observer learned there was additional help for the gardeners in the form of a white film on the ants' legs and abdomens. He recalled that scientists used to theorize the film was a sort of skin dander due to the ants never leaving the fungus garden. It came as a surprise to learn the true role of the film, actually bacteria, was to protect the garden from a tiny parasite mold that invariably hitched a ride on the cut leaf pieces and threatened the health of the entire fungus crop.

The ants produced the white film bacteria from a gland in their bodies, which, in return, produced an antibiotic called streptomyces which targeted the virulent parasite. Streptomyces was of great importance as the foundation for more than fifty percent of all human medical antibiotics.

The observant man was awed at this ant technology and certain there was even more to glean from his observations. He thought ants must have developed this incredibly potent form of medicine millions of years ago. What else might exist in the ant world that could be applied to the surface world of humans?

A pall of frustration overcame the man at the prospect that humans may not get the chance to unlock new aspects of ant technology and medicine from this colony. He was saddened because he had been smelling smoke for the whole month from land-clearing fires. Every day the fires moved closer to this ant observation camp. Those bringing the fires were also farmers who the observer knew would soon force him to abandon the millions of ants whose ancestors had been living there for hundreds of thousands of years—there at the cutting edge of the rainforest.

The human farmers would burn the trees and plants. They would disk the ground and plant new crops, and in two or three years the soil would be exhausted, and the human farmers would abandon it and move elsewhere.

Then…for the first time in fifty million years, there would be no farmers on that once vibrant land.

53

Arthur Livingston stood admiring his newly acquired entertainment center. It covered the whole back wall of the media room in his twenty-four room mansion on Maple Street. The house was still a monstrosity, but Arthur had to admit it was growing on him. Catherine had gone from one auction to another picking up painting after painting. The walls of their ostentatious, twenty-five thousand square-foot home resembled a gallery.

The place did make quite a statement. Thank goodness there was an endless reserve of trees left to be cut because Catherine's vision of their excessive lifestyle and spending was endless.

Even though Arthur hated parting with his money, he enjoyed bragging about how much everything was costing, not letting on that he managed to finance many of the paintings and other accessories with Will's savings.

Thinking of Will, Arthur wondered why he hadn't heard from the boy. After all, Will obviously knew by now that all his money was gone. Although he's taken the plane, it still didn't amount to half of what Arthur had stolen from him.

The one concession Catherine made in her verve for decorating, was that Arthur could have "his" room. He was king of his domain, or at least this part of it. The workers had just finished installing his new sixty inch 3-D TV. There was another TV room upstairs and a movie theater in the basement, but he wanted this room tailored just for himself.

The one "hobby" Arthur enjoyed was tinkering with new electronics. As soon as a new model for anything technical became available, even before it was in the stores, Arthur had to have it. He relished putting things together, especially systems like these. He sent his workers home early, preferring to tweak the final placement of equipment himself. Arthur still had to hook up the stereo equipment and DVD players and other gizmos he ordered.

He picked up the first box and opened it. *Ahhh*, he thought, *my speaker and amplifier package*. He pulled out cords and went to work.

Arthur ran his hand along the smooth wood of the entertainment center. He had never seen better grain. The cabinetmaker had done a fine job. The craftsmanship was as good as Arthur had ever seen.

He commissioned it to be made from the last shipment of mahogany he brought in from Brazil, which wasn't an easy task getting out of the country. Arthur sneered as he thought of the irate government official who called his office, yelling at him that his time was coming. *Well, let them try and prove something*. Arthur knew how to cover his tracks. They would never be able to pin anything illegal on him. Arthur Livingston was untouchable by any authority, and he was smug about it.

Arthur fed cord after cord through the back of the beautiful mahogany furniture. He hurried to finish before Catherine returned home. The craftsman had drilled holes so the plugs could easily be threaded through. Arthur tried to install the last cord. It wasn't going to fit. He pulled the plug back out and noticed an edge around it that was slightly larger than the hole it had to fit through.

I can fix that, Arthur thought. He pulled out his pocket knife and opened it. Reaching deep into the recesses of the cabinet, Arthur whittled out the hole on the back wall of the mahogany cabinet, making it a little larger. He dusted the chips into his hand and blew the fine pieces away.

"Arthur?" Catherine called from the doorway.

He closed the knife and put it in his pocket. Arthur's right eye began to itch. He blinked a couple of times, thinking some of the shavings must have blown in.

"I'm finished," he said, giving a satisfied chuckle and planting his hands on his hips. As he turned to look at his wife with a sardonic grin, a single drop of blood began to slide from his nose.

EPILOGUE

They had been flying for almost two hours when Julia heard the jingle of a text message coming over her cell. She ignored it, comforted as she was with the crooning of the plane engine and lack of conversation from Kosey and Alexis, both asleep in the seats behind.

A few moments went by, and Julia couldn't resist. She flipped over the iPhone and recalled the text message.

It was from Stephen. There were only two sentences.

Do not get comfortable. We have dead loggers in Sumatra.

FOR MORE INFORMATION ON THIS BOOK AND THE RAINFOREST, PLEASE CONTINUE TO THE BACK PAGES!

Figure 2 The wonder of the Amazon

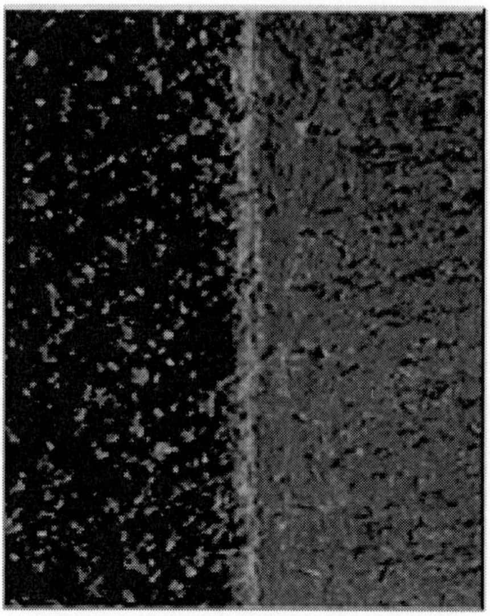
Figure 1 The cutting edge of the rainforest...

A NOTE TO THE READER

HOW THIS NOVEL CAME ABOUT…

This mysterious story sprang from a germ of an idea: *What if nature gained the ability to protect itself and stop humans from destroying it*?

The fictional plot is based upon real science, which is woven into the text as carefully and accurately as possible. The scientific facts support a theory so incredible, it is hard to separate fact from fiction. It is disturbing that should this story actually happen, mankind may be doomed on this planet.

I have done extensive scientific research on the subject matter covered in this book, including a trip to Brazil to study the Amazon Rainforest. Among the scientists consulted, I extend gratitude for the insights provided by the following: Dr. James Grogan, who calls himself a "tree-ologist" with Yale University; Frank Pantoja, ecologist with EKOAR (*Empresa de Assessoria e Consultoria Ambiental da Amazônia*) in Rio Branco, Brazil; Dr. James Maruniak, entomologist with the University of Florida; Dr. Domagoj Vucic with Genentech, a California pharmaceutical and biotechnology company; and the author's studies at the University of Georgia.

Contacting these scientists was mainly good luck. While reading an article on the internet from *Fortune* magazine about the best place to work in the US in 2005, the author was struck by the opening paragraph. It read, "Domagoj Vucic didn't come to Genentech for the rich stock options or the free cappuccino or the made-to-order sushi or the parties every Friday night. He came from the University of Georgia seven years ago because he believed Genentech could help him answer a burning question: What is it that keeps caterpillars infected with baculovirus alive for an entire seven days before they explode into a gooey puddle?" After reading about baculovirus, I called Dr. Vucic and interestingly, he returned the call. He gave insight into his work that is included in the book, including his group's work to develop a virus which attacks only cancer cells.

Dr. James Maruniak provided information about the black cherry tree and how it injects cyanide into its leaves to protect itself from tent caterpillars.

Dr. James Grogan spent many, many years studying deep in the Amazon in Brazil. I called him and explained that nature itself, with the trees used as the vector, were killing illegal loggers in my story. At first, he laughed at the theory being proposed. He said it could not happen. I asked, "If a black cherry tree can put cyanide into its leaves to protect itself from the tent caterpillars ravaging its leaves…what makes us any different as we devastate the forests with our cutting…in the psyche of the trees?"

Dr. Grogan was silent. And then he began to laugh again. "I have never thought of it that way…" he said. "Maybe the trees will win after all."

"Jimmy" made arrangements for me and a companion to visit the rainforest of the Amazon. Jimmy's friend and co-worker, Frank Pantoja, became our guide. He also became a friend.

We spent five days and evenings with Frank, his family, and an interpreter, Sol Das Oliveiras. Frank guided us many kilometers into the Amazon to experience the wonder of the forest. He and Sol traveled with us for days moving in and out of the forest and on a long river ride, immersing us in Brazilian culture while teaching its history and allowing us to live the life of the local people.

One evening while finishing a wonderful dinner outside a restaurant in Rio Branco, Brazil, Frank asked me to outline the book. He knew the information I relayed because of his own science background. He heard me describe some of the evolving, symbiotic relationships throughout nature and the ways nature has learned to perpetuate itself through the life of another plant or insect or animal, some of which are discussed in the book. At the end of the discussion, I proposed the theory that the mahogany trees, the jewels of the Amazon, the reason there is a spider's web of roads through the rainforest, were causing the mysterious deaths, and Frank began to nod. I worried what he might say, afraid he might laugh at the theory I was proposing.

Frank did not laugh. Instead, he smiled.

His response caused a shiver to run over me.

Frank said, "I think it may already be happening…"

ESSAY BY THE AUTHOR

Imagine the Amazon Rainforest. Most people conjure up a particular impression when simply hearing the word *Amazon*. Mysterious? Amazing? Remarkable? Miraculous? Inexhaustible? Curious? Sustainable?

The Amazon Rainforest, the largest rainforest on the planet, is a world of unparalleled diversity. Mysterious? Over half the plant species on the planet are located within its boundaries. The ever-increasing numbers include over 150,000 types of plants, 7500 types of trees, 2000 different birds and mammals, and more than 25 million categories of insects.

Amazing? Presently, one-fifth of the world's fresh water flows through the Amazon River, pouring enough water into the Atlantic Ocean each day to supply New York City's freshwater needs for nine years.

Remarkable? The forest provides 20 percent of the oxygen on Earth and is often referred to as "The Lungs of the World."

Miraculous? Scientists believe only 1 to 2 percent of all rainforest plants have been tested for medicinal purposes. At present, more than 120 prescription drugs come directly from plants in rainforests around the world. The US National Cancer Institute reports that more than two thirds of all medicines found to have cancer-fighting properties come directly from plants found in a rainforest.

Inexhaustible? Between 2005 and 2010, Amazon deforestation was almost 500,000 acres. While that might not sound like an immense loss from a forest of over a billion acres, man has been decimating the Amazon for more than 500 years.

What happens if the Amazon Rainforest is gone?

Curious? There would be no Amazon River without the forest—there would be diminished rainfall, too, since there must be a forest to recycle the water by returning it to the clouds to rain down again: evapotranspiration. Less forest means less rain.

And what of Earth's air quality? It's hard to predict. Ozone levels. Dust loads. Contaminants from fires. The list of pollutants goes on and on. The Amazon Rainforest is a major player in the conversion of carbon dioxide (CO_2) to oxygen (O_2). Less forest means more CO_2 and less O_2. Compounding the problems is when fire is used to destroy the forest and large amounts of carbon are released into the atmosphere during the burning process. So…there is less forest taking CO_2 and other gases out of the air and large amounts of CO_2 and other gases being released through burning. Less forest means less rain and less rain equates to less forest. Less rain equals more forest fires, and more forest fires which promises less forest—an interminable cycle almost entirely initiated by humans.

The loss of forest is great. The Amazon Rainforest is vanishing at a rate equivalent to seven football fields every minute. And for what? Farm and cattle land that in a few years, at best, are exhausted of nutrients and become unusable? The illegal logging of endangered yet valuable trees leaving behind a shattered forest? And, most importantly, roads which provide easy access to more illegal loggers and settlers? Firewood and charcoal, which when burned are gone forever?

Sustainable? The question must be asked: How long will we continue to allow the senseless destruction of the Amazon?

1999

The rainforest of the Amazon Basin is about the same size as the Continental United States of America.
Imagine America disappearing at the rate of one state per year.

That is about how long our rainforests have left
– 50 years…

(*…unless human beings are exterminated.*)

ABOUT THE AUTHOR

In 2006, S. W. Lee had the opportunity to visit one of the most mysterious and talked about places on Earth: The Amazon Rainforest. Fascination had been piqued two years earlier during a research study of the Amazon with a germ of an idea. Through that enquiry, Lee became aware of the hundreds of thousands of plants, insects, and animals that contribute to our everyday well-being – the global impact was astonishing. Through the exploration and the discoveries was the impetus to write The Amazon Murders and to fill the pages with captivating threads of real science. With the revelation of personal discoveries, Lee now looks at the world through different eyes. Peering into a deep hollow of logs and examining a spider's web no longer meets with revulsion or fear. Through newfound vision of the earth, realization bloomed – nature can go about its business with or without us.

Before The Amazon Murders evolved on the pages, Lee's writing career had commenced with a folk-life play for a small theater outside Atlanta. After interviewing older people in the community, their stories became vignettes, which developed into a two hour play performed by a cast of over seventy actors. Seven more plays followed, two of which were co-written, and five were directed by Lee, with casts of up to one hundred twenty. As time has the elusive ability to morph and change our lives, Lee continues to write and direct those stories.

Hobbies include reading, gardening, tubing down cold north Georgia mountain rivers, and climbing quiet trails to waterfalls.

Lee earned a degree in Language Education from the University of Georgia and went on to receive an M. Ed. and an Ed. S.

S. W. Lee resides in Georgia and takes great pleasure in the company of three granddaughters and an old minx cat that is definitely in charge of the house.

www.theamazonmurders.com

CPSIA information can be obtained
at www.ICGtesting.com
Printed in the USA
FFOW02n2340120215
11071FF

9 781618 684578